CHASING
WINDMILLS

Also by Joseph Pittman

CHASING WINDMILLS

A Linden Corners Novel

JOSEPH PITTMAN

LINDEN CORNERS PRESS

CHASING WINDMILLS

This book is a work of fiction. Names, characters, places, and incidents either are products or the author's imagination or are used fictitiously. Any resemblance to actual events or locales or persons, living or dead, is entirely coincidental.

Copyright © by Joseph Pittman
All rights reserved, including the right of reproduction in whole or in part in any form.

Published by
Linden Corners Press
NY, NY 10128

Visit www.josephpittmanauthor.com for more information.

ISBN: 978-0-9971998-0-2 (print)
ISBN: 978-0-9971998-1-9 (ebook)

First Published, 2016

This one's for... The Cornue Family

PROLOGUE

The Story of Charles Van Diver

Let me tell you a story. It's one you may know part of, but what you've read previously is simply not the complete tale. You want to know how it all turns out, though, don't you. I know I do. I've been watching a series of special moments unfold from afar, waiting for when love might strike. Life spins, a daily revolution, and eventually, one day, it reveals its true intent.

Think about it. Even the sun had to shine for the first time, the earliest drop of rain had to fall upon hardened earth, and that initial sheet of wind had to have swept across wide open fields. And just like those forces of nature, so too do stories need their beginnings, it's the only way in which to reach its ending. Destiny has to start somewhere. I know too

much about that, but I didn't always. It required an-
other first.

Once upon a long time ago the wind ran free
across the landscape of a newly incorporated vil-
lage, its blustery breath unfettered as it just passed
through. On stifling summer days, storms conjured
themselves seemingly from nowhere and they would
rage over darkened skies, rainwater pooling in the
low-lying fields. During harsh winters, falling white
snow would blanket the area in its downy, strangely
comforting embrace. In the reborn spring, flash floods
threatened the multitude of crops which sprouted
from tilled land, sometimes drowning its seeds before
their fruit could bear its full potential.

Nature had its yearly cycle. But so did people.

Together, they would combine to tell a story, one
that endured to this day, and perhaps, to another.

The village that became known as Linden Corners
didn't grow much over the years, but it prospered
anyway as though its landmark served as the magic
that kept its heart beating. That landmark was, and
remains, of course the Dutch-style windmill, stand-
ing proudly after not quite two centuries. Once use-
ful as part of tilling the land, it had transformed into
a symbol of hopeful wishes and pined-for dreams
for so many who had marveled at its power and re-
lied on its ever-turning sails. Built in the middle of
a verdant field of fresh grass and rolling hills, the

old windmill had brought families together, warm embraces mysteriously found in its latticed arms. Even on quiet days when the wind grew silent, the majestic windmill loomed over tiny Linden Corners like a guarded sentry, its unique presence beckoning visitors to town, drawing them inexplicably, into its unique hold.

The windmill never failed in its allure.

Legend persevered over the years that the windmill had originally been built for practical reasons, a way to assist the local landowners in clearing away the fallen rain that would pool in the valley and threaten to ruin the annual harvest. And while yes, those mighty sails proved their usefulness against nature's unyielding wrath, pumping the excess water into the nearby creek, it was an altogether different truth that came to define the windmill.

That's where the story begins.

With the building of the windmill.

His name was Charles Van Diver, and he raced out of the farmhouse and ran down the hill. His eager feet slopped in the soggy mess the overnight rain had created, but at an impressionable seventeen years of age, he didn't care for such inconsequential matters. The calendar had just turned from August to September and as such the warm summer months would soon recede into the past. A cool season of burnt colors loomed before them and for the wide-eyed Charles, who always looked at the world with hope toward tomorrow, there was no better promise than the arrival of a new season, a new morning.

"Charles, where are you going?" called out his mother, Verda Van Diver.

She stood on the back porch of the newly constructed farmhouse, a straw broom in her clutches. She wore a simple frock of yellow, but then again, she always did, no matter the season. Verda was a creature of habit, unlike her oldest child who was as hard to catch as a rabbit.

"I'll be back soon," he said, his voice echoing back.

"Breakfast in fifteen minutes."

It was barely six in the morning, but in a place like Linden Corners you rose with the sun. The animals were awake, the cows ready to be milked and the chickens producing eggs for that day's first meal. Verda, her blonde hair wrapped in her usual tight bun, had been up since four thirty gathering the ingredients in which to feed her growing family. Charles had come first, and as such he was expected to be the grounded one--the one who would take the family forward with practicality and a disregard for life's nonsense. Birth order meant nothing to Charles, not even in his toddler days. He had always looked upward to the sky, wondered where today's wind had been days ago and where it would pass through tomorrow.

Always wandering off, dreaming, that one, that's what his father Sven said.

Unlike his siblings, Anders, twelve, and little Sarah, seven.

Charles waved back toward his mother, his way of acknowledging that he'd back in time for breakfast. Still, his legs ran, slopping in the wet grass. It had rained on and off for the last week, afternoon thunderstorm were near-constants during these late summer weeks. Last night's insistent rain hadn't helped, and so the valley just behind the farmhouse was unusually swampy. In the back of his mind he knew he should be worried about the perennials, but in all of his years the family had managed to save the crops. He did his part, chores were done when schoolwork was not. But this day was Saturday, and he had awakened with a spirit he felt deep inside him. His heart raced, he grew a wide smile as he ran up the far hill, where he came to the gurgling creek. The water was high, not surprising, so the stones he usually used to cross to the other side were covered, slick. It was a good five feet wide, and he supposed had he gotten a good running jump he could have made it across. Charles Van Diver was lithe, with runner's legs and a slim build. The way he felt on this day, he might have soared across the creek and into the air.

He didn't. He didn't need to.

Because waiting on the other side of the creek, there she was.

"Why Charles Van Diver, what brings you here so early in the morning?"

Her words were mere pretense, spoken so anyone who might be listening could believe their meeting happened by chance. No one was about, the hour too early, and certainly, this was no accidental meeting. During last night's Summer's Wane celebration which took place in the basement of St. Matthew's, they had arranged it. Cara Larssen hadn't been allowed to stay late, not at the age of sixteen. She confessed during an exchange at the punch bowl that she wasn't much of a night owl. The morning was her favorite, she said, she liked to race the sun to the sky.

"Me too," Charles had confessed. "Meet me. At the creek."

She agreed, and here they were.

Cara had come to Linden Corners with her parents five months ago, just after the cold winter had finally swept out. They were visiting family that had come over from the Netherlands three years ago, Cara's aunt, her father's sister. They had arrived through New York, and soon journeyed their way up the great Hudson River, where other Dutch settlers had come in the early eighteenth century. Rumors of a new world and a fresh chance lured them to America, the sense of community and tradition landing them in Linden Corners. The Van Divers and Larssens were neighbors, and friends. All that separated them was this creek and its rushing waters

Charles looked over at lovely Cara, smiling, wishing he had done as he'd thought: leaped over the break in the land. She was grinning back, as though waiting for him to do just that. Oh, but his heart beat, a rapid sensation inside his chest. She was beautiful, with yellow golden hair like silk, and a growing bosom, which held his eyes, and she wore today a dress of blue, which turned her irises the color of the sky. What he wouldn't do to be forever in her company. But there was a reason for their meeting on this quiet morning.

"What you told me last night, it can't be true."

"Father has decided to return home. America is not his future, he said."

"Tell me when."

"Before the cold weather returns."

"In this region, that could be only weeks away," Charles said. "I can't bear it, you being taken by the wind."

"Charles, you are so poetic. You remind me of home. The way your arms swing when you run. You are like the windmills scattered over our land."

Charles smiled the way a young boy in love does when a grand gesture finds him.

Linden Corners, after that exchange by the creek, would forever be changed. He knew he would be.

"I have to return home before they find me missing," Cara said, turning back.

"I as well."

But before he could leave her presence, he stepped over a wet stone and nearly fell into the creek. Determination for the end result kept him balanced, focused. At last he crossed, and he swept her into his open arms, folding them around her with the freedom born of taking to the air. They had done the same before, at last night's dance. This morning, their relationship, so new and now so limited by time, took a dizzying, wondrous step forward. He kissed her, and what made his heart beat that much faster was the fact that she kissed him back.

Yes, when he returned to the farmhouse, his arms were indeed spinning, just as she had said. Just like a windmill.

"A windmill, where did such a fanciful thought come from?"

Sven Van Diver, brushing his long beard, could

hardly speak the words without laughing.

"I know how," insisted little Sarah, spooning oat-meal into her mouth. "Cara Larssen."

Charles felt his face grow flush; he thought he'd been so clever, so surreptitious in his feelings for Cara. But there was no getting around the fact he wore his heart on his sleeve. His mind recalled a pair of eyes spying on him and Cara last night and now he knew who it was, his meddlesome sister. Anders, his broth-er, seemed more intrigued by the idea of the windmill and thankfully brought the table's conversation back to it.

"I've seen pictures, Papa, I think it would look great on our property."

"It would cut down on the field's dampness," Verda admitted, her eyes darting back to Charles's filthy boots near the back door.

Sven Van Diver said he would think about it, but Charles watched him all through their breakfast, and all during the day, and he knew he was giving it cre-dence. It was just the type of project the denizens of Linden Corners needed before another long win-ter came; they would need to enlist the virile men of town to assist in its creation. Charles imagined them constructing the tower, then loading the sails until they were secure and only a passing wind could stir them. He thought about it for days, and it was on the fourth night of the following week when darkness fell

*and he readied for bed that his strong, large-framed
father came to his room and sat down on its edge. He
heard the squeak of wood.*

"So, a windmill, Charles. To help with our crops?"

"Just like the old country."

*"What do you know of the old country? You are
lucky to be born here."*

"Stories you and Mama tell. I'm a good listener."

"You're also a very good spinner of tales yourself."

*Charles again went flush, his visible emotions his
nemesis.*

*"No matter your motive, and I suspect it has more
to do with that pretty young thing at the farmhouse
up the road. Still, building a windmill on our land to
assist with the preservation of our yearly crops is practical and quite frankly, should have been taken care
of years ago. Our vegetable stand has suffered losses
the last few seasons, so our windmill has been a long
time coming. We begin construction next week."*

*Charles fell asleep with the picture of himself and
Cara, the two of them standing in the shadow of the
windmill. It was morning, their time, and the rest of
the world remained asleep. Its sails would turn only
for them.*

He awoke the following Monday to the insistent rat-a-tat of hammering, and once he realized where that sound was coming from, he tossed off his covers and dashed to the window. His view looked out across the vast land that sprawled beyond the farmhouse. At least a dozen men were gathered, wandering amidst a large supply of wood. His heart thrummed with excitement and it took all of his will to not run across the creek and bring Cara to the building site. He didn't want her to see it in progress. What he wanted was for her to see the final product, and of course it had to be done before she returned back home to her country. He wanted to bring home to her. Perhaps then her father might re-consider crossing the Atlantic again, the very idea doing little to quiet his heart.

The building of the windmill became almost a ritual for Charles.

For the next two weeks, he would awaken early to check on the progress.

He would come home from school and watch the men toil amidst the elements.

And at night, oh, at night, just before he feel asleep to sparkling stars, he would steal a long look at the day's progress, and then in his dreams he imagined the completed windmill. A fierce wind would blow through their little village, and the sails would spin, and spin, and spin some more. It was still summer, however, and the weather caused delays; hot temperatures and humidity came, enough to soak through the clothing of the men who labored under the hot sun, and one day, a soaking rain created another pool of water in the field. The windmill, his father stated with bravado, couldn't be put into operation any sooner. The way he spoke of it, building the windmill had been his idea. Not Charles's. No matter the reason, the windmill was steadily climbing toward the sky, and Charles' only enemy was the countdown of the clock. Cara Larssen would be leaving soon.

He couldn't bear such a thought. On this early night of September, he willed the windmill to spin, but only the tower was in place; the sails were still to be raised. He overheard his father that night, saying to his wife, "The sails go up tomorrow, except we've got a hell of a storm on the horizon. It might set us back a day or so. No sense putting it up and then having nature take it down."

Charles knew he didn't have a day, "or so."

He had to come up with an alternate plan.

Turned out, a storm did rage through Linden Corners, dropping buckets of rain along the valley. Wind was its companion, and it whipped fiercely across the land. Windows rattled inside the farmhouse. He heard the insistent clack of the back door, unhinged from its lock. The air was unseasonably cool, so the family had built a fire in the living room, and they had all gathered amidst the candlelight. Sven, Verda, along with Anders and of course young Sarah, huddling in her father's big arms for protection. Charles sat beside the fire, quiet, but that was not unusual. He had many thoughts as a boy, but he seldom shared them.

At last he got up, the heat of the fire having warmed him. His father was in the midst of a story of the time his parents were introduced back in the Netherlands. He spoke of endless fields of tulips, and of course he spoke of windmills that dotted the land. Such stories got Charles thinking and so he wandered off, putting on his coat and boots and going outside. He snuck down the hill, his feet sinking into the wet ground. The wind whipped at his hair. No moonlight to keep him company tonight, so he was left with just the dark shadow of the windmill that was taking shape. It was bigger than he had anticipated, with two floors and a metal railing that ran the circumference of the building. The entrance to it was already in place. It just lacked its sails. He set a wish upon the wind just then, asking the storm to pass for now; *let us finish first*, then return to allow the windmill to show off in its full, intended glory. He stood in the night for too long and eventually made his way upstairs, where his mother tucked him in.

"Mama, I'm not a child anymore," he said.

"No, I don't suppose you are," she said, knowingly.

"But you'll always be my boy."

His wish came true the next morning, the storm gone and the men back at work. How he wished school didn't beckon today, he wanted to watch as the sails were lifted, but at least it was an excuse to see Cara. And indeed, there she was, her soft golden curls as alluring as ever. They even got to share lunch together, though they were hardly alone. Anders was there, and so too were Cara's cousins whom she lived with. They spoke of her impending departure.

"Father's father is not well. That's the real reason for our return, I learned just the other day," she said. "We need to leave soon."

"How soon?" Charles said, his voice betraying him. He loved her, everyone knew it.

After school, he walked her home. The roads were soggy, and their feet grew wet. Neither seemed to care, so long as they were in each other's company. As they crossed an open field, he reached for her hand, and she took it. No, she clasped it. They snuck a smile at each other. Once she was home, her mother scurried her inside and he was alone, a feeling he didn't like. So he dashed across their land, reaching the creek and with a great leap—a leap of faith he thought—he landed smoothly on his property, and he emerged from the trees to see that the windmill was complete. Sails attached, spinning, the men standing in its grand shadow and applauding their own efforts. Their hard work had been rewarded, where once there was an open field, now stood a fully functioning windmill, built within the land called Linden Corners.

Charles Van Diver felt his heart skip a beat.

He had done it. His grand gesture of love loomed large in the field.

Two days from now would come the unveiling.

The day was Saturday, and all of Linden Corners was expected at the Van Diver farmhouse to celebrate the building of the windmill, a way for many to feel closer to the homes they had left an ocean away. Charles awoke to a bright sky, and the temperature hung in the high sixties. As nice a day as they had seen in weeks, almost as if Mother Nature had received an invitation to their celebration, too. She'd worn her finest, and so did Charles, dressing in what he would wear to Sunday service. He struggled with the tie, but eventually decided the effort was as good as the result. He skipped breakfast, ran down the hill, the grass still high and green. He leaped over the gurgling creek and continued his fast pace up to the Larssen's farmhouse.

He knew it was early, but everyone awoke with the dawn.

The farmhouse was unusually quiet. He only heard the cluck of chickens from the nearby coop. The morning's eggs hadn't yet been harvested. That was strange, he thought. But he would not be deterred, so he knocked, and then he waited. He turned back, and through the branches going to bare he would see the windmill's giant sails against the horizon. He exhaled heavily, his excitement palpable.

"My goodness, Charles Van Diver, you are an early riser."

She was Helena Craigg, Cara's elderly aunt, opening the door. "I'm sorry to come at such an early hour but...it's just so lovely outside, and the windmill... it's real, and it spins, and it's the most perfect day to celebrate. Oh, Mrs. Craigg, might I see Cara? She has to see the windmill. I have to show it to her. You see, I had it built..."

But she cut off his words, words that began with hope and ended with despair.

"I'm sorry, Charles, but Cara and her family left yesterday morning. The weather was so improved after that nasty storm, my brother Arnoud took advantage and started off. They are no doubt back in New York, and soon they will board a ship that will take them back home." She paused, and Charles's crestfallen expression must have spoken to a spot deep within her heart. She told him to wait, and

she returned a moment later, handing him a sealed, white envelope.

"She asked me to give you this."

Charles accepted it, but he wouldn't open it. Not here, not in the presence of another.

He shied away from the farmhouse, went back across the land. His feet knew where he was going even before his mind did; his mind was too numb to think. Still, he journeyed toward the base of the windmill, where the young, impressionable seventeen-year-old stared upwards at the sails, spinning just as intended in the gentle wind. With the envelope in his hand, he entered through the door for the first time, and he rounded a spiral staircase that would take him to the second floor. It was only when he was settled on the floor that he conjured the bravery to open the letter. He took a deep breath and then unfolded the thick parchment to read the words written upon it.

I LOVE YOU, TOO, CHARLES. THANK YOU FOR THE WINDMILL. I'LL CHERISH IT IN MY DREAMS FOREVER. GOODBYE.

He sat in the midst of his own creation, tears streaming down his cheeks.

He felt emptiness gather in his heart. How strange, since moments ago it had been so full.

———————

Charles Van Diver never forgot the lovely, golden-haired Cara Larssen. He never forgot the innocence which had spurred the idea of the windmill. He would never leave Linden Corners. He eventually married, and the Van Diver name forged ahead into the future, even as he and his youthful memories faded into family history. What did remain in Linden Corners, left to inspire others, was not only the majestic windmill, but the deep, heartfelt feelings of the man whose love had created the windmill. A man who hoped that one day, some day, the mighty windmill would inspire the kind of enduring love that had kept his heart aflutter. Done so until the natural course of life found its way, many years later, to quieting it.

Only in death had Charles Van Diver stopped chasing windmills.

And how do I know all of these details? How is it I come to tell you this story of love lost and found, and of others still to come? My name is Annie Sullivan, and I know a special thing or two about the windmill. Follow me, there's another story yet to be told. A most wondrous story.

PART ONE

Winter

CHAPTER ONE

THREE YEARS.

Three years since I'd called this city home.

Three years since my life had been turned upside down for good, spun into directions I'd never seen coming.

Three years since a young, funny, freckle-faced girl by the name of Janey Sullivan had magically healed my wounded heart.

And now, yes, three years later, the reason for that wounded heart walked into the church. It was almost as if the clock's hands had turned back, because she still looked amazingly beautiful, as though the elapsed time since last I'd seen her had somehow eluded her. Her soft, honey-blonde hair was longer, curling over her shoulders, her slim frame and crooked smile were as commanding, as devastatingly lovely, as ever. Her azure eyes sparkled in the candlelight's reflection.

Removing her overcoat, she wore a sleek silver dress and carried a black designer clutch. I would have recognized her anywhere, whether sitting at a fancy restaurant or sipping a cocktail at some upscale wine bar or sweaty after a workout at the gym, but here she was, in church, an unexpected guest at the wedding.

Once upon a time it should have been the two of us at the altar.

Proclaiming love for each other. It hadn't been real, only the idea of it had been.

I felt a rush of blood to my heart, even as sweat dampened my palms. There was nowhere to go, no escape from this moment unfolding before me. Her liquid eyes hadn't looked my way yet, but clearly she must have known I'd be present for such a momentous event. Thankfully I was in no position to talk to her, not now. With a crowd already assembled in the wooden pews, the lady organist ready to fill the ornate church with the sounds of the traditional wedding march, I caught the darting eyes of the man by whose side I stood. His name was John Oliver, my best friend, and I, Brian Duncan, was his best man.

But the look I tossed him could have brought an end to both relationships.

"What is she doing here?" I asked under my breath.

John, looking spiffy in his black tuxedo but guilty otherwise, wiped a bead of sweat from his brow. I doubted it was from any anxiety over marrying the beautiful, fiery Anna Santorini, whom he'd been dating for more than two years, including their yearlong engagement. He was a lucky bastard to not only have found her but managed to not screw it up--it was amazing she put up with his juvenile antics. Sometimes John did stupid things, not giving thought to the ramifications, and inviting her to the wedding ranked right up there. Conflict raged inside me, leaving me with the thought John might not live to enjoy the honeymoon. It didn't know if I felt anger or fear, and I didn't know if was directed at him, her, or myself for rising to the bait.

John spoke, his voice a whisper.

"She moved back to town a few months ago, got in touch with me. You know, we were friends before you two hooked up and..."

"Save it. You could have told me. You didn't have to invite her."

"Come on, Brian, what happened was a long time ago. You have a new life."

I did, right? Rather than ride the subways and work in a towering office building made of steel and glass, rather than eat take-out out from a carton at my desk while I logged long hours, rather than live in a small one-bedroom apartment with gates on the window, I'd gone rural, rustic. The farmhouse I now called home came equipped with a truck that was on its last legs, a precocious young girl who was fast approaching her teen years, not to mention the majestic old windmill that defined our land, all of which had given new meaning to my everyday life. I also served drinks at the local tavern, which I owned, and I was surrounded by friends, and recently, reluctantly, my family, giving the sparkling world of Linden Corners a tinge of angst. But the thing about having lived in New York City and walked its crowded sidewalks and indulged its quick pace is this: when you come back, so too do your instincts, and your suspicions. And I was feeling them right now.

I stared back out at the church's pews, and at last my eyes connected with hers from eight rows back. Even from this distance I could recognize a sudden flash of regret in them, unsure if it began inside her, or if were they simply a reflection of what lay in mine. Maybe it was as simple as a trick of the sun beaming through stained glass window.

She attempted a rueful smile my way. That same tilt of her head that I remembered when she posed a question. I had to wonder what that question would be today, and what made the matter worse, my mind was busy conjuring any kind of answer. I had no words for her.

My one-time fiancé was here. She'd betrayed me once. But in a way, she'd saved me.

Then, the moment passed between us, and in an ironic twist, the sounds of Mendelssohn began to fill the church. Bridesmaids and groomsmen readied themselves and began to proceed down the long aisle. The bride, all in pearled white and lace, appeared at the back of the church, ready to walk down the aisle and take this man at my side as her lawfully wedded husband. Their lives together were just beginning. For all I had gained over the last few years, what I had lost out on was laid out before me, and I had a front row seat. How were you to celebrate a wedding when the woman who'd denied you your own loomed before you? Digging into my pocket, I felt the ring box and hoped that when the time came for me to present it I wouldn't drop the ring. My hands were trembling.

All eyes were on Anna Santorini. Except mine.

Maddie Chasen had re-entered my life, and at the most inopportune time.

I never did understand the phrase "the wedding went off without a hitch,' seeing as though the "I do's" were successfully exchanged between man and woman. The vows spoken before a crowd of nearly one hundred witnesses were as heartfelt as I'd ever heard coming from my usually jocular, life-is-a-party friend. An already radiant, smiling Anna beamed when the priest said he could kiss the bride. So in fact, it did go off with a hitch. The unlikely pairing of John Oliver and Anna Maria Theresa Santorini were pronounced husband and wife, and after a prolonged kiss, they processed off the altar together and back down the aisle to the sound of applause. I followed suit along with Janine, Anna's sister and maid of honor, her arm linked in mine, almost as though she were keeping me from making a detour into the pews to say a formal hi to Maddie.

That would come soon enough.

The wedding party, including two sets of happy parents and the three other bridesmaids and groomsmen, formed a reception line on the steps of the Cathedral Basilica of St. James in downtown Brooklyn, while the afternoon's bright sun beamed down on the happy couple. I stood beside John, me playing the reliable best man despite the thumping coming from inside my chest, shaking hands and smiling till it hurt, nodding politely whenever someone said, "oh, yes, you're the farmer from upstate." I jabbed John in the side each time, always having thought that was a private joke between us. While I might have moved to Linden Corners, a beatific village in the Hudson River Valley, I was not, by any stretch, a farmer. The closest I came was the fact I lived in an old, rambling farmhouse. The only milking being done was by John for his corny cow references. As the line progressed, I kept my eye on the people as they approached, and there she was, just three people away. Maddie. She saw me, offered up that alluring smile again, albeit one with a hint of hesitancy.

"Yes, thank you for coming, it's a beautiful day in New York, thankfully not too cold."

It was February and why they had chosen this month to get married I didn't know; maybe a cut rate? But the inner heat I felt continued to dampen my palms. I wiped them on my tuxedo pants just before Maddie made her way to me. But it was all for naught, because she did not take my proffered hand. Instead, she kissed me on the cheek, her perfume nearly knocking me to the ground. Or maybe it was just her. As she drew back, I imagined a stain of red from her lipstick on my cheek. It would seem impolitic to rub it off.

"You look good, Brian."

I didn't know what to say. "Even monkeys can't wear a tux wrong," was what came out.

I flushed red but she laughed politely. "Don't sell yourself so short."

"You look good, too, Maddie. I didn't realize you would be here."

"So I gathered. You looked more scared on that altar than the groom," she said. "Well, I shouldn't hold up the line. Be well, Brian."

Be well? That was it? I looked good, and I should be well. So cool, so formal. I'd loved her once and thought I'd be spending the rest of my life with her. I'd even bought the ring and had the day planned when I would present it to her. A knot hit my throat, leaving me without anything else to say. Forgetting the line of people behind her, I watched as Maddie hugged John and kissed Anna, even though I wasn't sure if they'd ever met before, listened as she said her congratulations to the happy couple. Then, with one last, wistful look back at me, she put on her coat and headed off the steps and down the quiet sidewalk. John tossed me a look and I realized I'd been staring, as though watching her every move. Funny, I felt paralyzed.

"Go talk to her," he said.

"I...I can't. What kind of best man would I be?"

"You're relieved of your duties, soldier, for now."

"You sure?"

"Brian, you yourself said it's been three years. Wounds heal."

I couldn't say it was impulse that sent me chasing after Maddie, not when I had to think about what I'd say when I actually confronted her. John's less-than-subtle nudge sent me off the top step and I stumbled on the last one as I hit the sidewalk. Leaving the wedding party and its startled guests behind, I started after Maddie. She was about one hundred feet ahead and gaining distance; she'd always had that great New York pace down pat, as had I once upon a time. It was now being used against me and left me no choice but to call out after her.

"Maddie...Maddie, wait up," I said.

The sound of her name on my tongue seemed so strange, yet, with the rise of Manhattan's skyline in the near distance, it was also eerily familiar. This had been our stomping ground, the city that housed not only our memories but somewhere along busy avenues, our lost future. She spun around in the way that beautiful women can pull off, she all style and class. Her inquiring gaze penetrated me, confusing me. What was I going to say? What was there to say?

"I...I, look, this isn't easy..."

"So let me make it easy. Brian, I meant it when I said be well. There's no reason for us to rehash what happened, or what might have been. I just wanted to see you. That's all. John said you were happy in your new life and I'm glad for that. Taking care of Janey, she must be a full time job."

"You remember her name?"

"That little girl leaves quite an impression, especially if she doesn't like you."

Maddie had visited Linden Corners once, a short visit. It hadn't gone well for either of us.

"She didn't know you," I said, trying to be kind.

"You did."

I paused. "I thought I did."

She reached out, took hold of my hand. "Like I said, let's not do this. Time has moved on, I think it's a good idea if we take its lead. Good-bye, Brian."

"Wait, you came to the wedding. But you're not going to the reception?"

"It was a lovely ceremony and I'm glad I witnessed it. John's always been a good friend to me—to both of us. It's nice to see him settled, a bet I think we both would have lost," she said with a rueful smile. "That he actually committed."

"Anna's not the kind of woman to sit around waiting forever," I said. "She's a firebrand."

"They deserve every happiness," she said.

The words fell between us, as though they were too heavy for either of us to hold.

"So, uh, the reception?" I asked, trying to get us back on track.

She shook her head. "The idea of a party, it's not really something I'm in the mood for. Plus, I don't know anyone and I'd prefer not to be one of those guests sitting at a table filled with strangers and struggling to find even the smallest talk. It becomes a verbal resume exchange."

"I'm not a stranger," he said.

"That's sweet, Brian. But you have best-man duties. You don't need a distraction."

"You were never a distraction, Madison Laurette Chasen."

She patted my cheek. "Yeah, I was. Both the good kind and the bad."

Despite her betrayal three years ago, in which she'd

had an affair with our mutual boss and I'd found them in her bed together, Maddie spoke a certain truth. I'd been captivated by her from the start when I'd met her at a party John had thrown, drawn in by her obvious beauty, sure, but also the tiny lilt of a Southern accent in her voice. She'd been trying to get rid of it her entire life, she'd claimed, but even today I could hear it sneaking into her words. Emotions tended to bring out the real person, the one many people tried to hide.

"I don't leave New York until Monday," I said, not exactly the truth. But it couldn't end here, on a street corner in Brooklyn.

"Brian, I don't think...."

"Meet me, tomorrow. For coffee, or a drink...well, for you. I'll have seltzer, because as you know..."

Was I rambling? My mouth wouldn't stop nattering on, probably because my mind had ceased working. Had I really just asked Maddie to meet me? Didn't I have a ticket to return to Linden Corners on Amtrak tomorrow morning? Sunday was my day off from running George's Tavern, a day when Janey and I just got to hang out and play father and daughter. I'd intended to cut short my weekend visit with John to honor our routine. Yet here I was jumping into the deep end of the pool, except for the fact it was still winter, the water now a sheen of slippery ice.

Yet something I said must have melted her. Or maybe it was the tone in my voice, or the taste of the past. She laughed, holding up her hands. "Ok, I'll meet you."

I stopped talking. "You will?"

"If that's how I get you to shut up, yeah."

She took a business card from her purse, handed it to me. I avoided looking at it, fearing to see the name The Beckford Group. Had she gone back to the public relations firm she and I had once worked at? Was she still in touch with our old boss? I shuddered at the thought of that slime Justin Warfield? Is that why she'd returned to New York, to rekindle her affair with the hairy bastard? All those thoughts took a mere second to race through my mind. I slipped the card into my pocket.

"Call me, but not too early."

"You like to sleep in on Sundays," I remarked.

"You remember," she said.

"Not everything was bad," I said, unsure why.

"Enjoy the reception, Brian. Looks like the limo is waiting on you. Duty calls."

I looked back and saw John standing beside the sleek black limo. The door was open and he was tapping watch, waving me on. I had a toast to deliver, one I'd already worked out in my head. Given what had happened in the last hour, seeing Maddie, talking to her, knowing John had orchestrated the entire thing, well, I might just have to revise certain passages. Trouble was, I didn't know if I was mad at him or grateful.

You don't get many second chances in life. You had to grab them, or else they slipped through your fingers and became property of the air.

I'd lost Maddie once, letting hurt and anger fuel my motives to change my life.

But I'd also lost someone else during that time, someone wonderful and special, a woman named Annie Sullivan. Her passing had changed me in so many different ways. I'd learned patience, understanding, and not to not act on impulse. There were others whose lives were affected by your own decisions. Honestly, I'd learned what love really meant. I'd discovered that the biggest things in life came in small, irrepressible packages.

So why was I trading in my special day with Janey to spend it with Maddie?

The heart has many compartments. You can't hide in all of them.

Raising a kid is a curious thing. With Janey, it's not like I had nine months in which to get ready. To plan for her birth, sharing sonograms and feeling my wife's belly when the baby kicked, none of those privileges had been afforded me. I never had to decorate a nursery, build a crib. Just one day Annie and I were edging closer to a future, and I was helping the widow raise a then-seven-year-old Janey. Then came another day when fate stepped in and Annie was gone from our lives and Janey and I were thrown together, strangers who had nonetheless forged a connection deeper than either of us had imagined. Suddenly young Janey was my priority, my own life put on hold. Everything I did, every decision I made, all of it centered on Janey's needs.

So then why was I feeling guilty for taking a weekend for myself?

The wedding reception was winding down as the midnight hour approached. A last few dedicated dancers were still on the floor, even though the band had quieted things down for those wanting a romantic spin on the dance floor. I'd survived my share of moves, especially with the maid of honor, who seemed happy to get away from my two left feet and return to the arms of her boyfriend. I stole a moment away from the reception, nearly grabbing a glass of wine to take with me as I went outside into the night air. But I still didn't drink, even though the bout with hepatitis that had started me down this path was long over and I was completely healthy. Even though I owned a bar, people thought it strange that I didn't drink what I served.

It's just, all night long, without a glass in my hand I'd felt empty.

Not having someone in my arms, that had made me feel even emptier.

The Mercer Ballroom was located off Atlantic Avenue in Brooklyn. Once in the lobby, I walked up the marble steps to the third floor, where there were small balconies you could go out on. I opened the double-set of doors and emerged into a starry night. The temperature had fallen considerably, and I wrapped the lapels of my tux around my neck to ill effect. In the distance, Manhattan glowed, its towers lit, small boxes of light like insights into the millions of apartments that dotted the sky. How different urban life was from the rural existence I'd traded for. By this time at night, the only lights on in Linden Corners came from George's Tavern, and even then at midnight most nights they were doused.

Three years, I thought again.

Three years ago I'd had a successful job and was rising fast up the corporate ladder. I had the woman of my dreams in my arms and in my bed, a future dreamed about but one not realized. I'd bought Maddie's engagement ring at a small jewelry store of West 47th Street in the Diamond district, and before I'd had a chance to give it to her I'd discovered her in the arms of our lustful employer. From the way their bodies moved, it was clear they were familiar with each other's pleasure zones. I'd walked out before they'd seen me, and then I'd walked out on my job and her and my apartment, driving out of New York without explanation. Only John had known the truth.

John, the perennial bachelor who I thought I'd never see get married.

And today I'd stood up for him. Anna Santorini had changed him, for the better.

I harkened back to three Christmases ago when I'd brought Janey to New York. She had wanted to know what my life was like before she knew me, and thinking it was a way to help her through her grief, we'd come down to see the giant Rockefeller Center Christmas tree and the bright lights that lit up the stores on Fifth Avenue. Along the way we'd met up with John and Anna. And Janey, missing Annie still—it had been so fresh, still, just a few short months--had latched onto Anna fast. Their connection was strong, but it would have been with any woman, but still, I'd almost brought Janey with me to the wedding. My mother had talked me out of it.

"Brian, she won't have any fun, sitting by herself. You'll be busy being best man," Didi rationalized.

"We'll keep good watch over her," my father Kevin had piped in.

My parents had recently made a part-time move to Linden Corners, a fact I still couldn't wrap my mind around. They'd come for Christmas this past year and so far they hadn't left, busy setting up their new home in the farmhouse once owned by my friends, Bradley and Cynthia Knight. Changes were afoot all over, with my close friends having just moved to Texas, and now with John and Anna's wedding. Janey, too, changed almost daily, growing up, growing wise, and on occasion, cracking wise. She was ten going on thirty, but then again, when I met her she was seven going on thirty. Maybe some thing didn't change.

My life certainly hadn't, not since Janey had become priority number one.

So that was my reasoning, I supposed, for remaining behind in the city for another day. Maybe, in order to fully move on, I had to finally put the hurt and anger not just aside but away. I would call Janey in the morning and explain that I needed to take care of some personal matters back in New York, finally box up the last of my belongings that John still held onto. John had taken over my apartment lease when I'd left, and now he and Anna had their own apartment in Brooklyn, not far from her parents. Italians girls never strayed too far, even with a new husband in tow. The lease was coming up for renewal and of course there was no reason to hold onto the place. Letting it go, I knew that would be the final step in closing the book on my New York life.

So what was I doing trying to reread a chapter by seeing Maddie tomorrow?

Telling myself I was over-thinking our...what did

one even call it? Not a date, but not so much a meeting either. One sounded too intimate, the other too clinical. It was just a quick get together, to finally bury the past.

Feeling the cold begin to settle in my bones, I withdrew into the warmth of the ballroom. The music was done, the band packing up their instruments. John and Anna were the only ones left on the dance floor, both of them moving as one in a tight embrace. Guess they heard music in their minds, and why shouldn't they on a day such as this? Anna wrapped her arms around her husband's shoulders, and he leaned down for a long, passionate kiss. I felt weird observing such a private moment, it was just a reinforcement of what I lacked. So not wanting to rain on their joyous parade, I just made my way out of the hall and went back outside. The night shielded the tear I felt welling up.

I raised my arm and managed to hail a cab fairly easily.

"Manhattan. Eighty-third and Second Avenue," I said, the cross streets feeling natural on my tongue. I'd said them hundreds of times during my tenure in the city.

Thirty minutes later, after crossing the Brooklyn Bridge and battling late Saturday night traffic along the FDR, I was dropped off in front of my building, a five-story walk-up with fire escapes curling across the front of it. Suddenly exhausted from the long day,

I walked slowly up the two flights of steps to my old apartment, took out the keys and opened the lock with familiar ease. My life as I'd once known it came rushing back to me in a heady flood of memories. I was home, and tomorrow I would be meeting the woman I'd once loved.

Kicking off my shoes and shedding myself of the tux jacket, I padded over to the bureau. I placed the keys on the top and was immediately struck by the image I saw in the mirror above. No, it wasn't my reflection I was looking at, rather a postcard slid into the frame. I remembered buying the card at Marla and Darla's Trading Post, sending that postcard to John not long after I'd decided to stay in Linden Corners. I took hold of it and read the back: "I am not a farmer!" Smiling at the lame joke we continued to share, I turned the card back over and my eyes glazed over the picture of the old windmill that stood proud on my property, its latticed sails set against a deep, azure sky.

"Annie, is that you telling me something?" I asked to the empty apartment.

It wasn't like the open field in Linden Corners, where the wind ran free. It's howling like a voice from somewhere else.

There was no answer, not this time.

It's odd, here I was in New York, my old life threatening to reclaim me, and what pulls me back from the brink of indecision was the wondrous, spinning sails of the village landmark that had defined my new life in Linden Corners. But a small part of me had to wonder, could the power of the wind have been harnessed, those far-reaching sails taking command and spun time in reverse, swirling me back to when I thought I had everything I'd ever wanted?

CHAPTER TWO

PERSPECTIVE IS EVERYTHING. Me being the so-called adult, I called it stretching the truth. For a child of ten, it was far simpler: it was a lie.

"I thought you went to New York for a wedding."

"I did," I said, my voice not quite confident in my reply.

"So then why did you say you had some unfinished business?"

"Because I do."

Okay, that was truth speaking, but the details of which were not ones I wanted to get into with my daughter. Janey Sullivan had a way of seeing through me. I'd never been a very good liar, my poker face leaving much to be desired. It was a good thing she and I were not face to face. The phone kept things as anonymous as possible and at this moment that was a good thing. As much as I detested not being truthful with her,,being back among the pieces of the life I'd left behind brought with it complications that she didn't need to know about.

"It's personal business," I tried to explain.

"That sounds like an oxymoron."

Ten years old and she knew what an oxymoron was. "Janey, it's complicated."

"Brian, this is Linden Corners, we don't do complicated," she said. Sometimes she forgot to call me Dad, reverting back to a time when our relationship hadn't been as solidified. Usually when she found me either silly, or exasperating, like now.

"But I'm not in Linden Corners. New York defines complicated."

She grew silent on the other end and for a moment I thought I might have lost the connection. I was talking on a cell phone, which in New York was as ubiquitous as seeing rats on the subway tracks, but back home in the land where even time forgot to show up, reception could be a chancy thing.

"Janey?"

"Yeah, Dad."

"Yeah?" I asked, a slight annoyance in my voice. Annie had been a stickler for speaking properly and I'd done my best to enforce that.

"Yes, Dad?"

"That's better," I said, a hint of a smile on my face, because I could envision the one on hers. "Look, I'll be home tomorrow, it's just another day. This old apartment of mine...it's time to let it go. John is moving on, literally, so that means I've got to pack the rest of my stuff. This isn't my home anymore, so it's time to box up what's left and send it on."

"Send it here?"

"Well, that would make sense, since that's where I live now."

"So...um, you'll never return to New York?"

I allowed a small laugh. "To visit, sure, but this apartment...it's the last of my old life."

"You don't need it because you have a new life, right?"

As grown-up as she appeared sometimes, a child needed assurances.

"You," I said, "I don't need it because I have you."

Her giggle warmed my heart. "Hurry home," she said.

Easier said than done, especially considering the complication I'd run into yesterday. Not that Janey needed to hear about that...her. As I said goodbye to her, telling her to be good to her grandparents, I closed the phone and slipped it into my pocket. And that's when I stared at the blank walls of my once-upon home. No more artwork, no more frames, the walls were now an open canvas ready for new memories from some with their own brush. Mine were packed away, both in boxes and in my mind, and among them were the times I'd spent with Maddie. Sharing a rare, home-cooked meal at the small round table we'd bought together, sitting on the sofa in the dark while watching a movie with cartons of Chinese food at our feet, and in the bed sharing a night of passion or just holding each other after a draining day at the Beckford Group left us exhausted. So much had happened here since I'd moved in, but yet so much more had gone on after I'd left it, even if the lease kept me tethered, an opt out clause from Linden Corners if I'd needed one. Now that was expiring, John had married, and as for me...where was I?

Lost, I felt, somewhere between yesterday and tomorrow.

Which meant I was living for today, and today meant meeting up with Maddie Chasen.

Speaking of Maddie, I was due to meet her at two o'clock, an hour from now. I spent a half hour more taping up boxes, and when I was done I stared at my handiwork. The room was empty, most of the furniture gone. Just the sofa remained, a few throw pillows strewn about, and a lone blanket; it's where I'd slept these past two nights, and where I would spend one final one. Tomorrow I would arrange for the building's superintendent to be here when UPS came to pick up the boxes and ship them to Linden Corners. It was easier that way, logistically and otherwise. I wasn't sure I could close the door on a fully empty apartment anyway.

At last it was time to leave, and I tossed on a leather jacket, wrapping a scarf around my neck to keep out the cold. A quick check of my appearance in the bathroom mirror showed a man filled with apprehension. I think I'd avoided thinking about this meeting with Maddie by immersing myself in the packing and cleaning. Now there were no further distractions. I washed my hands, splashing cold water on my face. The shock returned me to reality, even if it wasn't one I was sure I was ready to face. But I stepped out into the hallway anyway and turned the lock. Down the two flights of steps I went and out into a cool, bright afternoon. I hadn't brought gloves, so I stuck my hands in the pockets of my jeans and made my way west down East 83rd Street. Maddie had suggested we meet at the boathouse in Central Park, not too far of a walk on this crisp, winter day. The air felt fresh, and filled my lungs with a burst of energy, enough to keep me walking at a good clip across the longer stretches of Manhattan's avenues. I at last arrived at Fifth Avenue and crossed at the light with a crowd of people who were headed directly for the steps of the Metropolitan Museum of Art. Maddie and I had gone to many exhibits during the two years we dated, and I looked on with regret and a bit of envy at the young couples who walked hand-in-hand up the expansive steps.

I entered Central Park at 79th Street, bypassing

a hot dog vendor, which reminded me I'd not eat-
en since an early breakfast of breakfast and coffee. I
supposed Maddie and I would end up dining somewhere, so I continued on, making my way around
the winding paths of the park. Not that I'd forgotten
how large Central Park was, but having spent the last
three years living in tiny Linden Corners, I thought
we could drop the entire acreage of our small town
right in Strawberry Fields and still have room to spare.
For a moment I imagined that, instead of Belvedere
Castle looming up before me, I saw the mighty windmill that defined Linden Corners. My heart grew full,
and I realized that though I'd only been gone a couple
of days, I missed my home. I missed Janey.

I missed Annie, too.

Annie Sullivan was Janey's mother, and we'd fall-
en in love, only to have our short-lived romance end
with her tragic passing. I'd been left with Janey in my
care and since then I'd done everything and beyond to
ensure Janey healed, moved on, never forgot, all while
racing toward her teen years, which, while nearly
three years away in time was ever-closer in attitude.
We'd shared three memorable Christmases together, and amidst our wishes, our hopes, our memories,
we'd somehow managed to forge a future filled with
promise. Something Annie had been cruelly denied,
but her enduring spirit lived on, daily, especially when
the wind blew and the sails of the windmill on our

property spun their magic dust. Annie's sweet, giving smile was still vivid in my mind, which made me lose my step.

I stumbled over a curb in the pathway that curved through the park, tripped, and landed flat on my face. I heard a couple of people nearby exclaim surprise, perhaps a giggle too. I knew the feeling. Just then a pair of shoes came into view when my eyes focused, and then they looked up to find Maddie Chasen staring down at me. She wore a nice wool coat and a soft, burgundy scarf. Oh, and a large grin on her face.

"I think that small town of yours has made you lose your street smarts."

"I meant to do that," I said, in my best Pee-Wee voice.

Maddie laughed, the lilting song enough to lift me up off the ground. I brushed away dirt and sticks from my sweater and jeans while I looked at her with a sheepish grin. Her smile widened, highlighting her already pretty features into a picture of beauty. With her honey blonde hair slightly blown by the wind, and a cream-colored turtleneck curling up around her neck, she looked lithe and lovely. A spot of light red lipstick gave color to her otherwise pale complexion.

"Guess it's a good thing I wasn't at the water's edge," I said.

"I called out your name, Brian, but you didn't hear me. Care to tell me where your mind was?"

Linden Corners, I thought. With Janey, and with Annie.

Being here now felt almost like a betrayal. A concept Maddie was familiar with.

I held my tongue. Any acrimony that existed between us should be put in the past, tucked inside one of those boxes inside my apartment.

I skirted her question and said, "So, how are you?" I asked.

"No complaints. Nice day for a walk."

I nodded, looking at the empty branches of the encompassing trees. Winter had left the park bare. "Thanks for agreeing to meet with me."

"I nearly canceled," she said.

I'd nearly done the same thing. Again I wiped at my clothes, even though there was no more residue from my fall. It was just something to do.

"So, what do you want to do? You'd mentioned grabbing a drink, or maybe a snack?"

She allowed a rueful smile. "Why don't we walk and talk? Take the pressure off of the two of us staring at each other across a table."

"Oh, uh, sure," I said, and then attempted to ease the tension I felt. "I can walk."

We started off away from the boathouse cafe, but not before I tripped once more. Maddie grabbed hold of my arm, steadying me, all while my senses took in the same perfume I'd taken in yesterday, an intoxicating mix of floral and pine. Or maybe that was caused by the scents of the park wafting over the wind. We exchanged a look that said too much. Once upon a time we'd always been there for the other, unconditional support. Now only she had propped me up.

We continued on through the park, virtual strangers, a deadened space settling in between us. As we walked it was like we were people who had agreed upon a second date even after the first one had ended in disaster. We had a second chance to make a bad impression.

"When did you move back?"

"About five months ago."

John had told me that Maddie moved to Seattle after our breakup, a parting of the ways that also brought an end to her high-paying public relations job at the Beckford Group, tossing away her ill-gained vice presidency along with the man she'd bedded for the title. It doesn't help matters when you betray your co-worker—the man you claim to love--by sleeping with the boss and then have both relationships blow up in your face and destroy your life. Of course Maddie carried her own wounds, I realized, and for a moment felt a wash of regret over how I'd handled things. I'd quit the job, I ended things with her without much of an explanation, and I moved out of New York and found a new life in the windswept world of Linden Corners. Only now did I imagine she'd gone through a similar change, albeit not one of her choosing.

"Why'd you return? Too much rain?"

"Actually, Seattle was lovely. Very picturesque, and when it did rain it seemed to already match my mood. It was a good place for me to hide, to lick my wounds, so to speak. But three jobs in a span of two years, I knew settling there was not an option. I just couldn't get..."

"Comfortable?"

"Isn't it crazy? This city of eight million people, all of them on their cell phones and none of them paying attention to where they're going...and I missed it. Crowded sidewalks and even more crowded subways. Crime, roaches, cabbies who think horns are toys and pedestrians are part of a pinball game." She smiled. "New York has its charms."

"You paint a vivid picture."

"And I wanted to be a part of it. Again. I missed the pace."

I smiled as a flood of memories hit me. "You always did crave the limelight. I remember that first day after you were hired at the Beckford Group. Wide-eyed, sure-footed, that Southern lilt to your voice which made you seem like an innocent among wolves. Until you got down to business and showed us your true colors. A shark in the office, your eyes afire at the thought of landing a powerful new client. It's what you made you so good at your job—your passion--and it's what got you promoted above me."

A sudden silence feel between us and I realized I'd made an awful gaff. Passion wasn't really the right word given the context. Her fiery drive wasn't the only reason she'd been handed a Vice Presidency.

She turned away, staring through the stark branches of the trees at the high blue sky. A few birds flew by and I figured she wished she had that ability right now. To fly away, forget this moment. I wouldn't blame her, but in truth there was no avoiding the mess she'd created, and the fallout from her ill-thought decisions. That didn't mean I had to hand it to her on a plate.

"Maddie, I'm not here to toss around blame," I said.

"Brian, we both know what happened, what I did. Can we move forward?"

"Tell me more about Seattle."

She thought about it, her mind gathering stories. "I bought a car, I drove those steep hills. I met some new friends and on weekends we would take the ferry across the sound to Bainbridge Island and go sightseeing, hiking, biking. I ate more salmon than ever before, and once went for a drive on Saturday morning and found myself in the parking lot at SeaTac. I watched the planes taking off. It was then I knew it was time to return to New York. The fact that I'd messed up another relationship..."

She grew quiet and I didn't know what to say. We were walking under a stone bridge at this point. Perhaps she'd quieted down because she didn't want to hear the echo of her own voice confirming that when it came to romantic entanglements, smart choices were not her strong suit. Before we had met she'd had other boyfriends; heck, I'd been engaged once before to my high school sweetheart Lucy, so we each brought luggage to our carousel. Those old relationships are what crafted who we became, and I suppose those that had happened since our break-up had continued to re-define us. Of course, for me, I'd only met one woman since Annie, and it hadn't lasted. It couldn't. The first time back up on the horse, you knew it was going to be a quick ride.

"And so you came back. Where are you working now?"

"Grady, Ebersold and Dinegar," she said.

I whistled. They were one of the top public relations firms in the city, a merging of three successful giants in the industry who created an even bigger company. "Impressive."

"I'm just a cog in a large machine, one of many account executives, smart enough to get hired, savvy enough now not to try and get noticed too much.

Experience isn't just knowing how to do the job, it's how to survive."

Where we had worked, the Beckford Group, is had been small and intimate. Perhaps too intimate for our tastes in the long run. Our boss Justin Warfield, the classic tall, dark and handsome type, was a slick guy and operator, and while I did admire his business acumen in landing clients, his personality off the field sucked. His seduction of Maddie while they were away on a business trip had been pure manipulation. Predator that he is, he had his way and tossed her aside when it suited him. Not just out of his bed but eventually his boardroom, too, and in its cruel wake he had destroyed everything Maddie and I had tried to build outside the office. Sure, she wasn't blameless and I was as angry then as I can ever remember, but Justin proved to be as caring as a hungry alligator and just devoured us.

Maddie and I continued to walk in the waning light of the day as she told me a bit more about the job she'd taken. She had a cubicle, not an office. She went to lunch with a couple of the other women her age, both married with kids, and she said she tried not to let it all bother her.

"I don't say much these days, I just listen."

Maddie Chasen had changed, and when I stared into her eyes I saw the sadness that lived there. That was the only part of her that was different. She was still beautiful and alluring and she could probably run that PR firm she worked for. Except the fire was gone. The look that passed between us spoke volumes of what might have been. Of what couldn't be.

"Come on, enough maudlin topics," she said, as we began a climb up a winding path.

Through the twisted brambles we went, turning, passing other Sunday explorers, and then at last we were approaching the gray stone stairs of Belvedere Castle. She took hold of my hand, more by instinct than reason, and my eyes must have flashed surprise. Even so, she was ready with an easy quip.

"We don't need you tripping again," she said.

So I allowed my hand to remain clasped with hers, and together Maddie and I climbed to the top of the castle, eventually sneaking through its entry and up inside its turret. From there we gazed out over the northern reaches of Central Park. I could see the reservoir, its water quiet in the growing wind. I could see the twin spires of a building on the Upper West Side that were featured in some old movie, and to my right I craned my neck to look for my apartment building. Yet the taller apartment buildings on Fifth and Park Avenues blocked any further eastern view I might have sought. It was almost like the place no longer existed. Boxing up its contents had eliminated it from the world.

Memories remained, though.

Memories that included Maddie. When she would stay overnight. When we would cook. When on rainy weekends we'd watch movie after movie. Maybe even that movie with the twin spires I could see now. The past was reaching out, it tempting tentacles trying to grab me and lure me back. Or was that Maddie's handiwork?

"People make mistakes," Maddie finally said after minutes of studied silence.

"I thought we weren't going there," I said, turning to her.

Strangely, we were alone in our castle, with the sun waning to the west, creating streaks of orange against an endless horizon. The temperature had dropped in the past hour, the wind picking up noticeably. Maddie wrapped her arms around herself and I zipped up my jacket. But as much as our body language said we were closed for anything more intimate, the fates had something else in mind. For any other couple, this would have been a moment where the early promise of romance would have built to a heightened level, to be captured by an embrace, a kiss that would carry on the wind. But Maddie and I had too much history, too much baggage to go there. A kiss would not heal the past, it wouldn't undo what we'd each done to the other.

But moments that shouldn't happen have a way of happening anyway.

Maddie took the lead. She drew me in, and she pressed her lips against mine.

She was needy and she was in pain.

Was I needy too? Had I pushed my emotions so far down I didn't know how to react?

That's when I melted into her arms and our kiss lingered. Warmth returned, if not to the rest of the denizens of the park but to us, my body suddenly afire for the woman I'd once loved and lost. She and I were now in our own private moment where the past meant nothing.

"There's still some dumplings," she said.

"And one egg roll."

"The won ton soup tasted great. Salty, hot."

"I could say the same about you," I said as I kissed her bare shoulder.

Strewn about my old apartment on East 83rd Street were a series of white cartons filled—at least they once were—with a selection of dishes from nearby Szechuan Garden, a restaurant on 2nd Avenue known for its heavy hand with the spice. It's just what our bodies had craved after what had turned out to be an explosive, unexpected reunion. Upon returning, we had worked up a healthy appetite, and as we waited for our delivery spent more time stroking the flame we'd lit, so when the buzzer rang I had to douse our fever, find my clothes, and regretfully open the outside world to this crazy slice of life happening inside here.

I didn't want anything, anyone, intruding on our moment. As though by admitting reality existed outside, its presence would eliminate the fantasy. You can't go back again, you cannot recapture the past, isn't that what all those experts claim? Recreating something special shows just how it impossible a task it is; recreation in itself means not real, a fabrication of the mind.

Now we were satiated, at least food-wise, as we put down the last of our Kung Pao.

"Brian," Maddie said, allowing that Southern lilt to catch in her throat. She didn't need to say anything else. One word and I melted all over again, kissing her lips, tasting that salty soup she'd referenced. It was good to replenish our bodies, our sweaty selves no doubt having been depleted of our natural supply. She kissed me back, her hand touching my chest as she did so. So close to her, I breathed in her scent, her perfume still strong, perhaps heightened.

She pulled back suddenly, taking one of the throw pillows from the sofa and hugging it. Hiding herself.

"Something wrong?" I asked.

"This..."

"Isn't even over. You want to dissect already how foolish we were?"

She reached out a hand, cupping my smooth cheek. "Oh, Brian, that's not what I meant. I can't tell you how special this moment has been...and how special you are. I never dreamed that today we would end up this way, certainly not when I accepted John's invitation to the wedding. I knew I would see you. And that's all I wanted. To know that you were well."

"You think he did it on purpose?" I asked.

"Not in any manipulative way. He's our friend, he wants us to be happy."

"Happy together?"

Now she looked away and I realized I'd gone too far. The mention of us being together was a nod toward tomorrow, and come sun-up I'm not sure either of us would be able to explain what had occurred here. One moment she's kissing me in Central Park, the next thing I know we are here and tearing at each other's clothes, and we're laughing like the kids we're not anymore, and then things turned serious as we realized what we were about to do, and then the world did nothing to stop it. No phone calls, no knocks on the door, no interruption of any kind. We kissed, and we touched, and suddenly we were locked together in a passionate rhythm neither one of us had forgotten.

"You haven't said much about your life," she said.

"My life is all about Janey," I said, her name sounding foreign on my tongue.

It was this place, this moment, this woman. I felt an odd disconnect with Linden Corners. My eyes glanced toward the bureau in the corner, at the propped up postcard of the windmill. Why hadn't I packed it? Had I left it for John? Or for whoever else rented this apartment next? No matter, it was a reminder that jarred me. It was real, this land I'd come to call home, and it was out there and it called to me. But so too did New York. Was it possible I could call Manhattan home again, bring Janey with me and enroll her in a good school, get a job in PR and return to the corporate world? Did I even know how to tie a tie anymore? Could I trade the freedom of Linden Corners for the crazy pace of the city? I wasn't even sure why I was contemplating such a concept. Did I think Manhattan came with a beautiful woman? Could I accept her arms around me rather than the mystical embrace of the windmill's sails?

"Tell me about her. Anything about Linden Corners," Maddie said.

"Janey's ten now, but she thinks she's thirty. She also thinks she takes care of me, and who knows, maybe she does. We're a good team, we've overcome a lot. I still run George's Tavern most nights, and our best friends, the Knights, recently moved away to Texas, but in Linden Corners there always seems to be this balance in effect, that somehow everything works out. Believe it or not, my parents came to town for a visit and so far...they haven't left."

"Didi and Kevin Duncan...in farmland?"

"Don't laugh. They bought the farmhouse right next door, from Bradley and Cynthia."

"Talk about pearls before swine," Maddie said.

I laughed at an image of my very formal mother clutching her pearls while feeding pigs.

"Anyone...you know, in your life?"

"If there was, I wouldn't be here," I said.

"Good point."

I paused before deciding to open up my heart a bit. "There was this one woman. We tried things out. She wasn't ready, and neither was I, but it was a first step in the right direction."

"You still run into her?"

"No, Trina...that's her name. She came to Linden Corners to reunite with her estranged father, and in the end, they reunited and left town. Ole Richie Raven's motel, the Solemn Nights, went up in flames right before Christmas. With nothing left in town, he joined his daughter and together they hit the open road."

"I remember the Solemn Nights," she said. "I stayed there one night. It was awful."

In a last ditch effort to reconnect, or at least to understand the reason I'd run off, Maddie had unexpectedly come to Linden Corners. It hadn't been a successful visit, and it had been the last I'd seen of her...until just yesterday.

"So if I came to visit, there's no place to stay?" she asked.

A wave of fear hit me like a typhoon. It must have shown in my eyes, because Maddie was suddenly backtracking, fumbling over her words and I was only half listening anyway. Her words were still reverberating in my mind. Was she thinking what had happened today was the start of something new, rather than the moment it was? At last, any words lost, she pulled away again, and this time she stood up and began looking for her clothes. Her blonde hair fell across her face, and I think that was deliberate. Hiding again.

I went to her and pulled her into my arms. Pushing the hair away, I saw wet eyes.

"I'm sorry," she said as she stared at me.

"No, I'm sorry. For reacting that way..."

"Brian," she said, her sorrow-filled voice heavily accented. Like she'd retreated further back to her past, to her Carolina childhood.

I kissed her, and she kissed me back. We were hesitant at first and before long our gentle touches grew stronger. Our bodies tightly entwined, this heated moment taking command and all the words and all the hurt and all the pain faded away, and were left with fire, with desire, with a consuming need for companionship. Taking hold of her hand, I led her to the sofa.

Lying down, she then pulled me atop her, and I felt her fingers dig into my back as she urged me closer. Nothing else mattered now. The world was out there, somewhere: my life, her life, separate. But in here, we were together, and as we rode out the wave of passion that had reunited us on this strange day, thoughts of tomorrow no longer existed.

I didn't hear the wind rushing through the canyons of New York.

I didn't hear the rain begin to patter against the windows.

Not until later, not until we were done, and the food cartons were empty and our bodies had at last found some sort of satisfaction.

Maddie didn't stay overnight, she claimed an early meeting the next morning. It sounded authentic. I didn't argue.

She kissed me at the door, and again spoke my name with her lilting voice.

"I'll see you sometime, Brian Duncan, maybe the wind will whisk me off to your land of the windmill," she said, and with that she left the door wide open and started down the corridor. I listened to the sound of her shoes on the stairs until they were no more. The front door opened and it closed. Maddie Chasen had returned herself to the real world. I was still stuck in the realm of fantasy.

But then again, hadn't I been for three years now?

CHAPTER THREE

MAYBE I HAD LOST MY New York street smarts.
Monday morning found me stuck in slow-moving
traffic, inside a cab that was trying valiantly to weave
its way down a backed-up Fifth Avenue. I should have
known better and gotten an earlier train. Yet I had
to secure all the cardboard boxes with my super, and
once that was done, I turned the lock on my New York
life and said a quiet goodbye. To my old home, and to
my old flame. They were both secured behind a door I
never anticipated opening again.

It was just after nine o'clock, my train was at ten
fifteen, and I was making little progress in my attempt to escape from the city. I had dreamed of Linden
Corners all night, but strangers kept intruding upon
it, not least among them Maddie. I had no idea, really,
where we had left our relationship. She had intimated
she might visit; I had more than intimated that wasn't

among the best of ideas, but when she'd spoken of the windmill it was like she was tempting me. My hesitation had brought about the end of our day together, funny if you think about it. Her affair with Justin Warfield had ended us the first time, and now it was our own interlude that had ended it again. Fault surrounded me as much as the cars and commuter buses that lined Fifth Avenue.

"You know, you can let me off at Fifty-third," I told the cabbie.

I would get out and walk toward the subway and catch the E train right into Penn Station. Nice that I hadn't forgotten everything.

"Sure, don't blame you."

I tossed him a twenty, feeling bad for leaving him stuck in traffic.

Then, the moment I hit the sidewalk with my weekend bag strung over my shoulder, I realized one last stop awaited me here, and so bypassing the entrance to the E train, I continued my way down Fifth Avenue, sideswiping hectic pedestrians who were making a fast-dash to their offices, most of them with Starbucks cups in one hand and a cell phone in the other. I pictured Maddie doing just the same and never felt the pull of Linden Corners more.

I walked beyond Rockefeller Center a few more blocks and at last I turned west onto 47th Street. The Diamond District, and of course that's where I had to stop before I returned home. So many stores on this block offered up sparkling jewels, diamond rings in the windows, golden baubles meant to draw you in. The store I wanted was mid-block, Eli's Jewelers, a more intimate store run by a wizened old man who knew, intuitively, about men, about women, and the bonds that brought them together....and sometimes apart. My heart beat fast as I approached the shop, unsure why. Not that I planned to go inside, maybe it wasn't even open at their early hour. Most of the others were still setting up, returning their wares to the display windows after being locked up overnight. But as I came to Eli's, a surprise awaited me.

The gate was down. The sign was gone.

A piece of paper hung in the window.

WE THANK YOU FOR YEARS OF SERVICE.

I felt a lump in my throat as I visualized the little gray-haired man with the thick glasses as he shuffled about his store, knowledgeably showing off his rings, bracelets, and other trinkets that gave him such pleasure, others such hopes. I recalled the sparkle in Eli's eyes when picking out the diamond ring for Maddie, but I also would never forget the nod of understanding when I came to return the ring a few weeks later. I would never forget his prophetic words of how we all must tilt at our own windmills; heck, I'd been doing nothing but that for the past three years. Wise old Eli knew about more than jewelry, he knew life, emotions. I hoped he was well, enjoying his retirement and that the store's closure was not for another, sadder reason. I stole one last look at the empty windows and discarded cabinets, and then realized I had a train to catch and should get a move on. Tilt away, Eli, I thought, and then resumed my journey.

I made my way to the corner of 47th and Sixth Avenue, went down the stairs to the F train and took it as far as 34th Street. I still had to walk two avenues, but soon enough I had descended onto the platform and taken my seat aboard Amtrak's Empire Service to Albany. I was going as far as the historic village of Hudson, where I would be picked up and whisked back into the open arms of Linden Corners. Having packed up my old home, it would be good to return to my new one. But as always, the question crept back into my mind: to do what?

My seat was on the right, so I sat and stared out the window as the city grew faint behind us. The George Washington Bridge loomed, and then it was gone, and the train whistled its way toward upstate. The tracks rode right along the edges of the Hudson River, providing majestic views of the water and of mountains that stretched upwards on the other side. As I stared out, my mind retuned to the events of the past weekend—the wedding, the reunion with Maddie--and wondered whether I was taking back with me any of those dreaded complications I'd told Janey of. I could just see Janey's face scrunch up in that fashion of hers; she'd no doubt grill me about that personal business which had delayed my returning by a day.

After last year's holiday, where I'd seen a potential relationship with Trina Winters take to the wind as she drove out of town—on Christmas Eve, to boot— I'd been once against set adrift. I had eaten up time by getting accustomed to having my parents a farmhouse away, and of course there were those nights where I worked George's Tavern and listened to the travails of Chet and the other denizens of Linden Corners. I was jogging in place, never getting anywhere but seeming- ly always on the go for others. Raising Janey was a full- time job, and without my friend Cynthia to act as my backup, the New Year had brought new challenges.

But it hadn't brought me any closer to figuring out what I was going to do with my life.

I needed a plan, and so far, one evaded me.

But the difference was this: I actually wanted a plan, I was ready to move on.

Had my dalliance yesterday with Maddie set the spark for this new energy coursing through me? Or was John's wedding my wake-up call? If he could mature, get married, start off on a brand new life, surely so could I. Maybe it was seeing Eli's Jewelers closed. A symbol, a reminder that time wasn't really our friend, it just ate at our days and nights and suddenly a week was gone, a month...three years, and you realized, where am I?

"Poughkeepsie," I heard over the train's speakers.

I smiled with irony. That wasn't what I meant, but the announcement was good enough, serving as a reminder that my stop was only forty minutes away. My future was just a couple stations up along the river, and as we jostled forward, my heart began to beat, and then to pound. My return to Linden Corners would prompt questions, not just from Janey but from my parents, and from friends like Nora and her mother, Gerta Connors. How was New York? The wedding? Did you see any old friends? Maddie's image was again flooding my mind, but her words about visiting Linden Corners reverberated more. Like a drum beat.

The Solemn Nights Motel had burned down two months ago. Which meant that Linden Corners was, as she'd jokingly stated, without accommodations for visitors, unless you counted the spare bedroom at the farmhouse. Like that would go over well, inviting Maddie into my home...our home. Complications indeed.

But as I lazily gazed out the window, the train clacking over the rails and the wide river swimming lazily by, the sky a series of dark clouds and gray coating, the kernel of an idea began to form, and suddenly my heart beat that much faster. Did ideas really just happen so simply? Could a passing seagull really make you think you too could touch the sky? Could a small island in the middle of the river with a house built upon it, change your mind about the myth of one being his own island? Could my future really have been decided by a not-so-innocent remark from an ex-girlfriend with whom I'd just spent the night? Had Maddie Chasen influenced my life yet again, and if so, was the universe laying out clues?

"Hudson next stop, twenty minutes away," came a sharp announcement over the train's speakers, jarring me from my reverie.

Suddenly I couldn't get home soon enough.

Snow had been falling since we left Rhinecliff, so when the train arrived in Hudson a fresh white coating was beginning to cover the streets and sidewalks. As if the open sky and lack of hustle and bustle wasn't enough to make the city fade in my mind, the snow served as a gentle reminder that I was back among the friendly confines of upstate. Seeing my friend Nora Connors leaning against the hood of her car waiting for me was another. I couldn't exactly say she was smiling at the sight of me, but then again, Nora wasn't exactly always known for her sunny disposition. She sometimes revealed an abrasive quality, which might have worked well for this former lawyer in the court-room, but not so much when picking up a friend at a train station.

With my weekend bag hung over my shoulder, I approached her car, a fiery red Mustang I'd once rear-ended.

"Hi. Thanks for picking me up."

"No problem, it's Monday. You know the Attic is closed."

A Doll's Attic was her store along Main Street in Linden Corners, a mix of nostalgia and memorabilia, formerly known as Elsie's Antiques until the town's busybody retired to trade gossip down at Edgestone. Weekends were Nora's busy time, when travelers, bargain-hunters and antiquers tended to make their way to the region. They would patronize my tavern, George's, too, so we worked hand in hand in helping our bottom line. We had also become closer friends in Cynthia's absence. Nora was divorced with a teenage son, she lived with her mother, and dated a man who lived just over the border in Massachusetts. Nearly eight years older than me, she and I had ruled out any kind of romantic subtext to our friendship. It was nice, sometimes, to just have a friend.

We hit the road, Nora behind the wheel, the roads a bit slippery.

"It's been snowing since the morning. How was New York?"

"Clear skies," I said.

"I wasn't talking about the weather," she said. "The wedding happened?"

"Yes, wedding's usually do. Unless you're watching TV. No drama for John and Anna."

"And you, any drama?"

Like my lack of a poker face, my body language spoke before I could think of a clever retort, and instead I found myself gazing out the passenger window at the passing countryside. Nora smirked. Her previous life as a defense attorney worked here. She was naturally suspicious.

"Oh, do tell. Did you get lucky with one of the bridesmaids?"

"Nora, do I look like the kind of person who would do that?"

"Well, something happened. Your face is redder than Rudolph's nose."

"Really, Christmas metaphors, in February?"

She was still smiling. "Maybe it's the snow that's put me in the mood."

"Not your boyfriend?"

It was a cheap shot on my part. Nora's other half was a decent guy named Nicholas Casey whose ancestor had been the illustrator for an old edition of *The Night Before Christmas*. Nora and I had tracked him down two holidays ago and they had struck up a rapport. This past Christmas had revealed some cracks in their cozy fireplace. Guess things weren't any better with the passing of the New Year.

"Touché, Brian, and very unlike you. I must have hit a nerve."

I wasn't about to tell her about Maddie. What was there to say? I didn't even understand all that had happened.

"Sorry."

We rode in silence for a bit, and only the mileage sign for Linden Corners brought me out of my quiet reflection. We were five miles out, and I in a few more turns of the road we would come upon the burned out ruins of the Solemn Nights Motel. There wasn't much left of the old structure, the fire having consuming it to the point where only the framework remained. It had been coated with snow and ice ever since, uninhabitable; the coming spring would bring with it demolition.

"What's got you so quiet?" Nora asked.

"Just got a lot on my mind."

"What else is new? Brian, you know, you think too much. Sometimes I think I can hear the gears turning in your head."

"Yeah, but this time I'm actually going to act on those thoughts."

She turned her head, momentarily taking her eye off the curving road. "A weekend in the big city and suddenly you're a man with a mission? Boy, that must have been some wedding."

"It was, actually. If John Oliver, perpetual frat boy and juvenile prankster, can actually settle down, then maybe I can stop wallowing in whatever morass I've been afflicted with."

"Sounds like you read a psychology journal on the train home. Big words."

I grinned over at her. "Big plans."

"Which of course you're not going to tell me, right?"

"Not now. I've got some logistics to figure out."

"Brian Duncan, I've never heard you speak this way. Is this about Janey?"

"Everything I do as about Janey. But I realized, if I'm really going to set a good example for her, then I have to take charge. It actually feels good. Finally I have an idea of what I want to do with my life, but now comes the hard part: going through with it."

"Ah, there's that famous Duncan doubt," she said. "Care to give me a hint?"

To our left as we neared Linden Corners, the burnt-out shell of the Solemn Nights came into view. Nora noticed me noticing it, my eyes glued to the lot. The old strip motel had been the first place I'd laid my head when I came to town, and it was the last place—until last night—that I'd been with a woman, Trina Winters, the daughter of the motel's proprietor, Richie Ravens. He had left town with Trina, intent on rebuilding their relationships after years of being estranged. A chain had been drawn across the old entrance to the motel's parking lot. The Vacancy sign was probably melted into the ground. Only memories remained.

"You going to rebuild that eyesore?" Nora suddenly asked.

I shook my head. "No, if I learned anything this past weekend, you can't go home again, even if it's a rundown old motel. No, you have to move forward. No more tilting at windmills for me" I said, "but that doesn't mean you can't chase them."

"Chase what, your dreams?"

"Exactly," I said, easing my head back against the headrest in her car. I allowed an easy sigh to escape from my lips, easing up the tightness I felt in my chest.

"You and that windmill, Brian Duncan. I don't think Don Quixote had it this bad."

"He only had Pancho to deal with. I have Janey Sullivan."

"He also had a woman he did everything for."

"Dulcinea will have to wait," I said.

"Are you sure about that?"

"That's it, Nora. I'm not telling you anything anymore. The prosecution rests."

Her laughter filled the small confines of the car, and together we zoomed back into the world of Linden Corners. I was home.

Except I wasn't yet. The time was nearing one-thirty in the afternoon, so Janey would still be at school and I didn't relish the idea of returning to an empty farmhouse. My stomach grumbled and I was about to suggest to Nora that we grab a bite at the Five O'Clock Diner when I noticed across the street Annie's beat-up old truck parked in the lot of George's Tavern. I asked Nora to drop me off there and she did so. I thanked her picking me up. She waved to me as she pulled out of the lot and back to whatever her day off would bring her.

Before going inside the tavern, I tossed my overnight bag into the passenger seat of the truck. The interior cab smelled of aftershave, a familiar scent because it was the one my father had been splashing on his cheeks for years. As I closed the door, I heard the creak of another door, and as I looked up there stood Kevin Duncan on the porch of the tavern. He was dressed in blue jeans and a red and blue flannel shirt. In his hand was a broom. The image was striking, my large, towering father who had worn business suits his entire life and who rarely looked up from his stock portfolios was missing only the pitchfork— and the dour lady—to complete the classic image. The pitchfork would be more believable than Didi Duncan in farmer's clothes.

"Hey, Dad," I said, "you looked relaxed."

"Why not, a nice, quiet, snowy Monday. Good day to shore up the old place," he said. "I would have picked you up at the train station, you know. Nora didn't need to go out of her way."

"It's okay. I like riding in her Mustang. Better than that beat-up old truck."

"We do have the Mercedes up at the house," Dad said. "Anyway, come inside out of this weather, let me get you a cup of coffee or something. It's too early for your top shelf, not that you would join your old man."

"First of all, you're right. Second of all, Mom wouldn't like you imbibing. Speaking of, where is she?"

"Back at the house, doing her crossword. She doesn't know what to do with herself."

"Moving to Linden Corners, it's certainly a chance of pace."

"It's not permanent, Brian. Just a respite, an escape.'

"Most people escape to Florida, not the wintery winds of Upstate New York."

"I'll have to fire my travel agent."

"More like your real estate agent."

Kevin Duncan actually laughed, an unusual sound for Brian. He'd always known his father to be as serious as a heart attack, until last fall when he'd actually had one. He'd been told by his doctors to change his lifestyle, and while it was good to get him out of the boardroom and the tight ties around his neck, sweeping the dusty floor of a small-town tavern probably wasn't what his wife had been expecting. Didi Duncan was someone who preferred having tea with the Daughters of the American Revolution, not hearing Martha Martinson at the Five-O crack wise about the latest road kill specials.

I made my way to the bar, where the stools were still upended on the long wood surface. I pulled two down, settled on one while Dad went for the coffee. I didn't really want it, not on an empty stomach. It was still rumbling. As I watched him go behind the bar and pour two cups worth, I marveled at how strange life could be. Rarely did I sit on this side of the bar, busy most nights behind it, serving the regulars. It's what paid the bills, not that I had to worry about things like rent. I owned the entire building, including the upstairs apartment which had been my first home in Linden Corners and was now where my relief bartender, Mark Ravens lived, along with his wife, Sara, and their infant boy, Harry. For the past three years, I had made threadbare ends meet, but being inside the bar and seeing it from the customers' point of view, I realized how unfulfilled I was slinging drinks for a living. Something had to change, people had been telling me that since Annie left us, but sometimes you bury more than people, you bury yourselves in things that allow you, if not to forget, than to ignore.

John's wedding had changed all that, a convenient excuse that I would have admitted to anyone who asked. Running into Maddie Chasen had actually changed my thinking, something which I'd never admit to.

"Brian, you okay?"

I realized Dad was holding out the coffee cup, steam rising before my eyes. I said sorry. I took the cup and I drank from it for good measure. I set it down haphazardly on the bar, missed the edge, and watched as everything went crashing to the floor. Coffee splattered, shards of the ceramic mug littered the floor.

"So much for my wiping the floor down," Dad said.

"Sorry, guess I was..."

"Distracted? You've been that way since you showed up. Are you still in New York?"

Was I? My body felt trapped in time zones, not there, not here.

"No, Dad. But...there's something I want to discuss with you. And I'm starving."

"Why didn't you say so, let's go across the street. That Martha lady cracks me up."

I wasn't going to try to dissuade him, it's just what I needed. So, I waited until he had put on his coat, and together we made our way through the snowy walkway and toward the icy banks of Main Street. We climbed over one, there was no traffic, and soon we were crossing against the non-existent traffic. A series of stores dotted the southern end of the road, including Marla and Darla's Trading Post and Ackroyd's Hardware Emporium, and I was shocked to see a flapping banner posted on the front of Chuck's long-time business. GOING OUT OF BUSINESS.

"When did that happen?" I asked.

That sign hadn't been there before I left.

"Oh, I heard some of the guys at George's talking about it Saturday night. Guess tough times are out there for everyone. Mom and Pop businesses are in trouble these days all over the country, with small-town America being the hardest hit," Dad said. "It's all discounted chains and strip malls, and even those are struggling."

Such foreboding words didn't sit well given what I hoped to discuss with him. Still, I felt bad for Ackroyd's. Even if Chuck and I had never become the best of friends, I didn't cherish the idea of the failing economy hitting Linden Corners. We'd always survived on our own, outside forces rarely affecting our borders. Perhaps the burning of the Solemn Nights had set a new tone for the New Year. But then wasn't it more imperative that I pursue my dream? Then I thought of Eli's Jeweler's in New York. What I surmised was that it wasn't small towns alone that were in jeopardy, it was small business. A way of life.

Forgetting Ackroyd's for now, we entered the warm comfort of the Five-O Diner, again, a place that held lots of memories for me. I'd enjoyed my first meal here, and despite her sass, I'd become good pals with the owner, Martha Martinson. She greeted us upon our arrival.

"Well, if it isn't Little Dunc and Big Dunc."

I gave my father an odd look; perhaps he'd been coming in more than I knew. Martha usually referred to me as Brian Duncan, Just Passing Through, which was a dig at the first words I'd ever spoken to her. Really, I'd only stopped in for a BLT and the decision ended up changing my life. The Five-O is also the first place I'd heard of the Solemn Nights Motel. So it was fitting that I would want to hatch my plan here. The Five-O was all about beginnings for me. Martha, at age fifty-seven, was already gray-haired and had a tongue as tart as Gerta's strawberry pie.

"Little Dunc?"

"Well, you're hardly passing through anymore, right, and now that Papa Smurf is here to stay I had to come up with something." Dad just laughed at the name, and that's when I realized what had given my father such a different outlook. It wasn't the jeans or the flannel shirt, it was the gray scruff on his cheeks. Papa Smurf indeed.

I wondered how my mother felt about what she would call a disheveled look.

"So, Little Dunc," Martha said, "how was that wedding?"

"Does everyone know what I was doing this weekend?"

"Pretty much, yup," she said. "So, you boys want a table or just the counter?"

"Counter's fine with me," Dad said.

I saw that three of the dozen stools were occupied, all by older men, and I wondered if they were Dad's new cronies, all of whom invited us to sit. Earl Cherington, Bucky Silver, Chet Hardesty, it was rare to see one without the other two, sort of like a triplet version of twins Marla and Darla. But I begged off their hospitality and asked that we have a private booth. Dad picked up on it, again giving me a curious look. I think I finally had his attention.

"Whyn't you bring over two tuna fishes on rye, fries, and some coffee," he said.

Martha said it was coming right up, and Dad and I moved beyond the grizzled guys at the counter, took a booth toward the back; the only other table occupied was by a mother with two kids, neither of whom seemed interested in eating, too busy climbing over the back of the booth. One of them, a five-year-old boy, stuck his tongue out at me. I'd take Janey any day.

Water poured into plastic tumblers by a waitress named Becky, I settled in and saw that Dad was staring at me.

"Okay, Brian, you're not one to keep things closely guarded. You've piqued my interest."

"Let me pose a question."

"Okay," he said again. At least he was agreeable so far. He might not be when I got done.

"Remember the Solemn Nights?"

"An ill-named establishment if ever," he said, with a shake of his head. "I'm sorry Mr. Ravens lost his business, but there wasn't much to recommend about it really. I thought your mother would rather sleep in a tent in the woods that one night we spent there. It's just a pile of burnt rubble and ice now, a shell. Don't tell me you're thinking about buying the property and rebuilding it? Owning the tavern has its appeal, but a motel? You'd make your mother keel over for sure."

"No, Dad, I only got the idea when I thought about the fact Linden Corners has no place for visitors to stay."

"Linden Corners doesn't exactly scream tourist trade. It's more passersby."

"What if we could make it a destination?"

"You running for mayor or something?"

"The country administers our government. No, Dad, but I think my idea could drive some interest in the region."

"Okay, Brian, enough dancing. You're not at the wedding reception anymore."

"I want to build an inn."

"An inn? Where?"

"On my property, on the hill above the windmill. Not one building, I think, but a series of them, maybe five or six small cottages; they would be individual units, offering guests more privacy. Imagine the view from up there, of the windmill, and of the Hudson way in the distance. The inn itself would be the place to see, the destination. It would give new life to the windmill itself, a chance for me to spread its magic to others." I paused as our lunches arrived and my stomach grumbled again. Seeing food before me, I dug in, the first bite tasting as though I'd not eaten for days. For a moment I recalled the empty cartons of Chinese food on the floor of my apartment, and Maddie's words about coming to Linden Corners for a visit rumbled inside my brain. If Maddie had sparked the idea, it was Annie's windmill which fortified it, making the inn's genesis conflicted at best. I wondered how Janey would feel about it. But I would deal with the emotional response later, first I needed to seek a bit of practicality. Which is why I'd invited my investment-banker-father to lunch.

"It's an intriguing idea, Brian. Not unfounded in concept. Execution, that's the rub."

"Money," I said. I was finally speaking his language, or as close to it as my bank account allowed.

"Lots," he said. "An unproven start-up business, you'd need permits, zoning approval, an architect, a contractor, builders, marketing, web design, the whole enchilada, as they say. It could be several years before it's operational, even more before turning a profit," he said, finally taking a bite of his sandwich. He chewed, mulled over my scenario further, and I did the same, realizing just how insurmountable it was. During the entire train ride, my mind had swirled with ideas, but now that I've given words to thoughts, it just sounded like the most ridiculous plan ever.

"Why don't we just skip it, Dad? How was the weekend? Was Janey well-behaved?"

"You know, Brian, it's that kind of defeatist attitude that got you here, isn't it?"

He meant my trademarked way of avoiding confrontation, of facing my problems. After I'd seen Maddie in bed with Justin, I'd said nothing—not to either of them. Only John, and what was said had changed everything for me. I'd told him I was leaving and I wouldn't be back. The open rode beckoned to me, a new life to be found somewhere on lost highways. I hadn't gotten that far from the city, but Linden Corners was its own world, the windmill easily transporting me into my own fantasy escape. Sitting here in a booth at the Five-O with my financial wizard of a father, if he couldn't help me with this issue, then both of us were at full tilt.

"Okay, Dad, I'm listening."

"Draw up a proposal and I'll show it to a couple of friends. Investors," he said. "To make this work, you're going to need partners, and I'll do my best to ensure the stay as silent as can be. They'll just be in it for the reward, and maybe a free guest room during the off season."

"You really think it's possible?"

"Brian, this is the first time in three years—heck, maybe in your whole life—that I've seen you genuinely excited about something. The Brian I know would have mulled this over for weeks, or even months and still not said a word. Which maybe is the case, but something tells me this plan of yours was hatched just recently. It's raw in concept, sure, but the passion is there. And that's what counts most." He paused and picked up a French fry, dousing it in ketchup. Didi wouldn't have approved of his diet. She wouldn't have approved of him conducting any sort of business, either. Yet here they were, the plate of fries, like ideas, ready to be devoured. Then Dad said, "You want to tell me her name?"

I blanched, my face growing red. "I don't know what you mean."

"Remind me, Brian, to always play poker with you. You're an easy mark."

"Gee, thanks, Dad."

"Okay, I'll skip that subject. Back to business. You got a name for this inn of yours?"

"Of course," I told him, pausing to take a deep breath before I spoke its name for the very first time. "The Windmill Inn."

CHAPTER FOUR

I SPENT THE REST OF that next week getting accli-
mated to my small-town routine again. It was like I
was suffering from a form of jet lag, the three days in
New York symbolic of the three years I'd been away
from its frenetic pace. Time lag, I suppose. I'd said
nothing of my Windmill Inn idea to my mother, nor to
Janey, preferring to allow the right moment to present
itself, rather than force it. It was one thing for Janey to
share her mother's windmill with me, quite another
to allow me to open it up to the outside world. This
farmhouse, this land and all that came with it, which
of course was highlighted by the mighty sails of the
old windmill, they would all be Janey's someday. I was
a mere caretaker. Years after the Van Diver family had
sold it off, the Sullivan family came to call it home, a
man named Dan falling in love with a winsome lady
named Annie Tessier, and together producing the

irrepressible child that had found her way in my life, and most assuredly, into my heart.

It was Friday night, late, and I'd just put Janey down to bed. Not that she needed me to at age ten, but after being away for four nights, she'd clung to me all week long like a puppy. I was her rock—and she mine—and when life's other demands stole moments from us, she retreated into her own world, a sort of anti-Janey who shut down and milled about the house quietly. I'd let her stew, knowing she'd eventually come around and open up. She didn't act this way to guilt me, or to try and keep me from living my life. Rather, given the losses she had suffered, it was only natural that she feared abandonment. The moment I was expecting came at around eleven-thirty, as I sat in my makeshift office in the guest bedroom down the hall. Sully, the black Labrador puppy my parents had surprised us with at Christmas, lay snoozing on the throw rug behind me. I guess she too had missed me; most nights she could be found curled up on the edge of Janey's bed. My mother had informed me dogs don't belong on furniture, but at her tastefully decorated Society Hill townhouse in Philadelphia, the same theory might hold true for certain humans.

I was busily clacking away on the keyboard of my laptop, working on my proposal for the Windmill Inn and feeling overwhelmed by all the details. Whenever I could this week, I'd played with concepts, ideas, any piece of information that I conjured that helped further shape my grand plan. Mostly I'd done it during daytime hours when Janey was at school, but tonight Mark had command of the tavern, and so after I tucked Janey in I had made my way to the office and shut the door, a cup of steaming tea, now cold and forgotten, was beside me. A sound stirred me from my concentrated state, and I turned to see if little Sully might be having a puppy nightmare. No, instead I saw Janey standing in the doorframe. I had not even heard it open.

"Hey, sweetie, what's going on? Why aren't you asleep?"

"We need new curtains in my room, the moonlight is keeping me awake."

Janey never mentioned such a thing before. It was just an excuse. But I played along.

"Okay, we can go shopping on Sunday."

"Why not tomorrow?"

"Because we're having people over tomorrow, remember. A big pot luck lunch?"

"Oh yeah," she said, though she didn't seem thrilled about it. Usually she liked when we hosted parties such as that. Linden Corners was all about community, and sharing a meal was first on its favorites list.

"What's the occasion? Valentine's Day is over, and there's no more holidays until Easter."

"Right. So we need to invent reasons to get together," I said. "Do you see First Fridays and Second Saturdays listed on the calendar? No, because we invented those holidays, and they bring friends and family together."

She wasn't appeased. "I think you're not telling me something. Why do we need this new holiday?"

"Well, it's not a holiday...per se. It's just, I want to talk to everyone," I said.

"You're being mysterious," she decided.

Well, she was right about that. I was going to spring my idea on everyone tomorrow, but I realized maybe that was the wrong approach, at least when it came to her. So I coaxed Janey beyond my office door and asked that she sit on the sofa. She sat on the carpeted floor instead, Sully stirring from her sleep just enough to cuddle with her. I smiled at the comforting scene, also knowing it was a defense mechanism on her part. Her stuffed purple frog, whom she'd finally given a name to—Dunc—was forgotten back in the tossed blankets of her bed, replaced by ticklish licks from Sully. Still in my chair and not wanting to talk down to her, I too eased down on to the floor, leaning my back against the sofa.

"Okay, Janey, talk to me," I said. "What's bothering you?"

She hesitated, as though considering where to start. Knowing Janey, she had a lot to say.

"What are all those boxes downstairs? They ones that came in the mail the other day."

"I told you, Janey. From my apartment in New York. I cleaned it out."

"What's in them?"

"Old clothes, photos, some CDs. Just stuff," I said, but she wasn't satisfied. So I spoke to her in our own poetic language. "Memories."

"Of your other life," she said.

"Janey, you know all about that. I took you to New York. You met John, and Anna."

"I like Anna. She's beautiful."

"Yes, John's a lucky man."

"They got married," she said.

"Sure, that's why I went down there. I was John's best man."

She seemed to mull this over, like it was breaking news. It wasn't. We'd talked about it.

"Did John and Anna ask about me?"

"Of course they did. Anna took a real shine to you. They promised to come visit soon."

That seemed to brighten her mood. "I'd like that. I guess I'm too young for a wedding."

"Well, maybe that one," I said. "I had to make sure John got to the altar."

"Didn't he want to get married?"

"Oh, he did. But...he's John I've known him a long time. It was my responsibility."

"Okay," she said.

"When we have time, we'll go through the boxes. I'll show you anything you want."

"Brian, do you ever want to get married?"

Okay, there was the shift in the conversation I was anticipating. Maybe we were starting to get to the heart of the matter. Janey had been concerned a couple years ago when she'd heard, first at Thanksgiving at my parents' house about a woman named Lucy whom I'd nearly married. She was my high school sweetheart, and kids of that age always think they've met the person of their dreams. Then she'd heard, from John himself, about Maddie and how I'd nearly proposed to her. Then came my time with Annie, which Janey had a front-row seat to, and she knew my intent to spend the rest of my life with her mother. In a fateful way, we had shared the rest of Annie's. Since then, my romantic prospects were about as promising as the economic outlook in Linden Corners. Janey was still young and impressionable, and I knew a woman in her life would go a long way. She used to have Cynthia, who was like a substitute mother, but she was gone from our daily lives. Assisting now was my mother, Didi, but her brand of mothering mirrored Emily Post more than Teen Beat. So Janey was left me with...me.

"Someday, Janey. Maybe it will happen. But she'd have to amazingly special."

"Because you wouldn't settle for less?"

'No, because you wouldn't," I said, and I smiled.

She giggled, her scrunched up nose a sign that I'd broken through the barrier she tended to put up. The light in her eyes danced in the night and I felt my heart melt. If only I had taken Janey to the wedding, my time with Maddie might not have happened. And then in a flash, I pictured Maddie dropping in on Linden Corners and interacting with Janey. Was she even the maternal type? Maddie was the cool blonde, and in Linden Corners, we breathed warm air, we lived without edge. We enjoyed the leisurely pace. But thought of Maddie's potential visit brought me back to the idea her comment had sparked. So I settled in next to Janey, petting Sully's scruffy face.

"I'm thinking of giving up working at the tavern," I said, my opening gambit.

"Oh. What will you do?"

"I was thinking of becoming an innkeeper. Do you know what that is?"

"Um, not really."

"Richie Ravens was an innkeeper, of sorts."

"You're going to rebuild the Solemn Nights?"

"No, I'm going to build a new motel, or hotel. Actually, it's an inn."

"What's the difference?'

"You can charge more when you call it an inn."

She looked at me dubiously, her eyes narrowing. I laughed so loud, I stirred Sully.

"Janey, you know I've had the best time the last three years with you. You and me, we are a team, and there's nothing one of us does that the other doesn't get a say in. Even a simple thing like what to do on a Sunday, or which tree to cut down at Green's Tree Farm each Christmas. So I won't do anything you won't like, or that will upset you. My idea, it's only in the planning stages so far. It's what I'm working on right now, and my father is helping out."

"Grandpa Kevin knows about money," she said.

"Right. And if I'm going to go through with this, I'll need his help."

"Okay, Brian, out with it," she said. "Where is this inn of yours?"

"Ours," I said.

She rolled her eyes at me. It was actions like that made me want to slow time. Where was my sweet, seven-year-old Janey who came tumbling down the hill that day I met her, so wide-eyed and eager to show off her windmill. She'd grown, she'd matured, some because of the turn of the clock, other because of life's twists. But here we were, at a crossroads, this moment between us the beginning of our future. The weight of my plan suddenly fell upon my shoulders and I had trouble getting up. But I did, encouraging her to do that same. Sully just lay her head on the carpet; she couldn't be bothered with tomorrow. She was content in the moment.

I brought Janey to the window. My office looked out on the same side of the farmhouse as did her bedroom window. It was a clear night, and the stars shined down over the windmill. There was no wind, not tonight, so the sails were dormant, as though waiting for life to jump start it into motion. That's what I was trying to do. But what I directed Janey's attention to was the hill rolled beyond the windmill.

"Imagine a series of buildings...five, six of them. Each self-sufficient. Places to stay."

"Oh, like little houses," she said. "All of them with a view of the windmill."

"Right. What do you think?"

"You think people would want to say in them, to pay to visit the windmill?"

"That's the theory behind my idea," I said. "After the Solemn Nights burned down, it hit me that there was no place for visitors to stay in Linden Corners. If I were to build my inn, it would help everyone in town. It would bring more business to the community. Which is a good thing in this day and age. But the construction will take a while, and it will disrupt our lives, and our land. I'll only pull the trigger if you give the a-ok."

She was silent a moment, as though absorbing the details, mulling over in her busy mind the implications of all I'd told her. I said nothing further, waiting for her to voice her opinion, her thoughts. Janey was practical, and she always took that extra moment to bring sense to emotion. But ultimately, she always voted with her heart, and I could already feel the conflict swirling inside her. The windmill was her mother's, and before then it belonged to her father once upon a time. Wasn't I Brian Duncan, Just Passing Through? It hadn't escaped me that tonight she'd called me Brian. Sometimes she slipped. But what she said now filled my heart.

"Sure, Dad, I love it. Momma lived to share her windmill."

I hugged her, feeling the tension slip away from me. Maybe the wind had taken it. Maybe Annie had. She was never far away.

———————————

March was just around the corner, and fortunately Mother Nature seemed fond of such an idea. It was a beautiful day that greeted us this Saturday, and by one o'clock in the afternoon the sun was still high in the sky, an indication that winter was on its way out, and spring would soon give new life to our little community. We were expecting a decent crowd for our lunch, dinner not possible because someone needed to open up George's Tavern tonight and that someone was me.

Cars started arriving just before one.

My parents were already here, my mother busy setting out plastic plates and with wrapping utensils into folded napkins, my father in charge of drinks. He had a cooler of soft drinks, beer, wine, and seltzer ready, along with some containers of crushed ice. The doorbell rang, sounding throughout the farmhouse. It was just one and the windmill clock in the kitchen began to spin. Just once. But it was enough to send me toward the front door, Janey and a barking Sully beating me to the door. She opened it and greeted the Connors' clan. Gerta, Nora, and Travis stood there, with respectively, a strawberry pie, a platter of macaroni and cheese, and an expression that spoke of wanting to be anywhere else.

"Hi, Gerta, oh, you brought your famous pie!"

"Well of course I did, dear. Goodness, Sully, let an old lady inside."

I pulled an excited Sully aside, but he continued to wag his tail as the Connors' entered the kitchen, where my mother welcomed them with a polite nod and my father handled the embraces and high-fives. Life in Linden Corners had changed my father—for the better—and not changed my mother—not for the better. He was casual, she was still ready for a charity event, complete with her trademark pearls.

"Oh Didi, you look lovely as always," Gerta said.

"Thank you, dear. Oh, my, look at you—baking again."

"She never stops," Travis said. "That's a good thing."

"Sure, a fourteen-year-old can eat anything," Nora said. "You don't have my hips."

It was a typical exchange between generations, and I watched them settle inside the warmth of the farmhouse with deep appreciation. If I'd learned anything in my time in Linden Corners, it was that neighbors were friends, and friends were family. A far cry from my New York apartment where my neighbors were strangers at best. I'd become fast friends with Gerta and her husband, George, who had passed away not long after I'd gotten to know him. His trust in me was implicit, and Gerta had put me in charge of his tavern. I'd renamed it in his honor. But running it was not enough to keep me going into the future, and I hoped Gerta didn't see my creation of the Windmill Inn as a sign of disrespect for what I'd been entrusted with.

As they busied about, the doorbell rang again and Sully and I did the honors this time.

"Welcome," I said, "Glad you could join us," I said.

Chuck Ackroyd stood on the porch, hands in his pockets. His surly expression was in place, as expected as his presence here was unusual. I'd sent out the invite, but Chuck and I could hardly be called friends. But here he was, responding to it.

"I don't know why I'm here," he said.

"Trust me, it'll be worth it."

"More windmill spinning, Duncan?"

"Actually, yes, Chuck. Come in, grab a beer. They're on the house here."

Chuck sometimes came to the tavern. He would order drinks but rarely talk to me, much less tip.

Another twenty minutes passed, and in that time arrived several other key people in Linden Corners, including Marla and Darla, who said they had asked their cousin Karla to work their shift at the Trading Post; Martha Martinson, owner of the Five-O, my friends Mark and Sara Ravens, who had baby Harry in tow, which gave Janey a chance to act like the big sister she'd been denied after Cynthia and Bradley and little Jake left town. The last to arrive was the elderly, slow-moving Thomas Van Diver, and at his side, busy body Elsie Masters, who'd agreed to drive him over. She no longer owned a business in town, but she was part of our history, and thus should be part of our next chapter. Seeing all of these fine folks from the village gathered inside the farmhouse, sharing a cup of soup before we got down to business, it warmed my heart. They talked, and they smiled, and they acted like they hadn't a care in the world at the moment, even Chuck, who was engaged in deep conversation with my father. Maybe seeking financial advice on how to keep his hardware store from folding. Just wait, I thought, planning my moment.

We finished lunch, everyone satiated by the myriad

of food. Sandwiches, casseroles, for the kids chicken tenders with a spicy sauce, so we all had our fill and now it was time to give our thanks for our bounty. For all we had, and for all we would soon have.

"Hey folks, hi...hey everyone," I said, waving my hand to the gathered crowd in the living room. Plates had been cleared away, drinks were refreshed, and finally I had the attention of the group. I'd even managed to quiet down Sully, who didn't know what to think of this big crowd inside his home. Janey had taken him into her arms and calmed her puppy self. "Thanks for coming today, and sorry if I've been a bit mysterious about my motives. As much as I enjoy the company of everyone here—and I do, more than you know, even you, Chuck--I have a very specific reason for gathering this particular group together, all of us who are invested in the future, in keeping alive our businesses. And Thomas, you represent the village past; after all, you lived in this very house as a small boy."

"Memories are everywhere, still," he said, with a twinkle in his eye.

"If you say I'm past my prime, too, Brian, I'll have a few choice words," Elsie said. "I've got more years in this town that any of us."

"Combined," Martha added.

There was a smattering of laughter, and Chuck even managed a crooked smile.

"Oh, you are as present as always, Elsie. All of you are, so much of a part of our lives. But I'm getting ahead of myself. I don't want to tell you here what's going on, so if you'll follow me outside...."

"I feel a trip to the windmill coming," Elsie said. " Didn't I predict that?"

"Yes, you told everyone at Edgestone this morning," Thomas added.

"Well, yes, you are right Elsie, informed as ever."

More laughter ensued, and the gang began chatting amiably, putting on their coats as we ventured outdoors. Through the back door we went, Janey taking my hand in hers and leading the tiny parade down the hill. Our destination: the windmill. Of course that's where I was taking them. Elsie wasn't gifted with anything other than knowing me. But hey, any good announcement came with props, and what better prop existed than the mighty windmill itself. The wind had picked up slightly, the sails were gently turning on approach. I smiled at the picturesque view; a Hollywood movie couldn't have conjured an image as beautiful, set against a hopeful, spring-infused blue sky. I brought them all to the base of the windmill, the sails sweeping so close to my head I felt my hair ruffle. It was just the feeling I needed. Like it and I were in sync.

As we gathered, they continued to murmur, trying to ascertain the reason I'd brought them here. I asked that they remain patient just a moment longer, and then, taking Janey's hand in mine, I entered the inside of the windmill. Janey giggled, since she was in on what I was planning and she was thrilled to be part of it. So we twirled our way up the winding staircase, emerging into Annie's studio. I opened the door that led to the outer rim of the mill, a catwalk that crawled its way around the entire upper tower. The sails passed close again, and it was perfect, just as I wanted. It was like the three of us were reunited again, Brian, Janey, and Annie.

"Brian, dear, you do have a flair for the dramatic, don't you?" Mom said, "This reminds me of the lighting of the windmill during Christmas. All those blinding white lights."

"This is even bigger, Mom," I said. "It's mind-blowing."

Not even her ability to remove silver linings from clouds was going to ruin my today.

"Friends, family, citizens of Linden Corners," I said, "picture this land as it is now, take a mental picture if you will, because in the coming months—assuming all works in our favor—I will transform this open field into a destination for visitors to our humble village. Imagine the hill that sits above the windmill, back there. Toward the trees that separate this land from what was once the Knight's farmhouse, now my parents'. I plan to construct a series of small houses—each of them self-sufficient in terms of water, electricity, the comforts of home. But what's different is the magnificent view of the windmill it affords, and in the distance, the sky, the moon, the waters of the Hudson River. Folks, I present to you the future home of the...ready, Janey. Say it with me, just like we rehearsed."

She nodded, smiling brightly.

Then together we said, "This is the future home of the Windmill Inn."

Our voices quieted, just as the sails passed by our faces, momentarily blocking the crowd assembled below. I wasn't sure what kind of reaction I was expecting: applause, or the kind of oohs and aahs associated with fireworks. But there was silence and for a moment I wondered if I had over-estimated my own enthusiasm. These folks had lived here far longer than I had, some all of their lives, and the rolling hills behind Crestview Road and the soaring windmill were a constant, a reminder that change and Linden Corners were mutually exclusive.

Finally, my mother spoke up and said, "So that's what you've been plotting all week," she said, turning toward her husband. "Kevin, I see your hand in this."

"Brian's idea, I'm just an advisor."

"So much for not working," she said.

I was worried my mother was going to kill the moment, but thankfully Gerta spoke up, her hands clasped together with excitement. "I think it's a marvelous idea, Brian. The Solemn Nights is gone, as is Richie Ravens. We need some place in town for guests to stay. Mark could rebuild the motel if he wanted, right?"

"I'm working at the RiverFront in Hudson. I don't need to run a motel," he said.

"And he's got his hands full at home," Sara added.

Baby Harry squirmed in her father's arm, and Sara leaned in and kissed his forehead as if to thank him proving her point.

"So, this idea, I see that it's a way to attract new visitors to our town," Martha said. "You planning on doing something like a B&B?"

I shook my head. "I'm not opening a restaurant, if that's what you're asking. Each unit will have a kitchen area if guests wish to cook. But I will not be providing food. A menu for the Five-O will be among the items waiting for them when they check in. So hopefully that will drive more traffic to your diner, Martha, and to the tavern as well, even to Nora's shop and the other places in town. For those guests who do use the kitchen, they'll need groceries, so Marla and Darla, you'll benefit too. Now, I realize six units doesn't mean a huge influx of people, and I don't think we'd want that anyway. But they would be high-end customers, since I don't plan on charging similar rates as Richie. No, the Windmill Inn will be exclusive, classy. And with so few units, we should have a waiting list to stay there. So, I can hardly see any downside."

"Doesn't help me," Chuck said. "Since I'm shutting down in a couple months. Business is just not what it once was. I can barely afford to restock."

"Well, maybe not, Chuck," I said.

"Why? Just why did you invite me here, Brian?"

"Because, I believe in keeping everything local. I want Ackroyd's Hardware Emporium to be the exclusive supplier to the building of the inn. The wood, the piping, the wiring, nails and hammers and whatever is needed, I want it coming from your store. You hire the laborers, and oversee everything. That ought to keep you around for a few more seasons, don't you think?"

He looked completely blind-sided. "I...I don't know what to say."

"You can begin by taking down that going out of business sign," I suggested.

I think after three years of antagonism I'd finally gotten through to Chuck. His baggage had more to do with Dan Sullivan, Annie's late husband, but once I'd arrived in town he'd played out his anger on me. I never held him in any disregard and now I was giving him a chance to help save his business. The expression he wore on his face was hard for me to read: could someone be reluctantly grateful?

"Look, everyone, this idea is going to benefit us all, but what it really does is finally gives me a purpose.

A future. When I came to Linden Corners, I was lost, and you all helped me find a part of myself. But I was kidding myself that I was fulfilled. Janey and I talked about this last night and she agreed that's it's time to move forward. My future has arrived, and with all of your help and inspiration, you can make it all come true."

Even as I heard the words, I realized what an undertaking this was going to be. The building of the inn would consume my life, and then once it was operational it would become my priority. It came with concerns, for sure, as I wasn't sure how it affected my job at George's Tavern. The upside, though, was that I would be spending much more time at home, at the farmhouse, and thus I'd be around for Janey as she continued to grow up. She was still a child, wide-eyed and excited, but I knew things would change, she would. Without Annie here, I was all she had, and as much as our friends were supportive and helpful, when darkness fell and it was time for sleep, it was just me and Janey. And a lazy Sully.

"So, Brian," Nora asked, "just how long do you think it will take till it's completed?"

"Hard to say," I said, "Dad and I are working out the logistics."

My mother again tossed her husband a stern look. The idea of staying in Linden Corners was to alleviate his stress level. But I recognized the fire inside my father's eyes because it was the same heat that had consumed mine all week. I could feel my fingertips tingling, excitement pouring all over me now that my news was out. It had given it voice, and the wind had taken hold of it.

"Oh, Brian, I have the most perfect idea," Gerta said, a revelation crossing her face. "In fact, I thought this was what you were getting at before you made your announcement. You just have to open the inn this fall."

I sputtered. "This fall? Gerta, I think that's beyond optimistic. Why then?"

She looked around at the group. Martha was nodding, and so was Sara. But it was Elsie Masters who spoke up and said, "Of course, we were just talking about it at the Five-O last week, weren't we?"

"What," I asked, "What's happening this fall?"

Gerta smiled, hugging her grandson Travis as she said, "Oh, Brian, it's just so perfect. This coming September is the one hundred fiftieth anniversary of the building of the windmill."

All night long, as I served drinks and hung back and watched my customers cheer, drink, and play pool, I wondered how I could not have known such an important fact. The windmill was going to turn 150 years old, and of course we had to celebrate such a monumental occasion. But could we really do so by christening the opening of the Windmill Inn? It seemed more possible we would be at a ground-breaking ceremony instead given the red-tape I might encounter. But if I had learned anything since moving to Linden Corners, it was that the residents, when they banded together, could accomplish anything.

When Annie was alive, she would regale me with stories of the windmill. We would lay in each other's arms in the upstairs studio of the windmill after making love, and I would marvel at such a magnificent place in which to spend time. It was her private place, as intimate as what we had shared. One night she had told me of the young dreamer Charles Van Diver, and his quest to have the windmill built for reasons that had nothing to do with the weather. Given how the love between me and Annie had blossomed within the windmill, it was easy to see that Charles's story was truth, not some fanciful legend that grew more romantic as the years had progressed. But what I didn't realize was just how long ago it had happened. A century and a half.

I was broken from my reverie by the jangling of bells above the front door, and I looked up to see Mark Ravens enter. He'd no doubt just gotten off his Saturday night shift from Riverfront Resort and he looked tired, rubbing his scruffy jaw as he sat down on a stool. He looked like he was carrying the weight of the world on his shoulders. I should know. Usually that was my look.

"Need a drink, Mark?"

"Gee, that sounds great. Man, it was crazy busy tonight. A woman's seventy-fifth birthday, family and friends totaling one hundred. Dinner, drinks, dessert. They kept us hopping. But I can't complain, Harry needs new clothes almost every week, growing as he is, and the tip from that one party was amazing." He paused and noticed that I'd already poured him a beer. The foamy head had time to settle. "Oh, sorry, was I rambling?"

"That's okay. We bartenders, we just listen," I said.

"Yeah, that's true."

Mark was my relief bartender, and he also lived upstairs in the apartment above the bar.

"So, Brian, cool announcement today, I think it's a great idea."

"Thanks. It's just good to have something to concentrate on. Slinging drinks to this crowd night after night, it's kind of lost its appeal."

"Hey," said Chet Hardesty, knocking back the last of his latest beer.

"No offense, Chet. I don't mean you," I said, and then poured him one on the house.

"Now that's an apology," he said, and took a drink.

I smiled, despite the lost profits. A happy customer came first, didn't it? I'd need such skills if I planned on running an inn.

"So, Brian, can I talk to you?"

"Uh-oh," I said.

"Yeah, well, I tried to talk to you this afternoon, but too many people were around."

"You quitting or moving?"

Beneath his olive-complexion he grew red-faced. I'd hit a nerve, and he took another sip of his beer to fuel his courage, his eyes darkening. "Okay, so this is the deal, yeah, I'm giving my notice at the bar, and I also have to tell you that Sara and I will be moving out next month."

"Oh, wow," I said, "a double whammy."

"Sara's Mom is all alone, and she's volunteered to help take care of Harry. Which means Sara can increase her shifts at the Five-O, you know, back to what she had before Harry was born. And because of that, I can just work Riverfront and not worry about picking up extra shifts here. I mean, in a pinch I could always come in. But I want to watch my son grow up, Brian. Not be out every night and get home too late to tuck him in at night. I know, corny..."

"Not at all," I said.

How could I object? Wasn't my plan for the inn based on the same concept? To be more available to Janey. What was going to be difficult was figuring out what to do with the tavern. The Connors family had entrusted me with its continuation after George passed away, and I'd done so for the past three years, even renaming the place in his honor to ensure his presence was never forgotten. It had previously been Connors' Corner, a riff off Linden Corners. I would have to come up with a grand plan for the tavern, one that would ensure that Gerta was happy that her husband's legacy wasn't forgotten.

"So you're not mad?"

"That wouldn't be fair of me, Mark. You've been a good friend, and that won't change. Go upstairs to your wife and baby, don't give it another thought. We'll work out the details later about your last day, both at the tavern and the apartment. But hey, it solves one immediate problem."

"What's that?"

"Until the Windmill Inn is built, there's one place for a visitor to lodge."

Mark finished his beer and retreated upstairs, and soon the midnight hour had passed and the crowd had thinned. Sometimes in the summer the antique tourists would require me to stay open later, but in the cold of February, they were few and far between. My regulars departed, Chet the last one. He waved me a goodnight, and I did the same, turning the lock of the front door as he left. I flipped off the overhead lights, and suddenly I was left in the glow of the jukebox in the far corner and the green-shaded lamps that hung over the bar. This was actually my favorite time of day, having the tavern to myself. This was about life's quiet moments. I thought about cleaning up but decided it could wait until tomorrow morning. It had been a busy enough day.

So I locked up and hopped behind the wheel of Annie's truck. It took a few turns of the ignition for the engine to start, and again I felt like the truck was on its last legs. Something I don't think I was ready for. Keeping Annie's belongings a part of Janey's life was so important, and I just couldn't bear to part with this one. I'd take it in to Chet's shop next week and see what advice he had for me. For now, though, I chugged along dark, empty roads and made my way back to the farmhouse, turning up the drive on Crestview Road. I parked, listened as the engine shuddered its way toward silence.

Out in the night air, I noticed a cold wind had swept in during the last few hours. I could see my breath illuminated by the moonlight. Bypassing the front porch and ignoring the creak of the porch swing, I wandered to the rear of the house. All was quiet inside, no doubt my mother asleep on the sofa. She'd watched over Janey tonight. So I took advantage of the moment and ventured forth toward the windmill, as I had so often done over these past years.

At the base of the windmill, I stared up at it, its sails gently moving.

"One hundred fifty years," I said, "it's too perfect. Too ideal. Annie, you would have loved to be here. This was yours, and it's only entrusted to me to keep it turning for Janey's sake. But you will always be the woman who loved the windmill, and your spirit never quiets. Tell me, Annie, tell me another story of the windmill's past. Who else fell in love while the sails spun their magic?"

Before she could answer, the phone in my pocket buzzed.

It wasn't a phone call but a text. Progress was slowly finding its way to Linden Corners and I wasn't sure that I liked being disturbed at a moment's notice. I flipped the phone open and read the words.

JUST THINKING OF YOU. STILL UP FOR A VISIT?

It was from Maddie Chasen

I stared up at the windmill again, and it sails spun, the wind blowing me back to a recent past I wasn't sure I was ready for. I would have preferred one of Annie's stories.

INTERLUDE

The Story of Lars Van Diver

Clocks may tell the tale of time elapsing, but it's really a mere countdown, not a reflection of life's journey. If you want to witness where the world has been, who its people were, just how many centuries have passed, there is no place more illustrative of life's passage than a cemetery. Visit any small town, walk through iron gates and along grassy hills, through the crunch of fallen leaves or wipe away snow that covers granite stones, you will see who came before you, who walked this earth and left it different from when they were born.

People started coming to Linden Corners as early as the sixteenth century, though the land hadn't yet found its way to the map. It was only through that elusive slip of time that more buildings cropped up, additional people came to till the land, to share in the community and to raise families. St. Matthew's Church was built in the early eighteen hundreds, its bell tower, once quieted by age, rang again, always on Sundays as it called forth its flock. There generations gathered to rejoice, and to remember loved ones who were no longer part of our daily lives. After mass, they could visit, stand before their graves, and acknowledge the others that populated the cemetery. Dates, names, epitaphs, all of them a record of time gone.

Here in Linden Corners, familiar names dotted the cemetery, that's how small towns were. Families thrived, they died, they grew from the ashes only to live again.

The Van Diver family had its own corner, found under a copse of trees. A series of granite stones, simple, and understated. The people might be gone, but their impact remained. When folks visited the Van Divers, their natural thought was of the windmill, the defining landmark of sweet Linden Corners. They built it, they maintained it, and they allowed the dreams of an entire village to spin toward the sky.

And it was a necessary trip to St. Matthew's cemetery one day that led to yet another story of love found beneath the spinning sails of the windmill.

Charles Van Diver, the architect, the dreamer of the windmill, was being put to rest.

Sunshine dappled down over the land, a lovely spring day that found the three Van Diver children gathered to say good-bye to their beloved father. Charles had lived a hearty seventy eight years, outliving his wife, Edith, by two years. He'd grown up in the farmhouse, and he'd lived there his entire adult life, raising three kids and continuing the Van Diver tradition of growing vegetables to feed the expanding village. And on the first weekend of September each year, he would perform upkeep on the windmill he'd asked to be built. He kept its spirit alive almost as much as the wind continued to give it life.

"You and that silly windmill," Edith would tell him on the day the village called Summer's Wane. The town would gather on the field for a picnic that included any and all. Linden Corners did love its celebrations. Edith understood the windmill's practicality. After so many years, he'd still never told her the story of Cara. Some things he kept locked in his own heart, and only toward the end of his life had he brought his three children together and told them the story of his impulsive youth and the golden haired beauty who inspired his heart. Life continues, though, that's what he told them, even as he knew it wouldn't for him, not for much longer. So on this lush breeze filled day, his time had come to take to the wind, and the family

stood silent, crying tears of sadness for their loss, but also celebrating a man who had never shown defeat. He was strong, courageous, deeply loving. But they also knew a different man now the dreamer.

"Aunt Sarah, did father really build the windmill for love?" asked an inquisitive young man with eyes that danced, even in sorrow.

"Oh, Lars, that fanciful tale. Told you, did he? A foolish boy, that's what Charles was. And now a foolish old man. Don't think he didn't love your mother. He would have walked to the ends of the earth for her. You were all his world. He never needed to see big cities, towering mountains. All he ever desired lived within the borders of Linden Corners. The windmill filled—and fulfilled—his dreams. His family was everything."

Sarah Van Diver had never married, living along the main street in an old Victorian house with two other women. They ran what today would be called a bed and breakfast called Masters Rooming House, welcoming visitors to their burgeoning village. She was now the matriarch of the Van Diver clan given Charles's passing. Anders, her middle brother, had died many years ago. He'd left town, gone to New York, and later made his way out west somewhere. Sarah didn't know if he'd ever married or had children. Anders had not been good at keeping in touch. There could be Van Divers elsewhere in the world.

But in Linden Corners, the Van Divers remained a strong presence.

Sarah, who at sixty-nine remained plump and plain, but with a giving heart, gathered in the light wind before Charles's casket, sending final wishes to wherever his soul had journeyed. Knowing him, as in life, he hadn't gone far. Also in attendance were Charles's children, the two women Gertrude and Theresa, along with their husbands, five children between them, and then there was Charles, Jr, his only son, along with his wife and two children. One was a young man, seventeen and fast coming of age. He was the one who had spoken earlier, his name was Lars, and he had been the apple of his grandfather's eye. They shared a common, unspoken bond. They both dreamed of special things, the windmill fueling them.

When the final rites were completed and the priest closed the prayer book, the Van Diver's retreated to the farmhouse they still called home, generations living under one roof. Yet Sarah had forgotten a certain trinket of Charles's that she wanted to share, at her brother's request.

"Lars, why don't you come with me, help your Grand Aunt," she asked.

Lars was only too happy to accompany his aunt back to the Victorian house, the shingle hanging on the front post swinging in the wind. It read Masters Rooming House, Vacancy. The two elderly ladies

Sarah shared the house with were seated on the front porch, rocking away, one of them knitting, the other watching the world walk by.

"Lars, dear, why don't you stay with Clarabelle and Sissy while I go upstairs," she said, "I won't be but a minute."

A minute is not a long measure of time, yet in the ensuing one, everything changed for Lars Van Diver. The front door to Masters' Rooming House opened and stepping out onto the shade of the covered porch were three people, a man in a dark suit and top hat, his face adorned with a large, twirling mustache; at his side was a handsome woman of some size, but with a happy disposition. However, it was the young lady who appeared behind them that had Lars wondering where his breath had gone. His grandfather, ever the poet, might have said the wind had taken it, and he supposed, had he given it thought right now, that this must be how Charles had felt when he laid eyes on Cara Larssen that first time. Lars felt himself unable to move, his eyes locked on the vision in gold.

He watched as the older couple acknowledged the two spinsters on the porch.

"Lovely day for a stroll," he said. "You have fine days of spring."

"Linden Corners knows from its seasons. If you're thinking of remaining, you'll experience them all, the *rain and the snow…"*

"And the wind," Lars said, impulsively.

Even Clarabelle and Sissy were surprised by his joining in of the conversation. He hadn't been asked, and manners mattered in such a time. Still, the couple turned toward Lars and he felt his face grow flush. Speak when spoken too, hadn't his mother always told him? But as the man turned to him, it was hardly annoyance on his face.

"Indeed, young man. The wind shares a unique pattern on this land, sweeping and grand."

He nodded, words closing his throat. "Yes, sir," he finally managed.

Clarabelle stood and said, "This is Lars Van Diver, the grand-nephew of Sarah, our third partner at the rooming house. He and his family live in the big farmhouse just beyond the village limits. If you come upon Linden Corners from the west, you'll no doubt notice the windmill that soars over their land."

"A windmill, you say. I hadn't heard," said the woman.

"Perhaps I can show it to you all," Lars said.

Just then Sarah returned and, having overheard the conversation, suggested they take Lars up on his offer a different day. "As I'm sure you'll understand, we have only just today buried my last surviving sibling, my brother Charles. Lars, you are welcome to show Mr. and Mrs. Larssen and their daughter, Cara, the windmill on any other day. Today, as etiquette dictates, must be for our family."

"Perfectly appropriate," said Mr. Larssen, "We are sorry for your loss."

"Our condolences," Mrs. Larssen added.

"I'd like to visit the windmill," Cara added, looking to Lars and she spoke. "Soon."

They moved on from the porch, emerging into the sunlight of the day, almost as if the glowing orb knew they were coming. Lars's eyes trailed after the girl named Cara. She must have been fifteen, perhaps a year older, and she was as lovely as spun gold, her hair shiny, skin like porcelain. She was as trim as her mother was round, and she carried a mischievous grin on her face; in fact, she looked back at Lars and with no one else watching, waved her fingers at him. He wanted to reach out and feel their touch.

"Come, Romeo," Sarah said with an obvious roll of the eyes. Romance had never seemed to capture her. "My goodness, as I live and breathe, my brother seems to have returned. Honestly, Lars, you and that windmill. Just like Charles. You think undying love can be discovered in an instant. Remember the hard lesson he learned, the girl of his dreams was taken by the wind, and he never recovered. You should heed such an example."

The only difference, Lars felt, was that this similarly-named Larssen family, as opposed to that which

*couldn't wait to leave Linden Corners, seemed intent
on staying.*

He hadn't missed the coincidence, either.

Grandfather, he thought, her name too was Cara.

*Lars assisted his aunt, but he thought of the young
girl and knew his life had changed.*

---

*That night, Lars found himself standing before the
windmill, where he tried to picture what the land
would have looked like without the majestic structure. How plain it would have seemed, so like other
hills that rolled around Linden Corners. Something
special loomed here, magic spun in the air, the windmill its conduit. He'd always been fascinated by it,
knowing how unique it was in this region, the only
one of its kind, strange given the Dutch ancestry that
was populated all along the Hudson River Valley.*

*He recalled just weeks ago, being called to his
grandfather's room, where the old man lay propped
up with an assortment of pillows, his breath shal-
low. Both men, young and old, knew time was short.
Charles patted the bed, asked that his grandson sit
beside him. He stared up at him with pride.*

*"You, my boy, are so like me. You see the poetry
in life."*

"Even on rainy days, I see the colors of the world," Lars answered.

The old man nodded. "Just as I said, you see pictures with words. Lars, I want to tell you a story," he said. *"I've only just told my children, and they nodded politely at the faded memories of an old man. You, I think you will see my story differently, the way I do..."*

That's the night that Lars learned the truth of the windmill, of the young beauty who had captured his impulsive heart. He spoke of the idea to build the windmill for her, as a way to keep her from returning to the old country, but in the end he'd been left only with the memory of her sweet aroma, the kiss they had shared, one so strong it had filled his heart for a lifetime. He chose, he said, to not look at her loss as an open wound but an imaginary badge. To have loved, and also to know he had been loved, it enabled him to move beyond dreams to reality and to live a life filled with promise and reward. He loved his wife, Lars's grandmother, and nothing could diminish that. "But sometimes, when you're young and you think anything is possible, your heart takes over from what the mind knows. If I can pass anything on to you, Lars, it is the spirit that lives within your soul. If you ever doubt it, just stand before the windmill and its sails will inspire you."

"Thank you for telling me, grandfather. The

windmill will forever spin, even when I have joined you in the sky."

"That will not be for some time, my boy."

His grandfather was right, of course. Because on this starry night when sleep should have claimed him already, Lars couldn't move. His grandfather's words reverberated in his heart, and he thought, with sadness, of his grandfather who lay in the ground. But that was just his body, not the soul he had spoken of, which was no doubt somewhere else. Somewhere floating on the wind. How was it that life happened as it did, that on the day he said his final farewell to his grandfather, a vision of the future materialized before him? How he wanted to see Cara Larssen again, he wanted to bring her here to the base of the windmill. Maybe she would be a struck in an instant by its wondrous beauty, just as he was by hers. But for that to happen, night had to end.

He retreated back toward the farmhouse. Sleep found him, dreams did too. A new day filled with promise loomed.

He heard Cara's simple word reverberate.

"Soon," she had said. A word with promise, yet elusive in meaning.

"Your name, it rings familiar to me."

She nodded, her smile bending toward a laugh.

"I know more about you, it seems, than you do about me."

"So it's not a coincidence," he said. "Your name is Cara Larssen."

"Named after my grandmother, yes."

"Tell me everything," he said, breathlessly.

Lars had needed to wait three full days to be reunited with the young woman who populated his dreams, Sarah had taken the reins by inviting the Larssen family to dine with the Van Diver clan, and they had accepted with alacrity. If they were going to move permanently to this region, didn't it make sense to get to know the locals and learn of daily life in this quiet part of the world? A far cry from the frenzied streets of New York City, Jasper Larssen had said as they toasted their arrival to not only Linden Corners, but the Van Diver farmhouse.

"Ellis Island just seemed to spit us out. They knew the plight of us Europeans. Everything is changing over there. Madmen are running countries. People are being persecuted. That was not the life my ancestors wanted for me. My grandfather, Arnoud, he spoke fondly of what he called the upper region of New York State, a place that made him feel as though he walked the fields of the old country. He never made it back here, but he wished that one day his family

would return to the shores of America, and this time call it home. It is with his wish in our hearts that has found us in Linden Corners."

"We couldn't be more pleased," spoke his wife, Anika.

It was during this evening as the families were getting to know one another that Lars snuck off with Cara, luring her with the promise of an exclusive tour of the windmill. She followed him down the grassy hill, and as they emerged over the bluff, dusk fell and she drew an intake of breath, all while Lars beamed proudly. With Grandfather Charles gone, the windmill had been entrusted to him, and today represented his first chance to show it off.

"It's just like back home," she said, and then she set off down the hill, racing to it as though her legs might just carry her all the way to where she'd journeyed from. Lars trailed after her, of course, he did. He'd already convinced himself he would follow her to the unknown parts found at the end of the world. Perhaps the wind would give them flight, transport them to a secret place that only they knew about. Lars wouldn't mind never returning from it.

For now, it was to the windmill they ran, and now Cara stood in its large shadow.

"Oh, Lars, it's beautiful. More magnificent than I imagined it would be after you promised us a tour."

"The tour has just begun," he said. "Follow me."

"Forever," was her reply, and in that instant, Lars Van Diver knew that, even when awake, his dreams could be fulfilled. He would marry her he decided in that instant, and they would share a lifetime of memories. They would have a family. They would be happy. He already knew he was in love, because love meant not being about to think rationally, and as he guided her inside the windmill and upstairs, she spun in the open space of the second floor with sudden glee, a squeal coming from her mouth. A mouth he wished to kiss, the sensation flooding him unlike any he'd ever felt. But he knew the timing wasn't yet ideal; lovely Cara deserved nothing short of chivalrous perfection.

He took hold of her hand, their first contact. The spark was electric, their eyes alight.

Hers were green, his blue, and together they melded into liquid aqua.

Outside they ventured, out onto the perimeter, where the sails spun ever so close to them.

Her breath drew deeply, her hands clutching at her bosom.

"Don't be afraid," he said. Perhaps the height had scared her, or the proximity to the spinning sails. He'd learned more about her, fear held nothing over her, she said.

"Never, I'm in awe. My grandmother, she told me all about it. How she used to sneak out at night

during the time the windmill was being built. She would check on its progress. She told me of the handsome young man named Charles. And now here I stand where she might have."

"That was my grandfather, and he asked that I took after it for him."

"I'm sorry for your recent loss," she said.

"What would make him happy is for me to have someone to share it with. To know of your connection to his beloved Cara...I can't put into words what that means."

Whether destiny was twirling around them, or each of them was searching for life's missing answers, they turned to each other, and then they smiled, and then, Lars, never feeling bolder than in this moment, leaned forward and pressed his lips to hers. It was his first kiss ever, and it changed him. He felt the last remains of boyhood shed from his skin right then and there, a powerful wave of passion threatening to overwhelm him. Yes, he'd fallen madly in love, and making things that much more perfect was the face which kissed him back, wrapping her arms around him. He thought his heart might burst from inside his chest.

As they parted, he sent a silent thank you to his grandfather, for his story, for his life. Charles missed out on his Cara, and Lars knew that he wouldn't be here if that had not occurred. But fate had brought a reincarnated Cara Larssen back to Linden Corners, *and while it was the windmill that drew her to this land, what would keep her here, for as long as destiny would allow, was the man who loved the windmill himself. Lars Van Diver.*

Their escape that day to the windmill hadn't gone unnoticed, and as the weeks progressed and the Larssen family settled into a new house on the opposite side of town of the Van Diver farmhouse, neither of them could be separated, or hide their feelings, not from themselves and not from their suspicious families. A decent interval was given, but it was during a snowy Christmas that found Lars Van Diver, a fresh age eighteen, asking for the hand of seventeen-year-old Cara in marriage. Their union was blessed by her father.

"I knew from the moment we saw you on that porch that my Cara's heart was taken," said Jasper Larssen, with the wistfulness of a father losing his little girl.

It would be another four months until they exchanged their vows, allowing winter to clear out and spring to breathe new life in to the region. They were married at St. Matthew's, and then the first night of their married life, as the night air still held onto cool air from the previous season, Lars and Cars stayed inside the windmill.

In this day and age, time could not be counted on to last forever, the world was changing daily. The threat of war once again dominated the headlines, and even in remote Linden Corners you could not escape the ever-growing scent of imminent danger. The world was shifting, you had to steal each moment. Only on quiet nights when the windmill lay dormant did Lars and Cara Van Diver think they could stop time.

It was two months after their marriage that Cara announced she was pregnant.

They named their son Thomas, and he was a fussy baby. He cried on a whim, and neither parent knew how to silence him. It was like he was trying to drown out the world's ills and maintain order within the farmhouse. Lars and Cara spoke often of the war, knowing America couldn't avoid entry for much longer. For nineteen-year-old Lars, he felt like his watch was taunting him, each passing day bringing him ever closer to an unwanted journey that would not be denied, one he desperately hoped would never come to pass.

And it seemed that was the case, as a year passed, and then another, and yet another.

The Van Diver family was able to subsist. The vegetables they grew on their land served as income, kept food on their table, keeping alive the promise of tomorrow. The war had forced others to leave town, including Cara's parents, who went to live with distant relatives in the south. More opportunity was there, factories that built weapons offering a new way of life for them. Lars had refused to leave, this was Van Diver country; they had been here for four generations.

Time always has other ideas, and eventually the hands of the clock caught up with him.

The letter arrived during the summer that Thomas turned five. He was too young to know what it meant, 'to be drafted." Soon Lars reported for duty, and wife and young son prayed for his safe return, Thomas often spending entire afternoons inside the tower of the windmill, knowing here was as close as he could get to his father. He could feel his spirit here, and he promised this was where he would remain until his father returned, falling asleep on the floor until his mother brought him home. For boys of that age, measuring time was ambiguous. His mother told him to be patient. We will be reunited soon.

Time, however, had other ideas, and finally it ran out for their family, as it had for so many others across the land.

Lars was gone, a hero. Cara sold the farmhouse, she had no choice. She and Thomas were forced to leave Linden Corners, following in the path of her family. Thomas's last image of the windmill was of a staid one, sails quieted, as though the morning they left, the land that had given life to the Van Diver family was in mourning. He spoke a sad goodbye to his father, and one day, when he was older, wiser, he thought about the windmill and heard the stories and sent a wish that one day soon, the windmill would give birth to another love story.

Oh, that trinket that Aunt Sarah needed to collect from her home on the day of Charles Van Diver's funeral! It was a piece of parchment, preserved within the pages of a book, one that had been passed down now through two generations of Van Divers. It was an edition of Clement Clarke Moore's **The Night Before Christmas**. Thomas treasured it so much he knew he had to sacrifice it, and he left the book behind before they moved, the traditions found inside its worn pages ready for another family to embrace it. But it was the words written upon the letter that Charles had treasured and hoped to one day pass down to his son.

It was the letter written to Charles from Cara, proclaiming her love for him.

Aunt Sarah passed it down to Lars, who had then entrusted it to his wife when he went overseas. But in truth, the letter hadn't been seen in years and upon her passing many years later, it had not been among her things. Her son Thomas knew nothing of *its existence. He never knew Linden Corners until his return, well into his eighties.*

Even though the Van Divers ceased calling Linden Corners home, the story of the windmill continued. Another family would come to call the farmhouse home, and they would keep the sails of the windmill spinning as though they knew of Lars's promise to his grandfather. It was a young family who, after the war, was intent on forging a new life. They went by the name of Sullivan, and one day, farther into the future, their name would become my name as well, and it would happen so unexpectedly. Oh, how my first sight of the windmill would capture my heart, leading me down an unforeseen path and into the arms of fate.

But that story, my story, it was for another time.

PART TWO

Spring

CHAPTER FIVE

ONE MONTH.

One month since my return to Linden Corners.

One month since my life had been turned upside down for good, spun into directions I'd never seen coming.

One month since a beautiful, lovely woman from my past who went by the name of Maddie Chasen had inadvertently set my mind thinking toward the future.

It was that future I was preparing for on this fresh spring morning, with Janey at my side, behaving in her usual non-helpful way.

"You're sure you're not going on a date?"

"No, Janey. Why would you say that?"

"Because, whenever you try to put on a tie, you get frustrated. I've seen that look before, like when you had dinner with that Trina lady last Christmastime"

She nailed me on that. It was true I was frustrated and that I was taking it out on the poor defenseless tie. A multi-hued blue tie with thin stripes, I was having trouble getting the shorter side to be shorter. A tongue-sized slip of material kept peeking out from underneath. So I started over again, and then again. By the fifth attempt I wondered why I was even bothering with a tie. Would wearing one really be the difference maker between yes and no? Actually, yes. Because you wanted to make a good impression, and also, I knew my father would be dressed in one of his finely tailored suits. I had to look the part, too.

Finally, I got the tie done well enough, tossed the jacket over my shoulders and buttoned it. That did the trick, or at least hid any tie-related imperfection. I stared at myself in the full mirror, ran fingers through my combed brown hair. It fell back in place, unchanged.

"This is as good as it gets," I pronounced.

"You look nice, Dad."

I smiled down at her and said thanks. A check of my watch said it was time to leave. Ten o'clock on a sunny mid-March Monday, my father and I had an appointment all the way up in Albany to discuss the Windmill Inn with a pair of architects. A firm that a friend of a friend of his knew, so a decent enough connection, enough to get us in the door. This was the first real step required to get the project underway, now that we seemed to have secured the initial round of financing. Dad had been working on that the past several weeks.

Sometimes I awoke in the middle of the night and thought: this is really happening.

"Come on, you, let's get going," I said to Janey. "Bring Sully."

It was spring break, so Janey was off from school all week. Today, while my father and I went to attend our business meeting, my mother was watching over Janey, and I'd promised to bring her up to the house. As we left the house, Sully came barking behind us, and I gathered us all into the truck. We could have walked up the hill and crossed over the stone bridge, but given the rain we endured over the weekend and my freshly shined shoes, I opted for the truck. It still looked odd, the battered old truck and the designer suit. Like my old world as a public relations executive returned, challenging, as my friend John would say, the farmer in me. Thinking such thoughts brought my mind around to the subject of Maddie Chasen and her text.

"Uh, Brian, you still here?"

I realized I'd been sitting behind the wheel of the truck, but I hadn't sparked the ignition. For three years, my life had revolved around this growing girl, but things had grown complicated for me. Yes, Maddie had contacted me and we had agreed upon her coming to Linden Corners for a visit. After weeks of delays, we'd decided upon this coming weekend. No one knew it yet. I'd told no one in town anything about my reunion with Maddie. I'd have to eventually. One thing I've learned living here, you can't keep a secret. All I needed was for someone like chatty Elsie Masters to see with me Maddie and soon the phone would be abuzz like she was working an old-style switchboard.

"Brian?"

"Sorry, just trying to organize my thoughts."

"I hope Grandpa's driving all the way to Albany," she said.

She was a smart girl, Janey—not that that was ever in debate. I started the truck, and soon we trundled our way down the driveway and up the aptly named Crestview Road, rounding the bend until we came to a familiar house with unfamiliar people residing in it. Not that my parents were strangers, but these past few months were the most time we'd spent together since my teen years, and having them here was far different than having Cynthia and Bradley Knight to rely on. Plain and simple, I missed my good friends.

We pulled into the driveway and I parked off to the side. My father's black Mercedes was pointed forward, giving us an easy escape. But that wasn't to be the case, as I needed to first say hello to my mother. She wasn't pleased with me these last few weeks, not since I'd gotten her husband involved in my "little fantasy," as she had taken to referring to the Windmill Inn. Last fall my father had suffered a heart attack and he was supposed to be taking it easy. She didn't think his being a backer to my idea counted. But that was Didi Duncan, ruling the roost with her iron fist, which at the moment was buried in soil.

"Mom, are you gardening?" I asked, as I came upon her near the front porch.

"Planting roses," she said. "This summer they should bloom into lovely flowers. Brian, I have to do something while we toil away in Linden Corners. Jane, dear, why don't you grab a pair of gloves from the garage and you can help me. Together we'll get these flowers planted in no time. Then I'll take you for lunch."

"Okay, Grandma, sounds like fun. I bet those roses will look so pretty when they grow."

Janey sped off with her usual enthusiasm toward the garage in search of garden gloves, leaving me with my mother for a moment. She stood up from her kneeling position in the soft grass, wiping away at her dirtied jeans, an unlikely look for my pearl-wearing mother.

"Not sure I've ever seen you looking so...relaxed."

"Unlike your father," she said. As she removed her gloves, I had an image of her slapping them across my cheeks. She didn't, but her stern expression might have been a virtual substitution. "I'm glad we have this chance to talk. Brian, you know as much I want to support your building of this inn, I'm concerned about your father. It's one thing for him to help you out down at the tavern, how stressful can it be to pour a beer? But this...it's a big undertaking, and the kind of work he's been doing—phone calls, emails, working his connections—well, this is what we came to Linden Corners to avoid. His doctors..."

"Mom, I'm aware of your concerns. But Dad is... that's who he is. He's happy."

"Brian, people can change. Goodness, look at me. I have dirtied knees."

I smiled. "I hear you, Mom. Once this meeting is over, I'll try and ease back."

Our conversation was interrupted by the arrival of my father, impeccably dressed in a smart, dark business suit. With his large frame, he looked imposing, and I suppose that's part of what had made him so successful in his world. He just looked like he knew how to make money. What client didn't want someone like him representing their financial interests? And now he had my future in his well-refined pocket.

"Well, look at my two handsome men," Mom said.

Dad kissed her cheek. "We'll be back later," he said. "Enjoy your day."

Janey then came running back from the garage and she wrapped her arms around my father's waist, staring up at him. "I might be getting taller, but you'll still always be a giant," she said.

"That's what makes me so able to tilt at windmills," he said, his smile wide.

She scrunched her nose and giggled. "You sound just like Brian."

Everyone laughed but my mother.

The offices of Kirby Spellman, Inc, a boutique architectural firm, was located in an eight-story building in downtown Albany, just a couple blocks from what many people in the capital district referred to as "the egg," an oval-shaped performance venue. I'd taken Janey there last summer, introducing her to symphonic music. I tried to find ways to enrich her cultural experience; and to do that required trips outside of Linden Corners. I promised we'd return, but so far I'd not lived up to that promise. Time plays by its own rules, sometimes I felt like I was always trying to catch up.

"Brian, don't dawdle, it's not good to be late," Dad said.

My remembrances had slowed my pace. I quickened my walk, not unlike a New Yorker would, and a few moments later we were entering the lobby of the office building, Spellman was on the fifth floor and we were expected, so the security guard simply instructed us to take the elevator. We did, emerging onto a floor with two offices on either side of us. Spellman was on the right, and we came to a receptionist, a young black woman with a ready smile.

"Kevin Duncan and Brian Duncan to see Kirby," Dad said.

"I'm Jenny, nice to meet you. Mr. Spellman is expecting you. If you'll follow me."

She got up from her desk and escorted us down a short hallway. A few other associates were in small offices with windows while others sat in cubicles, everyone busy clacking away at keyboards. I thought back to my days at the Beckford Group; I'd had a similar office, where I drafted press releases and came up with campaigns that would benefit our clients. Many of these offices had larger desks, from where their architects could design their projects.

Jenny knocked once, then opened the door upon request.

Kirby Spellman sat behind a desk, his ear attached to a phone. He waved us in, nodding as he said, "Look, that sounds like a project Spellman, Inc., would be thrilled to be a part of. Yes, put together your proposal, then we'll schedule a meeting. Sure, sure, anytime. Must run, another project awaits." With that he replaced the phone to the receiver, then stood up and it was then I noticed he was easily the same size and build as my father, his complexion as dark as the woman who'd greeted us. With his large hand, he shook ours. It was a strong grip.

"Kevin Duncan, it's been many years," he said.

"Indeed it has, I'm thankful Harry thought to reintroduce us, and how convenient is it that your offices are close to where I'm staying," Dad said. "This is my son, Brian. The architect, if you'll allow, of our special project."

"Ha ha, well put," Kirby said with a sonorous baritone. "Please, have a seat. Jenny will bring coffee. And I've also invited one of my associates to sit in on this meeting. Based on what you're briefed me on, Kevin, I think she's the ideal person to help out. She thinks big, and knows that even the most intimate project needs special treatment."

My mind was already spinning and the meeting had barely begun. My father had kept certain details about the behind-the-scenes work he'd been maneuvering quiet, but this was the first I was hearing of Harry Henderson's involvement. Harry was his friend and business partner whom I'd last seen at my parents' house in Philadelphia a few Thanksgiving's ago. That visit had been the first time Janey had met my parents, Harry and his wife, Katrina, among the guests, a buffer to counter the awkwardness of me showing up as the caretaker of a then eight year old girl. Though in truth, my wayward sister Rebecca had made a far worse impression by arriving with her latest boy toy, Rex, so Janey and I escaped that holiday with minimal damage. Still, to know that Harry Henderson was advising Dad on this project gave me comfort. He was wealthy, and he didn't get there by investing in pipe dreams. Maybe the Windmill Inn idea wasn't such a crazy one.

Coffee arrived, Kirby, my father, and I moving over to a rectangular conference table in the corner of his spacious office. As Jenny left, the door remained open, and then in walked a young woman, probably thirty, with dark hair that fell to her shoulders, curling naturally. A hint of make-up on her cheeks gave her a rosy glow, and the way she walked over to us spoke of sheer determination. She held out her hand and we both shook it.

"Kiera Bowen," she said, her voice strong and confident.

If this was the person to be assigned to my idea, I liked it. She wore confidence as well as she wore her tailored, dark-colored suit. Before she sat down, she handed over business cards to each of us. I read it: Kiera Bowen, Senior Architect, Designer. Nice title. I wondered what other projects she'd led, and how she had advanced in her career in such a short amount of time. Then I tucked the business card into my suit jacket, my hand settling over the manila envelope I had brought with me.

"So, now that we're all here, Brian, tell us about this inn. Kevin says it's...unique. Hard to come by these days, when ideas are as boring as a Big Mac for lunch."

I nodded, clearing my throat. It had been too long since I'd taken part in a meeting. "Yes, that it is, unique. But that's what makes this project so desirable. It's the windmill."

I didn't get very far before being interrupted from Kiera. "A windmill? Like those wind turbines you see all over the heartland?"

"No, Ms. Bowen..."

"Please, Kiera. Let's keep things informal."

"Very well, Kiera," I said. "When I say windmill, I mean like the old Dutch style."

"With sails, and such?"

"I could show you a picture," I said.

"Actually, I prefer to hear you speak of it. Pictures tell one story. I want to hear yours."

My father looked at Kirby, who nodded his pleasure. "She's sharp. Intuitive."

"Thank you, Kirby. Now, Brian, tell me again, about your windmill."

So I did. I launched into the telling of the first time I saw it, saying, "I didn't know where I was, where I was going—not on the road, or in life, I guess. I found myself on this country road that seemed to be taking me nowhere. Suddenly I crested over this hill and before I know it, there was this looming presence before me. It must have been a breezy day, because the sails were spinning in concert with the direction of the air, and, trite though it may sound, I think the sight of it took my breath from me. I had to stop, so I pulled to the side of the road. I had no idea that I was stepping onto private property, to me it was just an open field, green rolling hills and in the middle, there it was, this magnificent windmill. It was like walking inside a postcard."

"Well, you paint quite the picture yourself," she said.

"What happened after that...it's a long story. I could write a book or two about it. Suffice to say, the ownership of the windmill fell into my lap, and subsequently, I've been wondering what I should be doing with my life. Last Christmastime, the only motel in Linden Corners—that's where I live—burned down and the owner decided not to rebuild. So my mind began to churn over ideas. Then it came to me, to build a specialty inn on my property and become what I guess most would call an innkeeper, with a windmill the drawing card. Imagine waking up, and outside your window is this beautiful, classic structure, its sails already turning in the morning air, giving you the impetus to start your day fresh. It's a feeling I have each and every sunrise, and I want to share that with others."

She nodded, looking down at her notes. "Instead

of one main house, you want individual cottages, is that right?"

"That's the idea. Beauty and privacy. I also don't want to host too many people at once," I said. "I do have a young daughter who demands a lot of my time. So I'd like to keep it intimate for many reasons. No need to disrupt her life with too many guests, too many cars or activity. The Windmill Inn is designed to enhance our lives, but not overrun them."

"How old is your daughter?" Kiera asked.

"Ten," I said, going to my old joke. "Going on thirty."

She laughed, a pleasant sound that filled the room. My father was nodding as well, as he knew Janey's forthrightness all too well. Kirby remained as silent as he had since Kiera had joined the meeting. Clearly, this was her project if she wanted it.

"And your wife, I assume she's part of this as well?"

"Oh, oh no," I said, my throat tight. I hated these awkward moments when the real world intruded upon the safety I'd forged within the borders of Linden Corners. Back home I felt secure, and my wounds, while they may not be fully healed, at least no longer pulsed with hurt. Because being around the windmill on a daily basis meant being close to Annie's dream forever. "Another part of that long story. Janey's mom passed away."

"How terrible for that girl," she said, but I could tell my answer hadn't satisfied her.

I hadn't referred to Annie as my wife, nor had I said I was Janey's biological father. This meeting was taking a turn toward the personal, and while I didn't mind revealing certain details of my life, I preferred to keep some things to myself, at least for now, until I knew whether the Spellman firm was interested in taking things to the next level. Thankfully my father picked up on my feelings and he redirected the meeting back to business.

"What do you say, Kirby, let's show you two some pictures and you tell us if you're at all interested," Dad said.

He pulled out a flash drive, handing it to Kirby, who inserted it into a laptop that was on the conference table. Soon we were looking up on a screen that came down from the ceiling at a Power Point presentation. No need for the photos and proposal I had in the folder I'd brought today. Dad had it all ready with more high-tech approach. Three years removed from the business world, I think I'd lost my touch. Maybe John was right, maybe I'd gone all farmer.

For the next hour, Dad clicked through graphs, diagrams, and flow charts, giving each slide a sneak peek into our truncated timeline of events. He explained how quickly we wanted to break ground, given the upcoming anniversary of the windmill. When objections arose, he downplayed them with the ease with which he'd done so during his career, and as I watched him, sometimes rising from his chair and pointing out something on the screen, I saw how excited he was by the idea. He was in his element, something he'd been forced to give up last year and it was clear that he missed the chase. Kevin Duncan had spent his life in a business suit. A tie was as natural to him as a stock report. Health was one thing, of course, but when you stopped being who you were, I wondered then what was the point of waking up?

"Well, this is all very fascinating," Kirby finally said. "Kiera, thoughts?"

"Smart business plan, great that the financing is in place. The timeline is a bit aggressive, but that has less to do with me than it does to the builders, plumbers, and electricians who have to do all the work. Designing the look of the individual cottages shouldn't be too difficult. But to get started, I really need just one thing," she said.

"What's that," I asked.

"I need to see this windmill."

Her words were like magic, and I knew I'd found the right person.

"We're already prepared for such an instance," my father said, and he clicked the laptop a keyboard again, where a photograph of the windmill came up on the screen, the field around it as green as the summer sun allowed, the trees behind it adorned with bursting leaves, the sky reaching up toward a blue expanse. Even I drew in my breath and I wondered where Dad had found that photo, but it was Kiera Bowen's reaction I was most interested in. Because to take on this project, and to commit to our crazy deadline, it would take more than commitment. I would take passion, the eyes of a dreamer, and the heart of a lover.

"As beautiful as that image is, what I meant was I need to see the windmill," and then she paused, looking back at the photograph on the wall before staring me in the eyes and saying, "In person."

Even since Mark Ravens quit as my relief bartender, my shifts had been all over the place. I tried to maintain a regular schedule for Janey's sake, but given that she was on school break this week and my parents were around, there was flexibility. My father had volunteered to take a couple of shifts a week, but there was no way his wife was going to allow him the Monday night shift after a day long trip to Albany. He needed his rest, and after we returned back to their house, he eased into his recliner and with Sully laying at his side, he easily drifted off for a nap. Janey was staying not only for dinner but overnight, so I had the night shift to myself. I returned to the farmhouse in the sputtering truck, changed out of my suit and into regular clothes and made it over to George's Tavern only an hour later than usual, just after five in the afternoon. A thirsty Chet Hardesty had been waiting impatiently for me. With the sun still hanging in the sky, I felt like this long spring day was only getting longer.

Somehow the hours passed and the big sky darkened and ten o'clock found its way when I was really starting to feel the effects of the day. The adrenaline rush of the successful meeting had long worn off and I couldn't wait to close. Usually on Monday, I closed up at eleven, forcing the regulars to go home and spend time with their wives. I wondered if I could convince them to go an hour earlier. An unexpected guest kept me from doing that.

"Thomas, this is a surprise. Isn't it past...I mean, you're up late."

"You mean past my bedtime? I'm eighty-six, Brian, maybe I just woke up."

He laughed as his own brand of humor. I guess you had to be old to joke about sleeping habits.

"What can I get you?"

"Oh, a sidecar, that would be nice."

"I'm not even sure I know what this is, much less how to make it."

"Hmm, time advances too quickly, things of old get forgotten," he said. "A Jamesons."

"Would your doctors want you ordering that?"

"Do you see them around?" he asked.

Thomas Van Diver had come home to Linden Corners about a year and a half ago, intent on reliving memories of his youth. He'd actually been born in the farmhouse I now called home, and given his family's history mirrored that of this village, there wasn't anything I wouldn't do for him. He was dressed tonight with his usual bow-tie in place, this one a blue one with gold trim; no matter the day or hour, Thomas was if nothing else a man of refinement. He now lived at Edgestone, the retirement community just around the street. I poured him his drink and set it before him.

"On the house," I said.

"Keep that up, you'll need that inn to make ends meet."

"The bar is doing fine," I said.

It was easy when there was no rent to pay, just upkeep on the building. I'd been given the deed to the entire building—ownership of the bar and the now-vacant upstairs apartment--by George's widow, Gerta Connors a couple Christmases ago, a gift far too generous to accept, a gesture far too heartfelt to deny. I still hadn't decided what I was going to do with it once the inn was up and running. Figuring I had time to decide, I thought of Thomas's earlier remark about how quickly the hands of time move. Three years, my mind reminded me. My life had restarted three years ago, and as I poured a draft for one of my regulars, I recalled the first night that I'd come to what was then Connors' Corner. George had befriended me, put me in charge of the bar and gone home to his wife. Such was my introduction to Linden Corners, and it was that kind of homespun welcome I wished to impart to my guests of the Windmill Inn.

For now, though, I had the barflies of George's to attend.

I served up a couple more beers, gathered up a few empty glasses at the round tables, got the empty pretzel bowls and put them in the sink behind the bar. Perhaps I could get the message to Chet and the others to start packing up and go home. I finally rejoined Thomas, who was sitting quietly, barely giving his drink any attention. He hadn't come here for a drink, that much I knew. A man comes to a bar for company, sometimes the kind found in a glass, sometimes in the man providing that glass.

"Something on your mind, Thomas?"

"I was wide awake," he said, "practically wearing out the carpet in my living room."

"Things tend to be quiet at this hour at Edgestone, huh?"

"Quiet? You'd think the workers would need to a bed check to ensure we were all still alive."

"You sound bored, Thomas."

"I was always a night owl," he said. "My sweet Missy wasn't. Yet she would stay awake as long as she could, just to be near me. Some nights I'd look over after the late news ended and she'd be slumped over on the sofa, chin resting on her gently breathing chest. I would stare at her and think I was the luckiest man alive to have such a fine woman at my side. A man needs that, Brian, companionship."

I nodded. "Couldn't agree more."

"Can't spend every night at a bar, and I don't mean these folks over here."

He was focused on me, of course. "I thought the bartender was supposed to offer worldly advice to his customers, not the other way around."

"This inn of yours, sounds like it's going to consume your life."

"Actually, I think I need it. A purpose. You're right, running this bar isn't enough for me, not anymore, and Janey certainly deserves better. Mark Ravens, as you know, gave notice, and he and Sara moved out of the upstairs apartment. The last couple of weeks, my father has been helping me out, and it's been appreciated. Surely you're not suggesting you want to come work here, are you?"

"Oh, no, not here," he said, a twinkle taking shape in his eyes. "But I would like to offer my assistance on another matter. Consider me your historical consultant, if you will, on the Windmill Inn. I know lots of the old stories, perhaps they can be taken advantage of to help give color to your ideas. You don't have to answer me now, give it some thought..."

"I don't need to," I said, and I didn't. I understood where Thomas was coming from. He was not unlike my own father, a man who had worked his entire life and who now faced each day wondering how he would fill the hours. I'd given my father renewed purpose with this inn, and now I could offer the same to Thomas Van Diver. I shook his aged hand, and welcomed him aboard. "The Van Diver family is synonymous with Linden Corners, Thomas, and to have your blessing to share the windmill with the world, it means everything. Also, it would be my honor to invite you to be the first guest at the inn. It seems only appropriate."

"You honor my family with such a request, and I accept. Remember, Brian, the windmill wasn't built out of practicality, it was born of love."

He finished his drink, thanked me, and slowly made his way outside. I wished someone would have driven him back to Edgestone, but then again, he'd gotten himself here, so he'd get himself back home. I hoped I was as spry as he was at eighty-six. Heck, I was thirty eight now and some mornings I felt the ache in my knees.

Eventually, I convinced the others to do as Thomas had, and they departed George's with a grumble, as well as a promise to see me tomorrow. I flipped the lights off and turned the lock. I removed the apron around my waist, tossing it to the sink with the dirty glasses. It could all wait until morning. Grabbing my keys, I was eager to get home. But that's not where I went, because Thomas Van Diver's visit was still on my mind. It wasn't his request to join our growing team at the Windmill Inn that occupied me. It was his pointed remark about companionship. He'd lost his wife Missy shortly after returning home to Linden Corners, and it must be difficult for him, for anyone, after being married for so many years to suddenly find the world around you far emptier than you were used to. With Annie, she and I had only a brief time together, not that that lessened the impact of what our love meant. But the empty loss somehow, ironically, still filled me, as no doubt it did Thomas.

I thought then about Maddie, who claimed she was coming for a visit. A visit I'd still not told a soul about. The Inn was hardly ready, just now a figment of my overactive imagination. So then where would Maddie stay? The keys in my hand answered that for me. I went over to the back door of the bar, put a key in the lock, which opened up to a staircase leading to the upstairs. The apartment was empty, but it came furnished. So it was like a functioning hotel room. Since I was noticeably, and understandably, nervous about Maddie coming to Linden Corners, there was no way, given Janey's fragile state when it came to my dating life that Maddie could stay at the farmhouse. It just didn't seem...right.

Maddie could stay here. Wasn't that an easy solution to a problem?

But before Maddie Chasen was scheduled to arrive, I remembered I was going to receive another visitor, another woman to pass through the borders of our little town. Before my father and I had left the offices of Kirby Spellman, Inc., we had set up a time for Kiera Bowen to come visit Linden Corners, now just two days away. She said she wanted to see the windmill up close for inspiration, and I couldn't wait to show it to her. I knew a thing or two about how inspiring those majestic sails could be.

It was midnight before I closed up the bar, with a new day inevitably coming, and after that, another one, and another. Thomas was right. Time was moving fast. In this case, it was a good thing.

CHAPTER SIX

I HAD TO TALK TO SOMEONE about my Maddie dilemma, and I decided, barring calling Cynthia all the way in Texas, that Nora was going to be the unlucky recipient of this assignment. I phoned her at about eleven that next morning and told her I was bringing lunch.

"It's on me," I said.

"Which means you need something from me."

"Trust me, it's worth it."

She said she couldn't wait and then I heard the bells jangle from the other end of the line. She had a customer, so we said goodbye. Janey was at her friend Ashley's for a play date, though I'd promised her tonight it would be just the two of us. My father had taken my shift at the tavern. It seemed Janey and I weren't exactly making the most of her week off from school, especially given how distracted I was with the details over the inn. Our time together would give me a chance to bring up the idea of Maddie's visit. But first I needed Nora's advice on how best to broach the subject. Janey hadn't handled my dating life very well in the past, not that there'd been much of that in the past three years. Plus, she'd met Maddie years ago and hadn't been impressed.

Outside, a lovely spring day hovered in the sky, temperatures in the fifties, the ever-present wind there but virtually imperceptible. I felt just a slight ruffle of my hair as I got into the truck, turning the engine, only to have it go silent on me. I pushed back my hair as a sign of frustration and remembered I'd intended to take the truck into the shop this week. I'd sold the Pontiac which had brought me here, now preferring Annie's old transport. We didn't travel much beyond these borders, so I hadn't thought about getting a new car. Now with all of my expenses being directed to the inn, there wasn't budget for another car. So I said a silent prayer and hoped for the best. I turned the ignition again and this time the truck turned over, a shudder of complaint coming from the engine.

"Hang in there, baby," I said, running a hand over the dashboard.

I made my way into the main business district of Linden Corners, a blink and you miss it kind of village. Parking at the tavern, I put my hands into my pockets as I waited to cross the street. A Tuesday at noon on a beautiful day, we actually had signs of life out here, with cars turning in and out of the various store parking lots. The Five-O looked busy, but then again, it's where most of the local laborers went to for lunch. This was peak time. I noticed that the Going out of Business sign still adorned the front of Ackroyd's Hardware Emporium. Another reminder hit me: give ol' grumpy Chuck an update on the inn's progress.

Turned out, I could do that right now, as I found Chuck Ackroyd sitting before the counter at the diner, eating a bowl of chili. His weathered face naturally went into a frown when he saw me. It had been several weeks since I'd told him of my plan and since then I'd been so busy with the logistics—financing, design, zoning—I hadn't been ready for further talk of construction.

"Afternoon, Chuck," I said.

"Duncan," he said, sipping at a glass of water in front of him.

"I've been meaning to talk to you, you haven't been by George's lately."

"Watching my funds," he said. "Besides, you know where I work. You could come by any time and talk."

"We're talking now."

Just then our conversation was interrupted by Sarah, backing out from the swinging door to the kitchen. She had returned to waitressing fulltime now that her mother was helping out by watching baby Harry.

"Hiya, Brian, how are you? Here for lunch?"

"An order to go, two tuna fish sandwiches..."

"With fries and cole slaw, got it. Your usual lunch with Nora Connors?"

"Small towns are too small," I replied. "But yeah."

"Coming up."

While I waited, I took a seat next to Chuck and said, "The inn is a go, by the way. All the financing is set, if you can believe it, and I've had a meeting with an architect who is coming to town in a couple of days to survey the land. The county's zoning commission approved the idea almost immediately; anything that will help the local economy is foremost on their mind. So that means I'm going to need the resources of your store, just as I'd promised."

"You've been busy," Chuck said.

"I really need your help, Chuck. If I were to go to one of those major retailers, well, it just wouldn't be the same. Linden Corners folk stick together. We keep things local."

He nodded, then ate another bite of chili. I wasn't going to get much from him, it seemed.

Sara came back from the kitchen, my order ready. I went to pay when Chuck said, "Just put that on my tab, Sara, won't you?"

"Chuck, you don't have to..."

"Like you said, locals stick together. I think I can buy you a sandwich."

I extended my hand and he shook it. Not since that summer storm had nearly destroyed the windmill had he and I been in sync. We'd worked in tandem to bring about the repairs needed, but afterwards, he just reverted to his miserable self. Chuck's wife had left him years ago, after a not so discreet affair with Dan Sullivan, who had been Annie's husband. I thought of my previous remark about small towns being too small, a point well proven.

"So get your contractors lined up, and your suppliers. We're moving fast on this."

"Right, the anniversary of the windmill," he said. "Think you can pull it off?"

"I have to," I said.

"Why's that?"

Why was that, indeed? The windmill wasn't going anywhere, and as I'd surmised on the day I'd announced my plan, I could use the anniversary for our ground-breaking ceremony. Now, though, I'd committed Linden Corners to the biggest celebration they'd seen since the old Summer's Wane socials they had back in the time when the windmill was built. Which of course led me to yet another idea. Why not take this opportunity to plan another of those old socials? Get the entire community involved in the Windmill Inn's debut. But as wonderful as all that sounded, something ate at my insides, and it wasn't Martha's tuna fish sandwich. It was this sense that time wasn't so elastic after all, it was ticking down, almost like something was running out. I felt a wash of cold hit me and did my best to brush it off.

Then I went outside, feeling like a ghost was walking beside me.

Not Annie, someone perhaps from long ago. With my plan to celebrate the windmill's big anniversary, had I awakened the voices of the past? Was that Charles Van Diver whispering ideas into my mind? I shook off the strange feeling as I boarded the steps to Nora's shop, A Doll's Attic. I entered the store, the jangle of bells just as I heard earlier this morning ringing in my ear.

"Finally, I was going to send out the cavalry, or maybe just for Chinese."

"We don't have a Chinese restaurant in Linden Corners.

"A shame," she said. "Let me guess, tuna fish?"

Inside her store, she had set up by the large bay window a table and chairs, and that's where we tended to dine once a week. It hadn't happened on purpose, rather it grew out of our adventure two Christmases ago when Thomas Van Diver charged Nora with the difficult task of locating an old book. I'd helped out, and on several days we'd sat here with our sandwiches and brainstormed ideas. We'd solved the mystery and seemingly saved Christmas for him, and in the meantime Nora had found a new relationship after finally signing the divorce papers sent by her ex. We said none of this today, we knew our past. Right now, Nora was curious about what had brought me here on this day, digging into the sandwich with as much relish as she dug into my personal life.

"Spill," she said, "I know you've been meaning to for weeks."

"I ran into an old friend, when I went to New York for John's wedding."

"Hmm," she said, and I wasn't sure if she was thinking of commenting on the sandwich or my statement. By taking another bite, I think I got my answer. Keep going.

"My former girlfriend," I said, "Maddie Chasen."

She nearly dropped her sandwich, catching a piece of tuna and stuffing it in her mouth. "The one who slept with the boss?"

Maddie was notorious, apparently. "The one and the same," I said.

"She was there, at the wedding?"

"Yeah, how about that. Thanks John for telling me."

"Meaning he didn't."

"I was already up on the altar, in best-man mode, when she walked into the church."

"So, what did you do? Wait, you ran away to a

small town and fell in love with a windmill."

"Haha," I said. "No, I spoke to her, afterwards. We saw each other the next day."

"How much of each of you did you see?"

Now it was my turn to bite in to the sandwich, a large one that kept me chewing for what I hoped was eternity. Why had I gone down this path? Nora was a friend, but she was also cynical when it came to love and relationships. Maybe that's why I was telling her all this. To help me downplay Maddie's impending visit. It meant nothing, right? It's not like we were getting back together and she was going to move to Linden Corners to become a farmer's wife. Our one night in New York back at my old apartment, it had been about closing the windows of the past, not opening up doors to the future. Still, my silent chewing said everything.

"You hooked up with her?" Nora asked.

"Really, Nora, does that phrase apply? It's sounds so...impersonal."

"You slept with her, okay. How does that sound?"

"She didn't stay overnight," I said, "This time."

"What does that mean?"

"Could you stop looking like my misery is making you happy? This isn't easy to admit to. I mean, Maddie's betrayal is the sole reason why I set about changing my life. How I came to find Linden Corners, Janey, Annie, the windmill."

"So this was your way of thanking her? Very altruistic of you, Brian. But fine, in a moment of weakness you gave in to some ancient desire. You've moved on, she's moved on, but you both got caught up in the romance of your friend's wedding. It's not like you're going to see her again."

I didn't reply, and I fancied another bite of the sandwich. Nora reached over and held it from my mouth.

"Are you going back to New York to see her?"

"Worse," I said, "Maddie's coming here. This weekend."

"Brian Duncan, you are as predictable as snow in winter here."

"What's that supposed to mean?"

"It's why you're building that inn of yours. It's a subliminal message."

"Really, Doctor Freud. And what's my motivation?"

"That's easy. You want Maddie close, but not too close. You don't want her staying at the farmhouse, but you want the benefits that come with her visiting. But I hate to break it you, kiddo, Rome wasn't built in a day, and neither will your Windmill Inn. You say Maddie's coming this weekend. So with the Solemn Nights fried to a crisp, where are you planning on hiding her?"

Her comment about why I was creating the inn, I thought, qualified as "reaching." Maddie hadn't been a part of my life for three years now, I'd moved on and built a new life, and now I was building an even brighter one for myself and for Janey, so why would my desire to move forward hide a deeper shield of avoidance? Maddie coming to Linden Corners was the opposite of desire, it was innocent, a weekend in which we would discover that we had finally put the past behind us. I would show her around, she would return to New York and resume the frenetic pace that she so loved. There would be no hiding her.

I bit into the sandwich, my taste buds deciding the tuna had gone sour. I put it down.

"What does Janey say about all this?" Nora finally asked.

"See, that's where you really come in. What do I tell her?"

Nora allowed a hearty laugh that rattled the shelves of her store. "Oh, Brian, it's a wonder you've ever gone on a date, much less take care of a kid all your own. You haven't a clue about women, even when they're little girls."

Nora's words rang in my ears long after I'd digested my lunch. In fact, the indigestion I felt stayed with me for two days, growing worse by the Thursday morning of that week. I still hadn't mustered the courage to tell Janey about Maddie's visit. I had time still, I kept telling myself, but her arrival in Linden Corners was Saturday morning, soon. As I tossed and turned during the night, I had to ask myself the kind of questions that only those dark hours provide: why was I putting myself in this situation? Why couldn't I tell Maddie it wasn't a good idea? Was I holding onto some hope that a relationship was possible with this woman?

But on Thursday it was another woman I had to think about, switching gears from personal to business. Kiera Bowen was driving down from Albany for the afternoon. I had asked my father if he wanted to tag along but he begged off, saying he was taking his wife shopping. Said he owed her for all the worry he'd given her the last few weeks. Nora would tell me that that's how you appease the woman in your life. You read the signals, you follow through, and when you screw up, well, what's wrong with a little shopping indulgence.

Except I didn't exactly have a woman in my life. Unless you counted Janey.

"I'm not sure this week has been as fun as it could have been," she told me when I came downstairs to the kitchen. She was eating a bowl of cereal while I poured a cup of coffee. "I mean, sure, we had fun yesterday, even if it seemed like we were doing chores."

We'd raked up leaves that had been caught under a winter's worth of snow, and done some work in the old barn. We'd accomplished a lot, but the time spent together was more important. I was feeling guilty and her words cut right through me. Because I knew she was right. Today, while I hosted Kiera, Janey was spending time with Gerta. Usually I could have just dropped her off with Cynthia, and Janey would have been content as ever playing with baby Jake. Times might have changed, that didn't mean Janey's needs had.

"I'm sorry, Janey. When I talked to you about the idea for the inn, we knew it was going to disrupt our lives for a while. Today's an important meeting, it's the first real step in making our dream a reality. I'll tell you what, if there's time, I'll bring you home to meet her and you can tell her about the windmill, too. How does that sound?"

"Gerta promised I could help her make pies," she said. "So you'll have to call first."

Janey in defense mode. I knew it well. "I will check with your secretary," I replied.

Then she giggled. "You're so silly, Brian."

I leaned down and kissed the top of her head. "Good, some things should never change. Now, go get your stuff, and don't forget the blueberries we bought at Knight's fruit stand. You can make a blueberry pie today and maybe we'll invite Kiera for a slice."

"She sounds glamorous with that name," Janey said. "Is she pretty?"

"Janey?"

'Yes, Dad?"

"Go get your stuff."

She ran off with sudden glee, her giggles trailing behind her, mixing with Sully's barking. That dog liked nothing more to follow after Janey when she was in a bouncy mood. I had to admit, it was infectious, and I finished my coffee with a wide smile.

Ten minutes later we were ready to go, Janey in the passenger seat of the truck, Sully eager for her day's adventure, too. Again, the truck took a few turns of the ignition to catch, and Janey tossed me a look.

"I think the truck's almost done for," she said.

"Don't even think that, she's just rusty after the cold winter."

We pulled out of the driveway and headed down Crestview Road, turning on Route 23 and winding our way along back roads until we came to the Connors' house. It was a small Cape-style structure, a place Gerta had called home for five decades. She and George had raised four daughters and lived a beautiful life until he'd passed away. None of the daughters remained behind in Linden Corners, mostly because there was little prosperity for young people here, and only after her life had imploded had Nora sought refuge in the comfort of the land of the windmill and returned. When we arrived, Travis Rainer, Nora's son, was sitting on the sofa, earbuds plugged in, playing video games. He was going on fifteen at this point. It's what boys of that age did these days. He ignored us as Janey went dashing into the kitchen.

"Goodness, young lady, I haven't had that much energy since...well, near about your age."

Sully was running around the kitchen in circles, too.

"And Sully's got more energy than me."

"Then I guess I better prepare myself for an eventful day!"

I kissed Gerta on the cheek. "Sorry to leave you with the wonder twins."

She laughed. "Oh, I'm looking forward to it. Perhaps Sully being here will get Travis up off that couch. Lord, why the schools have to close for a week so boys can just sit around and do nothing. Perhaps we'll let him take Sully for a walk, that would do them both a little good and give us girls some quality time."

I wished them all a great day and reminded Janey to watch her manners—which got me an eye roll in return--then hurried back outside; I'd left the truck running for obvious reasons. Then I headed back toward downtown, where I'd asked Kiera to meet me at the Five-O. When I'd given her directions, I'd specifically directed her to come in from the east, where she would encounter the ruins of the Solemn Nights. To come from the west, she would have seen the windmill, and

I didn't want her to even glimpse it without me. So I parked at George's and again walked across the street. The sign on Ackroyd's Hardware Emporium was still up. Maybe Chuck wasn't being stubborn, perhaps it was a marketing ploy to draw in customers.

The Five-O was relatively quiet during this off hour, with just a couple of the booths occupied by ladies busily chatting. Just after eleven, I sidled up to the counter and waited for service. I didn't see a waitress, nor Martha. A few minutes passed and then I rang the little bell that was provided on the edge; why have it if not to use it? Then the doors to the kitchen swung open and Martha came out, a smile finding her frazzled face when she saw me.

"Ah, Brian Duncan, Just Passing Through."

"Thought you were retiring that name," I said.

"Okay, Windmill Man, what can I get for you?"

It was better than Little Dunc. "Just coffee, I guess. I'm waiting on someone."

"Got a hot date?"

"Meeting with an architect, actually. She's hopefully going to design the inn."

"Sounds promising, Brian. Who would have thought, a guy passing through town, stopping for a meal at a local diner would end up saving the little town's butt."

"I'd hardly go that far," I said.

"You've done more good for Linden Corners in

three years than I've done in thirty."

"Martha, without you, half of this town wouldn't get fed. Don't sell yourself short."

"I can't even give myself away," she said, her off kilter humor as intact as ever.

She poured me coffee and I sat and drank it, silently, every once in a while looking over at the front door. I knew I was early, I'd always been that way. First in the conference room for a meeting, first at a party, once when the host wasn't even ready. I arrived thirty minutes early for train rides. Time was a loose commodity, and I always made sure to pack enough of it in my pocket. Something Martha said, though, continued to tease my mind, and when she re-emerged from the kitchen, I asked her about.

"You said something about thirty years. Haven't you lived in Linden Corners all your life?"

"Yup, I have. But I didn't open the Five-O until I was twenty-seven. Thirty years ago this April."

"Martha, that's an incredible milestone. And just a few weeks away, too. What plans have you got?"

"Wasn't thinking of doing anything," she said. "One day in the life of a diner is pretty much the same as any other. Coffee brewing, bacon sizzling, eggs any way you want them. Sometimes I wonder why Sara and the girls bother taking down orders, we know our customers and we know what they like. What's so special about that?"

"The fact you don't see it says everything," I remarked. "Think about it, Martha, you know how Linden Corners' folk love to come up with excuses for celebrations. George created First Fridays, and I came up with Second Saturdays, and last Christmas Cynthia invited the entire town to participate in a Secret Santa exchange. The Five-O turns 3-0. Think about it."

"Not bad, Brian, I like that slogan."

"I did once work in public relations, sort of an offshoot of advertising."

"And now look at you, a farmer."

I rolled my eyes in true Janey fashion and reminded Martha and anyone else who might be listening, "I'm not a...."

But I gave up mid-sentence, as Martha was already laughing, her big voice carrying as she retreated back into the kitchen. I hadn't even noticed that someone had come in from the outside and settled down right next to me. I turned and saw Kiera Bowen sitting there, a smile highlighting her face.

"You're not a what, Brian Duncan? I'm curious to know the answer."

I'm not a lot of things, I thought, suddenly unable to answer. What I did know was, I'm an idiot. Looking at Kiera, it was like the wind had swept back into Linden Corners, breathing new life on its wide open land.

We stood in the parking lot of the diner, just over the swinging plastic sign that advertised the Five O'Clock Diner.

"Why is it called that?"

"Martha's little in-joke. It represents peak dining hours, both a.m. and p.m."

"Five a.m. sounds a bit early, even for breakfast," she said. "Unless you haven't been to sleep yet."

"Oh, does Ms. Bowen know a thing or two about late-night cravings?"

"I went to college, if that's what you're asking."

"Nice save," I said.

"Still, they have good coffee. I can feel the jolt of caffeine in my system."

Jolt was a good word, that's how I'd felt since she arrived.

Kiera had joined me for a cup, where I'd introduced her to Martha and explained what she was doing in town. Now, with a rush of caffeine coursing through my system aiding my already anxious self, I was glad to get back out into the fresh air. I turned to her, her style of dress different from the other day. She was in jeans and high boots, a brown leather jacket over a solid blue shirt, untucked. Still, she was as stylish as she had been in her tailored suit, and in the wind that seemed to have increased over the past couple of hours, her dark hair blown. I thought she might be wearing more make-up than the other day, but the rosy glow could have been natural. What did I know? Nora would say nothing.

"So, this is Linden Corners," she said.

I spread my arms as wide as I could. "Yup, this big. Literally."

She laughed. "It's charming," she said. "There is some lovely architecture here, a mix of styles to be sure, but classic and Americana all the way. That Victorian house down the street is magnificent. Oh, and I saw that old motel, that must have been some fire."

"Yes, nearly ruined our town Christmas party."

She turned to me. "The whole town celebrates Christmas together?"

"You have no idea. We even did a village-wide Secret Santa exchange, we all gathered at the gazebo across the street to pick names."

"It's like I've been dropped in to It's a Wonderful Life meets Brigadoon."

"Well, let me toss in a bit of Man of La Mancha," I said, "Shall I show you my impossible dream?"

She smiled at that one. "I thought you'd never ask."

I suggested we take her car, not wanting to get into the issue of the truck's reliability. She had a sporty SUV, silver in color, and I hopped into the passenger seat. I gave her instructions to turn left out of the lot, and soon we were coursing down Main Street in Linden Corners, where I pointed out various shops like Marla and Darla's Trading Post, Chuck's hardware store, mentioned too Nora's shop was housed in that Victorian she had commented on. I pointed out Memorial Park, where the gazebo stood, and told her about various town celebrations that had taken place there. During my first summer here, I'd watched the Fourth of July fireworks with Annie and Janey, but that one I kept to myself. Kiera was about to get enough of an introduction to the Sullivan side of the family.

I directed her to Crestview Road, where she turned left again into my driveway. Suddenly I was glad Janey wasn't here. It was one thing to introduce Kiera to the land, another to invite her into our home.

"Nice," she said when we'd gotten out of the SUV. "Lovely old farmhouse. I bet you spend a lot of nights hanging out on that big porch. I'm kind of envious, I live in a condo not far from the office. I do have a balcony, but it's small. Hardly room for a porch swing."

Her comment about where she lived made me realize I knew very little about her.

But I deflected her remark by saying, "The swing doesn't see as much action as it could. We tend to have long winters here."

"I grew up in the Syracuse area," Kiera said. "I know from snow."

And there it was, a hint of more personal information about her. I like how she volunteered the information, how naturally it emerged in conversation. Not like an awkward first date, where over drinks and dinner you played a back-and-forth game of twenty questions. Trina Winter and I had done that last winter, a forced date that had fizzled. Not that this was a date...I had to get my mind away from this topic. Sure, Kiera was pretty and I liked being in her company. But we had a job to do, and I suggested we get a move on. The sun was at its height, and on some days the bright rays beamed down through the latticed sails, creating striped shadows on the expansive green lawn. I wanted her to see that, for inspiration.

"Follow me," I said.

We started toward the back of the farmhouse and to the hill that, in winter, Janey and I used for sledding. It had a steep drop that enabled us to build up speed as we slid our way down toward the windmill. Today the snow was gone and the grass was regaining its thick luster, and so we trekked onward, finally reaching the crest of the hill; the top of the sails came into view, giving me pause. You could judge a lot about a person by their first impression of seeing the windmill, and as I waited for Kiera's, I found myself, ironically, holding my breath.

Kiera took another few steps forward, and as she did the whole of the windmill appeared. And not just the building itself, but the sails were in full motion on our windswept day, and with the sun so high, the sky opened up and created a blue vista of beauty. The trees, the hills that rolled beyond the windmill, and if you listened closely, maybe you could hear the gurgling of the creek. It's almost as if the windmill knew it was on display, and it was putting its best sail forward. I felt my own heart swell, almost like I was seeing it for the first time. Perhaps I was, but enhanced by the idea of my inn, or maybe from the woman standing beside me.

"Oh, Brian, it's..."

And she stopped. I gave her a silent moment, letting the windmill seep deep into her soul.

At last she spoke, finishing her sentence. "Glorious. Unbelievable." She paused, "Lovely."

"Yeah, I felt that way, too. No words, and then...a flood of them. And still none of them do it real justice."

She stood silent again, her mouth open. She was a student of life, of lines and shadows, the art of construction was part of her. If the Victorian house downtown had captivated her, and she'd displayed envy for the swing on the porch of the farmhouse, well, both were faint introductions to the true beauty that lived in this town.

"I've lived in New York State all my life," she finally said, "How have I not known of this windmill?"

"Linden Corners sometimes feels a bit isolated," I said, "I think we like it that way."

"Can I get closer?"

A silly remark, I told her, of course she can. I led her down the hill, taking her hand in mine to ensure she didn't slip, or simply because I wanted to. Her reaction was not unlike mine when I first pulled to the side of the road to inspect the windmill up close. That's where we were now, and I watched with swooning pride as she inspected the structure. She touched the wooden tower, as though feeling for its pulse. Leaning an ear against it, she could no doubt hear the churning gears of the spinning mechanism. At last she pulled back and observed as the sails passed above her.

"So," I said, "has inspiration struck you?"

She turned to me and said, "Brian, I want to build your inn. I want to be a part of this."

Her words were magic to me and our meeting could have ended right then and there and it would have been a perfect day. Except she wasn't ready to let go yet. She asked that I wait here while she returned to the car, and I did so, curious to see the evolution of what was in her mind. It wasn't a long wait, and soon I saw her reappear with an object in her arms, but instead of returning to the base of the windmill, she sat down in the grass at the edge of the hill. I saw her flip over something, and then she took out a writing implement. She had brought with her a sketch pad, and she was busily moving her hand across the page, looking up, then down, repeatedly. Seeing her sitting on the grassy field, drawing with such intent, I felt another intake of breath and I turned back toward the sails and saw them spinning still. Of course I thought of Annie upstairs in the windmill, in her painting studio and knew how empty it had been all these years. Then I pictured Janey racing down the hill toward the windmill, her arms outstretched to the point where the wind might take hold of her. Time was shifting, mixing past and present, leaving my mind jumbled.

"Should I join you up there?" I called out.

"No, stay right where you are. I want you in the picture I'm creating. You belong there."

It was almost too much to take, but I couldn't not look away. I stood my ground, realizing just how much my life had changed since that fateful day I'd found Linden Corners, and how much I could now change others. Some people went on journeys to find themselves; and sometimes the journey found you. Kiera continued to sketch, her hand working furiously, a deep smile lighting up her engaged face.

There was little doubt in my mind that the windmill had claimed another soul.

CHAPTER SEVEN

ASKING HER STAY FOR DINNER would have been
the easiest thing in the world. How I had wanted Janey
to meet her, but both would have to wait for another
time. Kiera begged off both ideas, for now, she said,
she really did have to start getting back to the office
before it got too dark.

"I'll be back, Brian Duncan," she told her me as she
stood before her SUV, "We have a lot of work ahead of
us, especially if we're going to make that anniversary
date next fall. It's a major undertaking, but somehow,
I think we will get it done."

When she departed, the word "we" stayed with
me, ringing in my ears like a song.

With my parents away for the day and a night at
the tavern looming, I'd made a phone call to Mark
Ravens, who I thought was off tonight from Riverfront
and maybe he'd want to pick up a shift, which he

readily agreed to. I felt bad about taking advantage of his own guilt about leaving me without a relief bartender, knowing it was one more night that kept him from tucking in his baby. He told me not to worry about it, saying Janey would probably remember the night with me more than would Harry without his father. I supposed he was right about that.

So tonight it was going to be just me and Janey, another "we" I liked. I went late afternoon to pick her up from Gerta's, where we were invited for dinner. I begged off this time, feeling like Janey and I needed some one on one time, a night when we could burrow inside the warmth of the farmhouse. Gerta nodded her understanding, just as Janey shot me a grateful look. She'd been at the Connors' house all day, she needed home, Sully, and maybe when she crawled into bed she'd reach for her trusty purple frog which had last Christmas finally gained a name, Dunc. Her two pets, one real and one stuffed but no less important, offering a bridge between her two families, Sullivan and Duncan. Annie and Brian.

Dinner was peaceful, Janey helping me make spaghetti and meatballs. We spoke of her day helping Gerta, and when the dishes were cleared we enjoyed a slice of the blueberry pie that she had made; she gleefully proclaimed she had rolled the crust and pinched its edges before going into the oven. I complimented her on the pie and that seemed to make her night.

What we did not discuss was how my meeting had gone, but I knew she'd bring it up eventually. Usually bedtime, when she wasn't yet ready to sleep and wanted to get some things off her chest before the night found her.

"Janey, go brush your teeth," I said, "It's getting late."

We were watching television, the program having just ended. It was nine o'clock and while it was spring break, I tried to keep a regular bedtime. She was still only ten, though, but she'd been through so much in her young life, she often appeared more mature. Tonight wasn't one of those nights, as she'd cuddled next to me—Sully along for the ride--on the sofa while we'd watched some competitive cooking show. Given how she'd baked a pie today, rolled meatballs, perhaps I had a chef on my hands.

She stirred from the sofa. "There's another episode on," she said.

"There's always another episode on, it's cable, no more," I said. "Brush, now. Get those blueberry stains before they settled in and make your smile all purple."

"Like Dunc," she said, emitting a giggle

I patted her on the rump and said get going and she did so, laughing her way up the stairs while Sully barked after her. I put our pie dishes into the sink, ran the water over the same purple stains I'd just mentioned, and then made my way up the stairs. I wasn't tired at all and I wondered what I would do the rest of the night after Janey had fallen asleep. Working the tavern had made me a night owl and often I didn't crawl in to bed until three a.m. Six hours was a long time when it was dark and quiet and you were alone.

Janey bounded into her room, already dressed in her comfy pajamas. She scrambled under the covers, a smile spreading across her face as she gazed at the photograph on the far wall. It was a portrait of Annie and Dan Sullivan, her parents, a reminder to her from where she came. I never wanted her to forget either of them. Dunc rested on her pillow, right by her head. Sully hopped onto the edge of the bed, resting his head on her leg.

"Gee, got any room for me?"

"Silly, Dad," she said.

While she often bounced between calling me Brian and Dad, at bedtime it was always Dad. I think she needed the assurance as she drifted off for the night that a parent was always there for her. She still preferred a night light to remain on, another sense of security. It cast a glow on the wall, my body creating a shadow, as though there were two of us. I could see Sully's tail wagging too. I sat down on the edge of the bed, kissed her forehead.

"When you start having guests staying at the inn, they won't live here, right?"

"No, Janey. We've been over this. The farmhouse will not be part of the inn. Off limits."

"Okay. Did that lady visit today?"

"She did, and I'm sorry you didn't get to meet her. She had to go back home."

"Where does she live?"

"Albany. Just a half hour away, but she's very busy, with lots of projects. She's likes ours."

"Will she build the inn?"

"She's going to design it," I said. "Her name is Kiera, you can refer to her as that."

"She sounds pretty. When will I meet her?"

"Next time. Not sure when, but she promised to be back. She'll be here a lot, supervising."

"Do you like her?"

"She very nice, Janey. I think she'll like you very much."

She scrunched up her nose, her signature move. "Why?"

"Because she understands how important the windmill is to you. She'll honor it."

"I like the sound of that. I like the sound of her."

I realized this was probably my best chance to raise the issue of Maddie. Shifting from the topic of one woman to another, I failed to see where I'd get any better opening. I adjusted myself on the bed, clearing my throat.

"Janey, there's something I want to discuss with you," I said.

"Okay," she said, but I could tell by her expression she was suddenly wary. Dunc found its way into her arms.

I don't know why the subject of Maddie was so difficult to bring up. Maybe because she represented my old life and I thought I'd left it behind long ago. John's wedding should have been the last vestige of that former life, and instead it had opened up fresh complications. Reminding Janey of that life, it didn't always go over so well. She was jealous of my past.

"So, an old friend of mine is coming for a visit to Linden Corners," I blurted.

"John? Is he bringing Anna? Oh wait, is it your sister, Rebecca? I like Junior, he's fun. No, wait, you said friend, so it can't be Rebecca..."

I think she didn't want me to tell her. Rambling on was another of her defense mechanisms.

"Her name is Madison Chasen...Maddie. Do you know who that is?"

She nodded but didn't say anything. She tightened her hold on Dunc.

"We ran into each other at John's wedding. We started talking. She said she'd like to visit."

"Is that why you didn't come home the day after the wedding?"

She didn't miss a trick, this kid. Her mind was a steel trip and I wondered if she'd been mulling this over in her brain since that day I hadn't come home. "Yes, one of the reasons. I did need to pack up my old apartment. Actually, Maddie helped me a lot, because, well, she actually sparked the idea of the Windmill Inn. I mean, not directly. She just made a comment and it set my mind to thinking."

"When is she coming?"

"This weekend. Just Saturday, actually."

"Is she staying here?"

"No, Janey, she has another place to stay."

"She wasn't nice to you," Janey said.

"Everyone makes mistakes, honey. I made my share, too. It's only through forgiveness that you can move on. Maddie and I are just friends. She wanted to see Linden Corners, to see that I'd settled well after our relationship ended. I want to make sure she's okay, too. Like I said, friends. But I don't want you to feel left out. Maddie wants to meet you."

"She did meet me, the last time she came to town."

"We were all in a different place then, Janey. We were all younger, including you. Maddie is looking for a fresh chance.'

"Are you going to marry her?"

I reached out, ran a comforting hand across her cheek. She squired beneath the covers.

"No, Janey, I'm not getting married."

"It's okay if you do, someday," she said. "That would give me a Mom, right?"

"Let's not get ahead of ourselves, Janey. Right now it's you and me against the world."

That made her smile. "I like that."

"Okay, good. Nothing's changing between us. Ever."

"Ever," she repeated.

I leaned in and kissed her cheek. "Get some sleep. And know, as always, whatever is going on in your mind, you can talk to me."

"I know that, Dad."

"So, are you up for an adventure on Saturday, help me show Maddie around?"

She waited a moment before answering. That's when she informed me, "Oh, Ashley wants me to come over Saturday, she and Erin and Jennifer are having a sleepover and it would be much more fun if we could all be part of it. Sorry, I forgot to tell you. But you and Maddie should have fun, too. You don't need a little girl tagging along. Goodnight, Brian."

She burrowed further under the covers, turning her back to me.

My heart dropped, my mind wishing I'd broached this subject a different way, or a different time. I turned to Sully, patted him on the head and told him to watch over Janey while she slept. He rested his head back on her leg, and I was grateful for his presence. Then I walked out of the room, my shadow following me.

Back downstairs, I rambled about the quiet farm-house, accomplishing nothing and growing increasingly frustrated. Finally, I grabbed the phone and dialed a number from memory. As I heard the voice on the other end, I sat down on the sofa and let out a sigh.

"Hi, Cynthia, glad you're home. Do you have a second for an old friend with an age old problem?"

"Anytime, Brian. I miss our talks."

We talked for an hour and I fell asleep afterwards with one piece of good news.

Cynthia Knight was pregnant with her second child. I was glad someone's life was moving forward. Maddie's looming visit—and Janey's reaction to it-- was only taking me backwards.

———————

A late winter storm was in the forecast, hardly unusual in this region. The cool air that had swept in on Thursday was just a preview of the high winds and snow that was in the forecast, perhaps a foot I'd heard on the news. Friday night, George's Tavern had an unusual number of people, which meant we were busy. There was a party of ten taking up the far corner, and from what they had told me, a reunion had been canceled due to the weather, but some folks had already arrived in town. So I was the lucky beneficiary. I asked where they were staying and they mentioned a roadside motel on the other side of Hillsdale. My locals kept their distance from what they consider interlopers, sticking to the bar stools like dried beer.

I barely had time to notice when my father walked in, as I was holding another rounds of drinks on a tray for the large group. Doing a double take, I nearly dropped the entire tray but I balanced myself and presented the drinks with aplomb. Maybe I was actually good at this job. Running the tavern had just sort of happened and, needing some kind of income, I'd stayed. I still wondered what I was going to do with the place come the fall, when the inn would be operational. But that was many months away, and for now I was a barkeeper, not an innkeeper.

"Hey, Dad. Kind of surprised to see you, not that I mind."

"Looks busy, Brian, that's good for business. Let me have a shot of Chivas, neat."

He wasn't supposed to drink but he'd been so helpful to me, how could I refuse. I poured it and said, "One."

"Janey wore your mother out playing Monopoly. It was that or baking cookies."

"Great, high finance or two women in the kitchen, Mom must have been thrilled."

"Janey in bed, Didi's reading but not long for this world. I told her I was headed home."

"Yet, here you are."

"This new life of ours, it's still tough adjusting," he said.

Not that I was looking to get rid of them, I'd gotten used to having my parents around and they had been a huge help with Janey after the Knight's move. But I had to wonder: just how long did they plan on staying in Linden Corners? They owned a beautiful Federal townhouse in historic Philadelphia, my mother's urban sanctuary after raising the three Duncan kids in the suburbs. A reverse transition, and now they'd taken it a step further by buying an old farmhouse in the country.

"With the exception of a trip to Philly right after the New Year, you two have pretty much stuck to Linden Corners. Except your overnight shopping trip the other day. Are you thinking it's time to go home, or even more likely, is Mom pressuring you to leave?"

He seemed to mull this over as he took hold of his drink. He sipped it, savoring the flavor rather than knocking it back in one gesture of instant gratification. He settled on a bar stool, my question still hanging in the air as he said hello to Chet, Gil, and a couple of the others. They knew him by now, of course, since he'd taken the reins at the bar many times. Who knows if he indulged the guys in shots, enjoying one or two on the house along with them? It wasn't the profits I minded, but I was concerned about his health.

"We'll be going back in a couple weeks," he finally said, "Doctor check-up."

"You feeling okay?"

"Fit as a fiddle. Despite your mother's hovering. I think her worry does more damage."

"Dad, she loves you. She doesn't want to lose you."

"Hmmph, Kevin Duncan isn't going anywhere, I've faced tougher closings than death."

Another group of people arrived, joining the reunion party already assembled in the back. Guess their party, whatever the occasion, was taking place here at George's. I excused myself and went over to take orders, and for the next half hour I was busy behind the bar, doing what these days came as natural. My father just sat there and watched, occasionally remarking on the energy I seemed to possess at such a late hour. Truth of the matter, my nerves were on edge, because once the night was over, it meant morning was soon behind it, and then Maddie would arrive.

Turned out, though, Maddie arrived before the dawn.

The door to George's opened and a burst of cold air swirled inside. Chet spun around and told the newcomer to close the door and she did. I didn't immediately recognize her, since she was bundled up, but once she removed her hat and let that honey-blonde hair fall to her shoulders, my mouth dropped open. I turned to the clock on the wall, seeing that it was just after eleven. Maddie Chasen was twelve hours early.

Dad had noticed her too; actually most of the men in the bar had. Despite the cold, she'd brought with her an air of freshness, helped out by the perfume she was wearing, detectable as she came wafting over to the bar. The scent took me back to our day in New York.

"What's a girl got to do to get a drink around here?"

I think a couple of the guys were willing to buy her one but I held them back.

"I'll handle this one," I said, coming around the edge of the bar. "Bartender's privilege."

The guys watched me as I greeted Maddie with an embrace, which she easily returned.

"What are you doing here?" I asked.

"Is that how you greet all of your guests?"

"No, I mean, I was expecting you tomorrow morning.'

"I was going to drive up, but the weather was questionable so, I thought, what would Brian Duncan do? So I took Amtrak to Hudson."

"And from there?"

"A cab. I had to call one from some fancy restaurant there…"

"RiverFront," I said.

"That's it. Sat and had a drink at the bar until the cab arrived."

"Still, a cab from there to Linden Corners couldn't have been cheap."

"Beats the cost of a car rental from Manhattan. Brian, you sound like you're not happy to see me?"

"We are," said Chet, holding out his beer. "Come on, Brian, get the lovely lady a drink. On us."

"Chet, you should worry about paying your tab before adding to it."

Maddie waved off my comment and said, "Where's your sense of fun, Brian? Hi boys, let me buy a round. Name's Maddie."

With that she went and grabbed a stool between Chet and Gil, much to their delight. As I went back behind the bar, my father's curious eyes trailed me. I could feel any number of questions boring their way into me from behind. But first I handled the drink orders, getting Maddie a very dry martini. I had little call for them, but luckily I had the stemware and the mixology skills. Soon they raised their drinks and cheered Maddie's arrival, a fantasy snow bunny emerging from the storm outside. Why was I left with the feeling that the storm had found its way inside?

"So, Maddie, you remember my father, Kevin Duncan?"

She set her glass down and said, "I knew you looked familiar, but I couldn't imagine what you would be doing in Linden Corners."

"Seems we have the same question," he said. "Very

nice to see you again, Maddie."

"And you, Kevin. I'm guessing Brian failed to mention my visit."

"Well, we haven't seen much of each other the past week."

She nodded, took a sip, and gave me a look that said she didn't believe a word of it. First, I had seen my father nearly every day this week, and second, and more devastating to my case, was the fact Maddie's visit had been on my calendar for weeks. I'd tried to push it from my mind, but eventually time finds a way to win. It always does. She was here.

I busied myself with bar duties while my father and Maddie got reacquainted, the other barflies getting in on the conversation when they could. As I served more drinks, I received a bit of ribbing on how I could have let a looker like Maddie go, and I took it all in stride, mentioning nothing of the reason behind our break-up. The moment was surreal enough with Maddie Chasen chasing drinks in George's Tavern; toss in the addition of my father, and I didn't know what year it was. Again, time was playing with me, and again I was losing.

Finally the bar began to clear just after one o'clock, the gang celebrating their reunion gone. My father was still here, as was Chet, as usual, and of course Maddie. I convinced Chet it was time to remember what his house looked like, and he took the not-so-subtle hint.

Before he left, Maddie said she had his tab taken care of, and he bowed in appreciation. Chet Hardesty was smitten, and he left the bar with a happy smile. It had probably been his best night at George's.

"Come back any time, pretty lady," he said.

"Thanks, Chet. You do make a girl feel welcome."

I turned the lock after he left, doused the main lights, as I always did. My father seemed to take the hint too.

"Maddie, it's been a pleasure," he said.

"Thank you, Kevin. I will see you tomorrow night," she said.

I turned. "I'm sorry, what's tomorrow?"

Maddie smiled at my father and said, "We're invited to their house for dinner."

I gave my father a look but said nothing.

"Wonderful, see you both then."

He departed, and finally Maddie and I were left alone. The bar was quiet, and normally I would be cleaning glasses, sweeping the floor, putting up stools. I didn't have time for any of that, because Maddie came up from behind me, and I felt her kiss on my neck.

"Now that's how you're supposed to greet someone," she said.

I turned, her body still close to mine. "Sorry, you took me by surprise, that's all."

"Brian Duncan, you may have changed your life,

but you haven't changed yourself. You are still a horrible liar."

I wondered if the same could be said of Maddie, but I was distracted by her kisses. I gave in to the moment, my brain shutting down. I spent too much time inside it, anyway. I enveloped her in my arms, and I felt a heady sense of heat swarm over me. She felt so soft, so intoxicating, more so than any of the booze that lined the shelves behind me.

"So, Brian," she said, as she pulled back with a devious grin on her face. "What kind of accommodations do you have for me?"

"Uh, upstairs," I said.

"How convenient. Why don't you show me to my room?"

I did, taking her warm hand in mine. I didn't get home until much later, which most folks in Linden Corners would call early. Again, time was toying with me, letting me enjoy the moment while paying for it later, tossing and turning in my own empty bed as dawn fast approached. The night was over, but I still had tomorrow to deal with. Actually, tomorrow had become today.

———————————

"Sorry I had to leave...you know, after."

Maddie cupped my freshly shaven cheeks, her warmth spreading through me on this cold day. It was ten o'clock, and we had just finished breakfast at the Five-O, just her and I. I had asked Janey to join us but she said her own plans took precedence, and soon Ashley and her mother were pulling into the driveway to whisk my defiant daughter for a day of denial. Or maybe that was how I felt?

"Since you weren't expecting me, all is forgiven," Maddie said. "Tonight is another story."

"Janey has a sleepover at her friends," I said.

"So do you," she informed me.

Yeah, but first we had to suffer through dinner with my parents. Why had my father gone and invited us? He didn't understand the ramifications, not that I did either. Clearly Maddie and I were going through a renaissance with our relationship, trying to put aside the incident that ended us, rediscovering why we had gotten together in the first place. Lots in common, and an attraction of the heart that apparently was still beating. I hadn't left Maddie because I was no longer attracted to her. No, it was her desires for another man, the one who signed both of our paychecks. I'd seen them in each other arms, making love, and that image had resurfaced ever since I'd seen her at John's wedding. Except it was me back in her bed.

"What's on tap for today?" she asked as we headed outside the Five-O.

The storm had stopped overnight, leaving in its wake a fresh blanket of snow all over the land. Linden Corners was as picturesque as ever, a winter postcard just like the kind Darla, or was it Marla, sold down at the Trading Post. I had told Maddie to dress warm, and to have hiking boots with her. So there we were, the both of us bundled up against the elements. Nothing like an early spring snowstorm to remind you that nature was in control. So why not enjoy what it had on offer. I said to Maddie.

"How about a hike in the woods?"

"Sounds adventurous," she said.

Since she'd taken the train up, the only vehicle we had to rely on was the truck, which of course I'd failed to take to the shop again. If the engine turned, we'd be fine. It had all-season tires, and could get us up the hills of Columbia County and environs. Settled into the truck, trying not to think of Annie beside me—this had been her truck, not mine—Maddie and I headed east out of Linden Corners, bypassing the burned-out shell of the Solemn Nights, and wending our way up a snowy, curving road. Open fields kept us company as we continued on, eventually climbing our way in the mountains, the truck finding its strength as it powered forward. It was as though it knew just where we were going, something it had over Maddie.

"This can't still be Linden Corners," she said.

"No, we're going up into the Berkshires, a friend of mine own a tree farm up in these hills, it's where we get our Christmas tree every year. I even chop it down."

"You, with an axe?"

"Better to swing it than to grind it?"

She wasn't amused by my comment, and neither was I. We grew silent within the confines of the front cabin of the truck, and it was only when the thick forest of trees opened up to us that brought her back to life. It was hard to deny the beauty spreading out before us, and soon we had parked in the lot of Green's Tree Farm, ours the only car. During the off-season, the Green family used their property as a nature preserve, and there were many trails you could walk. Last night's storm had left the ground with a fresh new coating of snow, the branches of the firs picturesque with downy white feathers. They wavered in the light wind. I helped Maddie down from the truck, my chivalrous gesture putting us back on solid footing, more so as we began to trek upwards on uneven land.

I took hold of her hand, helping her up a particularly steep slope.

"Not exactly a leisurely stroll up Fifth Avenue, is it?" she asked.

"Come on, there's a reward for our efforts," he said.

The promise of something to look forward to kept

her going, Maddie even passing me by as I stopped to catch my breath. I sucked down cold air, feeling the chill hit my lungs. But this had been my idea, there was no turning back, and at last I caught up to her, she grabbing my hand as we pushed on toward the top of the particular slope we'd chosen. The path cut between trees, marking its way as best it could despite the freshly fallen snow. Only our own footprints could get us back now, unless you counted the occasional prints from deer and rabbits that dotted the crunchy snow. At last we reached the peak, both of us standing atop a plateau that was slick with ice. We held onto each other to ensure neither of us slipped, but with one free arm I presented the view I'd brought her up here for.

"Oh, Brian, it's really lovely. Like we're at the North Pole," she said.

We were a few hundred feet above sea level, and spread out before us in all directions were small towns sprinkled in along the wide, sweeping land. More hills, more trees, snow falling around us now as this higher elevation. The spires of churches rose up, and way in the distance, if you concentrated hard you could see the outlines of the Hudson River, its wide expanse in winter usually coursing with ice floes; in early spring, the ice had melted and the water had returned to its natural current.

Maddie turned to me and said, "I'm sorry, Brian."

"Sorry for what?"

"Everything. The past, the suggestion that I come visit. My actions today."

"Here we are at the height of the world, and you're taking on its weight? Maddie, you don't need to apologize."

"Sweet, Brian. But I could tell last night...you weren't happy I was here. You didn't even tell anyone I was coming."

"Not true, I told my friend, I told Janey."

"And where are we?"

I was confused by the changing direction of this conversation, like the wind kept shifting it. "I don't understand."

"Brian, I came to see you in Linden Corners. And what do you do, you take me away from it. Like you don't want to share it with me, or make me want to feel a part of it. You have to know this wasn't easy for me either. As I boarded the train last night, the rational part of me kept saying don't get on, and at each stop I fought with my conscience to not hop off and return home."

"Maddie..."

"No, let me get this out, okay? When John invited me to the wedding, I knew I'd end up seeing you. Of course I would, you were his best man. I could have stayed away, but I went. And you came after me, and then we shared that next day...sort of like this, but citified. Central Park, then back to your place for Chinese food and sex. Neither of us expected that to happen, I know I didn't plan it that way. I just...I just wanted to see you. And once I did...after what we did, I guess I wanted to see you again. But your life here, it's beautiful and special, and it's uniquely yours. I don't belong."

"Maddie, that's not true. This is just...being with you again. You meant the world to me."

"And then I destroyed your world."

"I was already unhappy, what you did...it was a catalyst. Now I'm here, in Linden Corners and yeah, I love it. It's where I'm meant to be."

I paused and she offered up no words. But I could tell she had something more on her mind.

"Maddie, you're not one to hold back. What's really going on?"

"Why did you take me here?"

"Because, it's a beautiful view, and I thought you would enjoy it. Come on, that's not the real question. Maddie, stop beating around..."

She cut me off, her voice tinged with anger. "Why didn't you take me to the windmill?"

Words failed me. So did my thoughts. I just stood there amidst nature's bounty, with one of the most beautiful creatures I'd ever encountered on this earth, and I had nothing. The wind had already turned my face red, so the flush I felt inside me remained there, unable to fight its way out. I stared into her dark eyes, hoping not to see a tear. Because it would turn to ice, which is just how my heart felt right now. She was right. I'd not taken her to the windmill. I'd brought her far away from it. We couldn't even see it from here. It was like the windmill had faded into memory.

Finally, I said, "Because maybe I'm afraid."

"Of what?"

"Of what showing it to you means. When I left you three years ago, I went searching, not even sure what I was searching for. I like to think the windmill found me, plucked me right off the road and into its spinning world, one filled with promise. With Janey, and, for a time, with Annie. And now it's the focal point of my future."

"I get it. There's no place in your life for the past. For me."

"Actually, Maddie, if not for you, I never would have come to Linden Corners. If you trust in fate, perhaps that's how things were supposed to happen. Now, time has passed, flown by really, like the wind was controlling it. Even this weekend, it began as though time had stopped when you walked into the bar, and now...it's moving so fast. Our afternoon together is waning, and I don't just mean the light of the day. I mean, our window of opportunity..."

She stopped me, and she did so by kissing me.

I accepted the kiss, took her into my arms and kissed her back.

When she drew back, she wiped at her cheeks. "When did you become such a poet, Brian Duncan?"

"The windmill, I guess it inspires me."

"Will you show it to me?"

I should have taken her there this moment. But I didn't, as I said, "Later, when the time is right."

Later, like soon, was a fluid word, its relation to time loose.

CHAPTER EIGHT

I TRIED TO BEG OFF my parents' dinner invitation, but my mother would hear nothing of it when I called later the afternoon. Nonsense, she informed me, which was a clear indication that I wouldn't be winning any argument with her; she had been cooking and setting the table all day. Then she informed me I should have said something earlier about Maddie's visit, and before I could say reply, she told me I had surprised her, which coming from her, I had to take as a compliment.

"Usually you wear your heart on your sleeve, Brian. Keeping Maddie a secret, so unlike you."

"Guess I was wearing long sleeves lately," I answered.

She then said goodbye without a laugh, instead leaving me with the image of her unamused expression. It was that same face that greeted us at the front door of their farmhouse just a couple hours later, at seven p.m. sharp. My father answered the door, with Sully barking behind him. With Janey at her sleepover and me spending the day with Maddie, Sully stayed with them. It seemed my life was nothing but shuffling people and pets around, my routine having gone underground.

"Welcome, Maddie. You look lovely."

"Thank you, Kevin. I hardly brought anything nice for a dinner party. I wasn't expecting to attend one."

"We all improvise," he said, ushering us in from the cold. "I fear your timing wasn't ideal, weather-wise. Winter's last blast doesn't know from inconvenience. But such is life in the land of the windmill, eh?"

"I wouldn't know," she said, giving me a pointed look.

"I said later."

We'd come down from the mountain, where I brought her back to the tavern and poured her a glass of wine. I opened up for the night, getting it ready for Mark's shift, which he'd agreed to a couple weeks ago when I'd asked for his help, not telling him the reason. Maddie had gotten ready upstairs while the regulars settled in, and soon Mark was there, Maddie and I left, and now we were here.

As we entered the living room, which still retained the country-store charm wallpaper of Cynthia, the door from the kitchen opened up. My mother came out, looking stylish in her sweater and slacks, pearls back around her neck. She was in her element hosting dinner parties, usually for her society ladies or my father's business associates. Her effort tonight was no different, except for the company around the table.

"Maddie, dear, how lovely to see you," she said, a bright smile widening her face.

"Thank you, Didi. Very nice to see you too. You really didn't have to go to any trouble."

"Nonsense," she replied. "More notice would have been nice, but you know Brian."

"Hey, I didn't make the offer for dinner, Dad did."

"Men," Mom said, and then she took hold of Maddie's arm and drew her into the kitchen.

"Drink, Brian?"

I didn't drink, I hadn't touched a drop since my hepatitis scare almost four years ago. But if any occasion called for one, this one sure qualified. Still, I passed, and Dad poured me a seltzer, dropping a wedge of lime into the glass. He poured himself a whiskey and we clinked glasses, not sure what we were toasting.

"Those two ladies, they always did get along," he said.

"I'd forgotten," I said.

But it all came rushing back to me, memories unleashed like a damn that broke. The first time I'd even mentioned Maddie to my mother, she'd asked where she was from and when I said the South, she was immediately pleased, noting how well-bred she must be, her manners no doubt impeccable. With one notable exception, Maddie was the picture of grace, and when she needed to turn it on, well, that's when she dug out the lilting accent she normally tried to cover. Once they met, we'd attended the opera, Broadway shows, gone to fine restaurants in both Philadelphia and Manhattan, and she had been planning a family cruise. I'd been planning on popping the question, too, which had her seal of approval, when everything went, so to speak, south. I think Mom had been more devastated by the break-up than me.

"Your mother's been bustling about all day. I haven't seen her this happy in a while."

"She doesn't have much to do here in Linden Corners. She should volunteer. I know down at Edgestone Retirement Center they're always looking for people to come spend time with the residents. Thomas often remarks how bored he is, even with Elsie Masters constantly whispering gossip into his ears. He says sometimes he claims to be deaf. The advantages to old age."

"Hmm, that's an idea. She does still oversee the Knight's fruit stand, working with the men and women Cynthia and Bradley employed. But I'm not sure it's really her thing. Not that Elsie is her cup of tea either," he said. "Just give her time. She'll get used to Linden Corners."

It was an odd statement coming from my father, almost as though he was insinuating that their move had turned permanent.

"It's still hard for me to wrap my mind around," I said.

"What's that, Brian, dear?"

My mother and Maddie emerged from the kitchen, glasses of red wine swirling in glasses.

"Just, you know, having you and Dad around in Linden Corners."

My mother turned to Maddie. "Brian thinks he's the only who can change his life."

"He's rather myopic, isn't he?" Maddie said, hiding her grin behind her wine glass.

"So this is how tonight is going to go? Gang up on Brian?"

But I said it good-naturedly enough, which only drew more barbs my way, and soon enough the dinner party was under way. Small talk ensured, the weather, and what we had been up to all day, Maddie taking command of that, detailing our trip up into the mountains. She kept it G-rated, giving up no hint of anything romantic between us, either today or last night. Eventually, dinner was ready, salmon fillets with potatoes, a salad, and spinach. More wine, which I continued to beg off. I was fine with my seltzer. Best anyway to keep my wits around these two women.

My mother had set a lovely table, with her classic

China and silverware. I was surprised to see it here at the farmhouse, rather than back at the townhouse in Philly.

"Oh, I only brought up half of the collection," she said. "Maddie, I have service for eight."

Dad just nodded, chewing away at his salmon.

"Speaking of Philly, Mom, Dad says you're going back there this week."

"Just a quick trip, Brian. A doctor's appointment for your father. I have some errands, too."

"We'll, I guess it's inevitable that you'll be returning home for a long stretch, but the fact you'll be away next week means I need to speed up my search for a relief bartender. I can't do all the shifts, but I can't hardly close the bar down for a week, and I certainly can't keeping pawning Janey off on friends."

"See, Maddie, even in tiny Linden Corners the world's problems are large."

"Janey's not a problem, Mom."

"I suggested nothing of the sort, Brian. See, Maddie, he gets very defensive."

'Mom, I'm right here. Address me, don't attempt to explain my behavior to Maddie."

"Brian, Jane is far more adaptive than you give her credit for, that's all I was saying."

I hated when she called her Jane. "Mom, Janey's ten-years-old. She needs me."

She knew when to stop, especially on the subject of

my becoming not just Janey's guardian but her parent, with all rights associated with those of any biological parent. The subject dropped, she sipped her wine and ate a small bite of potatoes. Maddie did the same, perhaps feeling she had egged Didi on. Dad tried to save the day, of course, but the subject he chose wasn't one I was ready to talk about either. He asked Maddie her thoughts on the Windmill Inn.

"I don't even know what that is," she said. "Some place to stay, a hotel of sorts?"

"Brian, dear, what have you two been talking about all weekend? Maddie, why it's the only thing on his mind these days. Brian's grand plan for his and Jane's future. Of course it revolves, so to speak, around that windmill of his."

My mother was doing it again, talking about me like I wasn't here. I didn't take the bait.

"I was waiting to tell you, you know, later," I said, feeling like I was using the same excuse as before. I touched Maddie's arm as I spoke, my eyes trying to convey what my words might not have accomplished.

She nodded her understanding. Either that, or she didn't want to get into in front of my parents. Thankfully, I thought I'd dodged that bullet for now.

Dessert and coffee were served, even though I informed my mother that she'd done enough for one night, but etiquette dictated otherwise.

"I even went over to Gerta Connors, where she had

a pie coming out of the oven."

"Strawberry?" I asked.

"Fresh-baked," Mom said, nodding.

"I've never heard of such a thing," Maddie said.

"Gerta is a good friend of the family, her pie baking skills unmatched," I informed Maddie. "You've never truly been to Linden Corners until you've had a slice of her pies. The strawberry is her signature."

"Then I can't pass on that," she said. "It's like being initiated into an exclusive club."

Fortunately, the pie went over well, and full, we excused ourselves from the table, and finally brought the dinner party to a close. I was never more grateful to get out into the cold air, and I escorted Maddie to the truck after we said our thanks and goodbyes. When my parents closed the door, Maddie turned to me and planted a quick, strawberry-tasting kiss on my lips.

"Wow, Didi sure rides you hard. Does she approve of anything you do?"

"Oh, I wasn't sure you noticed, piling on as you were doing."

She kissed me again. "Silly, Brian."

Her words made me think of Janey, and suddenly I missed her. I hadn't seen her since the morning, and now, as the moon was climbing in the night sky, I wondered if she was still playing with her friends or if they had all dropped from exhaustion. I'd spoken to her earlier, just to check in on her, she said everything was fine. What wasn't fine, right now, was the truck. Maddie and I were situated in our seats, and I turned the ignition, only to get a choke from the exhaust. Nothing else. I tried again, then again, still nothing.

"Come on," I said, "follow me. Ready for another trek?"

"Where are we going?"

"Later has arrived," was my response.

We abandoned the truck in my parents' driveway, and then I guided her behind the house, across their property and toward the line of trees and the creek that cut between our lands. It was wet going, our boots sinking into the snowy field. We continued ahead, our shadows ahead of us, like they were guiding us. Through the trees we went, coming out right before the stone bridge. Then we crossed over it, and we were back on Sullivan property. Just over the hill, there she was, the mighty windmill, gently spinning in the wind as the moonlight reflected off its moving sails, creating dancing shadows on the white show.

"There it is, Maddie," I said, a catch in my throat. "My future."

She stepped forward until she reached the crest of the hill, her arms wrapped around herself against the cold breeze that swept past. She turned to me, beckoned me forward. I went to her and I took her in my arms, and we kissed, not once and not twice, and not any amount you could count, not when time lost its meaning. When we did part, I saw on her face the vulnerability that I'd first seen on her face the day she came to work at the Beckford Group. New York toughness hadn't yet hit this Southern filly, and that's what I saw again right now.

"You want to hear about the Windmill Inn, now?"

"No," she said, shaking her head for emphasis. "Brian, don't make me go back to that stark apartment, not tonight, even if you join me. Take me into your life. What you found, it's nothing but magic. Make me feel a part of it, if only for this night. I have to leave tomorrow anyway, and maybe I should be gone before Janey returns home. Our emotions are raw enough without adding pressure on a confused little girl. We'll deal with everything else...later."

I smiled at my excuse coming full circle.

"Well, I guess you'll have to stay overnight. The truck took tonight to die on me."

We made our way along the hill, returning to my home, where I invited her inside, and then, without further words, I led her upstairs and to my room. She entered, I closed the door, and pressed her against it, kissing her, feeling her body meld with mine. Our clothes fell away, our bodies reaching the bed. And then, under the warmth of the blankets, I entered her with a sense of anticipation, her cries releasing my apprehension. I didn't know what time it was, what year, what month or season, all I knew was that I was locked in the arms of something powerful, a rush hitting me with lost wonder. Linden Corners faded away from my mind, the woman I'd once planned on spending my life with suddenly back in my life.

Wasn't that what I wanted? What I'd always wanted?

Someone, anyone, to share my dark nights with. I'd spent too many empty ones alone.

I think a lot about time. It's natural I fear its evolution. Annie Sullivan thought she had all the time in the world, only to have the hands of fate win out over the hands of the clock. Maybe it was one of the reasons I wanted such an escalated schedule for the building of the Windmill Inn, because you never knew what tomorrow would bring, if you even had a tomorrow to experience.

Ten days had passed since Maddie Chasen had departed Linden Corners, leaving the life I had created for myself to find the one she was still searching for. Whether it included me, we'd agreed to not apply undue pressure. She'd parted with a kiss early in the morning, having called a cab to take her down to the train stop in Hudson. The cold air had dissipated overnight, and I was left with the image of her blonde hair flowing in the breeze, a smile on her lips as she waved back at me. I'd heard from her once since then, that same day when she arrived home and thanked me for a memorable weekend.

Life resumed its normal routine. I called upon Chet, who owned his own mechanic shop, who came over to give the truck a once over; he towed it to his shop, fixed this and that and I promised him a few beers on the house. Nora drove me over to pick it a few days later. It still gave me trouble starting, but at least it ran and I could get around town without help from others. School break was also over, Janey was back to school, happy to have homework to do, happy to have me around more often and not as distracted. My relief bartender had come from the most unlikely of sources, none other than Chuck Ackroyd. He'd seen my sign in the window the day I'd put it up and he'd applied, saying it would help supplement his income while he waited on me to begin placing orders for supplies on the Windmill Inn. Given that he still had the Going out of Business sign on the side of the building, I felt I had no choice but to give him the job. He was pleased to take as many shifts as possible.

My parents had still not returned from Philadelphia, and I began to wonder if they were second-guessing their commitment to Linden Corners. My father had bought the Knight's farmhouse outright, a cash exchange that

Bradley had only been too happy to accept. But I knew Kevin Duncan the businessman saw its purchase as more of an investment than a retirement home. My mother I think still thought he was crazy to have not only bought it but to have spent the entire winter inside its walls, but had appeased him in an effort to get him to listen to his doctors. Relax, something that was clearly difficult for him to adhere to.

It was a Thursday morning in early April when I was cleaning up breakfast dishes that the telephone rang. I looked over at Annie's windmill clock that spun on the far wall, saw that it was only just past nine o'clock in the morning. Janey had left for school an hour ago, leaving a day stretching before me with nothing on the agenda. That all changed with the phone call.

"This is Brian," I said, answering.

"Oh, Brian, it's Gerta."

"Hi, how are you?"

My voice was chipper at the thought of maybe having lunch with her, but there was a sharp tint to her own that gave me pause.

"I'm fine, dear. But I'm afraid I'm calling with rather sad news."

My throat closed on me, my hand tightening against the receiver. "Gerta, what happened?"

"It's Elsie Masters. She passed away in her sleep last night."

"Oh, I'm so sorry to hear that," I said, "was she even sick?"

"No one knows, Brian. My goodness, she knew everything about everyone, but I wonder how much we really knew her. The number of times I wished she would stop talking."

Elsie wasn't happy unless she a) uncovered some piece of gossip; and b) sharing her gossip with others. As she explained, what else were you supposed to do with such information? Keep it to yourself and it wasn't gossip. Guess she didn't see the larger picture. Perhaps she did now.

"Is there anything I can do?"

"A few of us are gathering at Nora's store."

"I'll come over soon."

"Thank you, Brian."

Nora's store, A Doll's Attic, had been in existence for just a year and half or so, when she'd come back to town after her divorce. Elsie was in retirement mode at age seventy, and she gave up living upstairs at the Victorian that housed her antique store, age having crept up on her. I thought of Gerta's comment and imagined there was truth in them. Elsie was so busy telling everyone's business, did anyone ever bother to ask her about her own? Had she been ill? How ironic that she felt she couldn't share her own fears. I felt a wash of regret for not having gone beyond the surface of a woman who had kept Linden Corners buzzing.

So I grabbed my keys from the counter and started off, only to hear the phone ring again. Thinking it was Gerta again, I retreated back to the kitchen and grabbed the receiver.

"This is Brian," I said.

"Oh, uh, hi. This is Kiera Bowen, of Kirby Spellman..."

"I think I remember," I said. "Hi, it's nice to hear from you."

"Did I catch you at a bad time? You sound out of breath."

"No, just some village news I got caught up in. What can I do for you?"

"I have designs for you. I've been working nearly non-stop the last week."

Even as I mourned Elsie's passing, I couldn't help but get excited about Kiera's news.

"That's great. When can I see them? I could maybe drive up to your office tomorrow."

"Oh, no, Brian, this can't wait. Let me come to Linden Corners and I'll show you."

I found myself looking forward to such a visit, and perhaps not only because of the designs she had prepared for the Windmill Inn. Kiera was dedicated to her craft, but seeing her on the hill that day sketching away, something else had transpired. She was in the moment, feeling the passion behind the project.

"Great, when would you like to come?"

"How about tonight, when I get out of work? Remember, time is of the essence."

Given today's earlier news about Elsie, Kiera couldn't have been more on target. Time wasn't a thing to waste, each second was precious. Phone calls sometimes seemed so impersonal to me. Yes, you exchanged information, and you caught up with a good friend. But mostly it was a recount of what had already happened. Didn't time prefer to move forward? There was nothing like tackling the future one-on-one, and I told Kiera that I agreed with her, the sooner the better.

"I'm not working the tavern tonight, so I'll be home. Me and Janey. Dinner?"

"Oh, so I get to meet the famous inspiration behind the inn?"

Janey was part of it, sure. Annie more so. Now Kiera had thrown herself into the mix.

"I'll see you around six."

"It's a date,' she said, and before I could comment again she had ended the call.

I pushed thoughts of the Windmill Inn aside, concentrating on the here and now. I hopped into the truck and drove toward downtown Linden Corners, thinking it was easier to park in the lot at George's and walking the couple blocks down to A Doll's Attic. But I could already see the hive of activity centered around the Victorian house down the street, so I kept going, pulling up to the curb and quickly joining the assembled group. There were about twelve people already, some of them I recognized from Edgestone and knew by name, others only their faces looked familiar. Still, it was nice to feel included in the remembrance of a woman who'd lived her entire life in Linden Corners, one who left it as suddenly as the wind shifted direction.

I found Gerta, who I hugged. A couple other older ladies greeted me, their faces worn by age, perhaps by defeat over losing one of their own.

"Elsie was one of a kind," I said to them. "One minute with her, you knew the entire history of Linden Corners."

"Some of it even true," one of the ladies remarked.

The others joined in. Clearly Elsie had left her mark with them as well. That was the thing about reputations, if you're going to have one, you may as well live up to it. Gossipy Elsie Masters subscribed to such a theory her whole life. I excused myself from the ladies and made my way up the steps of the Victorian, where I found Nora setting out a pitcher of tea on the wraparound porch. A lovely spring day hovered over our fair burg, the warmest temperatures yet this season. Gone was the snow from two weeks ago, the lush green lawns fighting to reclaim the land.

"Brian, hi. Mom said she called you," Nora said. "Isn't it awful? Elsie loved life."

"And she lived it to the fullest. She was a true

renaissance lady. She embraced the past with her antique store, but she never let a piece of information pass her by. She knew things not even the future did, and she was generally right. Any idea what happened?"

"Best to ask Thomas. He says he was the last person to talk to her."

I nodded, not surprised. Elsie had taken a shine to Thomas, even if he was fifteen years too old for her. But they had shared stories of Linden Corners' past, Elsie the keeper of so much town history, Thomas a man in search of such links to yesterday. As a boy, he'd only lived here for five years, but it was where his parents had met, where his ancestors had settled. Elsie knew it all, and from everything I'd heard, she would sit right on this porch during the slow periods at her antique store and tell anyone who would listen what she knew.

"Thomas," I said, finding him on the far edge of the porch. He was sipping tea, alone.

"Oh, Brian, so nice of you to come."

"I'm sorry. I know Elsie was…"

"She was a busybody from the word go, would tell you what she thought you should know, but she had a heart as big as the sky."

"Does anyone know what happened to her? I mean, it's just so sudden."

"Shouldn't we all be so lucky to go so peacefully," he said. "We had dinner last night, and she complained that something didn't agree with her. She turned in early, but you know me, I can't sleep well, and I don't like puttering around my small apartment by myself. So I just came back down to the recreation room at Edgestone, I took out a deck of cards and I just started playing solitaire. Next thing I know, there's Elsie, standing in the doorframe. She told me I should go to bed, and I said she might do well in taking her own advice. She laughed, Brian, a sound so full of life. Elsie then came and sat beside me, and we played a few rounds of gin rummy. She talked a blue streak, of course, about anything and everyone. Including you."

"Me? What would Elsie Masters have to say about me?"

"Oh, your Windmill Inn idea. She said it would be easier to restore the rooming house."

Masters Rooming House had been housed in this very spot, the spacious and numerous rooms of the Victorian offering up temporary lodging to visitors. One of Elsie's ancestors ran the place along with two other women.

"But instead the Masters family converted the upstairs space into their home. Elsie grew up there," I said, "at least, that's what she told me. She hated to leave it to move to Edgestone, but her knees weren't what they were, the steps were too much. Though after what happened to her, I wonder if something more was wrong."

I said, "She wanted to see her family home thrive, and to do that, she had to surrender it to the next generation. Nora got herself a nice bargain when she took over the house."

"It's certainly a piece of our past, a vital one."

"Yet the upstairs remains empty," I said. "Maybe Elsie was right, all Linden Corners needs is a few rooms to let, not some half-baked idea of an inn on the land of the windmill."

"Don't let today's emotion affect tomorrow. Don't listen to her, not even now. You, Brian Duncan, pursue your dreams."

"Speaking of, and I'm sorry for the short notice, but are you free for dinner?"

"Brian, a man of my age is free for dinner every night."

"I'm having company tonight. A woman named Kiera Bowen. She's the architect we hired to design the Windmill Inn's cottages. She's coming down from her office in Albany to show me some sketches. I'd love it if you were there. After all, you are acting now as our consultant. Plus, I know Janey would enjoy seeing you."

"Invitation given, invitation accepted," he said with a twinkle in his eye before gazing upon the porch. "You know, it's not just the Masters' family that worked here at the rooming house. A great aunt of mine, name of Sarah, lived here as well. For a small town, there's lot of history here, lots of family connections. It's why I came home, to upturn my roots. The Van Divers go back to the beginning of Linden Corners, Brian."

I nodded. "Without your family, the windmill would never exist," I said, "Which means I might never exist."

"Destiny has it all under control, Brian. We're all here for a reason, and we should enjoy our time. As Elsie proved, you never know when it will be over."

The doorbell rang at just after six, making Sully bark with excitement. I really needed to get that dog to learn not to go crazy each time a visitor arrived. Janey shushed him as she went running to answer the door, her voice calling out to me in the kitchen.

"Who do you think it is, Dad?"

"Well, it's one of two people. Thomas or Kiera."

I watched as she opened the door and heard her expression of glee. It was Thomas.

"Mr. Van Diver, I haven't seen you in so long, please come in," she said. "Dad told me the sad news about Elsie Masters. She was always nice to me, but she liked to ask a lot of questions."

"Yes, that she did," he said, "and as I've said before, you are to call me Thomas."

"But you're older, and I'm a kid."

"I'd like nothing more than to have something in common with a kid," she said. "Deal?"

"Okay, Thomas."

"Very good, Janey."

I echoed that sentiment as I approached the foyer and welcomed our first guest into the quiet warmth of the farmhouse, Sully notwithstanding. Despite the day's high temperatures, I did have a fire crackling in the fireplace, the smell of burnt cedar permeating the entire house. He was dressed for cold, a red sweater buttoned up, his trademark bow-tie firmly in place. I offered him a beverage, and he agreed to a glass of red wine. I did the honors, even as I gave Janey a glass of apple cider and for myself, my usual seltzer. I let Janey and Thomas catch up, excusing myself as I returned to the kitchen. I didn't get much else done, since the doorbell rang a second time.

"I'll get this one," I said.

No one seemed to mind, not even Sully.

Kiera Bowen stood on the porch as I opened the door, holding a large black leather portfolio in one hand, the other running across the edge of the swing. I remembered her commenting on how she liked it, not just its presence but the idea of it, and I saw in her dark eyes a sense of regret. Had it sparked her own memory, perhaps from childhood or maybe a past love? She didn't immediately see me, and she only drew back when Sully came running between my legs, the jangling of his collar stirring her.

"Oh, Brian, I'm sorry. Guess you caught me day-dreaming."

"Hope it was a nice memory," I said.

"It was, thanks," she replied but offered up nothing further.

I escorted her into the house, which she looked over with the eyes of someone who spent their life devoted to design. She commented on the high ceilings, the wainscoting, the sharp edges that led into each room. But as much as she enjoyed the quick tour I gave her, it was when I introduced her to Janey that the architect in her faded away in favor of a woman. Janey stood all proud, happy to share her home, and soon, her windmill.

"It's a real pleasure to meet you, Janey," Kiera said, extending a hand.

Janey shook her hand, giving me a look. She always thought shaking hands was a grown-up thing. Then said, "You have a pretty name, Kiera."

"Thank you."

"A couple kids in school call me Plainy Janey."

"They do not," I insisted. She'd never said such a thing.

She rolled her eyes. "Brian thinks I tell him everything. Some kids are mean, but it's just because they're unhappy with themselves. So I don't let it bother me. It's dumb, really."

"I've only just met you, Janey, and plain is hardly the word that comes to mind. You have a sharp mind, and you're quite pretty too."

Janey took an immediate shine to Kiera, taking her hand and drawing her further into the farmhouse. I trailed behind them, almost forgotten. As we went into the kitchen, Thomas stood up from his chair, albeit a bit unsteadily, but given he was eighty-six who could blame his slow start. Janey brought Kiera over to him.

"This is our friend, Thomas," Janey said. "He's much older than me but still he lets me call him by his first name."

"Kiera Bowen, a pleasure to meet you, Thomas."

"And you as well."

"Thomas is a consultant on the Windmill Inn project," I informed her, wanting to explain his presence.

"He was born in this house," Janey said.

It was probably more information than Kiera needed, so I moved things forward, pouring a glass of wine for Kiera and a refill for Thomas, a fresh seltzer for myself, and more cider for Janey. We then got down to business, settling down at the table, all of us telling Kiera how eager we were to see what she had come up.

She spread her portfolio across the round table in the kitchen, unzipping it to reveal a series of sketches, as well as schematics. Her drawings were done in black and white, done with charcoal pencils, illustrating the scene that we lived with each and every day, the wind-mill and the ridge that rose up behind it, but in her colorless world the picture differed in that five small cottages lined the hill. Each had two floors, and each came equipped with a deck that provided a view of the windmill. The architectural style matched that of the windmill, giving it a cohesive design. She showed an-other, this one with six cottages, but it looked crowd-ed, pushing them closer to each other, detracting from the privacy I hoped to offer. All of us pointed to the drawing of the five and agreed that was the way to go. Kiera said each building could be designed to be one complete suite, or each floor could contain individual units; they could be adapted depending upon the needs of the guests, and the price they were willing to pay. I liked that idea, and it would also give me more rooms to offer up during the busy season—ten instead of five.

The schematics were a bit more technical, and she said she also had them on her computer. They offered up dimensions, placement of windows, doors, all of the qualities that I required from her. Her presenta-tion was thorough, perfectly in sync with what my mind had conjured. Somehow I'd lucked out on the first try, finding a person who was able to visualize my dreams.

"It's perfect, Kiera," I said.

"I'm glad you like it. Janey, Thomas, what do you think?"

"I wish it was already built," Janey said, her innocent enthusiasm giving voice to how we all felt. Impatience was universal.

"I believe my ancestors would be proud to know their windmill was still so influential after so many generations. To think, the Van Divers left this land decades ago, but the spirit with which their lived their lives, it endures."

Kiera turned and gave Thomas an odd look. "I'm sorry, did you say Van Diver?"

"Yes, that's my name. Thomas Van Diver. Does it ring a bell with you for some reason?"

"Yes," she said, "it's a family name. My grandfather on my mother's side, he was a Van Diver. My mother's maiden name."

"How unusual," Thomas said, "it's not the most common name out there. What was your grandfather's first name?"

"Anders," she said. "A family name, too, I believe."

"Anders Van Diver. My goodness, perhaps you're a long lost relative, Kiera," Thomas said, repeating the name a couple times, as though testing it out on his tongue, hoping it would strike a memory inside of him. "No wonder the windmill inspired you. It's in your DNA."

"It's already in your heart," was what came out of my mouth.

My comment echoed Thomas's, but its impact fell

on Kiera Bowen with a fresh sense of wonder. I saw her dark, curious eyes connect with mine, and suddenly tonight's meeting had gone to another level, a deeper one. I heard the wind outside, the windows rattling. Almost as though it was knocking, wanting in on our possible discovery. Maybe it knew the answers already.

CHAPTER NINE

"GO AHEAD, GIVE IT A TRY."

"Oh, no, Brian, it's getting late, I really should be going."

"Yet you're still here. You could have left when Thomas did."

"I tried. You insisted on driving him home."

"Actually, I think it was Janey was insisted you stay with her while I did the honors."

"Janey's a charmer," she said, "She could talk your ear off. I mean that in a good way."

That wasn't always the case with Janey, she could go as silent as an old movie, and still be full of drama. Usually she reserved such behavior for me, when she either didn't approve of what I'd done or something dumb I'd said. She had a way of internalizing her feelings, locking them in her little body until she couldn't take it anymore. I hadn't seen that Janey tonight, and even when I told her it was time for bed, she hadn't protested. She'd hugged Kiera goodnight and thanked her for sharing her drawings of the proposed Windmill Inn and hopped to bed, Sully trailing after her. So it was just the two of us on this spring night, the air crisp, the sky clear and dotted with stars.

"Come on," I said, encouraging her again, "you know you want to."

We were on the porch, the swing practically calling her name and finally she relented. She sat upon the soft cushion that covered the wood slats. I'd only put the cushion out this past weekend when the weather had begun to improve. Kiera settled on it, began to gently rock.

"You said you had a nice memory of a porch swing? Care to share," I asked, sitting against the railing so I could face her. I used my arms to balance myself and not fall backwards into the bushes that lined the front of the porch.

"Just us kids with my grandfather. Summer nights, he would sit and sip lemonade and tell me and my older brother stories of his life. He was a fisherman, long-since retired, but whenever he told us of going out to sea, I always thought I could smell the salmon right on his skin. Like no matter how hard he tried to wash it away, he could never escape a lifetime of living on a boat."

"Did he live in Alaska?"

"Seattle," she said, "Before it became such a high-tech, coffee-loving city."

Seattle, where Maddie had escaped to after our break-up and my subsequent move here. I pushed such thoughts from my mind, this moment wasn't about Maddie, nor me. Kiera had the floor...the porch, and I wanted to know more. So I prompted her.

"I seem to recall you said you're from the Syracuse area. Beyond the letter S, those cities don't have much in common."

"My mother came east for school. Studied at Syracuse University. She met my Dad, a local. They stayed."

"Are they still there?"

"Mom, Dad, my brother Jack, his wife and three kids."

"Wow, a whole Bowen family tree. What about your mother's side?"

"After she relocated to Upstate New York, she said she lost touch. Not with her parents, both of whom are gone now, but with others, cousins."

"Sorry to hear that. Those would have been the Van Divers, right?"

"My mother's maiden name," she said, "yes. I don't know much of that side of the family. My father was one of four, so there are a lot of Bowens living in and around Eckert's Landing."

"Eckert's Landing?"

"A small town, not far from Syracuse. Born and bred. Nothing much happens there unless you like duck ponds and doughnuts."

"Sorry?"

"Inside joke," she said, with a wave of her hand. Planting her feet on the porch's floor, the swing stopped as fast as her conversation, and I guess she was thinking of home and the memories of her grandfather. Or maybe I'd touched upon a nerve she hadn't wanted to expose. Finally, she said, "So, how much do you know about Thomas Van Diver? Hearing his name, I couldn't have been more surprised."

"You, me, and he too. Thomas came to Linden Corners about a year and half ago. It's true, he did live in this farmhouse until he was five. His father, Lars, had been drafted into the army and unfortunately, he didn't return. He and his mother were forced to sell the farmhouse—the windmill part of the package—and he'd never been back, not until he came in search of his past."

"Did he find it?"

"That, and more. It was Christmastime when he came back. Nora and I helped him."

"Nora? Is she a girlfriend?"

"No," I said, "Nora's a friend. She's the one who owns A Doll's Attic, the store housed in that Victorian you so loved."

"She owns that beautiful building?"

I shook my head. "No, she just rents it. The house belonged to a lady named Elsie Masters."

"You speak of her in the past tense," she said.

"Actually, she passed away, only just last night."

"How sad, I'm sorry, Brian."

"Linden Corners will forever be silent without her," I said. "Like you said, born and bred."

"Brian?"

"Yeah?"

"Would you sit beside me?"

That was an invitation I was happy to accept, and soon I was beside her, the swing regaining its rocking motion. We sat in companionable silence, almost as though my earlier words about Elsie had proven prophetic. We stared forward, watching the night sky, its illuminated beauty not unlike how the windmill looked at Christmas, adorned with white lights bright enough to give life to the memories of those departed. I thought of Annie, of George, and now Elsie, along with a host of others I had never known who had graced the lands of Linden Corners. Time marched forward, but it also had a way of treating us to moments when we could stop and give thanks to a past that had shaped us.

"Did you know there's a place near Eckert's Landing, it's also called Lyndon?"

"Really?"

"Different spelling," she said, "and there is this

busy intersection, the locals call it Lyndon Corners.
I think that's why, when my boss Kirby asked me to
consult on your project that I sprang into action. It
spoke to me."

"But now, maybe it was something located far
deeper in your subconscious."

"You mean the Van Diver connection?"

"Stranger things have happened," I said. "Some
people would call that fate."

"Dreamers would. Pragmatists would call in
coincidence."

"Kiera Bowen, are you telling me you're not a
dreamer?"

"I...I guess I don't have to time to think that way.
Life is busy..."

I rose from the swing, held out my hand. "Time to
take a time out. Follow me."

"Brian, really, it's getting late, I've got a long trip
back to my apartment, an early meeting."

"Such a pragmatist," I said, allowing a smile to
grace my face.

She punched me on the arm playfully, but then she
put her hand in mine, and with my smile still in place,
I led her down the steps of the porch and around the
back of the house. We walked through the high grass,
our feet growing damp with the night's dew, and soon
we had come to the top of the hill, where she had sat
and sketched and I'd watched with a growing sense

of confidence that the world had led her here, to the land of the windmill, ready to bring fulfillment to the dreams that lived inside of me.

The windmill loomed in front of us, the sails spinning like they did, gently, reassuring. The moonlight glowed down on it, casting shadows upon the land. It was like the windmill was putting its best sail forward, again, ready to impress. As though it recognized Kiera. She paused, her hand touching her heart. I heard her exhale and if I'd had any doubt about her being the right person for this project, they were swept away in a rush of air. I let go of my worries, but not her hand. I drew her closer, down the hill. As we came to the base of the windmill, I withdrew a key from a hidden compartment in the tower, and unlocked it. The door opened, and I led Kiera inside, like Alice venturing into Wonderland. But the only crazy character she would meet was me.

"Brian, are you sure?"

"Of course," I said, "there's something about being inside the windmill that inspires me. I thought it would do the same for you...you know, for your designs."

That's not what I was talking about, and she knew it but didn't call me out on it. My flush face was evident, a glow in the darkness. Taking hold of her hand again, I led her up the staircase, winding our way to the second floor. Even after three years, I hadn't the heart to change things. All of Annie's supplies were still in evidence, her brushes and easel, a drawer full of her paintings stored.

"Brian, this is fantastic," Kiera said, turning around inside the open space, staring upwards toward the cap, which controlled the windmill's spinning mechanism. She ran a hand across the wood easel, her touch nearly a caress. "A painter's studio, inside the windmill? Whose is it? You don't seem like the painter type."

"No, it was Janey's Mom's. Annie."

"Oh, Brian, I shouldn't be here, I feel like I'm intruding."

"It's fine. Come on, let me show you one more thing," I said.

Then I opened the door to the outside, escorting Kiera out onto the walkway. She drew in her breath as one of the giant sails swept past us. I turned to her and said, "So, what do you think?"

She had nothing to say. The tear slipping down her cheek spoke volumes.

What happened next, it was a moment dictated by the moonlight and the sails, and by the surging rush of emotions that opened up our souls. I learned forward, she did the same, and soon our lips had touched. Gentle, soft, tentative, so much so we parted quickly, the surprise like an electric shock. The kiss continued to hang between us, as though each of us were still experiencing its magic despite it being over.

"Brian, that...it shouldn't have happened."

"I'm sorry. The windmill, it has its own power. I know what it wants."

"So do I," she said. "Brian, I really have to get getting home."

Her voice had changed. Even though she'd offered up those words several times tonight, I knew now was the one time to not question it. I nodded, feeling both awkward and shy. Our hands didn't connect again, not as we wound down the circular stairs, not when we walked back up the hill, or when we stood before her car in the darkness of the night.

"Kiera," I said, my feet shifting, my hands stuffed in my pockets. "What happened, I hope it doesn't change...you know, your interest in continuing with the Windmill Inn. I didn't mean to...make you feel uncomfortable..."

"Brian, you didn't kiss me, I didn't kiss you. We shared the kiss."

"That's a nice way of letting me off the hook"

"But if we're going to work together, it can't happen again."

"Sure, I understand."

"No, I don't think you do. Brian, I'm engaged. I'm getting married this fall."

Somehow I got through the next few nights working long shifts at George's Tavern, losing myself in my work and trying my best to forget Kiera's parting words. For all the personal information she had shared with me—her family, her job, her home, all of it spoken of willingly—only after our unexpected kiss at the windmill had she confessed of her pending marriage.

And if she could maintain her silence on that truth until the wrong moment to tell me, so too could I keep quiet about it. I'd said nothing to anyone. What was there to tell? Who was there to tell? We'd gotten caught up in a vulnerable moment, the romanticism of the windmill capturing us in its spun web for a fleeing moment. That's not to say I couldn't stop thinking about it, mostly when I crawled into bed in the early morning after closing down Geroge's Tavern and sleep eluded me. Which is one of the reasons I was so lethargic on this Sunday morning. Janey was quite the opposite. We had a big day planned, as she reminded me.

"And it was your idea, Brian. So come on, let's get going."

We'd just finished our usual Sunday breakfast of pancakes and bacon, even thought we'd gotten a later start than usual. More brunch, and so by the time we cleaned up the dishes and I got showered and ready, it was nearly one o'clock in the afternoon. Janey was impatient with me, as was Sully, who was riled up and running around the house as only a puppy can do. Our Labrador mix might have some Cheetah in him. At last I was ready and Janey and I went out back, Sully dashing ahead of us and tearing down the hill.

"Think he's been cooped up a bit lately?" I asked.

"He goes by moods," Janey said, "and yours has been weird the last few days."

Janey Sullivan, ten-year-old psychologist. I ruffled her hair and said, "I'm fine. Now, let's go."

"Oh, now who's ready?" she said, rolling her eyes.

I let her be her; why not, I was being my usual conflicted self. But I hoped that delving into our project today would cure me of my woes and get me focused back on the Windmill Inn. With the financing in place thanks to my father, Chuck Ackroyd ready with supplies and anxious to oversee the work of the various contractors we'd hired, Kiera's designs ready to take us from concept to reality, there was nothing to stop us from going forward with the ground-breaking. And this being Linden Corners, having such an occasion required it to be a town-wide celebration. I would host, with the after party scheduled to coincide with the 30th anniversary of the Five O'Clock diner. As I had told some of the regulars down at the tavern, both moments were rather ground-breaking.

For now, though, we had to spread the word beyond the denizens of George's Tavern.

Janey and I were charged with making the sign that

would be posted in downtown Linden Corners for all to see.

Entering the old barn at the back of the property, Janey and I approached a pair of wooden sawhorses, over which I'd placed a rectangular piece of plywood I'd purchased down at Chuck's store. I'd also bought different colors of paint and an assortment of brushes. On the far wall behind me, I'd nailed a drawing of what the sign would look like. Janey was actually gifted in the crafts, so her help was invaluable. I was more the director here, she the artist in residence. Thinking Kiera could easily have stepped into this role as well, but of course Annie would have been the ideal one to lead us forward. She couldn't, now, could she? Yet I felt that every move I made concerning the Windmill Inn was done so with her silent blessing.

It was a lovely spring day, the warmest we'd enjoyed yet, and so Janey removed her jacket, her old sweatshirt and jeans perfect for indulging in the messy art of painting. It didn't matter what happened with the clothes, the end result of the sign was what mattered. I'd dressed in similar style at her request, the two of us a matched team, ready to take that next step toward tomorrow. She grabbed a brush, and I opened the paint cans and stirred them, and soon we were under way. Our own ground-breaking, if you will.

An hour passed with us toiling away at the sign, our conversation minimal, focused on the project at hand.

Her lines were good, drawn first with a pencil to out-line the letters. Then she began to color them in, tak-ing careful pains not to go outside the borders. Finally, the sign began to take form, the words "A GROUND-BREAKING LINDEN CORNERS EVENT" in bright, over-size letters dominating the large board. Other details followed beneath it, indicating the date and time—next Saturday, noon sharp—with a post-cele-bration party to follow at the Five-O diner. ALL ARE INVITED, Janey painted.

"Just like when Cynthia did with the town-wide Secret Santa last year," she said.

"That's how we rock in Linden Corners. Everyone is part of is."

"How we rock? Brian, sometimes you say silly things. That's not proper English."

"Never mind, get back to painting. You missed a spot...there."

She studied her handiwork, dipped her brush in blue paint, and then swabbed at the board. Her touch was expert; perhaps she had a bit of Annie's talent hid-den within her. Some days she acted like a chef, others a painter, and I found myself wondering what career she would pursue when she grew up. She certainly leaned toward the creative side, but then I thought of Kiera, who had the same artistic bent to her, even though she had pursued a more technical approach, like she used both sides of her brain.

Suddenly I felt a nudge at my side, and I came back to the moment.

"Earth to Brian?"

"Really, Janey, 'earth to Brian.' That's not proper English."

"Silly, Brian," she replied.

"Yes, he can be that."

It was a new voice added to the mix, and we both turned to see my mother standing before the entryway to the barn, sunlight encasing her shape. I hadn't seen her or my father in a few days, just a dinner once after they'd returned from their trip to Philadelphia. She eased her way inside, and I could see her hair was as perfectly coiffed as ever, her dress casual but always stylish.

"Hi, Mom."

"Hi, Grandma."

"What's going on here?" she asked.

"Janey's putting the finishing touches on the ground-breaking sign."

'Once it dries, Dad and I are going to set it up down by the tavern."

She nodded, her lips tight. Then she said, "Jane, do you mind if I ask you a question."

I shot my mother a cautious look, one that said I wished she wouldn't. I never liked when Didi Duncan voiced something that was on her mind. But I'd also learned there was no stopping her either. I braced myself.

"Jane, I just find it confusing, you earlier called Brian by his name. Then you referred to him as Dad a minute later. I'm sure you can see that how those unfamiliar with your rather, uh, unique situation would find it...shall we say, uncomfortable."

"Mom..."

"Brian, it's a legitimate question," Mom said. "Jane is growing up. She should be able to explain herself."

I shook my head, wishing my mother was wearing her usual pearls, that way I could have strangled her with them.

"Oh, Grandma, it's easy. When he does something that reminds me of when I first met him, he's Brian. Because he...he just is. But there's times when I know he's my Dad, usually when I'm sad or thinking about things, and then I go to him and he helps me. But it doesn't matter what I call him, I just know he's always there for me and that he would do anything for me."

My mother had no response, she just grimaced, which I think was her attempt at a smile.

"Show me your handiwork," she finally said, dropping the subject.

I think she dropped it because she'd lost whatever argument she had prepared.

As Janey—not Jane--showed off her good work on

the sign, I stepped back outside, Sully laying in the warm grass before me, I bent down, pet him on the head, comforted by his presence. There were nights the past few years when the farmhouse had been so quiet, especially when I returned home from the tavern, Janey asleep or not even there, staying at a friends or over at Cynthia's. Having Sully around, he helped me, maybe even more than he did Janey.

"You're a good boy, aren't you?"

He rolled over, exposing his belly. I rubbed it and his tail wagged in the grass.

"That's why we got him for you, for just those moments."

I looked up and saw my father approaching, his large frame looking diminished. "Hi, Dad."

"Afternoon, Brian. Nice day out."

"Perfect. This is what I love about Linden Corners. The seasons are how they're supposed to be."

He nodded. "So, I looked over the schematics Kirby sent me. Everything looks in place."

"We're ready to break-ground. Both ceremoniously, and literally."

"Going to be a long summer," he said. "If we're to make the deadline."

In the near distance, the windmill loomed, doing as it always did. In just a few short months, time would mark the one-hundred fiftieth year of its existence, and what I had planned would mark the occasion with an appreciation for its past, for all the souls it had inspired in its long life, but also let it know it was part of a vibrant future, one that went hand-in-hand with mine. My heart grew fraught with a mix of emotions.

"We'll make it," I said, "we have too."

My father put a steady hand on my shoulder, said, "Anything I can do to make your dream come true, I'll do."

"You've already done more than enough. The way you put together the financing, I know I had to give up some of the equity in the inn, at least till it earns back its investment..."

"Don't even think about such matters, Brian. My investors are only too happy to help."

"Still, it's a risk."

"No, Brian, not with you in charge. You've taken charge of this project like I've never seen you. I'm proud of all you've accomplished, not just with the Windmill Inn. But your entire life in Linden Corners, and mostly, what you've done with Janey. You're a good man."

Those were deeply heartfelt words coming from my father, and perhaps I'd have thought them unusual in his earlier incarnation as the high-finance, business-minded giant I'd always seen him as. Linden Corners had altered him, just as it had me. For a father and son who had not always seen eye-to-eye, I took great comfort in this newfound relationship we had forged. If only I could achieve a similar détente with my mother. As commanding as Kevin Duncan could be, Didi was a force unto herself. You couldn't blame her. She'd lost her prized son, Philip, to cancer at a young age, her daughter Rebecca was a jet-setting mess who jumped from man to man, barely able to pay attention to her own son, Junior, and then there was her youngest son, me, who always had his head in the clouds. Didi was the type to slay giants, all while her son Brian was the kind to tilt at windmills. Metaphorically, we were so different.

My father and I returned to the barn, where he assisted with the final touches of the sign, Janey only too happy to share the moment with "Grandpa."

An hour later, we agreed the sign was done, dried, and ready to be put into place.

My father and I carried it onto the back of the truck, and Janey and my mother piled into the back seat. I turned the engine and it failed to start. I turned it again, still nothing.

"I thought you had this looked at," Dad said.

"Give it a moment," I said, and then willing it to start, I turned the key again.

It chugged to life and I breathed a sigh of relief. "Told you."

"Brian, you better just drive before it putters out again and we're left on the highway."

"Thanks, Mom," I said with a roll of my eyes.

"I saw that," she said.

"He learned that from me," Janey said.

"Oh, no, dear. Brian perfected that as a child. Just as you have."

The four of us laughed inside the tight space of the cabin, once again at my expense, but I didn't care. This was just family acting as family, bonding over another's idiosyncrasies, but not criticizing. We reached downtown minutes later, where I parked in the lot outside the tavern. Just a few hundred yards away was Memorial Park, a pair of granite stones embedded in the grounds standing like sentries before the entrance. Dad and I carried the sign across the lawn, placing it just between the rocks, like so many other signs had been placed in years past. Pancake Breakfasts, Fourth of July Celebrations, First Fridays, and now it was the Windmill Inn's ground-breaking that was taking center stage. We pronounced it perfectly placed, and Janey clapped, jumping up and down at seeing her afternoon's work on display for all to see.

"The whole town will see it now, and they'll come and celebrate our day," Janey said.

"Yes, it will be a memorable day in Linden Corners," I added.

"And I'll be right by your side, Dad."

As I hugged her, I felt pride wash over me. Only to have it doused moments later.

"So, Brian, who else will be by your side?" Mom asked.

"I'm sorry, what's that supposed to mean?"

She didn't even miss a beat when she asked, "Have you invited Maddie to your big day?"

"She actually said that?"

"Have you not met my mother?"

"Still, Brian, that's nerve."

Nora took a bite of her tuna fish sandwich, then paused and stared at me.

"What?" I asked.

"Well, since Didi acknowledged the elephant in the room, how did you respond?"

"I told her Maddie was checking her schedule."

"Liar," Nora said. "You haven't asked her."

"I'm complicated."

"That much I'll give you."

It was Tuesday afternoon, Nora Connors and I were having our usual lunch from the Five-O. We sat on the front porch of A Doll's Attic since the spring day was warm and inviting. Why be stuck inside an old house filled with dry memorabilia when outside the bright sun beamed down on the lush lawn of Memorial Park down the street. I could see the sign Janey and I had made, its presence announcing a promise to Linden Corners, even though today it seemed life had stalled here. She hadn't had a customer all day, the Five-O lot was nearly empty, and barely a car went by as we sat and ate our lunch.

"So, are you inviting Nicholas?" I asked.

"Oh, turnabout is fair play, huh?"

"Maddie and I only just reunited, and we haven't talked about...the future. You two, good or bad, you've been together for more than a year. Sure, he lives in Massachusetts..."

"I broke up with him," she said matter-of-factly.

"Oh, okay. You okay?"

"I'm fine. I'm actually great."

"Convince me."

"Brian Duncan, you're a nosy man. You taking over for Elsie?"

"Hardly. She was one a kind," I said, and with wistful humor added, "Then again, I do spend a lot of time here. Perhaps I'm embodying her spirit."

"I feel like Linden Corners has been so silent since she died," Nora said, gazing about. "So much of her still lives in this old house. I mean, she lived and worked in this house up until a year and a half ago. When she went to live at Edgestone, I don't know... maybe she'd given up. She'd done what she wanted with her life and was just waiting out the rest of it."

"When did you break up with Nicholas?"

"Playing psychologist with me, Brian?"

"Let me guess, the day after Elsie's funeral?"

She shook her head. "Nope, smarty pants, the same day. Afterwards. He invited me back to his house, and I told him I didn't want to. So he asked me what was going on, and I told him I just didn't want to be in a relationship. I wasn't looking for one when I met him, but he was charming, nice on the eyes, and he was so helpful in helping us solve the mystery of Thomas's *Night Before Christmas* book. So I went on a date, and then before I knew it we were a couple. My divorce was finalized during the time we were together, and I don't know, maybe I just didn't want to deal with the reality of being alone. But I'm not. I have Travis, and he needs me more than ever now that his father has moved overseas. I'm all he has, and vice versa."

"That's how I feel about me and Janey. Everyone's trying to marry me off."

"Girls are different," she said. "As she heads toward being a teenager, Janey needs a mom."

"You sound like everyone else."

Silence fell between us, and we ate more of our sandwiches. I took a sip of my iced tea.

Finally, Nora said, "So, are you going to invite Maddie to the ground-breaking?"

"Are we on repeat?" I asked.

"Fine, what do you want to talk about?" she asked.

I looked around, thinking again about Elsie. "Do you know what happens to this place?"

She shook her head. "I don't know if she left a will, or if she has any relatives. Whoever is placed in charge of her estate, they have their work cut out for them."

"How so?"

"The second and third floors of the house, it's where she lived."

"Surely she cleared out after she moved to Edgestone."

"She said she would, one day. She never got around to it. I mean, it was still her home. I was just renting. She was free to do whatever she wanted with the upstairs."

"You've never thought of living here?"

"It would be lovely to have my own place, me and Travis. But my mother, how could I leave her all alone?"

It was a dilemma we all faced, life's responsibilities weighed by our desires. Until Nora's return, Gerta had wafted about her house alone, George gone. I hated to think of those long hours, mostly at night, when memories were your only companion. No wonder my mother hovered over her husband so much. What would Didi Duncan be without Kevin Duncan? Who would she be? I steered the conversation back to Elsie's house.

"So all of Elsie's belongings are still upstairs?"

"You have no idea. Brian, I think everything she ever laid her hands on, or was unable to sell as an antique, is scattered all over those room upstairs. Got a few minutes? You've got to see it to believe what she left behind."

It was as good an offer as I'd had all day, so we wrapped up our lunch and tossed away the remnants in the garbage inside the store. She turned the lock, changed the sign to CLOSED. Then we ventured to the back of the store, where she opened a door that revealed a back staircase that led upwards toward the upper floors of the Victorian. For a moment I thought of Kiera and how much she would enjoy this, a chance to admire the molding, the doorframes and walls that were still intact even after all these years. Elsie had kept the house in great condition, I saw, each room adorned with antique furniture and lamps. It was almost like the past was coming alive before me, Masters Rooming House dissolved out of the past and was once again open for business.

But as much as I could see folks of yesteryear dressed in period clothes, they might have been ghosts walking amidst the myriad of antiques that filled the rooms. Nearly every wall of these high-ceilinged rooms was covered with old pictures, gilded-frames, trinkets from so many decades gone by, it was like a history of life in Linden Corners. I saw photos of ladies in hats, Nora pointing out one photo of the three women who ran the rooming house: Clarabelle Masters, Sissy Masters, and Sarah Van Diver.

"They ran the rooming house here," Nora said. "But here, let me show you something else. I know you're going to like this, an old reference to the windmill."

Of course I was curious about such a prospect, so I followed Nora deeper into the space that must have been Elsie's living room. On a far wall with faded wallpaper, Nora stopped before a frame of gold, a curly-cue pattern along its edges. But it wasn't the frame that interested me, it was what was locked inside it. I leaned in close to read the faded words.

I LOVE YOU, TOO, CHARLES. THANK YOU FOR THE WINDMILL. I'LL CHERISH IT IN MY DREAMS FOREVER. GOODBYE.

"Nora, do you know what this is?"

"Not really, but I figured you, the Windmill Man, might understand it."

"It's from Cara Larssen, the letter she penned before her father took her away from Linden Corners," I said, "she wrote it to Charles Van Diver. I've heard the story of it....Annie told me one night, she knew all the old stories of the windmill. Nora, this is an amazing discovery, and to think it was hanging on the walls of Elsie's house all these years."

"Not any longer," Nora said, reaching up to take it off the wall.

A faded space was left after the frame was removed, as though the letter had faded even more, its words invisible. Yet it lived, still, breathing in my hands. I stared down at it, then back at Nora. "But I can't accept it. It belongs to Elsie, or whoever inherits the house."

"Amidst all this clutter, I doubt the one item will be missed. Put it back where it belongs."

I nodded, knowing just where it should hang. Inside the windmill.

The ground-breaking ceremony was growing every closer, but so too strangely, was Linden Corners' past.

CHAPTER TEN

LINDEN CORNERS ALWAYS LOVED its celebrations. That was one of the most valuable lessons I learned, even before I'd decided to make this my permanent home. My first experience had been George Connors' pub holiday he christened First Friday, which celebrated the initial weekend of summer. Upon his death and with his widow's approval, I created Second Saturday as a way to honor him. We also liked our national holidays, Thanksgiving and July 4th, not to mention Christmas, my last three being among the most memorable times I'd experienced here in Linden Corners. Springtime was lacking in official holidays beyond Easter, and that had passed a couple weeks ago. So we residents would ordinarily be faced with a long stretch before Memorial Day arrived.

Which only served to heighten the anticipation surrounding Ground Breaking Day, as I'd heard the locals calling it the other day down at the tavern. On the morning of the day of the event, I was awakened with excitement. Janey came barging into my room, jumping up on the bed, Sully of course right behind her. He too leapt up, and the two of them bounded about the bed, she telling me to get up, get up, Sully happy to play along in his puppy fashion. He barked until I took hold of him and held him tight. Janey joined in and soon the three of us were tangled in an early morning tussle. As far as rude awakenings went, this one I'd take any day.

"Come on, Dad, it's a big day. And it's beautiful outside."

It certainly was, as I saw bright sunshine beaming through the lace curtains draped across the windows. This had been Annie's room, and I'd done little over the three years to add a more masculine touch to it. Partly I had been focused on Janey and small details like curtains and pillows hadn't taken precedence. Subconsciously I knew I'd kept it this way on purpose, it was familiar to Janey, another connection to her mother. Right after Annie's passing, Janey had slept here with me, curled up in the comforting blankets that probably held long to her scent, while I sat in the chair, watching her, crying over what this girl had lost, she so young, suffering through such a senseless death. I would stroke her hair, soothe her. Gradually she returned to her room, and ever since then this bed had been empty, just me, and sometimes not even I qualified. Some night, after coming home from the tavern, I stayed on the sofa.

Then it occurred to me, Maddie had stayed here. Just one night. But that might change.

Because Maddie was expected for Ground Breaking Day.

So was Kiera, of course.

Oh, what fun.

So I got out of bed, thinking this day could be very interesting. I'd gone nearly three years without a date, finally giving myself a chance at personal happiness with Trina Winter, knowing in the back of my mind that ours was a transitional relationship, for both her and for me. Something else was going on with Maddie, which confused me, and with Kiera, which had sputtered before it had taken off. How had my life gotten so complicated? I had told myself the only woman in my life would be Janey, and lately I felt I'd been distracted by more adult matters. I had to remind myself that today was a day all about moving forward, as much as for me as for Janey. This was our future, the ceremonial push of the shovel into the ground would be done by both of us.

So I showered and got ready in a hurry, Janey's enthusiasm my fuel.

When I walked into the kitchen, a surprise awaited me.

"Mom, good morning."

"Morning, Brian. You were expecting someone else?"

"Uh, not yet. But soon enough."

I knew she meant Maddie, and she knew I meant Maddie. What I wondered was what my mother had to do with Maddie's arrival in Linden Corners for the ground-breaking.

"She called me the other day," Mom said, giving voice to my question.

"I didn't realize you had shared phone numbers."

"Yes, the night we all had dinner. Brian, do you know what you're doing?"

"Many answers come to mind, but since I don't really understand where you're going with this, I'm not sure which one to offer. Are there clues in your enigmatic talk?"

"You needn't be petulant. Are you and Maddie back together?"

"Not that it's any of your business, but no, we haven't really discussed our status."

"But yet you invited her today."

"Didn't you suggest as much?"

"My point exactly. My idea, not yours."

"You know, Mom, it's too early for this. Where's the coffee? Where's Janey, by the way?"

"Oh, Jane went dashing outside, she wanted to see the set-up for today's big ceremony."

"Lucky her."

Didi Duncan got up from her chair, made her way over to the coffee maker. She poured in the grounds, clicked the switch, and I willed time to do two things: make the coffee appear, and to make my mother, for now, disappear. Only one of those wishes came true, and so I settled down with my steaming cup, looking across the table at my mother.

"Where's Dad?"

"Taking care of a last minute detail," she said.

"You don't sound pleased about it."

She shrugged, an unusual gesture on her part. She was usually so committed to her opinion and those she handed out to others.

I sipped at my coffee, looking back over at the windmill clock, seeing it was only ten after ten. Less than two hours until people would start to gather on the hill above the windmill, where we'd set up a make-shift platform, a giant ribbon in place between two posts. That's where I would tell the crowd that the Windmill Inn was a go, and that come fall, as the windmill itself celebrated its one hundred fiftieth anniversary, I would open the doors to the first guest. Linden Corners was taking a giant leap forward today, not to mention a leap of faith. Staring back at the clock, only a minute had passed, but at least time had advanced. Before long the ceremony would be over, and summer too would wane, time ticking down to my self-imposed deadline.

I was saved from further conversation with my mother when Janey came back in from the outside, her cheeks red from exertion. I had an image of the fearless seven-year-old girl I'd first encountered at the windmill three years ago, her arms twirling as she ran down the hill, greeting the windmill just as it did her. She might be ten now, but her enthusiasm was rarely dampened. I gave her a wide smile.

"Want some hot chocolate?" I asked.

"Brian, it's not winter outside, it's beautiful. Spring is here."

"Jane, I'll get you something. Honestly, Brian, have you learned nothing?"

There's an expression of being saved by the bell, and while the front doorbell did ring, and I got up to answer it, I wasn't sure I was being saved. No doubt it was Maddie, and my wary heart tightened in my chest as I awaited the meeting between her and Janey, and making matters worse, my mother was present to witness it all. Maybe Nora was right, maybe I knew nothing about women. But time waits for no one, that's another expression, and so I steeled myself and opened the front door. There indeed stood Maddie Chasen.

"Hi," I said.

"Hi," she answered back, a grin on her face. "Got anything else?"

"Oh, sorry," I said, and I leaned forward, planning a kiss on her lips. She tasted sweet.

"That's better," she said, stepping forward into the farmhouse.

She put her purse down in the foyer, leaving her smart leather jacket on. She wandered into the house, moving toward the kitchen. I caught up to her, entering the room at the same time, where I offered her a cup of coffee.

"That would be nice, thanks. Didi, hello. And my goodness, you're Janey?"

"I'm the only kid here," she said, a bit defensively.

"Janey," I said, a stern tone to my voice. "Say hello to Maddie."

"Hi, Maddie. It's very nice to meet you."

"We met once before, but it was a few years ago. Thank you for inviting me today."

"Lots of people are invited," she said.

Oh, this was going great, I thought sarcastically. I'd spoken to Janey earlier this week about Maddie's visit, knowing that she'd purposely missed out on her last one. There would be no chance of avoiding her this time, and I had asked that she be on her best behavior. Janey knew none of the details that had ended my relationship with Maddie, why would she? All she knew was that Maddie was the catalyst for bringing me to Linden Corners, and actually, she should be grateful for that. What happened to Dan Sullivan, her father, and to Annie, that was fate, events that were beyond anyone's control, and had I not come to town, who knew where Janey would be now, and in whose care. Truth was, Maddie's bad decision had led to a series of good ones. But wasn't that how life worked in this crazy world?

Mom served Janey a glass of orange juice, which took the pressure off the moment. Maddie gave me a helpless look and I tried to soothe her with my own expression: give it time. Fortunately, we were all saved from further conversation, as I heard coming from outside a honking sound. I turned my head, Janey did too, and Sully, laying peacefully on the floor, got up and started barking, running usefully to the front door. The four of us followed after her, my mother bringing up the rear as though she wasn't in a hurry; as though she knew the reason behind the honking.

I opened the door and stepped out from beyond the porch and into the bright sunshine. I saw a gleaming, dark blue colored truck coming up the driveway, coming to a stop just at the edge of the driveway. Cupping my hand over my eyes, I detected my father sitting behind the wheel. He got out of the truck, waving me forward. I did, surprise giving way to shock. Because on the side of both the passenger door and driver's side, were stenciled the words, "The Windmill Inn," the type style the same as Kiera had designed. A curly, scripted T, W, and I, followed by the rest of the letters in Times Roman; they were blue, set against a white backdrop.

"Dad, what is this...?"

"Well, no new establishment can have a rusting, unreliable working truck in which to get around. That doesn't send the most confident message to prospective guests. So...on behalf of your investors, we wish you a Happy Ground Breaking Day."

I was speechless and stationary, even as Janey dashed around the truck, Sully racing after her, both of them voicing shrieking pleasure that rose high into the blue sky. That's when I felt a comforting arm slide along my side, and I turned to see Maddie embracing me. My parents looked on with pleasure, both at the sight before them and at their pleasure in having pulled a fast one on me. I had to admit, it was a pretty damn good picture: grandparents, a little girl and her dog, me, and at my side, a woman who had once held a claim on my heart.

Dare I say, before me on this momentous day was the very portrait of a family.

"Thank you, everyone, for coming today. Mother Nature has blessed Linden Corners with a lovely afternoon, made even more special by your presence for the ground-breaking ceremony for what will become the Windmill Inn."

As I spoke, I stared out at the assembled group, numbering nearly one hundred people at last count. I knew most of them, familiar faces who I'd see at the Five-O, or at Marla and Darla's, or at the grocery store over in Hillsdale, or at Knight's Fruit Stand on the outer reaches of Linden Corners. Given the occasion, most business had shut down for a few hours so the proprietors could be here to witness this next step forward in all our lives, and our livelihoods. Martha Martinson sat in the front row, alongside Sara and Mark Ravens, baby Harry in his father's arms; twins Marla and Darla I saw were off to the side, being as social as they tended to be. Chet and his gang were here, too, which I appreciated, as were many representatives from Edgestone Retirement Center. Also sitting amongst the guests were my mother, Maddie sitting beside her, and near them was a man I did not recognize; he had dark, wavy hair he wore down to his shoulders, and a full beard grew across his handsome face. Sitting in such proximity to Maddie, I had visions of my old boss, Justin Warfield; he and the strange man among us had a similar build. Nora and Gerta were of course in attendance, as was a sullen looking Travis, who appeared to want to be anywhere but here, but what else was new? I was pleased with the turnout before me, but more pleased with those who were assembled behind me on the platform we'd built.

My parents, Janey, Kiera and her boss, Kirby Spellman, Thomas Van Diver, and Chuck Ackroyd, the latter of which I'd had to convince to join us up here. They all sat in chairs while I had taken command of the podium. Filling out the platform was a banner behind us, with a large logo of the Windmill Inn. It seemed like I was living inside a fantasy, the moment surreal. Just a couple months ago I'd been dreaming along the Hudson River on a train about what to do with my life, and here I was, today, ready to formalize the final step in moving toward a first one. I wasn't sure I had the strength to continue, overwhelmed as I was, but I stared out beyond the guests, I saw the windmill, its sails silent today, as though it too were eager to hear what I had to say. I took a deep breath, and then I pushed onward.

"For one hundred fifty years, our windmill has stood proud, a symbol of the enduring spirit of life, and today we set the countdown clock to what will be the most magnificent celebration of the landmark we all so love. Nearly two centuries ago, a young man named Charles Van Diver had the idea to build a windmill, not unlike those found back in the Netherlands, from where his family had emigrated, and we are still thankful for his passion. Windmills were built for practical reasons, but they were picturesque, and they gave the landscape an unqualified beauty. Charles knew from unqualified beauty, namely a girl who went by the name Cara Larssen, and for whom he had the windmill built. Fate intervened, as it so often does in our lives, and the windmill awaited another day for another set of lovers to fall under its spell. Today, the windmill continues to spin its spell, and to inspire lives and bring strangers together. So I plan to expand its influence well beyond our borders, and invite people from all walks of life to revel in what we get to see each and every day. Right up here on this hill, I will build, with the able assistance of Chuck Ackroyd and the team of contractors he has put together, five cottage of varying sizes, each of them built in the style of the windmill that stand before us. In opening up Linden Corners, I believe our other businesses in town will benefit, bringing our humble citizens more riches, and passing on to visitors the riches we hold so dear within our borders.

"I would be remiss in not mentioning the contributions of the many people who have helped turned my crazy idea into the reality unfolding before us today. First of all, my parents, Kevin and Didi Duncan, newcomers to Linden Corners but who have felt it pull as much as I did upon first arriving. My father's business interests have ultimately made this entire project possible, and I am forever grateful. For historical references and to help us remember that Linden Corners is nothing without its past, I welcome Thomas Van Diver to the team. As many of you know, Thomas called this land home before most of us were born, and he is a direct descendent of Charles Van Diver. Finally, an idea is only just an idea until someone can bring it to life, and for that I have to thank the architectural firm of Kirby Spellman, Inc, notably it's chief, Mr. Spellman himself, who saw the promise of my idea, and also had the wherewithal to recommend a visionary architect who has given the Windmill Inn its visual identity, and that person is Ms. Kiera Bowen. And finally, there's one more person to thank, and without her, I doubt this windmill would spin as it does, and I doubt I would be here before you today. She is a young woman of indomitable spirit who did more than capture my heart, I think she stole it and hid it somewhere in the windmill. Janey Sullivan, would you come up here and take a well-deserved bow?"

I turned to the wondrous girl who had, in the face of tragedy, but through the raw power of faith, become my daughter, and right now I welcomed her into my waiting arms. She was crying, tears of joy I hoped, but I knew she was thinking of who wasn't here. I was too, and I shared in her tears as we remained locked in our own private moment while the entire town watched. I barely registered the applause that was wafting off both the platform and the crowd before us. Annie too was applauding, the sails of the windmill taking to the wind.

But I knew I had to return to the present moment

and give the residents of our fair Linden Corners what they were expecting, a literal ground-breaking. So I called everyone to attention again, and with Janey at my side, we took hold of a pair of scissors and on the count of three we cut the pink ribbon, watching as its two ends, now separated, flapped in the growing wind. It was only the first step, as I then took hold of a shovel handed to me by Chuck Ackroyd, and Janey and I sunk it into the soft grass right before us, pronouncing the construction of the Linden Corners latest attraction, the Windmill Inn had begun. Amidst more applause, I welcomed select others to dig into the ground, before giving the shovel to Thomas, who dug into his reserves and tossed aside a big chunk of land. Finally, I had Kiera Bowen step forward, and with her hand over mine, our feet helped push the shovel into the ground, only to turn over another wedge of previously unturned soil. I'd accomplished as I'd hoped, a mix of past, present, and future helping out to mark the rite of passage that was Ground Breaking Day.

"Ladies and gentlemen, I hope to welcome you back here in a few months, where we will celebrate the one hundred fiftieth anniversary of our beloved windmill, which will coincide with the opening of the Windmill Inn. Now, to mark this occasion, we welcome everyone back to the Five-O Diner, which this week is celebrating its thirtieth anniversary of serving us good food and good cheer, and whatever else

Martha Martinson has found lying on the side of the road."

There was genial laughter, even from Martha, who nodded gratefully in my direction.

"Nicely done, Brian Duncan, Just Passing Through."

I suppose with her, I'd never live down that name, and I was fine with that.

The crowd began to disperse, returning to their cars that were parked along the side of the road, and as I watched them I realized I'd forgotten an important detail regarding my inn. Where would my guests park? Surely not on the side of the road, and I wouldn't want them driving right up to their cottages either, that would ruin the landscape I wished to preserve. That's when yet another shortcoming revealed itself: did I have an office? A place where the guests would register? I had told Janey the guests would not have access to the farmhouse—our home—so then what was I going to do? I hated to build another structure for that purpose. That was a question for Kiera, I surmised.

But that wrinkle would have to wait, as Maddie removed herself from the thinning crowd, coming over to me and Janey, both of us still standing on the platform.

"Well, that was quite a show, Brian. I didn't know you had such a flair for the dramatic."

"He's good with pronouncements like that," Janey

said, "grand gestures, that's our Brian."

"Janey, has anyone ever told you to speak like a grown-up?"

I rolled my eyes and said, "All the time."

Janey allowed a giggle and gave Maddie a fresh glance. "Sometimes it's fun being just a kid, too," she said, and with that she took hold of Maddie's hand, who then tossed me a look. I just had to smile, it was as natural as anything in this world to see a young girl bond with a woman old enough to be her mother, even when she couldn't be. Janey urged Maddie forward, telling her all about the milk shakes that Martha served, and I trailed after them with fresh dreams dancing in my head. Before we loaded up into the new truck, I stole a look back at the windmill, once the star of the show but now neglected as we all went off for our celebration. In a matter of days, the land would begin to be torn up, the construction on the inn underway. I didn't doubt that I was doing the right thing. I just wished that part was over, I didn't like the idea of Annie's world—or Janey's—turned upside down for any length of time.

Maddie, Janey and I got inside the front cab of the truck, breathing in that new car smell.

"It's quite an improvement," Maddie said when the engine turned over softly, and on the first try.

I still couldn't believe my father and his investors had purchased this truck. As we pulled out of the driveway, I stole a look back in my rearview mirror, where I saw the old truck sitting idle, and I was again reminded of the lonely windmill. Was I leaving too much of Annie behind? I remained silent the rest of the way, parking as I always did in the lot outside the tavern. From there, the three of us joined the throngs already filling up the Five-O diner. All beverages like soda and juice and coffee were thirty cents, with sandwiches and entrees just three dollars. The place was packed, and Martha had adorned her walls with banners announcing the thirtieth anniversary. I was certain the celebration could continue later tonight down at the tavern, but for now, Linden Corners was alive and well inside its cozy diner.

I located my parents, who had secured a back booth for us all, and we slid in, Janey sitting between my mother and Maddie. I took up next to my father.

"How does she run, Brian?"

"The truck is great, Dad. The gesture, above and beyond."

"Nonsense," my mother said, "You cannot represent the inn with that battered old truck. Sentimentality doesn't get you down the road."

I didn't want to get into things with my mother, not today, so I let her remark slip by. We were thankfully distracted by the arrival of Gerta and Nora, and soon the ladies were lost in some conversation. My father excused himself to go talk to some of the locals, which left me adrift at my own celebration. But then I saw Kiera, sitting and chatting at the counter with Thomas, and at their side was the bearded man I'd noticed earlier. Crossing the floor and shaking hands with some of the other locals who congratulated me on the ceremony, I finally was able to sidle up next to the counter.

"Hope I'm not interrupting."

"Hardly, Brian, this is all your doing, it's your party," Thomas said.

"Well, it's Martha's party now."

"So modest. Well done, Brian. Looking around the diner, the population of Linden Corners appears larger than I thought," Kiera said.

"They do tend to come out for celebrations," I said, looking now at the third person in the party. I extended my hand. "Hi. I don't believe we've met, are you new to Linden Corners? I'm Brian Duncan."

That's when Kiera jumped in, her words keeping the two of us from shaking hands. "Oh, Brian, I'm sorry. I didn't have time to introduce you before. This is Tyler. Tyler Danner. He's my fiancé."

"Oh," I said, her words hitting me like an arrow finding its target, and I felt the blood drain, if not from my face than my heart. Part of me had wondered if her statement about being engaged had been a ruse, a way to deflect the emotion behind the kiss we'd shared on her last visit. Our relationship, she said, was strictly professional, and now, sitting before was confirmation of her pending marriage. Now I did shake his hand, his grip strong and meaty.

"Thanks for letting me be a part of today," he said, his voice deep, masculine. "Kiera has talked nonstop about this project of yours since she landed the account. She and I look forward to being guests at your inn, maybe a quasi-honeymoon after the real one."

"Anytime. I think she might even get a decent rate," I said, trying to keep my voice steady.

As we spoke, I noticed Chet Hardesty watching from across the aisle from us, and suddenly he stood up and approached us. "Hey, I thought I recognized you."

I turned to see who he was addressing and saw that it was Kiera's fiancé.

"You are Tyler Danner, the ballplayer."

"Guilty as charged, except right now I'm more of a ballplayer in search of a team," Tyler said, running a hand across his fuzzy face. "The Twins invited me to Spring Training, but I got cut two weeks before the season started. Sad to say, I'm just waiting for an injury to bring me back to show; some team will come calling. That's how my whole career has gone."

"But I've seen you play. Like, on television. Huh, a real-life celebrity in our midst. Let me ask you..."

Chet launched a barrage of question at Tyler, which freed Kiera up to ask me her own series of questions that were on her mind. "So, Brian, you didn't tell me you were bringing a date," Kiera said, her tone playful.

"Oh," I said, my monosyllabic response falling flat, just as it had when I'd met Tyler.

"Janey seems to have taken a shine to her. Whoever she is."

"Oh, she's not a date. She's a friend," I said, but I'd stopped listening to what I was saying.

Instead, I looked back and saw the ladies in my life chatting away, Janey's head moving back and forth as though she were trying to keep up with the volley of chatter. It did look natural, generations of two families together, Gerta and Nora, blood relations, and Didi, Maddie, and Janey, relative strangers to each other with one thing in common: me. I realized I was staring, perhaps visualizing the scene as it should have been, because I saw someone else hovering around that booth, cast in her own glow. I shook my head, realizing Maddie was making eye contact with me, and she seemed to be indicating Kiera. I looked back and that's when I found Thomas, Kiera, and Tyler all staring at me.

"Did I miss something?" I asked.

Thomas spoke up, saying, "I thought her name was Maddie."

"It is, why?"

Kiera answered my question. "Brian, you just said that woman's name is Annie."

———————

The celebration continued long into the evening hours, moving from the Five-O to George's Tavern, with the drinks flowing as easily as the passage of time, the denizens of the bar also being treated to slices of Gerta's famous pies. She had baked an array of flavors, but I was so busy I feared I would not get a piece of strawberry. During a lull in the action, I looked up at the bar and saw Gerta with a plate, and she was handing it over to me.

"You were so busy. I saved you a piece."

"Gerta, are you ever not looking out for me?"

She smiled, her wrinkles tightening. "Brian, when are you going to learn that's what we do in Linden Corners?"

I came around the edge of the bar, kissed her cheek. "Reminders are always welcome."

"Do you have a moment? I know it's not an ideal time..."

"For you, any time is the right time," I said. "Dad and Chuck are both beyond the bar. Let's find a place where we can talk, you can tell me what's on your mind."

Amidst the music and the laughter, the comradery of friends and neighbors indulging their Saturday night fun, Gerta Connors and I went back into the office, where once her husband had toiled away his days and nights. He'd been a simple publican, proud of owning his own business and always going over his books while, along with his wife, raising four beautiful daughters. George was the type of man to emulate, and so far, I liked to think I'd done well in upholding his traditions at the bar. Family-wise, it was just me and Janey, not quite the coterie of ladies that populated George's house. We settled on chairs, Gerta looking around.

"This was George's private world," she said. "It's been so many years since I've been in his office."

"You're welcome anytime," I said.

She laughed, waving a hand at me. "Oh, no, why change tradition now?"

"What's on your mind?"

"Brian, I'm so proud with all you've already accomplished with the inn. I love the idea."

"I sense a but in there."

"Pardon me for being self-serving, you know that's hardly my style. Yes, I have a but to bring up. Have you given thought to what you'll do with the tavern? Surely your time will be more and more taken with the inn, first its construction, then running it. I don't see you working all day long, then coming here to work more long hours."

"That's true. One of the reason for the inn is so I'm closer to home, day and night. Janey's made enough sacrifices in her young life, so it's time for me to put the focus squarely on her. She needs to know I'm home at night, and if I have to run out and handle a work issue she'll know I'm still on the property."

"You don't need to explain that, Brian. I'm in total support. It's just...George's legacy..."

"Will never be diminished, not as long as I'm around. If I decide to hold onto the bar, I will just hire people to run it. If I decide to sell, well, it would have to be to the right person, and know that I would never make any move without first consulting you. You might have given me the deed that one Christmas, but to me the bar—heck the whole building--is just on loan. If I do sell, you'll get all the profits."

"Brian, the money isn't the issue. I appreciate though your sentiments. George was a good judge of character."

"I agree," I said. "Look who he chose to be his wife."

"It's a wonder you've managed to stay single, Brian Duncan. Any woman could do worse."

I didn't say that Nora and she differed on that subject, and at last we returned to the bar. It all looked under control, and with Gerta's words swirling inside my brain, I decided to go outside onto the porch to clear my head. The day had been overwhelming, the build up to it even more so. Combined, I was exhausted, and couldn't wait to set my head to pillow. Of course, I wouldn't be alone. Maddie would be staying at the farmhouse, our first night together with Janey also under the roof. When I'd mentioned it to Janey, she'd been silent, but I think today had changed all that. My ex and my daughter seemed to have become thick as thieves and I supposed I should be grateful to that. One on one, Maddie was charming, the beauty she wore on the surface just a hint of what lay beneath. It's what made me fall in love with her years ago. Time heals wounds, and I wondered if enough had passed for me to really give the two of us a second chance.

The creak of the door of the bar stirred me from my thoughts, and I turned to see Kiera step out, the light wind toying with her long dark hair.

"You okay, Brian?"

"Yeah. Just got a lot on my mind."

"Big day," she said.

"The first of many. For so long, I've felt like I was running in place, but now, having set this crazy project in motion, it's like I've set myself in motion too. I'm actually running toward something. Complacency has given way to anticipation." I paused, turning toward the night sky, where the stars sparkled as they had the night I'd shown Kiera the inside of the windmill. My trail of thoughts then made me think of the windmill itself, alone on the open field, the over-turned soil from the ground-breaking a blemish on the land. I'd have to get used to it. It would only get worse before Kiera transformed it to my dream.

"Want to go for a ride?"

"I'm sorry, now? Where?"

"Come with me, to the windmill."

"Brian, we know what happened last time…I have Tyler. You have Maddie."

"No, there's something else I want to show you, to inspire you."

I'd intrigued her, and so she took hold of my hand and we dashed down the steps, where we got into the new truck. I pulled out of the lot and drove back toward Crestview Road and the farmhouse. When we got out, I took her around the right side of the house, where before us stood the old barn, in desperate need of a paint job, a silent structure in need of new life, too.

"Okay, Brian, you've got me. Where does the barn figure into this?"

"The inn needs an office, a place for guests to arrive and register," I said. "We can convert the barn into my office, and maybe even create a common space on the second floor where guests can come and socialize, perhaps installs a makeshift bar. We'll have games, television, a library of books. We can host parties, events, whatever people are looking for. It will complete the entire package. What do you think?"

"I like it, Brian, I really do. And since we're on the subject of enhancements, let me show you another idea I have."

At this point, with my enthusiasm bubbling, I would have followed her anywhere.

She took my hand this time, and she led me back toward the platform where we'd hosted the ground-breaking ceremony. It was still set-up from this afternoon; I'd take it down tomorrow. For now, Kiera asked me stand on the edge of the hill, she standing before me.

"I thought we would create a walkway in front of the cottages, and now with your idea of turning the barn into the main office, I know where to start it from. But not just a path, but it would have a rail craft-ed of iron, one that would line the entire upper ridge here, giving not just guests of the inn but others who might want a view of the windmill. We can build an observation deck."

Already I could visualize it, and I told her so, turn-ing to her and catching her eye. I thought she might look away, but she held my gaze, drew me in.

"You've given me new life," I said, my hand cup-ping her face. "Me and Janey both. We're so grateful."

She tried to turn away, said, "Brian, this can't hap-pen. It shouldn't..."

But it did, again. I kissed her, and she kissed me back, and unlike the first time when we had parted with nervous energy dancing before us, we stayed con-nected. In the presence of the great windmill, with its sails spinning lightly, we kissed, our shadows kissed,

almost as though the connection between us had deep-
ened, doubled. At last we broke the kiss, our arms still
encircled around each other.

I detected a tear in her eye. She didn't bother to
wipe it, and it ran down her cheek.

"Brian...we should get back. I need...Tyler, he's
probably wondering where I went."

"Tyler's fine. The famous ballplayer is holding
court at the tavern and he's loving every minute," I
said, "and, besides...Kiera, there's something between
us."

"Yes, your ex and my fiancé, that's what stands
between us."

"That's not what I meant."

"But it's how it has to be. Brian, I don't think...this
project, I've done the work. I think I can't work on it
any longer. I'll talk to Kirby, he'll reassign someone..."

"Kiera, don't do this. The Windmill Inn, it's not
just mine anymore, it's become..."

She didn't give me another chance to finish a sentence that had deeper implications. She turned and
ran off, disappearing into the dark of the night, leaving me alone in the one place in this world that never
made me feel that way. Lost in the emotions of the
moment, her words stinging me, I started down the
steep hill, my stride strong and determined. So much
of my life I'd run from problems, from confrontation.
I no longer wanted to be that man. I wanted what I

wanted, and my heart was telling me I wanted to be with Kiera Bowen. Was it just transference, her love of the inn drawing me to her, or was it something else, a piece of her soul that I'd locked onto? She might have run from this moment, but I doubted she could walk away from what we'd begun to create.

I came before the windmill, running my hand along the splintered edges of the tower. Still, it felt soft to the touch, as though I knew what lay beneath its hard exterior would never hurt me. I stepped inside the windmill, journeyed up the stairs and into Annie's studio, where I sat down on the floor, my mind silent, as though it were listening for another voice which might swirl around the windmill, in or out; I hoped Annie's spirit was here.

"Are you there?" I asked. "We had such a short time together, but you live inside me, and inside Janey, and everywhere I turn lately I see you. The world you helped bring back to life, it still lives—more so, it thrives. The windmill, even as it stands proud as a symbol of our future, the past is not forgotten. Annie, I want to honor that past as much as I can. Tell me another story from yesteryear, unlock for me another of the windmill's precious secrets."

I paused and drew in my breath.

"Tell me your story, Annie. Make me feel close to you again."

INTERLUDE
The Story of Annie Sullivan

There are many things people do in the name of love. Foolish plans, desperate actions, irrational thoughts that really threaten to do more harm than good when it comes to relationships. They can be done in the name of romance, and mostly they are, but human nature reacts intensely when familial issues rise as well, or when an object becomes the focal point of all your attentions. That object can be another person, or it can be a structure that unexpectedly, wondrously alters the path of your life, your very soul.

There was once a young woman who came to a sweeping land previously unbeknownst to her, her arrival based more on obligation than out of a sense of love, but in truth, she never would have taken on her task if not for the loving memory that fueled her on cold dark nights, stirred her and kept her eyes from needed sleep. Her unforeseen journey became something more, it turned surprising and unexpected, and awoke feelings she'd thought long since dormant inside her. As so often happens in life, death leads to new life.

At age twenty-one, she had lost her mother while a third year nursing student in college. It was as though time had clashed, her mother's illness and her higher education racing to whichever destiny would be fulfilled first. Time was cruel, as it could be, and the young woman was left adrift, lonely in her life and alone in this world. Her father had long since abandoned them, the routine of marriage and fatherhood unable to tether him to the ground. He'd taken to the open road and not been heard from in more revolutions of the moon than she could count. Some nights, as a girl, she had wished him back, thinking that her words contained strength, and that the universe existed to grant those wishes. No answers came, and eventually she slept with dreams that had been tucked away into the far reaches of her mind. She and her mother, together against the forces that existed beyond their home. Until her mother was taken and she found herself without her anchor. Again, she was set adrift, until one day a phone call changed everything.

It changed her, forever.

I knew all about her story. Because this was how Annie Sullivan came to find, first refuge, then love, inside a place called Linden Corners. How she came to be called the Woman Who Loved the Windmill, it was a circuitous route, and it opened up a crater inside of her and began to fill it up. She discovered her destiny one day on an open road, perhaps not unlike the one her father had taken, one she felt mirrored her own directionless life. Until she crested over a hill, and was captivated by the most wondrous sight she thought, for now, she'd ever seen. I am this woman, Annie Sullivan, and this is my story, one I realized only too late was just another in the history of the grand windmill.

"Hello?" she asked, answering the phone on the third ring. She hadn't been expecting a call.

"Annie, this is your Aunt Bobbie," said a weak-sounding voice.

Roberta Tessier was her mother's older sister by seven years. She hadn't heard from her since the funeral, when the more reserved of the two Tessier sisters returned to her reclusive life. Something must have happened for Annie to be receiving this call, and indeed it had. Her aunt was sick, the same cancer *which had claimed her mother, and it was like a second chance had been handed to Annie. While she couldn't help Margaret Tessier, maybe she could bring comfort to her aunt, and so when the request came, Annie abandoned her studies and journeyed from the lake side town of Danton Hill, driving beyond the nearest city of Rochester, four hours later finding the lush, rolling hills of the Hudson River Valley.*

She hadn't seen the windmill on her first day, she'd driven with determination to her aunt's house on a bluff above the Hudson River. It was a sprawling Victorian-era home, with lots of open rooms and corridors, too much space for one person, but as Aunt Bobbie explained one night as they lit a fire and drank tea, her life hadn't worked out as she'd hoped. Her husband had been a successful banker, made his fortune, bought the house, and the two of them had retired here to live out their golden years. Bobbie confessed she had never wanted children, but now lived her older years in the throes of regret.

"That's why I'm so blessed to have you at my side, Annie. The last of the Tessiers."

Her family's legacy wasn't something she'd ever considered. But now she thought about it, how strange that two sisters would bare only one child between them, a girl, now a grown-up who one day would get married, and in the simple exchange of "I do" would bring about the end of her family's surname.

But on that night, she clasped her hand over Aunt Bobbie's frail hand, and said, "Right now, there are two Tessiers."

"For now," the sickly Bobbie said.

For several months, Annie drove her aunt to doctor appointments, played cards and drank tea with her as winter turned to spring, where they could sit on the patio and enjoy the view of the languid waters of the river below them. Annie sometimes, when her aunt was napping, would venture further out on the property, sitting on the edge of the hill and stare at the water, thinking where the current had been earlier today, where it might be tomorrow. Rivers were a strange being, transient in a way even as they remained locked between lands. Almost a reflection of her life, her current status as caretaker, her own life on hold as she watched the inevitable decline of her aunt. For that's what it was; the doctors tried all they could, but the end was near. After, she had to wonder, what came next? She did not see herself going back to school, not for nursing. What she'd seen, first with her mother, then with her aunt, she wanted life's affirmation of tomorrow, not its end game.

"Dear, perhaps you need some air, it's such a lovely day," her aunt said one morning. "Some space in which to call your own."

Annie had been sitting on the bluff, and today, as she had for the past week, she had brought with her *a sketch pad. It had been years since she had drawn, but with her days stretching endlessly before her, she had to find something to occupy empty time. She loved landscapes, the land around her, but already she had sketched the river several times. That's why Bobbie's suggestion of hitting the open road had such an impact on her; she could chase the river, and see where it took her.*

Indeed, it was a lovely day, and once Bobbie had begged off going with her, claiming this was something Annie needed to do on her own, the grateful niece got in her car and took to the road. Columbia County was rife with winding, careening country roads, sometimes leading into small towns, at other times just driving past old farmhouses and towering silos, and as she forged on she considered stopping to draw, but something kept her going. She was enjoying a freedom she'd not felt in years, like she'd been released from life's hold, gravity giving way to the power of the wind. She drove, she soared, and she crested over a hill.

And then drew in her breath.

There it was, magnificent, wondrous, but, not unlike herself, wounded, imperfect.

She pulled to the side of the road, stepped out and walked along the grassy field until she came closer to a structure so unexpected, she thought she might have been transported back to a past that existed before she'd even been thought of. What she found was an old windmill, the kind she'd only seen in photos, with four sails that spun in the wind and gave poetry to the surrounding sky. What marred an otherwise perfect scene was the fact that the windmill was in a state of disrepair, its sails broken, pieces missing. Like it was reaching the end of its usefulness.

Annie Sullivan had found something more than a drawing.

She'd found something she could rebuild and bring back to life. It was called a purpose.

"Does someone actually own that old windmill, or does it just stand there...alone?"

Annie had returned to her car, not before taking a series of photographs, and she'd found herself entering the borders of a small town that went by the name of Linden Corners. It seemed as forgettable as so many towns that dotted the countryside, not just here but all over the country. She considered stopping at the local diner, a place called the Five O'Clock, but then just a short stretch further she saw a sign that might lead her to answers to her questions. A large Victorian house stood there, not unlike the one her aunt lived in, and a sign indicated stated it was the home of Masters' Antiques.

Who else would know about something from a by-gone era than an antique specialist?

She entered the store, a jangle of bells announcing her presence. A middle-aged woman lifted her glasses off her eyes, peering at her with intensity, from behind a counter.

"Afternoon, miss. Something I can help you with?"

The store was over-crowded with furniture and knick-knacks all over the place, her front counter nearly swallowing her up. Annie thought the woman behind the counter escaped her counter as a way to avoid being swallowed up her voluminous inventory. She stepped forward at last, a smile gracing her face.

"I was wondering, do you know much about that old windmill in the field?"

"New to Linden Corners, are you? You've come to the right place. Name's Elsie Masters."

"Name's Annie Tessier," she said.

"Pleasure, dear. Are you just passing through?"

"I...no, my aunt lives down the road, closer to Hudson. I'm... taking care of her She's not well. She kind of gave me the day off, and I went driving, and, well...here I am."

Annie wondered why she was providing so much detail; she could envision this woman at the end of the day meeting with friends over at that diner and discussing the strange young woman with the hesitant questions, asking about the windmill. Just another in a long line of people who came to her store and walked out without buying anything.

"Oh, that old windmill once stood so proud, it's a shame what's become of it!"

"So someone owns it...and allows it to look so... lonely! Its sails hardly spin."

"Back when the Van Diver family lived here, that windmill spun like magic. And for a while after they left, the new folks kept it up, but the newer owners, I guess they just don't appreciate its legacy."

"Legacy!" Her eyes widened at such a perceptive word.

"Oh, my dear, you are smitten. I could tell you stories of the windmill. My family has been in Linden Corners three generations, including two aunts of mine who lived in this very house. They, along with one other woman, ran a rooming house. But that all can wait for another day, if it's the windmill that so interests you, I suggest you visits the Sullivan farmhouse. Parents have gone the way of the wind, if you'll indulge my own flight of fancy, but their son still lives there, when he's not working up in the capital city of Albany. An ambitious guy from what I hear, doesn't give much credence to our fanciful stories of the windmill."

"Yet he owns it," Annie said.

"That he does."

"So that's where I begin," she said.

"Annie, just what do you have in mind?"

"Something so precious shouldn't be allowed to die. We have to honor our past."

Annie's day in Linden Corners was not yet complete. She thanked Elsie for the information, then she drove back from whence she'd come, parking her car along the side of the road again. Up the hill she went, past the windmill, her head turning back as often as she could to ensure her steady footing, and soon she came upon an old farmhouse and barn. A gleaming car was parked in the drive, and she found herself walking past it and up the steps of the wraparound porch. A wooden swing lay silent; the day was quiet, the wind tempered in the bright blue sun of this early spring day.

She knocked, and when she heard no response from inside the house, she knocked again. Determination had found Annie Tessier, or maybe purpose had. Maybe the car in the driveway was misdirection, perhaps the owner and his wife or whomever, were out in their second car. She didn't know what to do, so she sat upon the porch swing, her mind dancing with images that not even a hand upon the sketch pad might reveal. She didn't even hear the voice the first time he asked the question.

"Oh, I'm sorry..." she said, instantly standing up. "I didn't think anyone was home."

A man had appeared in the doorway, dressed in a

dark suit and tie, not quite what she was expecting. A farmer, maybe. He was young, perhaps a few years older than her, with wavy brown hair. He had a curious smile on his face.

"And who might you be, Goldilocks? Did you find the swing just right?"

It was the opening salvo in what would be, for a time, a fairy tale come to life.

––––––––––––

His name was Dan Sullivan, she learned, and when she asked him about the windmill he laughed.

"That old eyesore, it's a month from being torn down."

"No, you can't do that," she said, her voice filled with sudden despair.

He was still smirking when he said, "And why can't I?"

"Because, it's beautiful...I mean, it could be."

"My parents bought this land, including the windmill, and they bought the old thing out a sense of obligation. Someone who served with someone else in World War Two. But they're gone and I've got my own life and have no use for old wives tales. What you inherit isn't always what you asked for. What I know I've got is valuable land down there, and it could be

developed if Linden Corners wasn't already so de-
pressed. Small town America, it's on the wane," he
said, "We need to find ways to reinvent a way of life."

"You sound like a politician," she said.

"Dan Sullivan, assistant clerk to State Senator
Harold Ames," he said, proudly.

It was her first taste of Dan Sullivan's ambition,
and she found it infuriating. How could he possess
such beauty on his land and treat it with such...deri-
sion? Annie Tessier realized that in the months since
she'd been living with her aunt, caring for her, she'd
been lost while searching for an elusive thing called
the future. Her future. She didn't know why she was
so concerned about the fate of the windmill, but
she'd latched onto it, and she was going to convince
Dan Sullivan that the worst decision he could make
would be to tear the windmill down.

"Fine," he said, "convince me. Can I buy you
lunch while you state your case? I'm starved and
while there's no decent restaurant in town, I suppose
the diner will suffice."

Annie was thrown, by both his invitation and
his willingness to listen. She also hadn't had lunch,
and her stomach was grumbling. So she accepted,
and soon found herself inside the homey walls of
the Five O'Clock Diner, she and Dan breaking bread
across the table, almost as though it served as the di-
vide between the windmill's existence and memory.

She spoke so eloquently of its beauty, of how it had touched her so profoundly, and when he asked her why she found herself unable to give an answer that would stand up in court. She was losing her case.

"Okay, Annie, if you could do whatever you wanted with the windmill, what would it be?"

"I'd repair it, restore it to its full glory. Fix those sails, and let the wind pass through it." She paused before saying, "Everything in life has a purpose, even a building. To not let it reach its full potential is denying life's natural course. Things break, but you don't always have to destroy them. Then can live again."

"Annie Tessier, is there something more to your motivation?" he asked.

A tear slipping out of her eye, rolling down her cheek. She didn't wipe it away. Then she said, "I'm tired of losing all that I love."

It was as if those very words altered the course of not just Annie's life, not only Dan's, but all of Linden Corners, her voice rising amidst the daily life of people who worked, lived, loved, endured, giving new breath to a town starved for attention. Annie Tessier had come to town, and in just one afternoon, she'd transformed herself and the man sitting across from her. He invited her back to the windmill, and there she was allowed to more closely inspect the beat-up structure, detecting imperfections in the tower as well as the sails, jotting down notes on a pad she'd brought with her. Dan watched, first in amusement, then in wonder, as Annie spoke about the simple re-pair work that was necessary to restore the windmill. It would cost money, she said, money he didn't have, he confessed, saying that was one of the reasons to tear it down was to allow commercial development on the property.

"Besides," he said, "I don't plan on living here much longer. My career is just beginning."

Beginning was a curious word at the moment, and as it turned out, a game-changer. For the next month, Annie Tessier would come to Linden Corners as of-ten as she could, to the point where her anticipation of the coming day kept her wide awake; why sleep, she thought, when your dreams already knew the sun. She spoke with the owner of the Five-O, Martha Martinson, and with George Connors, who owned the tavern across the street, and of course, with Elsie's help, she got the word out that the windmill was go-ing to be restored. But everyone had to do their part. Annie began a fund-raising project, with each of the business owners participating, asking their clientele for donations. She'd even spoken to the surly local hardware store owner about doing the repair work, and he agreed.

"Thank you, Chuck," Annie said, shaking his hand, knowing that without his help her plan was stalled in the planning stages.

But as much as Annie had found a reason to wake up every morning, Aunt Bobbie continued to decline, and it was one morning when Annie awoke to find that Bobbie hadn't. The morning was gray, awash with rain, the elements unable to keep Annie from walking out on to the bluff she and her aunt had shared and there she cried, adding her tears to the rain. She thought not just of Bobbie but of her mother, Margaret, and as she stared out at the river, she knew where her journey would next take her. Not back to her studies, not back to Danton Hill, but to Linden Corners. She spoke to no one of her loss, not then, and it was a week before she returned to the town she had embraced. She first said good-bye to her aunt, and seemingly to her mother, again, and when she felt ready to face the world again, she found herself standing in the shadow of the windmill on a windswept day, where pieces of the broken sails fell to the ground.

When she turned around, she found Dan Sullivan beside her.

"I'm sorry about your aunt," he said.

"How did you hear?"

"Elsie Masters has an ear for these things," he said.

Annie allowed tears to fall again, and Dan took her into his arms, and he said, "Why don't you live here, Annie?"

"In Linden Corners?" she asked.

"No, here. At the farmhouse, with me," he said, and that's when he bent down and kissed her lips, a gentle move that cleared her tears and pieced back together her broken heart. What she wished to accomplish for the windmill, Dan Sullivan had just done for her. She found herself accepting his offer, and that night, he took her inside her new home, and he kissed her again, and she allowed herself to be brought upstairs, and there she found new wonder in the arms of a man who a month ago had been ready to end the windmill's life. Instead he'd reawakened a damaged woman who had known nothing but sorrow the last few years.

It was another month, as summer was at its height, when Dan brought Annie to the hill that rose up behind the windmill, to a creek that separated his property with that of the farmhouse to the north. A stone bridge rose over the water, and it was there that Dan told her this was where he came during his youth, where he would hunt frogs that hid among the rocks and gurgling silver waters. He confessed it was the one place on the land that made him happy, and he wanted to continue that tradition, and that's when he pulled out a ring and asked Annie Tessier to transform into Annie Sullivan.

They were married three months later, right after the windmill's restoration.

The sails spun, and the residents applauded its return to glory. On her wedding day, Annie stood on that same stone bridge, staring down at her handiwork. She had done this, she'd brought new life to this town, and in the process she'd done it for herself. The specter of death which she felt had haunted her these last few years was gone, taken by the wind, so strong that it also lifted her veil just as Dan bent to kiss her. The windmill had given birth to another love, and it spun each day, like the passage of time, knowing it had been given fresh powers of magic. In an act of love, it had been given the gift of tomorrow, a privilege not granted everyone.

Fairy tales can't last forever, but before they crumble under the weight of expectation they can create the potential for another story. Annie recalled the day during the rebuilding of the windmill, when Chuck Ackroyd, in a bad mood, came to her on the ridge of the hill, a piece of paper in his hands. He said one of the workers found this on the second floor, tucked beneath the floorboards. "He almost tossed it, thinking it was just garbage," *he explained.*

But when Annie set her eyes on it, she knew it was a piece of the past, and there was only one person who might know its importance. To Elsie Masters she went, where she examined the slip of aged parchment, reading its tender words: *I LOVE YOU, TOO, CHARLES. THANK YOU FOR THE WINDMILL. I'LL CHERISH IT IN MY DREAMS FORVER. GOODBYE.*

"Why, this must be the letter Cara Larssen wrote to Charles," Elsie claimed, commenting also how fragile it was.

Annie suggested they put it in a frame, preserve it just as they were doing with the windmill, and there it remained on the walls of Elsie Masters' antique store, until a woman named Nora Connors moved it upstairs, just another object piled among Elsie's numerous belongings. One day it would be found, and its story would inspire someone else, this much she was sure of. Yes, Annie, thought, the windmill would continue to spin, it sails reaching out like giant arms, ready to embrace those who fell under its spell.

That spell was cast upon Annie and Dan's daughter, born two years into their marriage. And as much as she recalled the day her sweet baby came into their lives, another day stood out by virtue of its wonders. Annie remembered the day Janey first ran to the windmill.

Of course it was summer time, she was nearing her second birthday, and the grass was high. Dan should have mowed it this past weekend, but he

*was so busy with his new job, preparing for an even
higher purpose. He wanted to run for a state congres-
sional seat, and he worked long hours in the state
capital, sometimes not even coming home. Ambition
had found him again, which left her with their precious daughter, and as such, he missed the special
moments that renewed your faith in life. She saw
her daughter get up after falling in the soft grass, giving voice to an infectious giggle as she did so. She
smiled, her heart thrumming. That's when she got
up, and she began to walk again, her little legs finding their footing, and soon she was moving ahead
with determination.*

*Annie trailed after her daughter, hovering to catch
her if she fell again.*

*But she didn't. She picked up her pace, and she
reached out her hands, almost like she was a tiny
windmill, mimicking what she saw before her. That's
when she took off, down the hill, her legs nearly un-
stoppable as she raced forward, racing into the wind,
and that's when Annie realized she'd given birth to
the windmill's next generation.*

*"Janey, wait for me," she called out, and she
laughed and she laughed and laughed more.*

*Annie caught up with her, and she took hold of her
and she spun her into the air, and she heard Janey's
infectious giggle, even as she heard a second voice,*

another one filled with the joy of laughter. Annie spun to see a woman crossing the stone bridge and coming down the hill. She was pretty, about Annie's age, and had a friendly face.

"Hi, sorry to intrude. It's just...what a wonderful sight to behold."

Annie smiled and felt like she'd just met a friend. "Annie Sullivan," she said.

"Cynthia Knight. My husband Bradley and I just moved into the farmhouse next door."

It was another of those fateful moments, and Annie began to realize that no matter what life had in store later, tomorrow, a year from now, she knew the majestic windmill was in the best of care. Janey Sullivan was its caretaker now, its future, and only down the proverbial road would she come to know its power and her own destiny.

I already knew mine, and when the wind granted me a return to watch over all I missed, I thought back to that day when I first came upon the windmill. Life changed that day, a sharp turn of the earth's axis, but that was the thing about the windmill, even as people came and went, even as seasons were swept away, it was a constant, waiting for the next person to fall under its spell. I am Annie Sullivan, and while my time may be over, I take comfort in the ever-turning sails of the windmill and eagerly await what happens next.

I just know it's going to be filled, in true Linden Corners fashion, with love, with memories, and with the bittersweet notion that tomorrow comes with no guarantees.

PART THREE
Summer

CHAPTER ELEVEN

SIX WEEKS.

Six weeks since the ground-breaking ceremony.

Six weeks since my life had been turned upside down for good, spun into directions I'd never seen coming.

Six weeks since an ambitious, talented, raven-haired beauty who went by the name of Kiera Bowen had magically opened up my wounded heart.

It also been six weeks since I'd last seen her, her figure running off into the darkness, her promise of abandoning the Windmill Inn project coming to fruition shortly thereafter. I'd had no choice but to move forward, a new architect taking over her designs.

During that elapsed time, the ground up on the hill behind the farmhouse had been turned over, a necessary but messy first step in the construction of the Windmill Inn. Chuck had brought in his contractors and they had dug up the ground, putting into place the piping that would handle the plumbing needs of each cottage, as well as laying the electrical wire that provided electricity, cable, Internet, all the modern conveniences you needed to attract a high-end clientele. As much as I wanted the inn to harken back to a time that people seemed no longer to revere, I knew I still needed the basic accoutrements of any hotel.

What pleased me were the daily progress reports; we were on schedule for our September deadline. Today, this bright Monday in mid-June, was an auspicious one, as the actual building of the cottages was scheduled to start. My parents would be present for it, but not Janey, since she was still in school another week. I didn't want to make a big deal of it anyway, after the Five-O party, I'd grown weary of Linden Corners celebrations. As well as that day had begun, its end left me unsatisfied, and, woefully alone. Kiera wasn't the only woman to leave my dreams in their wake. When I'd returned to the tavern after my disastrous kiss with Kiera, I found out that Maddie had slipped out of town too. It was my mother who handed me the note she'd left, sealed inside an envelope for my eyes only.

BRIAN. I WISH YOU ONLY THE VERY BEST WITH YOUR WINDMILL INN. BUT I'VE COME TO REALIZE THAT THERE IS NO ROOM THERE FOR ME. ALL MY LOVE, MADDIE.

I hadn't shared the letter's abrupt contents with

anyone, not that night, and not since. The Brian Duncan of old had returned, burying his pain and instead was moving forward with renewed drive. Respecting Maddie's wishes, I'd not tried to contact her, and besides, deep down, hadn't I known that Maddie and I were just an extension of my past? Never did I think she would commit to a life within Linden Corners, and maybe watching me in action the day of the ground-breaking was when the truth had dawned on her. My wounds dug down far deeper when it came to Kiera; yes, I was attracted to her, but it was more than a physical reaction. Kiera understood the windmill, she got the inn. She got me. I had left her a voicemail a few days after she'd left, and it remained unreturned, unrequited. I later spoke with her boss, Kirby Spellman, and he told me that Kiera had taken a leave of absence from the firm.

Both relationships were over, neither of them had been expected. It was time to move on.

The Windmill Inn's life was for me, and it was for Janey, too. Everything I did, then and from now on was done for her sake, ultimately giving her happiness precedence over mine. What else explained the past three-plus years, where I had placed my existence on hold to care for an irrepressible girl who had faced more tragedy than her years deserved? How she had maintained such a sunny outlook on life gave credence to the enduring spirit of youth, and so, taking a page from Janey's book, I too was ready to move forward.

Out of the kitchen window, I could see the laborers beginning to arrive, a dozen large-framed men who had been hand-picked by Chuck Ackroyd, all skilled at building houses and sticking to deadlines. They understood the time constraints involved, and were present today, on schedule, ready to give rise to a project that so far still lived inside my mind. Each day that passed, each turn of the clock, brought the inn—my dream--that much closer to fruition. I sipped at my coffee, watched as the men went into the barn to gather their tool belts and prepare for the day. Thankfully it wasn't too warm yet, temperatures in the mid-sixties.

A knock on my front door broke me from my concentration and I went to answer it, not sure who it could be. This being Linden Corners, I just opened the door without worry, where I was greeted by Chuck.

"Morning, Chuck," I said, surprised to see him.

"Hey, Brian. Got a second? I, uh, need to talk to you about something."

"Sure, come in. Coffee?"

"No, thanks."

I brought him into the kitchen in case he changed his mind, offered him a chair. Again, he refused. Was he nervous about something, or still not totally believing that our chilly relationship had turned as warm as the weather? He shifted from one foot to the other, then finally looked up at me.

"Sorry, I just...this is hard for me. You saved my

business. You also gave me a job at the tavern when I needed some extra income. Hard as it is to say, I owe you a debt of gratitude."

"Think nothing of it. I was glad to help out as I could," I said. "But, Chuck, don't tell me you're quitting the project."

"No, not at all. See that's the thing. With the construction beginning in earnest today, all of my time will be taken up by it, and by day's end I'll be exhausted from working in the sun all day. So I just don't see how I can continue to act as your relief bartender. Look, it really helped me out the last few months, that extra bit of cash. But now..."

"Chuck, no worries. I'd rather you put all your efforts into the construction."

"Great, thanks. I...we haven't always been the best of friends..."

"Chuck?"

"Yeah?"

"Let's see if you still feel the same way after the summer. I can be quite the task-master."

He nodded, a hint of a smile hitting his usually sour expression. Then he excused himself, as he said he should get to work, and then he departed, this time through the back door, where he joined his men in preparing for the day. Setting down my coffee, I realized I had a new problem on my hands. There was no way I could cover every night at George's, especially with the school year coming to an end and Janey's bedtime pushed back an hour; that just meant more time when I wouldn't be around. Mark Ravens had spelled me occasionally, but his reason for not wanting a permanent position matched my own. More time with your child, and I couldn't blame him. My father had helped out some nights, but I knew how my mother felt about him keeping late hours. D-Day had come for George's Tavern, and as much as I didn't want to admit it, I had to put it up for sale. Hanging onto the bar would be out of sentimental reasons, but again, I had to think of the future, of Janey. In a few months, I'd be home way more often, working out of the new office in the converted barn, within earshot of Janey, morning, noon, and long into the night.

I didn't know what I was going to do. I hated to disappoint Gerta, not after all she had entrusted with me.

But I knew solving this problem wouldn't happen today, so I ventured outdoors, walking to the edge of the hill. The windmill turned, gently, seemingly undisturbed from its routine despite the sound of incessant hammering. It was almost as if the windmill approved of what was happening. I hoped so. There was a lot riding on this venture, and while right now we were upsetting the status quo, I had to have faith it was all worth the effort. For a time I stood there, watching the manly laborers as they took to the tasks set before them, creating from nothing the future of this town. At last, though, I left them to their duties and walked over to the barn, where I noticed my parents pulling up the driveway.

"Morning," I said.

"Good morning, son," Dad said, emerging from behind the wheel of his Mercedes.

"Sorry if we're late. Your father was on a call, it took longer than expected."

"No worries. I told you I didn't want to make a big deal of today."

"No more dramatic gestures?" Mom asked with a noticeable smirk.

"I'll save that for the windmill's anniversary celebration."

"Speaking of," Mom said, "I had my own interesting phone call last night. Rebecca."

My wayward sister. "Where is she these days?"

"Paris, she claims. But she's also promised to try and be here for the unveiling."

"I'll believe that when I see it," I said.

"That's what I said," Dad concurred.

"It's no wonder Rebecca keeps us at arm's length. Brian, perhaps you could reach out to her as well. Since the Windmill Inn is a family affair, it would be nice if we could all be together. If nothing else than to honor Philip."

Philip had been my older brother, and he'd died from cancer as a young man. Filled with promise, highly athletic as well as intelligent, he had been the prized apple in a cart of Duncans, and I still wasn't convinced Didi Duncan had ever recovered from the tragic loss. Whenever she worked my last nerves, which was often enough, I would remind myself that tragedy had shaped her as well. We honored Philip every year, since he was the person responsible for the Christmas ornaments that adorned our trees every year: reflective, colorful orbs with our names written across them in silver glitter. He'd left them for us his last Christmas, and we had hung them each year with deep appreciation of his message of family.

Now, as the sun rose and temperature rose, I escorted my parents into the shade of the old barn, my mother suddenly taking charge by pointing out some ideas she had been thinking about. Of where the entrance to the office would be, whether the interior of the barn should be sectioned off or just be a wide-open space. She liked my idea of the upper level being transformed into a common room for the guests, as escape from the privacy of their cottages.

"Mom, Hal is working on all that, no need to trouble you," I said.

Hal Wallis was the new architect from Kirby Spellman, Inc. He was a by the book guy; boring and uninventive. I wasn't happy with him, but at least he was using Kiera's basic design.

"Hal. I've seen his so-called enhancements. They're

not half as good as Kiera's ideas."

"Didi..."

"It's okay, Dad. I agree. Look, let's leave the work to the professionals. How about lunch down at the Five-O, my treat."

"Actually, before we go, there's something your mother and I need to discuss with you."

My father's words felt ominous, my mind harkening back to a couple weeks ago when they returned to Philadelphia for another of his regular check-ups. I searched their faces for any hint of bad news, but the way they looked at each other, I felt I was in for a surprise of another kind.

"Okay, I'm listening," I said.

"Well, your mother and I have been doing a lot of talking, and thinking," he said, "About our future."

"Neither of us is getting any younger," Mom said, "But we're not exactly ready to retire to Edgestone either. What we decided was this: we need a new lease on life, a new adventure to get our blood flowing again."

"You're buying an RV and traveling the country," I said.

"Hmm, not likely," Mom said.

It was hard to envision that anyway.

"We've sold the townhouse in Philly," Dad said. "Linden Corners is our home now."

You could have knocked me over with a feather.

My jaw dropped, unspoken words in the empty air between us. My mind raced: sure, they'd been living in Linden Corners since just before Christmas of last year, they'd purchased, on a whim, Cynthia and Bradley's home shortly thereafter, and aside from the two weeks they'd spent in Philadelphia, they had remained here, settling in, getting comfortable. My mother, I recalled, even had her precious china for dinner parties. My father had taken shifts at the bar, and he'd gathered his investor friends to help make the Windmill Inn a reality. Had all the clues been sitting before me? It seemed so unreal.

"Does your silence mean you don't approve?" Mom asked.

"No, no...not at all. I'm just...surprised."

"You're not the only one who can chase windmills, my dear," she said. "We all have our dreams."

"And yours are?"

"We'll get into that later," Dad said, "we just wanted you to know, the Windmill Inn will be a true family business: you, your mother and I, and Janey. No one else."

"Except your investors," I said.

"Brian," Dad said, taking hold of my shoulders in an effort to steady me. "There are no other investors, just your mother and I. The only financial assistance my friend Harry Henderson gave was in buying our townhouse from us. His wife was always envious of the place, and now she owns it. Linden Corners is where we belong."

My mother added the final touch, the words so strange on her lips but ones which sent my heart swelling. "With our loving son and his daughter."

"I don't know what to say."

"How about welcome home?" Dad stated.

Home wasn't a building, home was a feeling. I took my parents into my embrace, silence dictating just how I felt.

"They did what?"

"They sold the townhouse."

"And they're moving here permanently?"

"The moving truck arrives next week, the last of their belongings."

"I don't believe it."

"Say that three times fast, and then try and sleep on it," I said.

"You do a look a little peaked around the eyes."

"Thanks, Nora."

It was Tuesday, and she and I were sharing our usual lunch at her store, but I ordered chicken salad for a change of pace. We were sitting outside, another warm day settling over the village square, a light breeze ruffling the wax paper the sandwiches came wrapped in. I drank from my iced tea, grateful for the shade of the wraparound porch. I felt calm and refreshed, as unlikely a feeling as I'd experienced in months. From the moment I'd decided to move forward with the Windmill Inn idea, I felt I'd been running a marathon, and while I might not have reached the finish line, I'd been given a respite. I always looked forward to our weekly lunch, but even more so today.

"It's like a giant weight was lifted off my shoulders," I said.

"Usually your mother make your shoulders reach for the sky."

"Yeah, funny. Maybe she's changing too. Can you believe she used a windmill metaphor on me? Of all people? My mother, who disapproved of my decision to change my life. And what does she do, follows in my footsteps. Chasing windmills. I feel like I've been doing that for the past three years. No longer battling my own problems, no more tilting, now it's time to allow my dreams to take over."

"When the inn is built, maybe you can write poetry," Nora said.

"I'm so glad to have you as a sounding board."

"My point is, Brian, you've got everything organized. Stay grounded."

I nodded, took a bite of the sandwich and chewed thoughtfully. Was that even possible, to keep the wind from taking me into its embrace? From swirling with my mind, filling it with lost images of Annie. Forgotten thoughts about Kiera?

"So, did you finally decide what to do with the letter we found?" she asked.

She meant Cara's love letter to Charles, and I admitted that I hadn't. I wasn't much in the mood for discussing letters, love or Dear John, or those that were put into words, as Kiera had done before she went running off that night.

"Something you're not telling me, Brian?"

For six weeks, I'd avoided the issue of both Maddie and Kiera. Maybe I was ready, given today's sense of renewal, of a fresh start. Finally, taking a deep breath before I jumped in, I said, "Maddie ended things with me, and I also kissed Kiera, who freaked out and quit the project."

She blanched, dropping the sandwich on her plate. "Um, when did this happen?"

"The day of ground-breaking ceremony."

She calculated this in her head. "Two months?"

"Six weeks, actually," I corrected, "and a couple days, to be precise."

"Wait, you messed up your relationship with two women on the same day?"

"Like you said, I don't know anything about women. It showed that day."

"How did Maddie break it to you?"

"In a letter, short, not sweet, but to the point. She said she didn't fit in here."

"Is she wrong?"

I'd had all those weeks to ponder that question, so I answered quickly. "Not really. She's too...and don't take this wrong way, but Maddie Chasen is a bit too sophisticated for our sweet Linden Corners. When I reunited with her the weekend of John's wedding, I sensed a change in her, but maybe she was telling me what I wanted to hear. When she suggested she come for a visit, I was a nervous wreck—apprehensive about what Janey would think, or so I told myself. Part of me wanted her to come here and have her fall in love with the windmill like I had. She could finally see for herself why I stayed here."

"And the other part of you?"

"Couldn't get the image of her and the boss... together."

"Tough one to let go," she said. "Have you spoken to her since?"

I shook my head. "She asked me not to."

Nora set her sandwich down, shaking her head as she did so. "No wonder Maddie feels left out. You were supposed to go running to her, Brian, tell her she was wrong. If, in fact, you really thought that. Now you've left her hanging."

"After this amount of time, I doubt she's sitting around waiting for my call."

"Okay, let's set Maddie aside for a moment. Tell me about Kiera and this kiss."

I paused before I said, "It wasn't our first one."

"Brian Duncan, I thought we were friends," she said. "But yet, here you are, holding back on me. Talk, and don't stop till I know everything."

"The spirit of Elsie Masters lives," I replied.

"And don't you forget it. Now, Brian, spill."

Spill I did. I told her about seeing Kiera for the first time, so professional in her tailored suit, so passionate about our project. How her first visit to Linden Corners had me dreaming of Annie—the way she sketched on the edge of the hill, drawing the sails of the windmill as though she'd already fallen in love. How could I not be affected by that? It had set my heart aflutter, like it hadn't been since...

"Annie," Nora said. "I get it. Some might call it transference."

"What do you call it, Nora Connors, lifelong cynic?"

"It's not what I think, Brian, it's what you, the poet, thinks. Love at first sight."

"Nonsense," I said, though I spoke the word with far less conviction than my mother did.

"Fine. Let's move on. You still haven't told me about either kiss."

"I brought Kiera to the windmill, inside, and then out on the catwalk. A light breeze was in the air..."

"Romantic," she said.

"Do you want to hear this or not?"

"This would be so much more entertaining over a glass of wine," she said. "But go on."

It was the day that Elsie Masters died, I explained, and all of our emotions were raw after spending the afternoon on the porch of what had been her home, right where we were now. "Thomas joined me and Janey and Kiera for dinner, where we talked about the plans for the Windmill Inn, explaining to Kiera that Thomas was my historical consultant on the windmill. I think, later, when it was just the two of us up on that catwalk, Kiera began to feel the pull of Linden Corners, as though it was her destiny along with mine. Through an odd twist of fate, we learned it was possible Kiera's ancestors came from this village. Maybe that's what pushed us toward what happened. Anyway, we kissed, briefly. That's when she told me she was engaged."

"Ouch," Nora said. "But then there was a second kiss."

"The night of the ground-breaking. We left the tavern because I wanted to share with her an idea I'd had, and she said she had one too. Again, it was night, the windmill spun, the stars, all that, and the moment thrust us together again. Our kiss the second time was deeper. I knew then it wasn't the romantic atmosphere that had drawn us to each other, it was mutual desire. But after she pulled away, she told me this couldn't happen. She went off into the night, and when I got back to the bar, she was gone, having left with her fiancé, Tyler. Maddie was also gone, the letter left in her wake."

"Let me pose a question, Brian."

"I don't think I'm going to like it."

"Is it possible Maddie witnessed the kiss between you and Kiera?"

The idea hadn't even occurred to me. Kiera and I were at the windmill, Maddie back at the tavern. But the timing could have worked. Maddie would have had time to follow us. A wash of regret hit me like a flood, perspiration forming on my brow. If this was true, then what I had done was just as Maddie had done to me. Had she and I come full circle in our betrayal? If so, I hated the thought that she had left because of that, and I said so aloud.

"The question remains, Brian, do you want to know the truth about Maddie, or have you decided, after all this time, to just let it go? Given your history, I think you need to know. You never gave her a chance to explain her actions, you just walked out on her and the life you two had planned. She deserves your honesty. And you, you need to close that chapter of Maddie once and for all. That is, if you really want to pursue whatever exists between you and Kiera."

"Kiera is gone, out of the picture. She's marrying Tyler, the baseball player."

Nora got up from her seat, grabbing the wrappings from our sandwiches. Apparently, our afternoon tete-a-tete was coming to a close. An SUV had just pulled up to the curb outside the store, an indication it was time for Nora to get back to work. It was also time for me to get going, I had the shift at George's tonight.

"What you just said, I'm not sure that's going to happen," Nora said.

I turned to her, my eyes curious as to why she would say that. She cocked her head to the sidewalk, where walking up the cement path was none other than Kiera Bowen, and seeing her walking toward the great Victorian house, I felt a fresh row of perspiration on my brow. It wasn't from the heat of the day, but rather from the reaction of seeing her. Like she had appeared out of the ether, a willowy vision taking form.

"Kiera," I said. "What a surprise."

"Hi, Brian," she said, coming up the steps.

"What are you doing here?" I asked. There was no other way to say it. Blunt is better.

"Actually, I came to see Nora."

"Me?"

"You deal with the past, don't you? Your store, it's built on nostalgia, on lost items?"

"Among other things, but yes. What can I do for you?"

"How are you at ancestry?"

"If I can help find an antique book gone missing for

decades, I suppose I can find an old relative. Who are we looking for?"

"Not one person, but a family. The Van Divers," she said, "I want to know if I'm related to the family that built the windmill."

———————

This first day of the summer season had been filled with one surprise after another, the events more akin to a ground-breaking than the actual day we'd celebrated six weeks ago. My parents had confessed all, Nora had informed me that I knew nothing about women (again), and then the biggest surprise of all was the unexpected return of Kiera Bowen. It was nine o'clock at night, and I was still reeling, not only from her presence, but by her request to Nora.

The bar was quiet tonight, just a couple of my regulars, all of them busy watching a ball game between the Mets and the Nationals. The score was 4-2 Mets, bottom of the sixth. I didn't much care who won, but I left it on because the Yankees were not playing today, and besides, George's preferred team had been the Mets, so I turned them on out of tradition. Earlier in the night, the burly guys from the construction site had come over for some hard-earned beers, and I'd instituted a two-for-one special for the rest of the summer for them. Who I hadn't seen appear was Kiera, not since I'd left her and Nora to their business, feeling left out the moment they went into the shop and closed the front door. If Nora was transforming into the new Elsie Masters, I could only imagine the questions she was peppering Kiera with.

From the television I heard the roaring sound of the crowd, heard Chet and the others yell at the screen. I turned back out of curiosity, where I saw a player trotting around the bases; he'd just hit a home run.

"To think, that guy was in our town just a couple months ago," Chet said.

"I'm sorry, what did you just say?" I asked.

"That's Tyler Danner, he just smashed a two-run homer, tied the game."

I grew more interested, focusing more on the screen as the player crossed the plate and received a high-five from the guy he'd knocked in. Indeed, the home run hero was Tyler, his dark beard as unmistakable as the curly-cue "W" on the caps of the Washington Nationals. So he was in the nation's capital, and Kiera, his fiancé, just happened to show up in Linden Corners today. My mind played with the coincidence, and decided there was more to the story. I would get the details moments later, as the front door to the tavern opened just as the game was going to commercial. The inning had ended on a strikeout. When I saw Kiera, I hoped it wasn't prophetic.

"Hello, Miss, may I help you?" I asked, walking out from behind the bar.

She attempted a smile. "A white wine would be nice."

"You sure? Have you tasted our wine?"

"I'll survive," she said. "Do you have a moment?"

"Let me get the guys a refill and then you can have all the time in the world," I said.

She watched me pour a fresh round of beers for the guys, who cheered when I announced the round was on the house. When I changed the channel to an out-of-market baseball game, they were less than pleased but I said too bad and left it at that. No explanations needed for the peanut gallery. Then I poured a white wine and a seltzer for myself and joined Kiera at a table. I told her the wine was courtesy of the house as well.

"Keep that up, you'll run yourself out of business," she said.

"I've got new priorities," I said. "So, how are you?"

"I'm...good. Brian, I came, first, to apologize. How I reacted..."

"Kiera, there's no need. We both acted impulsively."

She accepted that, taking a sip of her wine and wincing. "We're going to have to work on your wine selections."

That "we" sounded promising, I thought, but let the comment drop. No need to get ahead of myself.

"Did you have a productive meeting with Nora?"

"I surprised her, for sure. Guess you never told her I might be one of 'those' Van Divers."

"Actually, I'd mentioned something about your family, but never got to the name."

"She's going to talk to Thomas, first, see what he knows. Then do a search."

"You could have done that yourself."

"I'd rather an impartial person do the hard work. I'll trust the result better."

I nodded, sipped at my seltzer. Sounded like Kiera had family issues of her own.

"You didn't let me finish, Brian. What happened between us, I let it."

"Kiera, it was just a kiss."

"Two, in fact," she said. "Tyler and I are finished."

Considering I'd just seen him hit a two-run homer, her words didn't surprise me. But I let her tell her story without prompting her. It was like she need to tell someone, anyone, but the fact she wanted to tell me made all the difference.

"Tyler's career always came first. I mean, when I met him two years ago he was playing ball for the Triple-A affiliate of Washington, the Syracuse Skychiefs. He's spent his life in and out of the majors, and now that he's thirty-seven, he's a reserve player, one of those journeymen—his phrase—that moves from team to team each season, filling in when there's an injury. Before this season he told me was retiring at its end, he was tired of never knowing where he was playing. I agreed to give him one last season, but when he got cut by the Twins in spring training, he said that was it, he was done. Let's get married. I've never wanted a life on the road, and I didn't want to have my husband gone six months out of the year."

"And then he got a job," I said.

"How did you know?"

I explained what she'd just missed, and she just shook her head. "He's a lifer, that's what I had to realize. He'll transition from bench player to coach without missing a beat."

"Which leaves you...where?"

"Here," she said, "In Linden Corner, and ready to supervise the construction. I've already spoken with Kirby, who has agreed to put me back on the project. But I told him I had to speak with you first, to see if you wanted me back."

"I never wanted you gone," I said.

"So, I guess I'm back."

I raised my glass, and encouraged her to do the same. She did, and we clinked.

"To new beginnings," I said.

We drank, and I saw the tension that had been evident on her face dissipate. My fears too drifted away, and I leaned back in the chair. Tomorrow couldn't come soon enough, to see her on site, supervising the construction of the cottages just as had always been intended. I realized she was jumping into an intense job, and I mentioned it was going to require much of her time.

"It's a long drive back every night," I said.

"Then we'll have to change that," she said. "Ironic, isn't? I'm constructing a hotel, and I have no place to stay."

"Funny, I happen to have a place for you."

"Brian, I'm not ready...for anything. I can't stay at the farmhouse."

"That's not what I was going to suggest. I happen to have a spare apartment just upstairs, fully furnished. Would you like to see it?"

She nodded, and we rose from our seats. Before we ventured to the back stairs, she turned to me and said, "Brian, would you do me one favor?"

"What's that?"

"Buy the guys a round of drinks on me," she said, "And put the game back on for them. Who knows, maybe Tyler will strikeout in his next at-bat."

Score one for the home team, I thought.

CHAPTER TWELVE

A WEEK HAD ALREADY PASSED, and I was gearing up for First Friday, the annual celebration of summer at George's Tavern, a tradition started years ago by George Connors himself, with an able assist from his wife, Gerta. He'd serve up drinks, she'd have pies aplenty, and the residents of Linden Corners would usher in the summer solstice with cheers and laughter, the sense of community richer only during Christmastime. This year we had decided to tie First Friday in with the annual Fourth of July fireworks, and to ensure the word was properly spread, flyers were posted to telephone poles, and up on bulletin boards at the Five-O and at Edgestone, at Marla and Darla's Trading Post and other stores along our little strip. The party itself was two days away, so as much as it was on my mind, the Windmill Inn insisted on taking precedence.

Kiera had returned to the site, and she was busy overseeing the daily construction. I had to admit, she looked sexy in her yellow hardhat, her dark hair tucked beneath it. She looked even better when she stopped for lunch and let her hair fall to her shoulders. It was a high point of each day, not that I told her. I could enjoy certain benefits from afar. Bu she was doing amazing work, whipping the guys into shape; I think they liked working for her. I also think they were looking forward to the bonus my father had promised upon timely completion of the project. I knew it was still a longshot that the inn would be ready for occupancy by September, but with each passing day Kiera worked hard to dispel my doubts. The frames of the cottages were in place, giving the landscape a new shape.

But today I was taking Kiera away from the site. I'd promised her a break, and I'd also told Janey I'd spend the day with her. Might as well kill two pretty birds with one stone, and so it was on the morning of July second that I awoke with fresh determination and a ready smile. I quickly got dressed and was downing my first cup of coffee when Janey came bounding downstairs.

"Dad, it looks like it's going to rain," she said.

Indeed, dark clouds hovered over Linden Corners, which might impede the progress on the construction site. Freak summer storms were a staple around here, but usually they waited until the humid months of August to whip up their frenzy. Today, though, the men were already at work, as though they knew the weather could put a damper on their work, and were going to do their best to get in as much work as possible. The same was true of my plan, though we were not so dependent upon the outdoors for what I envisioned doing today.

"We can't control Mother Nature," I said, "But we also can't let it affect our day."

"You seem different," she said.

"Oh, how so?"

"I don't know. You're not as tense."

"And what, pray tell, does a ten-year-old know about tension?"

She rolled her eyes. "If you only knew."

School was over for the year, she was well provided for, and she was surrounded by people who loved her—which included, Sully, who sometimes thought she was a person—so what cares did she have? But whatever was eating at her, I knew Janey would eventually come to me and spill her guts. She just needed time to work things out in her mind, not unlike how I behaved most times. Answers didn't always come immediately, not to her or me, and you had to let them stew inside you until they you were ready to seek them out. Janey and I, we were not dissimilar.

"Are you ready?" I asked.

"Had breakfast, took Sully for a run outside. Ready as I'll ever be."

"Have you forgotten to use pronouns and such?"

"Just like Momma," she said, "such a stickler for proper grammar."

She didn't often reference Annie, not lately at least. I knew she thought about her, but with all the building going on around the farmhouse, perhaps she was as turned upside down as the land and I wondered if I'd not been sensitive enough to her concerns. Not that she'd protested any of the ideas for the Windmill Inn, she'd been fully on board since the beginning, but now that it was fast taking shape, the skeleton-like cottages stealing some of the windmill's thunder, it was only natural for her to feel a sense of loss. Before I'd come along, it had been Janey and her mother, the two of them bonded by the windmill.

I let her comment slide, urged her to put on her sneakers, and once she did, we headed out into air as thick as soup, no doubt a precursor to the storm. We hopped inside the front of the cab of the new truck, I felt that Annie was riding alongside us, Janey's comment having conjured her. As we drove toward downtown, I wondered if there was going to be enough room too for Kiera given our past baggage. Three was company, four a crowd, even if one was ephemeral.

I pulled into the parking lot at the tavern, honked my horn as prearranged.

Kiera stepped out immediately, just as the first raindrop hit the windshield. She dashed to the door, opened it and slid in. Janey shuffled over, sitting between us.

"Hi, Kiera," she said.

"Hi, Janey. Doesn't look like the weather is going to cooperate with us."

"Brian says we're not staying outdoors," she said.

"You call him Brian?"

She giggled. "Only when he's being silly. You sound like my grandma."

"Pay her no mind," I said.

"I'll do no such thing."

So that's how it was going to be, the two of them against me. It sounded familiar, and as I drove off, leading us out of Linden Corners, I did so with a knowing smile. This day would be lots of fun, I hoped. I pushed down on the accelerator as we journeyed up a hill, following the yellow signs when indicating it would curve. The new truck performed without issue, its engine silent as he took to another hill.

"Way better than Momma's truck," she said.

I was reminded of the day I'd taken Maddie up in the mountains with that old truck and how we had barely made it there, much less back. I had much more confidence in this one, as well as with the two ladies in my care. We zoomed again around a curve, rising up further into the hills. For several miles we drove, until the river came into view just beyond the historic town of Hudson. Janey asked where we were going and I said all in good time.

"He can be very mysterious," Janey said.

"I think it's fun, an adventure. Anticipating what we're doing is part of the surprise."

I let the two of them debate the issue, concentrating instead on the road ahead of me. The turnoff I wanted was hidden by brush and I didn't want to miss it. When last I'd come this way, it had been December and now had nearly blocked the driveway. It had been two Christmases ago, just after Nora had opened A Doll's Attic, when she had been summoned by an elderly lady named Katherine Wilkerson. She had need of an antique specialist. Nora and I had visited her, where we'd learned her tragic story of losing her only daughter, Mary, overseas during a *sinterklass* celebration, and as such, she was looking to part ways with the items her daughter had sent back home while on her travels. Among them were Christmas ornaments from an assortment of European countries, and while Nora questioned her desire to sell them, it was clear that in Katherine's mind, trinkets were just those, memories hers to treasure.

We turned up the winding driveway, the woods around it neglected to the point where branches tried to reach out to us; we were already in its web, drawing ever closer to the main house that lay beyond the overgrowth. As I silenced the truck before a large Victorian mansion, not unlike the one that housed Nora's store, but far more rundown, I began to question if I was doing the right thing. The lawn hadn't been mowed, and the brush too grew over the pathway; grime lay thick on shadowy windows, and cracks in the paint made the house seem like the set of a horror movie. The fact that the rain had increased, battering the truck as we parked only added to the mood.

"Where are we?" Janey asked.

"We're here to visit a nice lady," I said, "and I expect best behavior."

"From her, or us?" was her reply.

She was not unfounded in her suspicion. Nonetheless, we made a mad dash for the porch, and hit protective cover just as the front door opened. Katherine Wilkerson had aged considerably in the near-two years since I'd last seen her, her face a maze of deep wrinkles, her hair more gray and unkempt. But when she saw me, she smiled and I saw that the light in her hazel eyes was as alive as ever. She was lonely, she didn't see much company, but I had no doubt she had tea at the ready, our arrival as welcome as sunshine, the latter which just wasn't going to happen. A clap of thunder rushed us inside, Katherine closing the door behind us.

"Goodness, storms come on so quickly around here, don't they?" she asked.

"But that means they pass quickly, too. Just a summer storm," I said. "Mrs. Wilkerson, I'm very pleased to see you looking so well, and thanks for agreeing to meet with us. This lady here is Kiera Bowen, whose working with me on the Windmill Inn, and this young one here..."

"Let me guess, Janey Sullivan herself," she said.

"How do you know me?"

"I know all about the windmill, young lady. I know all about you."

"I can't say the same," Janey replied.

Her remark might have come off as rude, but Katherine just chuckled, asking us to join her for tea in the living room. As we followed her, Kiera's eyes opened up, as I knew they would. Not only was the structure beautifully designed and preserved, the antiques that filled the room gave it an old-world feel, as though we'd stepped back into the past. From my last visit, I knew that each room was similarly adorned, with treasures from yesteryear filling every nook and cranny. Once upon a time, Katherine and her husband Chester had bought this house in retirement, taking advantage of the many antique stores in the region to help give new life to the old home. They'd owned it not ten years, and had enjoyed their time here until her writer-husband's death. Since then, Katherine had wandered its halls alone. I had enough trouble thinking of myself rambling around the farmhouse on quiet nights; it had to be more intense for a woman of Katherine's age and loss.

"You have a beautiful home, Mrs. Wilkerson. Such history within its walls."

"Thank you, Kiera. And please, call me Katherine. Now, tea?"

So we sat down to tea. I took over the pouring, much to Katherine's pleasure. She liked to have someone dote on her, and unfortunately there was no one around to do that on a regular basis. Janey gave me a look when I handed her a cup, since it wasn't usually something she drank. But I nodded, and she took head. We are all grown-ups here, this was important, and so she stepped up. I dropped two cubes of sugar in her cup just to ensure it was sweet enough for her. Kiera took hers plain, and I added milk into mine and Katherine's. We settled onto the sofa, Katherine in a beautiful wing-backed chair.

"Brian, Nora has told me all about your Windmill Inn. I think it's marvelous."

"Thank you. It's a lot of work. Kiera here designed it. Modern, yet keeping alive the spirit and style of the windmill. We want our guests to feel like they're entering another world, not just from the exterior but inside as well."

"Which is what brings you here,' she said, skipping right to business.

"Nora told me you were thinking of selling the house, and its belongings."

"I have no need to for all this space," she said, "It's

taken me a while to realize it, but as I get older, I just cannot keep up with the needs of the house. I could pay all sorts of people to help trim the branches and mow the lawn and such, but in the end, that just drains my bank account. My husband did well in life and left me well off, but why should I throw good money after bad? As difficult as it's been to admit, I cannot endure another winter stuck up in these hills. Don't get me wrong, my view of the river is as lovely as ever, and had today not been stormy I would have suggested you all enjoy a picnic out on the bluff."

"Another time," I said. "So where will you live?"

"Given how nicely I've been treated by Nora, and by you, Brian, I see no reason not to move up to Linden Corners. I heard about poor Elsie Masters, of course, she used to visit me just so she could drool over my furniture. She'd also fill me in on the goings-on about town, not that I knew the people she was talking about. I've been in touch with the administrators at Edgestone Retirement Home and inquired about Elsie's room. It's mine if I want, and I said yes immediately. This house will be listed in the coming weeks."

"And the contents of the house?" I asked.

"Yours,' she said, "if you think they will help bring life to your inn."

"We'll pay you a handsome fee," I said.

She waved her hand. "We'll work out the details later. I'm sure you'll be fair."

"Katherine, this is wonderful, and I don't just mean the furniture. As someone who has felt the unique hospitality Linden Corners offers, let me be the first to welcome you to your new home. If there's anything any of us can do, don't hesitate to ask."

"Oh, Nora is taking care of everything," she said. "Kiera, Brian tells me you're an architect. So no doubt you have an appreciation for a home like this. May I give you a tour?"

"If it's not too much trouble."

"I don't get upstairs much, so that floor I'll leave to you to discover on your own."

As Kiera set down her cup, she rose and looked around the room. "It's so homey," she said, "how long have you lived here?"

"We bought the house about ten years ago. The last owner had died, and her only relative decided it was best to sell rather than hang onto it. She was young and had her whole life ahead of her. My Chester handled all the details, or at least, he had his financial people do it. We just bought it for cash and moved in."

This part of her story was news to me, and the details rang inside my head.

"Mrs. Wilkinson, do you know the name of the family you bought it from?"

"Oh, my, it's been some time. I think it was Tess... something. Oh, I just can't remember."

I felt my heart race as the words formed on my lips. "Was it Tessier?"

"Why, I think it was. How remarkable, Brian. However did you guess it?"

"Because, you're looking at the last of the Tessiers, right here."

We all turned to look at Janey Sullivan, she the ideal picture of innocence, the perfect blend of yesterday's memories and tomorrow's dreams. She gave me a look, her nose scrunched up when she was trying to understand.

"Janey, your Momma once lived here," I said.

———————————

Independence Day arrived, and with it came the annual Linden Corners celebration known as First Friday, hosted by George's Tavern. Which meant me, with a strong assist by Gerta Connors, who provided food and dessert, as well as, behind the bar, my father and, making a special appearance for the occasion, Mark Ravens.

"I wouldn't have missed this event," he said.

I was glad to have my friend and former relief bartender back where he belonged.

Among the crowd was his wife, Sara, along with their six month old boy, Harry, who had captured

Janey's attention. She missed her buddy, Jake, Cynthia and Bradley's son, who she had attached herself to like glue on paper. I'd be remiss in not missing the Knight's too; I'd never done a First Friday without them, and had it not been for Kiera, I might have withdrawn into my shell, a host with a lonely soul. Kiera was talking with my mother, the two of them seemingly thick as thieves and I had to wonder if that was a good thing. My mother had always taken a shine to Maddie, and she and Kiera were night and day, city and country. My mother straddled that fence these days, transitioning from society gal to farmer's wife. Was that the bouncy Green Acres theme song I heard in my head?

It was seven o'clock on that Saturday, with half the town already enjoying the day-long affair. Memorial Park was the ultimate destination, where some families had already set up grills and picnic blankets, getting perfectly situated for the night's expected fireworks; others hadn't yet ventured there, content sitting inside the tavern, positioned along the wood bar, enjoying a drink. Marla and Darla were positioned as they always were on First Friday, at the far edge of the bar, taking turns in knocking back shots of tequila. We all had our holiday traditions. As my eyes drifted away from them, I saw Martha hanging with Nora, the two ladies happy for the day off from their daily duties, and in the corner I saw Thomas, as well as some of the other residents from Edgestone, and I was pleased to see that they were taking under their wing Katherine Wilkerson. For too long she had lived alone in that rambling house, and now she was getting a taste of the community that awaited her after her move. I didn't see Chuck Ackroyd, but he'd been working nonstop this past week, he and his coworkers having done yeomen's work in getting up the framework of the cottages. I wouldn't blame him if he was asleep back at his house.

All in all, it was a great turnout. When I finished surveying the room, I walked back behind the bar, poured myself a seltzer.

"You are the weirdest tavern owner I've ever known," Chet said, remarking on my drink of choice. "I've never seen you take anything stiffer."

"I run the bar, I'm not a customer."

"Still, on our day of independence, you can relax. Let me buy you one, Brian."

"Thanks. Maybe when the inn is finished, then I'll have some champagne."

"Then I guess I'll have that beer I was going to buy you," he said, sliding his glass forward.

I refilled his glass, smiling as I did so. Chet was a good guy, and even though I thought he spent too much time here, who was I to argue with his patronage? He probably contributed half of our weekly profits.

"Okay, who else needs a drink here?" I asked.

But my father and Mark had everything under

control, both of whom were mixing, pouring, all while taking fresh orders and engaging the customers. Maybe I'd over-booked my staff, leaving me the odd man out. So I made my way across the room, checking in on Janey. She was holding Harry, cooing at him, scrunching her nose when he didn't react.

"Sara, he just sits there, he doesn't do anything," Janey said.

"Ha, come visit at two in the morning, you'll see he's plenty active. I think he's got more than a bit of his father's night owl in him," she said. "And given that I'm a morning person, it makes for an interesting schedule. Thank goodness for my mother, she takes the reins when I have to get up for work. The Five-O morning rush doesn't care you've been up half the night feeding a baby."

"Where is Denice?" I asked, referencing Sara's mother.

"With friends. Last I saw, over at Memorial Park. I think she needs a break from playing grandmother."

"How could she need a break? If I had a baby sister or brother, I'd never want to be away from them."

"Well," Sara said with a slight blush, "you might think differently after experiencing it."

"Plus Dad would have to get married, first," Janey said.

"Okay, I think I'm done with this conversation," I said. "Thanks, Sara. Janey, don't spend all your time here. Travis is somewhere, you and he like to hang out, don't you?"

"He's got friends his own age. They don't like a pest of a ten-year-old. Especially a girl."

Travis, Nora's son, was fourteen. I suppose Janey had a point.

I continued to play amiable host, stopping by and greeting the residents of Linden Corners, many of whom wanted an update on the progress down at the windmill, a subject I was only too happy to discuss. Not that they were potential guests necessarily, but it didn't help to spread the word and hopefully have a relative of theirs make a reservation. I assured all who asked that we were on target for the one-hundred fiftieth anniversary of the windmill. Another celebration to look forward to, they said. I moved on, finally finding my mother and Kiera. Kiera gave me a look that begged of being rescued, so I asked if I could borrow Kiera.

"She's not a library book," Didi said.

"Still, I like the cover," I said.

Kiera groaned, slapping me playfully on the arm. But she got up and joined me outside on the back porch, which at the moment was devoid of other partiers. Out of the corners of my eye I'd seen my mother join Nora and Martha, and I was happy to see her integrated so well into Linden Corner's society. She'd probably suggest they start a local chapter of the DAR, and I smiled at the thought of Didi Duncan becoming the First Lady of Linden Corners.

"Something funny?" Kiera said.

"My mother. I was just thinking how well she's adapted here. If you had told me a year ago that my parents would buy the farmhouse next door to mine, move here fulltime, and give up the high-profile life they'd always led, I would have asked if I'd been hit in the head and was hallucinating. For nearly three years I practically begged them to visit, and always something kept them away. Then, the moment they arrive, they're changing their life."

"For you," Kiera said.

"Please don't say that."

"Well, maybe you gave them the push they needed."

"What do you mean? What has my mother been filling your mind with?"

"You know, Brian, Didi is a strong woman, who doesn't let many things affect her. She's played the role of dutiful wife, hosted dinner parties and made a name for herself in society circles, all in the name of her husband's career. But there's a real woman beneath the façade. She loves Janey, you know that?"

"She calls her Jane," I said.

"Her way of grand-parenting. Let's face it, Brian, when Janey grows up, will she go by that name? It's cute, and it works now given her outgoing personality.

But one day...maybe not so. But that's a topic for another time. My original point about your mother, she's lived her life doing everything for her husband. Last year she almost lost him."

"She told you about the heart attack?"

Kiera nodded. "You don't spend all that time in your prime only to lose someone just as the golden years begin."

"Your parents?"

"Not yet ready for their golden years, but getting closer every day."

"Aren't we all," I said. "Will you invite them to the Windmill Inn debut?"

"We'll see," she said, non-committing.

"Don't want to talk about it?"

"We have enough drama. Let's just leave it you and me for a while, okay?"

"Sure, no problem."

There might be issues there, but as Kiera said, there were topics for another time. I wanted a return of her smile.

"I'm glad you're here," I finally said.

She smiled at me. "I'm glad I'm here, too."

I leaned forward and planted a kiss on her lips. She didn't pull back, and she certainly did not run away. She actually fell into my arms, and I caught her, held her, kissed her again, and as I did I felt magic swirl around us. Darkness was beginning to mover across the sky, the light of the sun hidden behind the western mountains, creating a blaze of orange streaks across the horizon. It was almost like the moment existed only for us, and I didn't want it to end. This was my fourth First Friday in Linden Corners, hard to believe, and it was the first one in which I'd had someone to share it with. Firsts indeed. I kissed her again, and when we parted the bright smile on her face matched mine.

"So," I said, additional words failing me.

"Yeah, so," she said.

"Not a bad conversationalist, huh?"

"A man of few words. And too many thoughts."

"I think you're getting to know me."

"You wear your heart on your sleeve, it's easy to see."

"You're not the first to tell me that. Hopefully the last."

Those were potent words, and I saw Kiera shift uncomfortably.

We should rejoin the party, I suggested, and she readily agreed, but for a moment neither of us moved. We just stared at each other, our hands still locked together, four arms like the sails of the windmill, happy to be quiet and unmoving for a time on the soft night. A sudden commotion and a scream inside changed all that, our connection broken in a heartbeat. I dashed back inside, heard the crash of glass against the floor. Running to the bar, pushing my way past a group of curious onlookers, I finally got a look at what had caused such drama.

My father was lying on the floor, his hand to his chest.

His eyes were wide, fluttering.

"Dad," I said, dropping to his side. "What's wrong...?"

"I...I can't breathe," he said, his face flush, sweat breaking out on his brow.

I sprang into action, asking someone to call for an ambulance. One of the guests here was a doctor, and he went over to my father to attend to him, and I watched, fear eating away at me. I held onto my mother, tight, as she wiped at tears that streamed down her cheeks. Time ground to a halt, a shroud hovering over the festivities. I stood, I waited, protecting my mother, and only after I felt another arm encircle me and I saw Kiera at my side did I realize that I had someone to comfort me as well.

I wished my father wore his heart on his sleeve, too, so we could see what was wrong.

———————————

In the distance I could hear the explosion of fireworks, and I could envision the bright colors that painted the sky, blues and golds, reds and greens, spirals of light spinning back down to the ground to a chorus of oohs and aahs. How I so desired to be there, on a blanket set upon the grass, with a lady named Kiera in my arms, a sweet-girl named Janey right beside us. Behind us, my parents, the complete family portrait, as Americana as you could get, and in Linden Corners, all that would be missing was the shadow of the windmill in the background.

Instead, we were in the waiting room at Columbia Medical Health down in Hudson.

My mother stood, staring out the window, Kiera with her arm around her. I sat beside Gerta, who had insisted on joining us. I knew why, even though her reasons had gone unspoken between us. Nora had taken Janey back to the Connors house, saying she would stay overnight with them, and I assured Janey everything would be fine and I would see her in the morning. The last place I needed to bring Janey was to the hospital, especially this one. This was where we had lost Annie; Janey was scared enough for her grandfather, she didn't need the reminder of her mother, lingering here until the infection claimed her. She'd hugged me so tight I felt my lungs constrict, and then I told her to be a good girl for Nora.

So here we sat, no news being good news, or so they say. It had been just about two hours since my father had been brought in by ambulance, my mother staying at his side the whole time. Kiera and I rode with Gerta in her car. As I stared forward, trying to push images of Annie out of my mind, I felt a hand upon mine. I turned and saw the comforting face of Gerta Connors.

"He'll be okay, Brian. I'm sure it was just a scare. He never lost consciousness."

"I hate this," I said, "not the waiting. The long goodbye."

"What do you mean?"

"Obviously my father has a heart condition. He suffered a heart attack last fall. He changed his routine, his diet...heck, he left the big city behind and became a country bumpkin. That does not appear to be enough. Eventually we will have to face that fact that he's dying, slowly perhaps, but the clock is ticking."

"Brian, even when you're dying, you're still living. Knowing his fate, it gives him—and those he loves—a chance to renew all that life is about. The good things, the loving things. How I lost George, so suddenly, I never got the chance to say a proper goodbye. He went off to work that day, just as he always did. And then he didn't come home." She paused, shaking her head. "I don't know why I'm telling you this. You were in the next room."

"He'd just poured a beer for me, even though I told him I didn't drink."

"But you drank it," she said.

I nodded. "It's the last one I've had."

"You have remarkable discipline."

"I'm just focused on other things," I said, "Janey. And now, Mom. Thanks for being here, Gerta, but if you want to go home, it's okay. There's no telling when we'll know anything."

"I'll stay," she said, with a warm smile that felt like an embrace.

I stood up, made my way over to the nurses' station, where a red-headed young woman sat behind the counter. She looked up sympathetically. Her tag read Jeanine.

"Any word?" I asked.

"The doctor will be with you shortly, Mr. Duncan."

I willed her words to be true, and soon enough they came to life. An older man with a beard of salt and pepper appeared around the bend in the corridor, a white coat, a chart in his hands, an unreadable expression on his tanned face. He asked for the Duncan family, and my mother turned just as I waved him to our side.

"I'm Dr. Savage," he said, by way of introduction. "I'm the attending cardiologist on staff."

"How is my husband," Mom asked, not wasting time on niceties.

He nodded his understanding and said, "Kevin is resting comfortably. We have him on an IV drip to get some fluid into him, and we also ran some tests. I'm happy to say he did not have a heart attack, though I do see damage from an earlier episode."

"Last fall," Mom said. "We saw his doctor in Philadelphia last month. He got a clean bill of health."

"Yes, he appears fine."

"So what caused him to react as he did? Dropping to the floor?"

"My guess? A combination of heat, exhaustion, and dehydration."

"You mean he exerted himself too much," Mom said.

"Not necessarily. Just a perfect storm of circumstances, and his body revolted. But not his heart," Dr. Savage assured us.

"Can I see him?"

"Of course. We'll keep him overnight for observation. You may stay with him if you like."

"I like," Didi Duncan said with her famed authority. "Brian, you don't have to stay. See to Janey, assure her that everything is fine. I'll let your father know you were here."

I began to protest but then decided not to add to her anxiety. I kissed her on the cheek, and watched as my mother followed Dr. Savage back from where he'd come. I turned to Kiera and Gerta, a sigh of relief easing the tension built up in my body.

"What do you say we bring this long day to a close?" I asked.

CHAPTER THIRTEEN

MIDNIGHT HAD LONG SINCE PASSED when we returned to Linden Corners. I drove Gerta's car back to the lot at the tavern, where my truck awaited me in the silence of the night. Gerta then assured Kiera and me that she was perfectly fine in driving the last mile back home, even at this late hour and I reluctantly let her. On the drive back from the hospital, we had called Nora to tell her the good news, where she informed us that Janey was fast asleep. No sense disturbing her now. I was instructed to follow her lead and go home and get sleep, too.

"Come get her first thing in the morning," Gerta told me before driving off. "Pancakes for breakfast all right with you?"

I smiled, and thanked her. "Janey will want them with strawberries," I said.

"Brian, am I ever out of strawberries?"

Gerta drove off, leaving me and Kiera together in the otherwise empty lot. I didn't know if First Friday had continued after we'd left, or if Mark had closed down and urged everyone to watch the fireworks in Memorial Park. All I knew now was that the tavern was as quiet, only the porch light offering a dim glow in the dark night. I liked how it reflected off Kiera's dark hair, wisps lightly dancing in the air.

"Thanks, Kiera. You've gotten more here than you signed up for."

"Do you mean tonight, or this whole Windmill Inn project?"

"Yeah, probably both."

She reached out, took my hand. "I'm glad your father is okay."

"But that episode is only going to send my mother into over-protective mode."

"You mean she wasn't already?"

I laughed aloud, my voice echoing in the quiet of Linden Corners at night. There was no one about on the streets, not a single car passing by, nor any late-night revelers still at the park, perhaps indulging in post-fireworks intimacy. Time belonged to us, and Kiera continued to hold my hand, and I wished for the frame to freeze, despite the heat that hung between us. I sensed it wasn't just from the temperature.

I learned forward and kissed her, something I enjoyed doing apparently.

"Thanks again," I said. "I should let you get some rest."

"Brian," she said, the tone of her voice intimate. "I'm not sure you should be alone. Not tonight."

Was that an invitation to join her upstairs, where she'd been staying on the many nights she didn't return to her apartment in Albany? Or was I supposed to sweep her off her feet and carry her back to the farmhouse? Too much time had passed since I'd felt this deeply about a woman, and here she stood before me like a shadowy vision. Did I reach out and take her into my arms, and if I did, would she disappear into the ether, a ghost-like presence like I'd seen that day of the Five-O party?

"I...Kiera, I don't want what happened tonight to create an artificial sympathy..."

"Brian, we both know what's going on between us. We both know what's inevitable. What better time than now, when we both have experienced just how tenuous time really is. You take your moments, you make them last for as long as you can."

My heart beat wildly inside my chest and I didn't know what to say.

"What you said earlier, that it's time to end this long day? Is that what you really want?"

I shrugged. "It's summer, I guess the days are supposed to be long," I said. "And hot."

Hot was how things went soon after, the two of us

locked in passionate kisses, our bodies tight against each other, arms bringing us so close we might as well have morphed into one. She was sweet-tasting, her scent intoxicating. Parting was difficult, but we could hardly continue here in the tavern's empty parking lot like a couple of teenagers. It would be the easiest thing in the world to take her upstairs to her apartment—the one which had been my first home in Linden Corners—but its bare rooms were impersonal, and so I asked her to come home with me.

She nodded her acceptance, smiling deeply.

I escorted her into the new truck, the engine catching immediately. Touching her cheek, I then shifted into gear and turned onto the dark, empty street, headlights guiding me. Crestview Road was not far, but in this moment I felt like it was pulling away at me, as though prolonging the agony of mine and Kiera's first time. Was the farmhouse ready for us? An idea formed in my head, and suddenly the turn off road appeared. I took it, then going up the driveway. I parked, we exited, and then as I took her hand in mine, I asked her to follow me around back.

"Brian Duncan, what are you thinking?"

"Only of you," I said, "and perfection. Which I can't seem to discern one from the other."

She tightened her grip on me, smiling. "Nicely said," she offered with a laugh.

We came to the old barn, and I led her inside. We

hadn't yet begun the restoration of the barn, especially given it was the storage area for the boards and other supplies being used for the building of the cottages, keeping them safe from the elements. I led her through the maze, where we came to the stairs that led to the second floor. Sensing our night had turned into an adventure, she took the lead, climbing the slats that were nailed to the wall. Upwards she went, me bringing up the rear, and at last we emerged through the hole in the floor and were lost in a world that was all ours. The farmhouse was quiet, as was my parents on the other side of the creek, and in the near distance, the windmill spun gently as it always did. I took Kiera into my arms, kissing her, tasting her, touching her.

She stepped back, unbuttoning her blouse as she did so. All I could do was watch as she let it fall to the floor in a willowy dance. I followed her lead, taking off my shirt, and I allowed it to join hers, pieces of ourselves merged. We came together again, our skin making first contact, the feel fiery and alive. I kissed her shoulder, even as I took hold of the clasp of her bra, felt it unhook. I peeled it off her and brought her closer to me, feeling her breasts press against my bare chest. Our kisses intensified, and we moved to a pile of old blankets that I kept stored up here. I spread them out before drawing Kiera down. I kissed her neck, her breasts, my tongue leading downwards. I heard her gasp.

Soon, she'd removed the remainder of her clothes, and I did the same, and for a precious gift given by time, we simply stared, our eyes locked on each other, our bodies craving contact. She was as beautiful as I'd imagined, inside and out, and I told her so and she kissed my lips, my neck, the center of my chest where my heart thrummed. I took a deep breath, and it was almost as thought I'd taken that breath for us both. She eased back down on the blankets, drew me to her, all of me.

Our love-making began with a quiet push, growing as passion consumed us.

I felt her fingers dig into my back, I felt her warm breath on my neck.

For so long, I'd maintained a distance with my own heart's desires, and at last I gave way to something deeper, my soul. Her touch urged me on, and we quickly grew into a rhythm that kept us in sync. Warm air and heated actions created a sheen of sweat on our skin, and her salty taste was matched only by her salty language. We built up to a moment of desperate release, and at last the moment happened, and I kissed her, hard, deep, and she responded in kind. Our bodies grew flush. A few moments later, we fell back against the blankets, both of us staring upwards at the wooden beams of the barn's ceiling.

I took another deep breath. Kiera kissed my chest, laughed but said nothing else.

We lay in silence for a while, fingers caressing shoulders, lips exchanging gentle kisses.

At last, I clambered up from the floor, took hold of her soft hand and guided her up too. Grabbing a blanket, I brought it with me, urging Kiera to follow me. I moved to the front of the barn and proceeded to open the hay door. The thick wood door opened wide, exposing us to the outside world, or maybe opening up the world to what we'd just experienced. Kiera stood before me, and I took the blanket and wrapped it around us, the warmth unnecessary in the summer heat, but comfort came in different forms. She leaned her head back against my shoulder, and she sighed with content.

"It's beautiful," she said.

The moonlight shimmered down on the land, and we could see the outline of the five cottages that would be the Windmill Inn, and further down the hill, lay its inspiration, my dream. The windmill itself, and from where I stood, it was waving toward us, almost as though it was giving its blessing to this next chapter in its existence. The windmill has been built out of love, and it had inspired other loves, but it had also seen its share of tragedies, and yet it continued to spin, and to give new life and future dreams potential. You just had to believe.

I turned Kiera to me and I echoed her words. "Yes, beautiful, indeed."

"I think my life just changed tonight," she said.

"Oh, mine changed the moment I saw you sketching your ideas on the hill," I said.

"Brian Duncan, what's next?"

"I believe we have an inn to finish building," I said. "And then I think, I mean, we have something else to build."

"A life?"

"Do they teach you that in architecture school?"

"No, Brian, I'm learning about life from you. What you've built here, in Linden Corners, your sacrifice in raising Janey, the way you have breathed new life into small-town America, everything that you have accomplished since you came to town, it's something to envy. As wounded as you may have been by the direction your life was going in, what you did was take charge. You might have run away from your problems, but what you ran into was your destiny."

I grew quiet, thinking about her words. Linden Corners had captured me, and Janey's big heart had consumed me. I thought of Annie, of all she taught me and how much I lost when she took to the currents of the wind. I knew she came back, I always felt her presence swirling on our property, and I hoped she knew how much she meant to me, even as I tried, strived, to finally move forward. For three years I'd put my life on hold for the sake of others, and I regretted not a minute of it. But feeling Kiera in my arms, hearing how much she understood my inner soul, I realized that when I awoke tomorrow the many questions I usually faced would feel answered.

Still, there was still one last piece of the past I had to excise, and I said so.

"Brian, do what you need to do. Close the door on whatever you need to."

"It's not in Linden Corners," I said.

She nodded; she understood the scenario without me having to give voice to it now. She just said, "I'm here. I'll be waiting. I like what we've built."

We remained standing, staring, at the ever-turning sails of the windmill for a time, and soon the crack of dawn was nearing, and we knew we needed our rest, it was going to be a busy day, so we finally made our way to the farmhouse, and I invited her into my house, my room, my bed, and before we slept we made love once last time, the two of us alone again, the forces of the outside world forgotten.

I first came to New York City with ambition my only true possession, and for years it fueled me more than any jolt of morning coffee could, joining the huge throngs of people on the subway, all of us pursuing the American Dream in the nation's biggest city. You could almost feel the city's pulse beneath the crowded sidewalks, almost as if the released energy made you walk that much faster. For years I thrived on such an existence, meeting new friends, furthering business contacts, working late hours in search of that elusive raise or promotion, all the while hoping that amidst this city of strangers you would find the one person who would personalize it.

One day I thought I had.

My friend John Oliver had been hosting a party at his apartment on the Upper East Side, he'd invited coworkers and old college pals, the latter of which included me. It was a spring night, a Saturday, and as we'd knocked back beers as though we were still in throes of academia—we were on the wrong side of thirty at this point—I saw the door open and in walked this woman, she with two friends, neither of them I really gave notice to. My heart skipped a beat as I shook hands with her, telling her it was nice to meet her. Her name was Maddie, and when I asked her if she was from the South, her lovely face soured. She confessed she was trying to lose it, to better fit in the shark-infested world of public relations. We realized we were in the same business, so our common ground led us to a date, a second one, and soon we were not only in a relationship, I was recommending her for a job at my company, the Beckford Group. She got it, we worked great together, it all seemed as if we were building a life. I'd even bought a ring. Life was in a collision course with happiness.

I'm still uncertain when it was that fate stepped in—when I first met Maddie, or when I handed her resume to my cutthroat boss, or when Justin Warfield interviewed her, but no matter, what happened, happened, it was supposed to happen that way. Because hours away, in a small town that I'd never heard of, another course of fate was rushing toward its conclusion, and a little girl would be left alone in this world, adrift, facing teary uncertainty with each waking morning. I'd thought it before and I thought it now: in some strange, roundabout way, Maddie Chasen was responsible for Janey Sullivan being the center of my world, and if I had to relive it all, there's only one thing I would change.

Annie.

Now, it seemed I had Kiera, but I felt I still had to close a chapter in my life.

Maddie.

Which is why, on this Monday morning, mid-July, I was headed back to New York City.

Right where my story had begun.

I'd again taken the train, and I walked the streets now on what turned out to be a horridly humid day. I felt the sweat on my brow and run down my back after walking just two blocks, headed north from Penn Station. An overnight bag rested on my shoulder, adding to my misery. The air was as stale as any summer I remembered, and I missed the open land of Linden Corners and its near-constant breeze. But I had a mission to conclude, so I forged ahead, my shoes clacking hard against the concrete. By the time I arrived at Eighth Avenue and 51th Street, I was dripping, and I ducked into a pub called the House of Brews, savoring the cool air-conditioning. It was just after the noon hour and I sat at the bar, where I ordered a seltzer. Perhaps something stronger would have settled the nerves rising inside me, but it was best to keep my emotions in check.

I slapped down a ten dollar bill, got back change and left a generous tip. We bartenders do that. Then, I washed up in the restroom and headed back out into the heat. It felt like ninety degrees and I was glad my destination was around the corner. I caught the light, crossed Eighth, and made my way past the Gershwin Theatre, coming to the corner and walking up the steps which gained me entrance into the lobby of Paramount Plaza, a high rise office building that was eerily familiar and where the offices of Grady, Ebersold, and Dinegar were housed. It was a large public relations firm, and I found it ironic that they had taken the entire floor that had previously housed the Beckford Group, where I worked. Coming full circle, indeed. I was here for my own public relations, and truth be told, I wasn't exactly expected.

Thankfully the lobby was cool. I settled in to wait, easing the bag off my shoulder, and in order to fit in and not gain undue attention, I took out a small cell phone. I hardly used it. In place of fancy technology, Linden Corners used the Five-O diner and George's Tavern and other businesses where people could meet and, dare I say, talk. Face to face. Given my surrounding, such an idea seemed positively antiquarian. I watched as men and women walked past me, their ears glued to smartphones, talking, texting, generally not paying attention to anything around them. Which at the moment, thankfully, included me. I was never more grateful for the intimacy of Linden Corners and all I'd found there.

The lobby was large, with high ceilings and large canvases of art adding color. A bank of sleek metal counters were spread out before me, a host of uniformed security men behind them. If you were going upstairs, you needed an existing appointment and had to be announced. I'd done no such thing, and I was here on a hunch, anticipating a pattern I'd known about Maddie Chasen from when we worked together. She insisted on getting out of the office for lunch, and it didn't matter the time of year, the weather outside. She refused to be cooped up all day. The time was twelve-thirty. I leaned against the wall, pretending to play with my phone, but all the time listening for the ping of the elevators and watching as the lunch mob descended from above and out into the melting streets of Manhattan.

The minutes clicked away, hundreds of people passed me by. None of them Maddie.

Finally, at ten minutes after one, I saw her. And almost like clockwork, she saw me.

Her eyes widened, and she stopped in her pretty tracks, a couple of people bumping into her. I made a move toward her but she shook her head, and I wasn't sure if that meant I should leave and forget this fool's errand, but then she came over to me. She'd only gone about fifty feet and appeared out of breath. I suppose my presence had knocked the wind out of her. Well, so had her disappearance done the same to me. Maddie Chasen and I were starting off on equal footing.

"Brian," she said, "what are you doing here?"

"I had to come to New York on business," I said, a half-truth. "So, uh, surprise."

"You could have called, or texted."

"Not my speed. Maybe a letter would have worked."

She frowned. "Is that what you came to say? To rub my face in the way I left?"

"Actually, no. Look, Maddie, let's not be antagonistic here. Too much as happened, some of it good. I'd like to remember those times."

"Ok, fair enough," she said, but even as she spoke her words sounded hollow. Her green eyes danced around the lobby, as though she feared being noticed by a co-worker.. Or maybe she was expecting a friend to meet her for lunch.

"This won't take long," I said. "Do you have plans, or can you join me for a sandwich?"

"Uh, no, Brian. I have an appointment. Can we meet later, after I get out of work?"

"I'm going back tonight, Janey's waiting for me."

"Janey, or Kiera?"

I'd struck an exposed nerve, and her abrupt letter made more sense. Had Nora been right, and Maddie had witnessed me kissing Kiera the night of the ground-breaking ceremony? "Is that why you left so suddenly that night? Not even saying a proper good-bye? Because of Kiera?"

"Well, you were a bit busy saying hello to her, right there at your precious windmill," she said, her tone harsh.

I nodded. "Guess I'm defenseless. I did the same to you. No explanation."

"Right. You just walked out. You didn't give me a chance to explain."

A simple kiss was not as severe a betrayal as sleeping with the boss, but I wasn't going to split hairs on the nuances of such a word. Maddie hadn't stayed around, she didn't know that Kiera had gone running off right after that kiss. For all she knew, Kiera and I consummated our relationship that night, when, indeed, it had been just a couple nights ago.

"I'm sorry," I said.

"Brian," she said, again looking around. She appeared nervous. "What happened between us, then and now, is over. We both made mistakes, and neither of us felt compelled to find out why we did what we did. I accept your apology, and I wish only the best for you. But, really, you caught me unaware and I really must get a move on. Lunch time is only an hour, they run a tight ship at the firm."

Again, she glanced around nervously, and I surmised she was trying to get rid of me. Should I prolong this encounter and see what transpired, or just leave? Finally close the book on whatever we had shared. But I hadn't said all I had come to say, and I knew this was my only opportunity to clear the air.

"Just another minute, Maddie..."

"Brian, really..."

"I also wanted to thank you."

"Thank me?" she asked, a derisive snort escaping her. "For what, driving you from New York and into your little world of the windmill?"

"No, not back then. It's what you did for me this year," I said, earnestly. "You woke me from self-induced complacency. Seeing you at John's wedding, I realized we'd all moved on—heck, if John can get hitched, and you could return to New York and restart your career, then maybe I could finally do something for myself. You set me on the path for creating the Windmill Inn. It's strange, how a simple comment can alter a man's life."

"I'm happy for you, Brian. That's all I ever wanted for you. What we shared this year, it meant so much, but both of us knew we were fooling ourselves. You were never going to move back to New York, and I really didn't see myself donning jeans and flannel shirts, shucking out the barn. When I asked to come to Linden Corners for a visit, I suppose I just wanted to make sure that you were truly happy, and I got my answer. But it's more than Linden Corner's having changed you; you have changed that town. The residents not only adore you, they depend upon you. You're their heart."

I shook my head, downplaying her words. Compliments never went down easy with me.

"Thank you for saying that. I guess, well, we've said all we can say."

"Take care of yourself, Brian. And Janey. And if you stop acting like a fool, Kiera too."

I was about to open my mouth and reveal that Kiera and I had become a couple, not to rub my newfound happiness at her, but to assure her that the pain we'd both endured had been worth it. A ping of the elevator stopped me, or maybe it was the way her eyes darted about, then widened. My own eyes followed hers, and that's when they fell upon the moving figure of a man approaching us. He was dressed in a pricey blue suit, a crisp white shirt with a couple buttons undone displaying a rich triangle of chest hair. His hands were holding a freshly removed tie. I couldn't believe what I was seeing, the two of them together. Again.

"Well, Duncan, what a surprise. Thought you'd moved to Holland."

I wouldn't rise to his bait. "Justin, how interesting to find you here, too."

"Not so, I work here."

"You work..." I turned to Maddie, who simply nodded, her eyes shaded.

"Maddie and I ran into each other a couple of months ago at some fancy new restaurant opening. We got to talking, and one thing led to another...you know how it goes," he said, his smarmy smile not having lost any of its impact in three years. "Soon I found myself being head-hunted by her firm. Beckford is small potatoes. But fear not, Bri, we're not working on the same accounts—just on the same floor. So, Maddie, dear, shall we get a move on? Sorry I'm late, a client I just couldn't get off the phone. Brian, good to see you. Be a stranger."

Justin Warfield slipped an arm around Maddie's waist, his touch as familiar as ever. As if he'd not made his point already, he leaned down and kissed the top of her head. I continued staring, Maddie staring down at the floor for an escape from her embarrassment. Her expression said it all, and it ended it all. Everything. The past, the present. I realized I would never see her again. I hoped I would never see Justin again, too.

They left the lobby, Maddie asking him what he wanted for lunch.

I didn't hear his reply, as he whispered into her ear. She laughed. "Justin, that's not on the menu."

They disappeared into the streets of Manhattan, leaving me in the cool lobby. I grabbed my bag and I too swirled my way through the revolving door, a changed man from the one who had been transported inside nearly an hour ago. As though by going through it, time had sped up, but in my mind, the image of Justin and Maddie sent me into a time warp. I walked in a daze, down Broadway, not paying attention as cabs honked at me as I darted across a street against the light. I knew I had to focus. I'd achieved what I'd needed to, and in the process Maddie had done her part in ensuring our lives were no longer connected.

My feet controlled my brain right now, and I ended up on 47th Street between Fifth and Sixth. I felt the sweat on my brow bead again, wiped it as I continued down the block. Why I was going here failed me, since I already knew old Eli had closed up his shop. No longer could he offer me advice on my life, not that he ever knew how much he had influenced me. I guess I needed to stand in the shadow of his store one last time and remember. So there I stood, but it wasn't closed. I saw a younger man with a long beard behind the counter, polishing some piece of jewelry. I stared at the sign above the entrance. Aaron's Jewelry it stated in simple type, only accompanied by a phone number.

I entered the store and he looked up.

"Good afternoon, sir. Can I help you? A nice trinket for a special lady?"

"No, uh, not today. I wonder, could I ask you a question? About the man who used to own a shop in this location."

"Oh, Eli. My uncle."

"Your uncle?"

"Yes. He retired last year. But I only opened up two months ago."

"Is he..?" I didn't want to say the word.

"Oh, no, Uncle Eli is well. Old, tired maybe, he now spends his days listening to my Aunt Ruth and I think on some days he misses coming to the store. But it just became too much, the daily grind. Sometimes you have to give up something you love in order to bring happiness to others, that's what he told me."

"Sounds like him. Wise."

"Did you know him?"

"Not really. He once sold me a dream," I said.

Not it was his turn to laugh. "That sounds like him, too."

"Would you be able to get him a message?"

"I can do you one better," Aaron said, picking up

the telephone. "I'm sure he'd love to talk to you, if you're willing to trek uptown."

I knew about treks. How far could this one take me?

Turned out, plenty, and I wasn't just talking mileage.

Aaron estimation of uptown was understated.

I'd been planning on staying overnight in Brooklyn with John and Anna, whom I hadn't seen since the wedding, and had only spoken with a couple times since then. But as much as my trip was about bringing a final close to me and Maddie, I was ensuring my friendship with John endured. But Brooklyn would have to wait, as I traveled to yet another borough: the Bronx. The trip took a while, as I rode the #1 train to the last stop at 242nd Street and Broadway. I don't ever remember having come up here in all my years of living in the city, and as I rode the elevated subway—as Janey would say, an oxymoron—I was amazed at how different it felt up here. Smaller stores, discount retailers, Irish pubs and restaurants, but bigger chains were prevalent as well. Once the train pulled into the final stop, I walked down the metal stairs back to street level, emerging on the western edge of Van

Cortlandt Park, a wide expanse of green lawn that rivaled Central Park. I looked at the directions Aaron had provided me, hopped a waiting #9 bus, and kept a close eye on the next few stops. We weren't far from the Westchester border. The sky was brighter, the canyons of Manhattan far off. I got off the bus at a street named Moshulu Avenue, crossed the wide boulevard that was Broadway, and started up the road, a hilly stretch with a mix of delis, barber shops, insurance agents, along with residences. I had been told I would run into a side street called Liebig Avenue, and it was there that I would find Eli Allon.

I was staring at the piece of paper, then back up again as I looked for the right address. But then I realized I didn't need it. I recognized the man immediately, sitting on a wicker rocking chair on the front porch of a brick house. He was dressed in a short sleeve dress shirt, a pair of suspenders attached to his gray pants. As I opened the gate and walked up the path, he smiled at me, his weathered face brightening at the sight of me. In his lap he held a thick book, a marker indicating he hadn't gotten very far.

"Mr. Allon?" I asked.

"You always called me Eli. All of my customers did. They were like family."

"Of course. Eli, I'm Brian Duncan. Not sure if you remember me."

"I ran my little store for forty years, I serviced

thousands of customers," he said, "and if I didn't know a name, I surely knew a face. Come join me up here, Brian, we'll have a chat about windmills and such." He patted the hardcover book, his gesture its own invitation.

"You have a remarkable memory," I said.

"What I remember is a face saddened by loss," he said. "I see a flicker in your eyes."

"You're a very intuitive man as well."

"Forty years, you get to know how people tick." He patted his thin chest. "In here."

I took the seat next to him, another wicker chair; this one stationary. I was happy to have my overnight bag off my shoulder. "You traveled down to the city every day for forty years from all the way up here?"

He nodded. "A long trip, I admit, and as the years progressed it started getting longer. It's not that my body cannot handle the work anymore, but as the young ones say, the commute was taking its toll. A smart man knows when it's time to alter the routine. Now, most days I sit on this porch, taking in the sunshine, listening to the birds, taking a walk up to Riverdale Avenue a few blocks away and stopping for a bagel and some company. Of course, once winter arrives, I'll have to change all that again. Life is all about adjustments."

"And your wife?"

"She does what she's always done. Worry about me. Now she does it locally."

I smiled, yet a pang of jealousy hit me. "How long have you been married?"

"Fifty seven years this coming fall, November fourth."

"I'm sure your wife appreciates that you remember," I said, giving me a launching pad for my visit. "Speaking of, how is it you remembered me? When your nephew called, you didn't hesitate in telling him it was fine to send me here for a visit. As though you knew exactly who it was."

"I had a hunch," he said, and again I saw his finger rub the spine of the book.

"Well, whatever part of the universe brought us to this moment, I'm grateful for it."

"You have something on your mind, Brian Duncan?"

"I really just wanted to thank you," I said, the words sounding strange on my tongue. Not that I didn't believe them, it's just that this man and I had only interacted for a combined thirty minutes in our lives and yet he'd made a significant impact. "Almost four years ago, I wandered into your store with a lovely woman on my arm..."

"A blonde woman, I remember her accent. Southern, but trying to disguise it."

He really was remarkable. Like I was sitting beside a medium.

"We perused the selections of rings, Maddie

pointing to a couple that caught her eye."

"Caught her heart," he said.

"I'm sorry, what?"

"Yes, your eye catches it first, but it's merely taking a picture for the remainder of you. It seeps into your heart, and your soul. The sparkle a gem creates is one of a kind, its effect unique, as unique as the person gazing upon it. I can tell when a person had made such a connection—the eyes linger, the photograph develops inside you. Once you see it, there's no denying its draw. That's how I survived on a street filled with so many stores. They sold jewelry, I sold..."

"Dreams," I said.

"Like wishes, they don't all come true," Eli said.

"I came back and bought the ring that struck Maddie's heart," I said.

"And just a few months later, you were back, without the girl, but with the ring."

"I needed to return it."

"But you didn't."

I shifted in my seat, bent down to the overnight bag. From a front compartment, I pulled out a ring box, whereupon I set it on the table between us. I sensed the felt glowed, as though the ring inside it was a talisman, a symbol of the possibilities of life. But to me it represented the wrong path. Eli reached over and held the box in his hands, but just as I'd not opened it in the three-plus years since mine and Maddie's breakup—it had been in the boxes I'd shipped up a few months ago--neither did he flip the lid. Perhaps in his experience he knew not to tempt fate, to invite Pandora to the party. Then he did the unexpected. He handed it back to me, and when I took it in my hands, I felt the heat, almost like it was pulsing.

"Never blame the stone," he said.

Wise words again, and any I might have had in response seemed insignificant.

"Keep the ring, Brian."

"I could never give it to another," I said.

"No, I don't suppose you could. But one day, perhaps long after you and I are gone from this fine world, it will be discovered, and it will be treasured. Not unlike our beloved windmills, eh?"

"I found one," I said, "A windmill. A real one. I'd never have stopped if not for the words you spoke to me that day. All of us, we must tilt at windmills, that's what you said. Eli, I found a life new in the land of the windmill, and for so long, yes, I tilted at it, but I wasn't really fighting the building, I was at war with myself. The windmill tamed me. It inspired me. It breathed, it spun, and as a result so did I."

He patted the book. That's when I looked at the spine. Don Quixote. Cervantes. Did Eli really remember me, or was his use of the windmill metaphor something he used on everyone? I felt a hint of betrayal wash over me; had I put too much credence in his words? Had I allowed a trite line that a businessman used to sell engagement rings to transform my life? Had my life's transformation been built on a lie?

"I read it once a year," he said. "It speaks to me."

"And you used it, you manipulated me."

"Oh, no, Brian Duncan. You are seeing things wrong. But it's okay, you were wounded; perhaps you still are. Yes, I have said those words to others, but herein lies the difference: many people go through life with their ears closed. They are not receptive to change. They don't listen. You, on the other hand, Brian Duncan, you not only heard my words but you embraced them. In finding your windmill, it proves that, despite what had happened between you and this Maddie, you hadn't shut down, not your mind, and not your heart." He paused, allowing his words to once again sink into my pores, to rush through my bloodstream. "You are done tilting, you say? What is it now that you're doing?"

"Chasing windmills," I said.

He nodded. "Tell me more," he said. "I feel our business is not yet complete."

And so we sat, and we talked, and then the night began to take its inevitable claim on the day, and still we sat, and we broke bread together, where I met his beautiful wife, Ruth, who served dinner and filled my soul with stories of their life, stories I would take home to Linden Corners and forever relish. Seeing these two precious people, gems themselves, share their life together, reading their minds, finishing their sentences, I thought about the ring that accompanied me on this journey, and what it had meant. A symbol of what Eli and Ruth had, one I'd always desired.

When I finally left, shortly after eight that night, Eli walked me back onto the porch.

"Come to Linden Corners, Eli," I said. "Stay at the Windmill Inn. For your anniversary. Be my special guest."

He nodded but didn't commit. "The wind has already seen fit to blend our lives, even for a wisp, Brian Duncan. Perhaps that is enough. Tomorrow holds its own secrets, and we want to know them. That's what keeps us waking up with sun."

CHAPTER FOURTEEN

"HAVEN'T WE done this before?"

"Six months ago," I said.

"Seems like a lifetime."

"So was this trip."

"You find what you were looking for, Windmill Man?"

I smiled, it was nice being on familiar turf. "That, and more. More than I bargained for. More than I expected."

"Is that good or bad?"

"Both, kind of in between."

"Okay, if you're going to speak in riddles..."

"Nora?"

"Yes, Brian?"

"Just drive."

She did as asked, concentrating on the road out of Hudson, from where she'd picked me up at the Amtrak train station. Life had been a series of déjà vu moments the past two days—Maddie and Justin, Eli and his wise advice, a laughter-filled stroll down the past with my friend John--so it was only fitting that it continue as I made my return to Linden Corners, ready to put away those repeats and return to original programming.

Our conversation resumed as we hit the county roads.

"So, did you see Maddie?"

"Sure did." My tone dripped with sarcasm.

"Too much of her?"

"Maybe if I'd arrived a half hour later, and knew where she was going to be."

"Riddles again?"

"I staked her out in her office building's lobby, and we talked. But she was waiting for an old friend of ours."

Nora's eyes left the road for a long moment, focused on me. "For once I don't think I want to hear this."

"Concentrate," I said. "But yeah, that slime ball Justin Warfield. He strutted about like the macho jerk he is, saying he and Maddie ran into each other recently. He insinuated they resumed their relationship that night, and yesterday, he was hooking with up her... what do they call them? Nooners?"

She nodded her understanding. "It's probably for the best, Brian. You know it's over. For good."

I said nothing, allowing her words to drift out the open window and take to the wild wind. Wherever they ended up, they were gone from my life; I would no longer let them linger inside me soul. I stared out the window, silent again and Nora respected it.

At some point during this past spring, bulldozers had come and leveled the land where the Solemn Nights Motel stood, its burned out shell gone and replaced by an open field which today, as we drove past it, showed signs of renewal. Tufts of grass grew up among broken concrete, and who knew, maybe someone would come one day and buy the land and rebuild. A little competition for the Windmill Inn wouldn't be such a bad idea. Being the only game in town meant you were a winner by default.

As we hit the village limits of Linden Corners, we quickly came upon the business district, where Nora pulled into the driveway of the Victorian, and it was there that I noticed a slight change here as well. Just how long had I been gone? Little more than twenty-four hours, really, but in that time it felt as though Linden Corners had grown up a bit, but maybe it had been this way for months and I was only now just waking up from my own life. On her front lawn was a new sign, much larger than the shingle that announced "A Doll's Attic." A hand-painted sign read: "A Doll's Attic: A Purveyor of Antiques & Nostalgia." I tossed Nora a look.

"All those tuna fish lunches we shared, pouring my heart out to you about Maddie and Kiera," I said, as we got out of the car and meandered over to the sign, "and meanwhile, you were holding out on me. Don't get me wrong, I think it's the right direction to the take the shop, but I could have helped..."

She stood before the sign, almost posing before it, a proud smile on her face. "Brian, you're not the only one whose had to face the difficulties of making over your life. Besides, you had your hands full with the plans for the inn. But to say you didn't inspire me to rethink my approach would be a lie. Elsie's passing got my mind to thinking, and then, icing on the cake, the most unthinkable happened next."

"Which was?"

"In her will, Elsie left me the building, and all of its contents."

"That's amazing. But didn't Elsie have anyone else...?"

She shook her head. "Apparently not. The Masters family ended with her. She wrote a note to me, saying she could think of no one else she wanted to entrust the Masters' legacy. I appreciated the contributions her family made to Linden Corner's history; and she thought I could keep that alive while adding to the Connors family's future. I haven't told my mother yet, and I hope you'll keep it quiet until I do, but I'm thinking of moving upstairs."

Nora and her son, Travis, had been living with Gerta since they had moved back a year and half ago. Seems we were all changing, answering the call, even long after it had gone to voicemail. But see, that was the thing, you could preserve those messages, keep them until you were ready to act upon them. Nora was, just as I was. We weren't alone, it turned out. As Nora started up the steps of her business and future home, I followed after her, only to be met on the porch by Kiera, who apparently had been inside the old Victorian waiting for us. I smiled at seeing her and she mirrored mine, and then we kissed briefly. It was sweet and tender, a silent exchange of having missed each other passing between us.

I gave Nora a look, because she didn't seem all that surprised.

"We had dinner yesterday, while you were in New York," Kiera explained.

Nora grabbed my hand and squeezed it. "I'm happy for you. For you both."

"Thanks. Now, is there a reason you brought me here instead of to the farmhouse? And is Kiera's being here not such a coincidence?"

"He's grown very impatient since building that inn of his," Nora said. "He used to just let the day dictate his actions. Back-seat Brian."

With each passing month, my nicknames had grown increasingly worse.

"He's on a deadline, you know how men get," Kiera said.

"You know, I am standing right here," I said.

Both women laughed and I got the sense their dinner last night had gone on for a time, and probably involved a bottle of wine or two. Glad I'd missed it. If they talked about me in the third person in front of me, I can only imagine what damage was done when I wasn't present. Still, I was glad they had bonded, especially if all I'd given thought to on the train ride back from the city came to fruition. But that would all have to wait. Nora invited us onto the porch, where four chairs were set up around her small metal table; an antique I hoped she never sold. This was our spot, and I treasured our lunches together, always a Tuesday, just as today was. Kiera returned from the inside with a pitcher of lemonade with fresh lemon slices among the ice, and wrapped sandwiches and pickles from the Five-O. On the current of the wind I thought I smelled bacon, but of course, that could have come from the exhaust from the diner itself. Turned out, that wasn't the case.

"What's the occasion?" I asked.

"A celebration," Nora said, "except we're still waiting on one of our lunch guests."

Of course, there had been four chairs.

Nora disappeared into the store, leaving the two of us alone. Kiera poured our drinks as I came up behind her and asked if she knew what was going on. I could smell her perfume, and it made me wish I'd not gone running off to New York so soon after our first night together. Confidence in relationships were not my strong suit, and to have given our tenuous time such an early test was tempting fate. She just brushed it off.

"Nora's being very secretive," she said, "wouldn't even drop a hint last night. I imagine it has to do with the job I hired her for."

"Your ancestry?"

As if by saying the word, I'd conjured our final guest, my question answered. Thomas Van Diver approached, slowly ambling down the sidewalk. I dropped down to the pathway to Nora's, concern of how aged he looked. He was eighty-six, and as well enough as he got around, time had a way of speeding up the years when you'd gone golden. He waved me off and I respected his wishes. He trundled up the steps with the aid of the railing, and then took a deep breath, the red polka-dot bow-tie at his neck lose around his skin.

"How are you feeling, Thomas?" I asked.

"I got up this morning. I got myself here. I'd say time was being good to me today."

"Thomas, come have a seat," Kiera said, and when she approached, he was happy to allow her to escort him to a waiting chair. Nothing like the attentions of a pretty lady to suddenly admit to his frailties and enjoy the attention. At last, Nora returned, a file fold-er in her hands. This wasn't just our casual weekly lunch; this was business, and she was not only pre-pared, she was excited.

"Okay, good. We're all here. Have a seat. Thomas, thank you coming."

"You took me away from sitting around. How dare you."

We all laughed, even as we took our sandwiches and unwrapped them. The Five-O did a mean BLT, adding a slice of Swiss to it, and then grilling the entire thing, giving the bread a nice brown crust. A generous amount of bacon highlighted the sandwich. After all, it was the first listed ingredient. Thomas licked his lips.

"What a rare treat," he said.

So we dined and we made small talk, our conversa-tion peppered with questions about my trip. I avoided talk of Maddie, and to discuss the meaning behind my visit with Eli would take too long, so I kept the focus on how well John and Anna were doing, the happy couple living in a house next door to her parents in Brooklyn, and how the entire family had, last night, gathered for a huge pan of lasagna.

"I asked John and Anna if they would come to the grand opening of the inn," I said. "They will be here."

"That's great, Brian," Nora said. "They are sort of responsible for the inn. Going to the city last winter for their wedding kind of set the whole thing in motion."

Fortunately I had a large piece of sandwich in my mouth, so I didn't have to disagree.

What I added was, "Finally, John will come to Linden Corners and see I'm not a farmer."

We finished our sandwiches, refilled our glasses, and then Nora got down to business.

She cleared her throat, almost as if getting ready to address a jury, and said, "I used to think that being a defense attorney was the height—and highlight— of my professional life. Nothing got my blood going than when I was in a courtroom, facing the prosecution and doing all I could to disapprove their case. To speak before a judge and have him or her side with me. Little victories on the way toward a larger one. In life, you have to be ready to adapt, and did I ever, when I came home to Linden Corners. Friends back in Chicago told me I was nuts to give it all up, but I did, and here I am, Travis and I are making a new life. But what I found along the way was that if you really want to understand where you were going in life, you had to understand its past. Living with my mother for the past year and a half has taught me so much. I've probably learned more from her as an adult than I did as a child."

The three of us just sat silently, silently taking in her message and waiting for what came next.

"Okay, sorry to go off like that, I just had to set the

stage. Kiera, a few weeks ago you came to me with a request, not unlike one that Thomas had for me when he returned to Linden Corners. How funny that both of your stories would coincide."

"So, it's true?" I asked, "Kiera is a Van Diver?"

"Brian, do you understand the art of storytelling? Don't flip to the last page."

I silenced myself by taking a prolonged sip of lemonade. I couldn't help my anticipation, though, how amazing would it be that the woman who had helped me bring the Windmill Inn to life was doing so, not because it was her job, but because it was her familial destiny. I'd found Linden Corners, and Thomas and Nora had returned to it, and now here was Kiera's turn, and as I gave her a look, she smiled my way and took hold of my hand. I squeezed it, support for her in what was about to be revealed.

Nora opened the file folder, put on a pair of glasses, and began to explain.

"The Van Diver family came to the Hudson River Valley in the early eighteen hundreds, having arrived from Europe. Linden Corners was barely a blip on the landscape at that time, but gradually it began to form, and the Van Divers were instrumental in creating a close-knit world of immigrants. They lived off the land, even as they built up around it, and soon Linden Corners came into being. Chief among those early developers was Hans, the patriarch of the Van Diver family, who, along with his wife, Verda, raised three children: oldest son, Charles, middle son, Anders, and the youngest, a girl, Sarah. In fact, it was Sarah who was one of the owners of this house in which we sit, she being one of the three ladies who ran Masters' Rooming House. Charles, the oldest, was known as the dreamer, and it was he who was responsible for the building of the windmill. He built it for a girl, only to lose that girl when she returned to the old country. Charles never forgot her, and the windmill served as a constant reminder. But he did eventually marry and have children, all of whom lived in Linden Corners."

She paused, checking our faces to see if we were with her.

"We know about Sarah, and course, Charles. What happened to Anders, the middle son?"

"Anders Van Diver left for the city when in his early twenties, and for a time he disappeared off the face of the earth. But in checking with various records agencies, I found mention of an Anders Van Diver on the west coast, specifically the Pacific Northwest."

"My grandfather was a fisherman in Seattle," Kiera said, "Also named Anders."

Nora nodded. "Indeed. Himself a grandson, named after his grandfather."

Kiera drew in a breath. "So it's true."

Nora nodded. "The Elder Anders had a son, and subsequently that son had three children. Among them was his oldest, whom he named in honor of his recently departed grandfather. So, the younger Anders, he married had two children, one of them he named Sarah in memory of the aunt he never met.

"My mother," Kiera said, "Sarah Van Diver. Until she married my father." Kiera stopped, her mind no doubt filled with faces, of her past, of the past that preceded her, thinking about her unknown family that came before her. "We never heard much about my mother's side of the family. The Bowens were many, and they were nearby, all over Central New York. To travel back to the West Coast, it was too costly, and besides, I think my mother was happy with her new family. But, Nora, you have no doubt? I'm descended from the Van Divers of Linden Corners."

"Without a doubt," Nora said.

"Which makes us…cousins, I guess," Thomas said.

"This is remarkable," Kiera said. "Isn't it funny, it's almost like life meant to take me here."

She paused, and we all did. We allowed her to absorb the past and make it part of her.

"And I have you to thank, Brian."

I wanted to tell her destiny deserved all the credit, having led her down a path these past years, the wind gradually grabbing hold of her and taking her further east, to Albany and to a firm that would one day land an account about an old windmill and a man who dreamed of spinning its dreams toward tomorrow. It was not unlike the same course I'd followed. Here I was, and here she was, our lives converged, seemingly, along the same road, the turning sails of the windmill the one bond between us.

The passage of time had done its job, bringing these four unlikely people together—me, Nora, Thomas, Kiera, all of us bonded by the inevitable. We raised our glasses at that point, and we cheered. As we drank I caught Kiera's eyes and they sparkled with light, and while it may have been a trick of the afternoon sun sneaking its way onto the porch, I knew better. She sparkled like a diamond, shiny, precious, and deserving of its beauty.

I smiled inwardly, my mind turning back to last night. Eli was a crafty Sancho Panza to my Quixote.

Summer was running away from us, almost to the point where I imagined that when I stared at the hands of a clock I could actually feel the earth move. But maybe that effect also came from the non-stop work being done down by the windmill. Over the course of the month of June, and now, with July waning, the Windmill Inn had done more than take shape, it altered the entire landscape behind the farmhouse. The five cottages were fully built, their walls and roofs were up, and what was being done now was the inside work, rooms, walls, flooring, all being performed with a steady sense of accomplishment. I checked with Chuck every morning and night, Kiera at my side as she checked the building schedule and announced we were running on time. While most people might have been surprised with the alacrity that these men brought to their job, I wasn't. This was Linden Corners. I knew how we worked as a community to bring about change, and that was certainly what was taking place.

As the days turned to weeks, and time swept past us, I tried to maintain a regular routine for Janey, ensuring she had the joyful, sun-speckled summer she deserved. Autumn and a new school year would come soon enough, so I spent as much time with her as I could, taking her on hikes on sunny days, watching movies or baking pies with her (and Gerta) on rainy ones, which thankfully were not all that frequent; they might have impeded our progress on the inn. My parents were invaluable in helping out with Janey, especially since I'd come to no workable solution when it came to George's Tavern. I worked five night a week, my father taking the other two, despite protests from his wife, but as he explained, he'd not suffered a heart attack, he'd just been pushing himself too hard, and his new doctor down in Hudson had pronounced that he was healthy as a horse.

"Stubborn as an ass, too," Mom had added.

Still, she spent a lot of time with Janey, and she'd also done a lot of work on planning the office layout in conjunction with Kiera.

As for Kiera, we kept the status quo. On some nights she returned to her tiny apartment in Albany, reporting to work at the office before coming back to Linden Corners to oversee the final stages of construction. One those nights she stayed in town, she would insist on returning to the upstairs apartment at George's, and some of those nights—when Janey was at a sleepover with friends, or if my mother agreed to stay at the farmhouse overnight—I would stay with her. It was clear we enjoyed our life together, but neither of us had spoken of the future. An uncertain future, one which kept me from asking Kiera to stay overnight at the farmhouse. I wasn't sure if Janey was ready for that, or if I was. Too much was riding on the successful, and timely, building of the inn, and so we let the inn's priorities consume us, allowing us to ignore the obvious, even as the unspoken words hovered between us as we slept through the night after making love.

Love.

That word was the elephant in the room, and so far we let it just hang out. No need yet to unpack that trunk and see what awaited us inside.

In other words, Linden Corners went about its

business, but in the air, as the wind swept its way across our open land, you could feel the buzz. We were building toward something, literally and figuratively, and on some mornings when I went down to the windmill with my cup of coffee, I could see some of the residents—and maybe some visitors just passing through—stopped to see the progress of the inn. I remember standing there for a couple hours one morning as Chuck's men climbed ladders and attached to the roofs of each cottage a weathervane, a windmill of their own. None could compare to Annie's, but they were a nice touch. How I watched as the wind caught them and spun them, like children born of the windmill.

I couldn't wait for September to arrive and for the anniversary celebration we had planned, but first, August arrived, and with it came oppressive heat, and afternoon thunderstorms, which created a work stoppage that we could ill-afford. Kiera had begun work on the pathway that would guide guests from the barn down to their cottages, but the ground grew increasingly soggy, keeping them from laying down the cement. These were problems we had anticipated; after all, you could not control the weather, and no matter the season, each came with their complications. We just had to hold out that hope was on our side.

But as the Windmill Inn's unveiling was fast approaching, I was left with the feeling that my life was about to shift once again, Priorities would be re-aligned, and so far I'd done nothing to fully embrace what it would all mean to me. It all came to a head as one afternoon as I was arriving at the tavern where I found water dripping out of the front door, along with dirty drops falling on the outside façade. What the hell had happened?

I dashed up the porch, unlocking the door and walking into a flooded bar. The wood floor was buck-led, and a faint scent of mustiness pervaded. I held my nose as my eyes gave study to the damage. What I knew on first assessment was that there was no way I could open the bar tonight. I'd have to have the build-ing checked for structural damage, and if it was bad, real bad, it might mean I'd have to start from scratch. Had the former Connors' Corner finally met its end, just as its owner, George, had done so? It had been a year of loss, from the burning of the Solemn Nights, to its proprietor, Richie Ravens, leaving town with his daughter, Trina, to the death of Elsie Masters, the end of whatever Maddie and I had attempted to rediscov-er. All of those I could handle. This, losing the bar, was not an easy let-go. I'd known a decision was soon coming for my future with the bar, but the Windmill Inn wasn't ready for me, and I wasn't ready for it.

I hated the idea of telling Gerta what had happened.

I spent the next hour mopping up the water, wait-ing for a plumber to arrive to find the source of the problem. It was Chuck who showed up, personally, and I thanked him for coming. He grumbled out a no-problem, and went to work. No matter how much he appreciated the work I'd given him on the inn, we'd never be best friends. There was too much baggage between him and Sullivan family, and while I wasn't one, my relationship with Annie and Janey had made me an honorary one. Chuck's wife cheating on him with Dan Sullivan had led to the demise of both families.

"Pipe broke," Chuck said, coming down from the upstairs. "Seems okay up there. Most of the water came down to the first floor. I've shut off the water in the whole building, and I'll send one of my guys tomorrow to replace the piping. You may want to us to check the rest of the place, see if any of the support beams were damaged beyond repair. You're looking at a big problem, Brian, it's not an easy fix."

"Thanks, Chuck. For your time, and I guess your honesty."

"Shit happens," he said, and then he left, leaving me alone with the rest of the clean-up.

Or so I thought.

"Oh, man, what happened here?"

I turned to see my former bartender, Mark Ravens, standing in the doorway.

"Broken pipe, water everywhere."

"Need help?"

"You're here, you know where the mops are," I said, and then added, "Thanks."

Mark and I went to work, mopping, wiping, and doing our best to return the bar to a state of habitation. After two hours, we thought it looked pretty good, but still, I was wary of opening up. No sense inviting trouble. But we were here, and so I offered Mark a beer and he accepted, taking a seat on one of the freshly dried bar stools. I sat next to him, a seltzer at my side. I really wanted a beer. Disasters like this sometimes called for something stronger. But I stuck to my guns.

As Mark sipped his beer, I finally asked him what he was doing here. "No work tonight?"

"Got laid off," he said matter-of-factly.

"Oh, Mark, I'm sorry."

"I knew it was coming. Business has been slow. Besides, I haven't been happy there."

I nodded, took a sip of my seltzer. "Got any ideas?"

Mark smiled, giving his perpetually scruffy face as openness. "Actually, yeah," he said, but then he looked around at the water-logged bar. "Though what happened today kind of changes my approach. But maybe everything happens for a reason."

"Care to explain? I'm all ears."

"You know, Brian, you did more than just offer me a part-time job when I most needed it. You opened up the chance for me to have the life I wanted—and though I'm not fully there yet, I'm getting closer.

Taking the job here at George's, I don't think Sara and I would have bonded like we did. Sure, I knew her from high school, but we ran in different circles. But then she started coming here after working her shifts at the Five-O, and you know, we got to talking and..."

"And now you're married, with a great kid."

He nodded. "Yeah, and another on the way."

"Mark, that's great...oh." I saw his predicament. A second kid, no job.

"Yeah. Don't get me wrong, I love the idea of having a big family. Sarh does too."

"But the timing is off?"

"Whatever. The time is never right. You just have to live."

"Sounds about right."

"You took charge of your life, Brian. This inn you're building, it's fantastic. I'm jealous."

"If you're asking me for a job..."

"No, not at all. That's your dream. I have my own. You inspired me."

"I'm glad I could help. Is there anything else I can do?"

"Yeah," he said, "and actually, maybe the pipe breaking helps me out."

"Nothing like finding the silver lining in storm clouds. Spill, Mark. Tell me, and I'll make it work. Financially."

"I want to buy the bar from you. No, the whole

building. I always wanted my own place, a restaurant, not just a bar, and well, since you're going to be attracting a more upscale crowd with the inn, I was thinking that the Five-O might not be their desirable choice of places to eat. I want to open a restaurant in this place, me and Sara want to. Uncle Richie, believe it or not, he left me the deed to the property where the Solemn Nights stood. If I sell it, that would be my start-up capital. What do you think? Will you sell it to me?"

Before answering, I took a look around, at the glasses and at the taps, at the stools where my regulars sat, I thought of the First Fridays and Second Saturdays, about my father behind the bar, and of an inexperienced bartender than looked a heck of a lot like me, and then I saw George Connors emerge from his office and go behind the bar, pouring out that last beer he'd ever tapped. A tear escaped my eye, and I wiped it away as I got up from my seat and went behind the bar. Mark, his expression filled with curiosity, just watched. I ended up pouring two beers, a fresh one for Mark, and one, actually, for me.

I raised my glass, and Mark did the same.

"All of us," I said, smiling, "must tilt at our own windmills."

He smiled, nodded, and we clinked glasses and drank. The beer was bitter on my tongue, but like the night I'd had that last one George had poured, I drank down the last one that I would pour. I was glad to know that in Linden Corners, I wasn't the only crazy dreamer.

It was later that night, and I enlisted help on my next endeavor. After dinner Janey and I had left the sink full of dishes while we played a game, just the two of us, and it was only after she went upstairs to get ready for bed that I went and cleaned up the kitchen. At my feet was Sully, who had grown considerably in the past few months. Our puppy was growing, and soon we would have a full-size Labrador running about the farmhouse. She'd probably one day control the bed, pushing Janey to the edge, but then again, wasn't Janey growing too? Seems the world inside the Sullivan farmhouse was giving way to the inevitable. And speaking of, there was something I needed to discuss with Janey, and so slapping my leg and encouraging Sully to follow after me, the two of us padded our way up the stairs and into Janey's room. It was almost eleven o'clock, all was quiet within our home, the lights dim. Janey was just getting settled under the blankets when we arrived.

"Sully, come here puppy," she said.

Sully leaped onto the bed, snuggling in beside her.

I sat on the edge of the bed, petted the dog's head as he lazily let his tongue lag. As close as Janey and I were, it was nice to have a buffer, and a cute one at that. Janey leaned down and kissed Sully's head, and the dog stretched out with contentment.

"He's getting big," Janey said, echoing my earlier sentiment.

"Aren't we all?"

"I'm going to be eleven in two months," she said.

"What do you think of that?"

"Well, it's not quite a teenager. But it's two ones, and if you think about that, it's kind of cool. I'm number one, twice over."

I smiled. "You have a unique perspective on the world, Janey."

She grew silent a moment, and I knew she was churning thoughts in her head. I waited till she was ready, rubbing Sully's head as I did so. The dog yawned and dropped her head onto Janey's leg.

"Dad?"

"Yeah?"

"I'm sorry about the tavern."

"Thanks. It's kind of a good thing. It keeps me home at night now."

"Is Mark really going to buy it?"

I'd talked to her at dinner about what had happened today. "That's what he wants."

"Just like you want with the Windmill Inn?"

"Grown-ups like to have a sense of purpose."

She grew quiet again, her questions no doubt about to go down a new path. Her behavior was typical Janey, and truth be told, I looked forward to whatever came next. These nights together, they were precious. Just she and I, ready to tackle the mysteries of, if not the universe, of Linden Corners.

"Kiera sometimes lives at the tavern, upstairs, where Mark and Sara lived. You did too."

"That's not going to be possible anymore, not until repairs are done on the building."

"So, will she always go home after work? It's a long ride."

"Do you have a solution for her?"

"She can stay here," Janey said.

"Is that so?"

"Brian?"

Oh-uh. She'd changed from Dad to my name. She was distancing herself, and I steeled my heart for what was going to come next.

"Janey, you know you can tell me anything. And ask me anything."

"Do you love Kiera?"

"You don't hold back, do you?"

"That's not an answer, Brian," she said, "but if it helps you, I love her."

I ruffled her hair, a sweet gesture. "Love is complicated," I said.

"Adults," she said with a roll of her eyes. "If you like her, why can't you tell her?"

"It's not about feelings, Janey. It's about moments, about opportunity. Kiera is here to work and ensure that the Windmill Inn gets done in time for the big anniversary party. Whatever else is happening, it's going to have to wait. We can't always act on our impulses."

"It's okay if she stays here, even if it's with you."

"Well, I'll be sure to let her know she's welcome here."

"This is home," she said.

"It's our home," I said. "But if you want to ease your mind, I would like very much if Kiera considered this her home, too. You know that she and I have spent a lot of time together the past few months. I could never have accomplished so much without her. The Windmill Inn stands as a reality, partly because of my determination, but mostly because of her dedication."

"Brian?"

"Yes?"

"Remember how some nights you tell me some of the stories of the windmill?"

"Sure. The ones your mother told me."

"I like the one about Charles Van Diver, and how he built the windmill for that pretty girl."

"Cara," I said.

"Did you ever notice," she said, "that Kiera sounds a lot like Cara?"

We talked for a bit longer, but it was that lone comment that settled within me. I kissed her good night, and I left Sully at her side, and I went down the hall and into my bedroom. But I wasn't yet ready for bed. From my bureau, I withdrew a small box, the same one I'd shown to Eli a couple weeks back. I'd offered to return it to him, just as I had nearly four years ago. Neither time would he accept it, and so I still possessed it.

Eli had told me I would know what to do with it.

Taking hold of the box, I went downstairs, through the kitchen and out the back door. What I did next surprised even me, as I'd not seen it coming. I journeyed along the upper ridge beyond the farmhouse, past the cottages that now dotted the landscape like soldiers standing at attention in the shadow of their general. To the stone bridge I went, the exact spot where Dan Sullivan had proposed to idealistic Annie Tessier. I dropped to the ground, and I dug a small hole. Then I placed the box inside it. I stopped and I looked at it and questioned my decision, and then I buried it with the dirt I'd just dug up.

As Eli said, what occurred between people was hardly the fault of the diamond.

It would sparkle again, and it would for the right person, the right couple.

Like Charles Van Diver, I had placed a gift for the future upon the land, and one day the ring would be discovered, and it would tell another tale of found love within the reach of the giant sales of the windmill.

A wind swept passed me, and even though it was still August, I detected a chill.

Autumn was around the corner. So too was the one hundred fiftieth anniversary of the great windmill. Time became like tonight's wind, it was moving fast, urging all the residents of Linden Corners forward, to an unwritten future that only destiny seemed to understand.

I had my plan in place, a day in mind, and I couldn't wait for time to speed up its arrival.

Little did I know that other surprises awaited me, some as spectacular as the windmill itself, others as bittersweet as the memories that kept our hearts beating. This was Linden Corners, after all, and a day of celebration couldn't happen without a bit of magic touching us, teaching us, and challenging us.

CHAPTER FIFTEEN

IT WAS THE NIGHT BEFORE the one hundred fiftieth anniversary of the Linden Corners windmill, and
to me it felt as if the ghosts of yesteryear were all
gathering for the occasion. The dinner table was set
for six, but it may as well have been set for so many
more, because I felt the warm presence of those who
came before us. My parents were hosting a simple dinner party, themselves, me, Janey, Kiera, and Thomas.
But I felt that Cynthia and Bradley Knight were here,
and I could hear baby Jake's howling as he so often did
on late nights when he couldn't fall asleep. I thought
also of the Larssen family, who had built this cozy
home, and who, for a time, had welcomed relatives
from the old country, not least among them a young,
impressionable girl named Cara. I couldn't help but
think it was Cara who was ultimately responsible for

us all being here today, because if not for her beauty, inside and out, I doubted the windmill would spin today. That it would ever have spun.

As I watched Janey and Kiera together, setting the table, I thought of Annie.

Cara gone, and Annie, too. Was Kiera a symbolic blend of the two of them?

I could only smile at such a thought.

I was returned to the moment as my father came down the stairs, dressed in jeans and a casual shirt, a countrified uniform that I was still getting used to. He had a wide smile on his big face, even as he looked thinner than usual.

"You look happy, Dad. You feeling well?"

"Top of the world, Brian. And don't start harping on me like your mother. We've worked hard for this day, and I fully intended to enjoy it. Dinner with family tonight, and then our village-wide celebration down at the windmill, what could be better?" He stopped, and he took hold of my arm, his eyes connecting with mine. "I couldn't be more proud of what you've accomplished here, Brian. It's one thing to take care of a little girl who has lost everything. It's quite another to take on the travails of an entire town and fix them too. Philip would be proud of you, too."

Dad had never spoken to me this way, and I swallowed the knob of emotion that hit me.

"Thanks, Dad," I managed to say.

"So, how about a before dinner drink? Seltzer for you, Brian?"

"I'll have a glass of red wine, along with Kiera."

He said nothing, just merely nodded. He did the honors, and Kiera came over to join me. Janey received a glass of sparkling cider, and my mother emerged from the kitchen in time for her gin and tonic, while my father pouring himself a whiskey. We were missing someone, so I was reluctant to offer up a toast yet. But just then the doorbell rang and Janey went bounding over to answer the door.

"Hi, Thomas," she said.

"You sweet thing, good evening. It's quite exciting, isn't it?"

"I don't think I'll sleep a wink tonight," she confessed.

Thomas Van Diver entered the house, his eyes filled with wonder as he looked around. It was almost as if he was embodying the soul of his ancestor, Charles Van Diver, who had often come calling for young Cara Larssen at this very house. My father handed him a glass of wine, and then I called for a toast.

"To family, past, present, and future," I said. "The Van Diver's started it all, and then the Sullivan's continued the long-held tradition of the windmill, and today, it is the Duncan family that brings everything full circle. So, to Charles and to Lars, to Cara and to Sarah, to Anders, to Dan, to Annie, we celebrate all they did to ensure the continuation of Linden Corners' long-held beliefs, not least among them was that if you put your trust in the turning sails of the windmill, anything is possible. Love, life, a future that goes beyond your own mortality. They created a world that would endure for generations to enjoy, and that's my goal too. I'm a caretaker, just as they were. The windmill remains ours, for a time, but like nature itself, it is fiercely independent, and defiantly uncontrollable."

We cheered and we drank.

"If that's your warm-up for tomorrow, I can only imagine the dramatics you have planned for tomorrow," Mom said.

Kiera dismissed my mother's cynicism, leaned forward and kissed me and told me what a great speaker I was. She tasted sweet, better than the lingering wine on our lips. As we parted, I noticed Janey looking at us, her eyes dancing with delight, with maybe just a hint of something more behind them. I paused, wondering just what Janey Sullivan had up her own mischievous sleeve. But it would have to wait, as my mother called us all to the table. As kids she used to ring a bell at the base of the stairs, calling to her three kids from wherever we might all be; Philip was always the attentive one, first to the table, and then I would wander in, usually from outside and needing to clean-up. It usually took a couple shakes of the bell, to my father's growing annoyance, to get Rebecca to show up, and the wait was never worth her sullen appearance. That was life in the young Duncan household, and if I'd learned anything, apples don't fall from trees and people rarely change.

A loud honking sound took the place of my mother's dinner bell, stopping us all as we started to pass around the steaming dishes of meat and potatoes.

"What the hell is that?" Dad said in characteristic frustration.

"Sounds like a duck's gone out of control," Janey said.

But my mother, with her steely instinct, knew exactly the cause, and she tossed her napkin down on the table and proceeded to the foyer of her new home. She threw open the door, where a pair of headlights illuminated the house. I shook my head, figuring out just who had intruded upon our dinner. Unannounced as always, sweeping in like an uninvited wind, there she was: my sister, the one and only multi-named Rebecca Louise Duncan Samson Herbert, and coming up behind her, in his customary shyness, was her teenage son, Junior. I waited another tense-filled beat to see if some strange man would accompany them, as so often was the case with my oft-divorced, oft-dated sister. Thankfully, no one else was there.

"Bon jour, Mother," she said, an air kiss passing between them. Despite the heat of summer, a stole adorned her shoulders and she tossed it back over her shoulder. With her make-up and her walk, she was aiming for sultry chanteuse and ended up looking like someone cheap you'd find on the *ponts* over the Seine.

"It's evening, Rebecca," Mom said. "If you're going for a French affectation, then get it right."

It was like Rebecca heard not a word, as she swept further into the room, going right over to our father and hugging him.

"You are full of surprises, Rebecca," he said. "Like always."

"Better than boring old Brian," she said with a laugh, "Hello, brother."

"Ever heard of a phone?" I said.

"See what I mean? Geez, Brian, relax. You did invite me to your shindig, didn't you?"

"I believe there was an RSVP. That too is French," I pointed out.

"Enough of this nonsense. Junior come over here and sit beside your grandfather. Brian, get a couple more chairs and plates, let's eat before this fine meal goes cold. You can all bicker like old during dessert."

And so that's how it came to pass that the entire Duncan family would be present for the big day, and while Rebecca had a way of stealing even a storm's thunder, I was determined that she not be given the latitude so often granted her. We had all spent too much time and energy to have Rebecca upstage us all at the last minute. As it was, her dramatic entrance waned, and we ate and talked, making introductions all around, Kiera eyeing me with a raised eyebrow. I just nodded, unspoken words passing between us. I basically said don't rise to any of her bait. And Junior, he was thankfully nestled between Dad and Janey, a protective cocoon of grandfather and cousin, safe for now from his mother's over-the-top antics.

Dessert was served, pie of course, and coffee, and soon the dishes were cleared, the night inching ever-forward toward tomorrow. I thanked my mother for a great meal, but it was time to get Janey home and to bed. She agreed.

"I'll get Rebecca and Junior settled upstairs, we have plenty of room of course."

"Wait, I thought I'd get to stay in Brian's new hotel," she said. "That's what I came for."

"It's not open for business yet," I said.

"Thought tomorrow was the big opening. What's one day?"

"Tomorrow we christen the inn, and only one guest will stay, a gesture born of the past."

"You always did talk that way, even as a kid. Who gets to stay?"

"I do," Thomas said, his hands resting on his plump belly. He was content not only from his meal but from his standing as Linden Corners' elder statesman, and he relished representing the Van Diver family as the first guest to ever stay at the Windmill Inn. It was only fitting, and his response didn't go over well with Rebecca.

"Then I want the next night, and then, as you might say, Brian, I'm gone with the wind."

"That's a movie," Janey said.

Her comment broke up the building tension, and it even made Rebecca turn red. She was only too happy to pound her way up the stairs and seek out her room, Junior and my mother trailing after her.

"Well done, Janey," Dad said. "Not everyone gets the best of Rebecca. Never be afraid to speak up. Now, why don't I let you all get back to the farmhouse? Thomas, I promised you a ride home, so what do you say we escape this den of drama and get some air?"

"Very appreciated," Thomas said, getting up from his chair.

I watched as the two of them made their way toward the front door, disappearing behind it as if the wind had indeed swept in and taken hold of them. Fear struck at me, my mind wondering just how differently my life in Linden Corners would have gone without either man. Thomas had awakened in me the responsibility to our fair town's past, and my father, well, he turned my entire idea into the reality we just celebrated tonight. I hadn't realized I'd stopped in my tracks, halfway between the living room and dining room, and it was only Kiera's touch that brought me back.

"You okay?"

I nodded. "Yeah. Just, sometimes..."

"Your Dad is fine," she said, kissing my cheek. "Come on, let's get Janey to bed."

But that was easier said than done, because as the three of us left the house, I remembered we hadn't driven over, and instead had crossed through the woods and over the stone bridge, and so we needed to retrace our footsteps. The night was cool, giving sense that autumn was creeping ever-closer, and in the sky the moon was hidden behind a growing number of swirling clouds. The forecast did call for rain overnight, but I hoped it wasn't severe, and that it would pass long before the start of our celebration. As we crossed over the bridge, Janey between us, holding our hands, she suddenly broke loose and went running forward.

"Janey..." I called out.

Kiera held me back. "Let her, Brian. Let's see what's on her mind."

"What makes you think something's on her mind?"

"Do you know your daughter?"

I smiled. "Yeah. Good point. There's always something churning up there."

Kiera and I continued to walk in the direction where Janey had gone, and when we rounded the grassy lawn and came to the newly installed walkway, we saw Janey was leaning against the iron rail of the observation desk. Centered between the five cottages, the deck extended out over the hill, giving an unimpeded view of the windmill. We strolled lazily, just enjoying the moment, the culmination of months of endless work. Each cottage had a front porch light, and they were lit, the only light in the darkness of the cloudy night, and they cast a glow upon us as the three of us stood on the deck.

"It's so beautiful," Janey said. "We did a great job, all of us."

"That's true, Janey, it shows what dedication can produce," Kiera said, coming up behind her and placing her hands on her shoulders. As much as I enjoyed the view of the windmill, seeing Janey and Kiera locked together in sweetness, it gave my heart tender pause. The moment here was perfect, unplanned, but then I had to wonder: maybe it was. Not by me, but by Janey. I thought of my earlier comment about Janey being up to something and realized she had orchestrated us being together, perhaps the last time the three of us could enjoy the peace and solitude of the old windmill. Tomorrow we hand the windmill to the world, so tonight, it was all ours. I came before Janey and ruffled her hair. She looked up and scrunched her nose, and I smiled, thinking of that seven-year-old girl who'd captured my heart four years ago.

"You okay, Janey?"

"Yeah," she said.

I didn't bother to correct her this time. I didn't want to distract from what was on her mind.

"Kiera, can I ask you a question?"

"You can ask me anything," Kiera said, bending down to Janey's height. "Always."

She paused, gave me a look, and I gave her one back, wondering where she was going with this. I saw a tremble hit her lips, a wavering that gave way to a tear escaping her eye. I wanted to ask her what was wrong, but she had Kiera's attention and I had to just stand there and wait.

"Janey, talk to me," Kiera said.

She took a deep breath, a move I knew well. She was going to take a leap of faith, and there was no stopping her until she'd spoken her wishes.

"Kiera, we have fun together, don't we?"

"Lots," she said.

"I like that. This past summer, you've always been there for me."

"And that's going to continue," Kiera said.

"Are you sure?"

"Of course. Janey...I'm not going anywhere."

"You're going to live here?"

"Well, I don't know...that's something Brian and I have to talk about."

"But Brian is so slow," Janey said, "He'll never get around to it."

"To what, sweetie?"

She paused again, and I waited to hear her next words. I couldn't speak. I was busy wiping at my own tears.

"Kiera, will you be my new Mom?"

It was like the wind knew what she was going to say, because it grew silent, the windmill's sails slowing, as if too waiting for the answer. We were like the wind, the three of us, a wish had been put out there and it demanded to be granted.

"Oh, Janey," Kiera said, taking the girl into her arms and holding her, tight. "I've never heard more beautiful words in my entire life, and I've never been more honored to know they come from you, from your heart. I wish I knew what to tell you. Because to be your Mom, I would need to be Brian's wife, and well, that's something we haven't discussed yet. It's a very big decision, for all of us—not just for Brian, or for me, but for you too."

"So you don't want to be?"

"No, I never said that...I...I just..."

She turned to me for help, but I was too busy figuring out how to make this all right. A girl who'd lost so much, who needed so much, and even after four years together I always knew, deep down, that I wasn't enough for her. Not as she grew older, not as she matured and sought advice that only another woman could impart. I was silly Brian, ready to take a tumble down the hill just to get a laugh more than I was prepared to meet all of her inner needs. But hadn't this last year been all about bringing security to Janey? That's what I thought I was doing, but of course, it was not enough, it couldn't be. All of this flashed in my mind in seconds, and finally I realized just what I needed to do, a day early and ill-prepared, but maybe that was the way to do it, impulsive, not planned, like I'd first done when I'd left New York and come to Linden Corners.

So I dropped to one knee, joining Kiera and Janey. The windmill remained silent, so did they, but I could see the hopeful smile building on Janey's face, the wide-eyed surprise hitting Kiera's face. Both appeared so open to tomorrow, so hopeful, and I felt my touched heart beating wildly inside my chest, and then I finally said it. The words I spoke were not traditional, they were not what a girl expects to hear when the man of her dreams invites her to share his life. Because it was more than just my life.

"Kiera Bowen, would you do Janey and me the pleasure of becoming our family?"

She held her hand to her mouth, tears sliding down her cheeks. Janey clasped her hands, her feet jumping on the deck, the biggest grin I'd ever seen taking command of her. And then Kiera Bowen spoke, and her words were like magic, conjured from inside her own beating heart.

"I will," she said, and then she fell into my arms

and sobbed, and Janey joined us, hugging us, shaking us, bouncing up and down with obvious glee.

How long the three of us remained locked in our new family huddle, I couldn't say. I saw not the light, not the dark, I felt not the wind, nor the cold. Nothing existed beyond our own world, one we'd created in a moment crafted by destiny. Not even the rain, which had begun to fall, could dampen the early minutes of our new life together, and we only broke when the raindrops became much more insistent.

We broke free, wiping the rain from our faces like they were a flood of tears

"I think we need to get home," I said.

"But Brian, you didn't give Kiera a ring," Janey said.

"Janey, can you leave some of the details to me? You always steal my thunder."

She giggled. "Silly, Brian."

"Actually, tonight I think it was a case of Silly Janey," Kiera said.

She giggled again. "Like father, like daughter."

Kiera then leaned down and tickled Janey, and she laughed again.

"You're silly, too, Kiera," Janey said. "Like Mom."

———————

Is this how Charles Van Diver had felt, knowing that today the finishing touches would be put on his windmill, and he'd be able to call upon the girl of his dreams and walk her across the creek and show her what he had built for her, what she meant to him, all while dreaming of a lifetime of tomorrow's they would share together. I could only feel his pain when his dream failed to come to fruition, but to know that what he started continued to inspire generations one hundred and fifty years later, I had to give the young man credit. What he gave birth to, it persevered, continued to stand as a symbol for what it had always been intended for. Love lived here, on this land, and in the soil and in this farmhouse, and on the currents of the wind that passed through those enduring sails of the windmill.

It was almost as if Charles's dream had been finally, fully, realized.

I awoke to the smell of bacon, and to the barking sounds of Sully, and when I went down the stairs into the kitchen, I saw the most beautiful sight, a woman and a little girl, laughing, talking and cooking, sharing time just as time meant for it to pass. I kissed my wife-to-be, then the daughter who I'd never ever expected in my life, and then Sully came running up to me and wanting in on the action, I pet him on the head, and then opened the door and watched as he took to the air, charging his way down the hill, not unlike the little girl with whom he cuddled nightly. She must have told him some of her secrets.

What I also noticed down on the great expanse of lawn around the windmill were people, the residents of Linden Corners staking an early claim to their spots for today's celebrations. The lawn looked like the start of a patchwork quilt, blankets strewn about, not yet connected, but by the noon hour I knew the quilt would be complete, all of us bonded, bound, by one thing: our hope for Linden Corners and all of its tomorrows. So I ate my pancakes with contentment, happy to have both Janey and Kiera sharing a meal. I had no doubt it was the first of many.

The rain had indeed washed out overnight, thankfully not leaving much water in its wake. The windmill might have, when first built, actually served its purpose in helping to rid the land of its excess, thus preserving the crops which grew all around it. Its pumping system had long been removed, and its inner mechanism today only managed the turning sails as they shifted with the ever-changing directions of the wind. Today the sails turned as lightly as ever, the wind light, the sun beginning to emerge from the last of the clouds that held tight to the sky. A soft yellow glow had begun to erase the shadows on the land, giving way to bright, celebratory sunshine.

We finished breakfast, and got ready for the big day. As I showered, my mind was a jumble of words, none of them ordered, all of them pertinent to the day. I knew I had to make a speech, and the expectation was there that it would be a doozy—everyone always made fun of my gestures, anointing them as overly dramatic. Maybe I would surprise them today. Maybe I would let what we had built do the talking. As I dressed and made my way back downstairs, I was on the verge of accepting my new approach when I saw that I had a new audience for the day's events.

"Where are the cows, Mr. Farmer-sir?"

"John," I said, my voice filled with exclamation. "You made it, I kind of can't believe it."

"Anna said if we didn't, then I sucked as a friend."

"That was made clear the day of your wedding," I said, a thinly veiled reference to Maddie. "Speaking of, where's Anna?"

"Kidnapped already by Janey, and by some pretty lady named Kiera. You holding out on me old-sod?"

"It's all part of the day's program," I said.

I then embraced my good friend and told him how glad I was that he was sharing today. As we parted, he said, "So, do you have chickens too?"

"No, but I do have a windmill," I said.

"So you keep saying. I just thought it was metaphorical."

"Right. John, if you had dared to come here in the last three years, you might just see the world differently. Come on," I said, slapping him on the shoulder and leading him back outside, past the barn—where there was another farmer joke—and then he shut up. It wasn't just the simple presence of the windmill that had his mouth agape, but the entire scene. The broad, leafy expanse of land, a foreign concept to those who chose New York City as a way of life, the great blue sky, and at last, the Windmill Inn itself, the five cottages fitting beautifully into the landscape that won our hearts every day. John was a convert from the moment he saw it.

"Brian, I had no idea...I mean, you suck at describing things. This is great, it's..."

His words failed him and I just nodded, clasping his shoulder. It was good to have my best friend here, and I felt that now that he was here it might not be his last visit. The fact that he had found Anna Santorini and now I had Kiera, perhaps a deeper bond could be established among us all. Now we just had to get John to be a father and he'd finally start to understand that life wasn't always a great big party.

Except today it was.

My partial tour over, we returned to the barn, where I found Kiera and Janey showing our work-in-progress office to Anna. I kissed her cheek and welcomed her to Linden Corners, and she smiled at me.

"I think I'm officially jealous," she said. "I'm sorry we never got here until now."

"Now is what counts, Anna. This day is one

hundred fifty years in the making, so whoever is here today gets to witness something truly remarkable. I can't be more pleased to have you both here, and for you see Janey again."

"And to meet Kiera," Anna said with a knowing smile. "Something you not telling us?"

Kiera obviously hadn't said anything about the events of last night, and I supposed she was waiting on me to tell my friends that we were engaged. But in my heart, I knew our bond wasn't yet complete, because I'd not put a ring on her finger, and so I kept silent, passing a silent exchange with not just Kiera but with Janey. She was ten and she was excited and it wouldn't be beyond her personality to spoil the surprise. I had to leave Anna hanging.

I said I had some final details to arrange so Kiera took charge of our guests, and as I went back into the house, I saw more friends begin to arrive. First my parents, with Rebecca and Junior in tow, then the Connors clan, Gerta, Nora, and Travis. The entire group assembled before the barn and said hello with hugs and kisses, handshakes, Sully bouncing around between their legs. Linden Corners' special brand of hospitality was on full display, all of them embracing the spirit of the day.

I then went back into the house, bypassing my room and instead going to Janey's. On the wall was a portrait I'd had framed and given to her for Christmas—it was a depiction of Annie and Dan, in happier times, a nightly reminder for Janey that no matter where the future took us, she would always know where she came from. But life was about to change, mine too, because we'd found a special lady in which to share our lives. Kiera Bowen was going to be my wife. It was a concept I had trouble wrapping my mind around. For so many years the pursuit of companionship had defined me—my high school sweetheart, Lucy, who I had proposed to but never gone through with the marriage, choosing instead to move to New York; Maddie Chasen, a sophisticated beauty who had both stolen my heart and stomped on it; then Annie Sullivan, who had stolen much more than my heart, my very soul, and she'd awakened a truth buried deep within myself. Time had stolen her from me, even before I had the chance to let her know I wanted to share every moment with her. I knew she knew that, because before she left us she entrusted the life of her only daughter to me. If that wasn't love, devotion...trust, then I knew nothing about anything.

I reached forward and caressed the frame, thinking of Annie and how we had lost her just four years ago, almost to the date. She was missed, and she would be forever, but I had to think of Janey, and her needs, and as much as I wanted her to have a mother figure in her life, it was more than that. I wanted her to have a mother, and not just any woman. My dalliance with

Maddie earlier this year had been just that, a hurdle to overcome and allow me to realize that what I wanted had appeared before me as if the wind had dropped her down in the heart of Linden Corners. In truth, hadn't it? Kiera Bowen had come home, she'd found her past connection to this town, and she had discovered that it also represented her future. Her future with me, with Janey, to share her life with us inside the walls of this farmhouse, surrounded by the ever-spinning sails of the windmill.

I realized that time was slipping away from me, the clock headed toward two o'clock, when I had told the residents that the festivities would begin. But I had one last, special item to fetch, and I had my friend John's arrival to thank for reminding me about it. To find the item, it required a visit to the attic. I went out of Janey's room and in the hallway I pulled down the stairs that led to the confined quarters of our third floor. A series of boxes surrounded me as I crouched up there under the slanted roof, some of the boxes filled with Janey's schoolwork art projects, some of them our Christmas decorations and other memorabilia of the Sullivan family. But I came to the newer boxes, which were the ones I'd had shipped from my apartment in New York. It was to one of those I went and began digging. I smiled as I found my desired object.

Yes, today was going to be special. More so than I'd ever considered possible.

The sun had fully broken through the clouds, leaving us with a late summer Saturday, as perfect a day as we could have asked for. For the past hour, I had walked the grounds, shaking hands with any and all, listening to congratulations on how beautiful the inn looked, and how some in town had doubted whether we would make our deadline, and then I gave tours of the cottages, a steady stream of guests walking along the pathway, taking pictures, feeling their way around the lovingly created rooms, all of them filled with restored antiques collected from Elsie Masters, Katherine Wilkerson's old home, as well as from other dealers in the region. Each house had its own identity, and eventually, each would be branded with their own name. I hadn't yet announced that. At last, though, the moment of truth had come, and from the observation deck, I called out to everyone to take their seats along the great lawn, all of them sitting amidst the giant windmill as it welcomed us all, turning its sails with an openness that defined Linden Corners.

On the deck with me were several chairs, VIP seating for everyone who had played a role in the construction of my dream. There was Chuck Ackroyd and his dozen men, and near them I saw the Connors' clan, Gerta, Nora, and Travis, who for the first time seemed happy. Perhaps all he needed was attention, and being up here on the dais certainly qualified. Sitting next to him was Junior, who also seemed pleased to have a friend to hang out with, and beside him was Rebecca, who was busy texting on her phone. I saw my mother urge her to put the phone away. Meanwhile, my father was helping Thomas get settled, and sitting next to him was Katherine Wilkerson, who looked as surprised as any to be here. I had asked her to be part of the celebration. The cottages would not be what they were without her contribution. Also on the stage was Martha Martinson, who had fed the construction workers these past few months, and next to her was Sara Ravens, baby Harry, squirming in his arms and probably wanting to run free. Mark was doing his best to keep the boy entertained. Finally I had asked John and Anna to join us. It was crowded up here for sure, but it was important for me to acknowledge all of them. My life was empty without them all.

Two other people occupied the deck, each of them flanking me.

One was Janey, of course.

The other was Kiera.

Our hands were linked, and I felt Kiera's touch warm me as I stepped before the podium. A microphone had been set up; my regular speaking voice would only carry so far, and I wanted everyone to hear what I had to say. That included those who couldn't be here in person, but who I knew their spirits had been blown in by day's currents.

I paused, taking in the magnificent scene before me, and I drew in a deep breath, realizing that all of this was my doing—the inn, the crowd, even the windmill, which had been damaged so badly in the storm four years ago and restored to its former glory. It was a testament to the power of people, of bringing everyone together, community acting as a continuation of what our ancestors had built long ago.

I had nothing written down. Whatever I said, it would come from the heart, my inspiration on either side of me. I smiled my way at Janey, and she rolled her eyes at me. Get on with it, she was saying. That only made me laugh. She had a magician's touch of knowing just when to soothe me, and I felt my nerves dissipate. Kiera remained silent, uncomfortable in her starring role. But I gave her a smile too, this woman who would be my wife, even if no one knew, even if her fingers were devoid of such evidence.

Then I launched into my speech. "In Linden Corners, we like to talk about symbols, about their meanings in our lives. They can be so simple—a Christmas ornament with our name written across it, a clock upon the wall in the shape of a windmill, even something as random as a postcard. Of course all of us here in Linden Corners know of our ultimate

symbol—the windmill itself. It spins daily, never failing to show us the passage of time and the power of
nature. We live under its shadow, but also under it
spell. When I first arrived in Linden Corners, it was
the first thing I saw, and to say it left an indelible
impression upon me would be—as all of you know—a
vast understatement.

"What was it about the windmill that drew me in?
It didn't hurt that it came with a happy, grass-tum-
bling little girl whose smile could light up any dark
night. It didn't hurt that it also came with a defiantly
independent woman who laid down daily challenges,
even as she opened up her own wounded heart. It was
these two ladies, and so many other characters who
live within our borders who drew me to this town,
who encouraged me to make this my home. My grate-
fulness knows no bounds; there is no way I can repay
the kindness that had been extended to me by all.

"But I was talking about symbols, and today stands
before you a rather dramatic symbol. The Windmill
Inn. It is one of the keys to our town's endurance,
our taste of tomorrow. For not only will we be inviting strangers to our land to fall in love in the shadow of the windmill, we will be sharing what we've
always known—that when you harness the power of
the wind, you realize just what matters most. Grab it,
take it, taste it, before the next wind takes hold of it
and you lose all you loved. If the windmill has taught

me anything, it's that time is the only constant, and if you don't live in that very moment, life's possibilities might just pass you by."

I paused to ensure I still had everyone's attention. I was going on longer than I intended. Contrary to my mother's opinion, I hadn't planned on being dramatic today; I wanted to keep it to the point, christen the inn and allow everyone to enjoy the day. But after nearly four years of life in Linden Corners—holidays and celebrations, loves, losses, lessons learned, friendships—this was the culmination of all I'd sought, all I'd found, and all I still hoped to discover as time marched onward. This was my moment, yes, but as the sun caught my eyes and blinded me, I realized it was the moment in the sun for so many who had come before me. I liked to think that floating in the wind around me were the people of our past— so many Van Divers, chief among them Charles, and Lars, his grandson, both of them dreamers, and Janey's parents, Dan and Annie, certainly Annie, and people who might not have known the truth about Linden Corners—like Thomas's late wife, Missy, and my own brother, Philip, whose confidence and giving nature still informs me today.

Then I dug into my pocket and I pulled out the item I'd taken from the box inside the attic.

"I spoke of symbols," I said, "and I'd like to share one with you. This, what I hold up before you, is a simple postcard. I bought it four summer's ago at Marla and Darla's Trading Post. It was the last one on their spinning rack. It's a photograph of the Linden Corners windmill, and while I had the privilege of waking to it every day, there were people who were unaware of not just its existence, but its power. I remember putting a stamp on it and dropping it in the mailbox. I sent to back to where I'd come from, to New York, to my friend John Oliver, who stands with us today. Sending the card was my way of setting the windmill out in to the world, to no longer hide behind our borders. It was for all to see, for all to experience. It is from this postcard that the Windmill Inn was born. I will have it framed now, and it will hang in my office, a constant reminder of the possible.

"And so, without further delay, ladies and gentlemen of Linden Corners, friends, family, guests, loved ones all, I present, as promised several months ago at the ground-breaking ceremony, the fabulous, beautifully conceived, lovingly built...Windmill Inn."

The crowd broke into applause, and I was glad they did, because I was out of words. I just stood on the podium, watching as the windmill turned its sails in approval, and then I turned back to see what everyone else was seeing, and atop each of the cottages, the weather vanes spun, kids themselves, learning to spin, trying to earn to praise of its older soul. My heart swelled, and I felt Janey and Kiera embrace me, and as

I felt their warmth, their love, course through me, I realized I wasn't done. Not yet. One final surprise awaited everyone, not least among them was me. I hadn't planned this part. I was just going with the flow.

"If you'll indulge me one last moment," I said, "and then the party can continue long into the night."

Kiera and Janey backed away, giving me m space, but I asked them back.

"This concerns you...both of you."

I turned back to the crowd, but what I was about to do wasn't for them. It was for all that were assembled behind me—my parents, my friends, those who had been instrumental in making my life in Linden Corners the special one it was.

"The story of the windmill dates back one hundred fifty years to the day," I said, "and today we celebrate the spirit with which it was built, the men who labored in the hot sun to bring it to life, the families that have taken its unique presence into their hearts and maintained it, ensured that it would continue to turn for generations to come. It all began with the Van Diver family, and when circumstance dictated they sell the land, the great windmill was handed down to the Sullivan family, who, after a time, restored it to where the sails lived to turn again. And the one day a man appeared, a stranger to these parts, a broken man with no path in life, no discernable direction. That was me, Brian Duncan, and as much as I like to think

I discovered the windmill, I know now, after all these years, after all these memories—both wondrous and bittersweet—that the windmill found me. It awakened me.

"Those three families—the Van Divers, the Sullivans, the Duncans—are all represented here today. Thomas Van Diver was born here, and returned to our land just over two years ago. But another Van Diver, as we've discovered, is in our midst. Kiera Bowen, the architect who took my idea and made the Windmill Inn come to life, is a direct descendent of Anders Van Diver, the brother of Charles, whose love for a woman caused him to dream the windmill into existence. And of course, no one can forget the giving presence of Annie Sullivan, whom you all dubbed The Woman Who Loved the Windmill, and her daughter, Janey, who stands before you today as the future caretaker of our beloved windmill. But what you don't know is that our three families have agreed to become one, to finally bring a sense of completion to the spirit with which Charles Van Diver brought to this land. Indulge me if you will, Kiera, Janey, will you step forward?"

Both of them did so, Janey quickly to my side, Kiera a bit more hesitantly.

What are you up to? she seemed to be asking me.

Well, Janey might have stolen my thunder last night during the passing rainstorm, but today it was all sunshine and verdant lawns, and the ever-spinning sails of the windmill. So I dropped to one knee, and I took from my pocket what I'd purchased last month from Eli, and this time it was me who got the chance to invite Kiera Bowen into our family.

"Marry us, Kiera Bowen. Me, Janey, complete our family. Fill our hearts."

Even though the crowd held its collective breath, I was relaxed. I already knew the answer.

"Yes, Brian Duncan, yes Janey Sullivan, I will marry you," Kiera said.

The crowd erupted into applause, and soon we were swamped by people, all of them filled with good wishes and cheer. But I remained focused on the two people who mattered most.

As I felt Kiera's embrace, and I felt Janey's excitement as she bounced upon the deck, what drew my attention away was the windmill itself, its sails turning with growing speed, a strong wind now coming off the mighty Hudson River. I thought about where that river led, down to a city that had once filled, if not my dreams, but my ambitions, and once I'd exhausted those, what was left was a shadow of the man I wanted to be. Life had given me challenges, and a wizened old man with rings to sell and dreams to peddle, told me that all of us had to tilt at windmills. We had to confront our fears, and only then would we make ourselves stronger. I was no longer tilting at windmills, and I don't think I was chasing them anymore, either. I'd found my place, my heart was content.

The windmill's sails paused, suddenly, like they were winking an exclusive hello at me. It was a connection that existed just between us.

Hi to you, too, Annie.

But then, sometime later, as the day turned to night and the celebration waned, I asked Kiera to join me, and together we ventured to the windmill. There was one last piece of the puzzle to solve. Upstairs to Annie's studio we went, where I presented Kiera with a rectangular shaped box.

"What is it?" she asked.

"Just open it."

She did so, the ribbon and wrapping paper falling to the floor. She pulled from the box a gold frame, and inside it was a piece of paper, a letter written one hundred and fifty years ago. I told Kiera the love story of Charles Van Diver and Cara Larssen, and as she wiped a tear, I then suggested we place it where it belongs. I'd already put up a hook, and as I put my hand over hers, we hung Cara's words on the wall inside the windmill, she and Annie linked forever in this tiny space. I then kissed my future wife and said the words my heart longed to say.

"I love you, Kiera Bowen," I said.

"I love you, Brian Duncan."

Later, as we left the windmill, the wind grew

strong, and I watched as the sails started to turn with determination. Was Annie still among us? Had she come to wish us well? That's when I saw Thomas Van Diver—the Windmill Inn's first guest--ambling down the cement pathway to his cottage, his shadow trailing after him. I realized, as sorrow struck me, that maybe Annie hadn't come for an altogether different reason. She lived on a different plane, she took to the wind as others had before her, as others would after her. No, as happy as Annie was for me, and for Kiera, and especially for Janey, both of us who would lead her beautiful daughter into womanhood, Annie Sullivan had arrived with a purpose. She'd blown in to claim someone for her world.

EPILOGUE

The Story of Janey Sullivan

Seasons came and seasons went until countless years had passed and the men who had crafted her, labored in the hot sun to build the magnificent windmill, were like the wind itself, blown into the past, into the memories we coin as history. As for the windmill, it was allowed to fall into disrepair for too long a time, and the once-heralded landmark—a classic token to a lost era—became nothing more than an eyesore to a generation that no longer embraced its ancestry. There was talk, and not just once, of tearing down the old windmill.

Until he came along. The man who loved the windmill and restored it to its former beauty and grace. At last, the wind would again pass through its sails, a familiar friend returned to define an otherwise lost landscape. He thought it sacrilegious to deprive the windmill of its true purpose, and by restoring its spirt to the building, he breathed vibrant new life into the community around it. He could never know, though, never imagine, that his love for the creaky old structure would inspire a sense of mutual caring—even love—among the townsfolk. But it would, even in the face of awful tragedy and sorrow. The windmill would generate an invisible power of healing—and would bring together two most unlikely souls.

Those words were spoken once, so long ago in your time, not so much in mine, with only one change. The "she" had become a "he," but even so, the powerful message holds true today. A new generation has begun to grow toward maturity, led by a girl named Janey Sullivan, sweet Janey with her giggle and scrunched up nose, my beloved daughter who had seen so much, more than her young mind should have to. But she was strong, that one, I'd been able to teach her that much during our limited time as mother and daughter. She was Brian's now, and Kiera's too, and they were an ideal couple. They would allow her to grow, to soar to her greatest potential. Of that I had no doubt.

But lessons are learned hard in life, and for Janey, for all of them really who called Linden Corners home, it was one last loss which gave new appreciation to each moment they were given. I was there, *too, somewhere, sending energy and strength to them on the waves of the wind.*

"Ashes to ashes, dust to dust, we commit our brother to the earth. Rest easy, and know that you are loved, now and always. Like those who came before us, your time on earth is over, but your life lives on, in your wife, your children and grandchildren, and in a town that you came to far too late in life but embraced with the fullness with which you did everything else. All that you did, you led by example, a selflessness we can all learn from. That is your legacy. One of devotion to family, one of loving one another."

Father Eldreth Burton of St. Matthew's Church gazed solemnly at the assembled crowd, a small one at the behest of the family, asking those here if anyone had something further they would like to add. Before the service they had discussed this, and decided to save their thoughts, their prayers, their sorrow, for their inner selves. Yet one voice spoke up, and all eyes turned to Janey, dressed in a simple black dress and a tear rolling down her cheek.

"You don't have to do this, Janey," Brian said, leaning down to whisper in her ear.

"It's okay, Dad," she said, and stepped forward,

inching that much closer to the casket. In her hand was a single rose. "I remember when I first met this giant. He had such a booming voice, and I thought he was scary. It was at Thanksgiving, the first trip Brian and I took together. That's when I met a man who I would come to call Grandpa, and what I learned from him was that you can't always believe what you see. Sure, he was in...intimidating, at first, but then he smiled, and then he swept me into my arms and twirled me around and I thought, he doesn't even know me but he knows I like windmills, because that's how I felt at that moment, and of course the windmill made me think of Momma, and that comforted me. When Grandpa moved to Linden Corners, our bond only tightened. We played games, we talked about dreams. He gave me Sully." She paused, and then said, "I'll miss him, like I miss everyone who dies. But I have my memories, and that's the one thing about memories—nothing can take them away."

It was the first day of autumn when Kevin Duncan was buried, a cool breeze had snuck up overnight, but above them soared a blazing sun and a sky so blue it looked painted. Nature would soon grow quiet, rolling up for the winter until such time passed that life began anew. He had enjoyed the day of the Windmill Inn's unveiling to the fullest, taking his position as the man behind the idea, and reveling in his son's accomplishment. He'd kissed his future daughter-in-law on the cheek and welcomed her to their family. He'd told his wife he would see her in the morning. Then he'd gone upstairs to bed that night, filled with pride, and his sleep had turned into an eternal one. His heart may have given out, as it had been doing for a year now, but they all knew how big it was; his body may have been silenced, not his impact.

So now, a saddened Duncan family said their final goodbyes to their patriarch, each of them leaving a red rose upon the casket, until finally filing away. Janey took hold of Kiera's hand, following after her Grandma and Aunt Rebecca and Cousin Junior, more of a family than she could ever remember having in her entire life. The Duncans weren't many, but they outnumbered the Sullivans; in fact, on some nights before sleep when she looked at the portrait of her birth parents, she realized she was the only one left.

She'd heard that word today several times: legacy. Was that hers? To ensure the Sullivan name? But wasn't that silly, because one day she would get married and she'd cease being who she had been all her life. It was a conundrum her young mind couldn't quite get beyond.

Janey turned back toward the grave, where she saw Brian still standing there.

"I'll be right back," she told Kiera.

"Oh, Janey, give him a moment."

But Janey knew otherwise, and she went to the man who had become her father, and she just wrapped her body around his, arms encircling his waist. No words were spoken, none were needed. They just stood there, together, as they had, as they did, and they shed tears and realized they had been here before. Janey was older, wiser of course, she'd always been that, and as much as Brian had seen her through her dark days, now it was her turn. He leaned down and kissed the top of her head.

"Thanks, Janey. What would I do without you?"

"That you'll never have to find out."

Indeed, she was there for him all day, and in the weeks still to come. Her birthday was just around the corner, and in the week leading up to it, she wondered what it would feel like to turn eleven. Life was moving ahead, just as Father Burton had promised it would, the turn of the clock as reliable as the sun waking her up each morning.

———————

Janey Sullivan tossed back the covers and dashed to the window. The windmill spun, just as it had always done, and why today should be any different she didn't know. All she knew was that another year had passed, she was one more year older, and *she hoped it was going to be a special day. It was pancakes for breakfast, then school, and both Brian and Kiera drove her, much to her pleasure and excitement. It was all she could do during the long day of lessons and schoolwork not to think about the rest of the night. It wasn't so much what gifts she might receive; instead, Janey Sullivan had a plan all her own. She wanted only one gift today. She'd thought long and hard about it, each night since Grandpa Kevin had left them.*

Soon, but not soon enough, the school bell rang, and she ran out into the afternoon sun. A woman stood on the sidewalk beside her gleaming car, waiting for her.

"Hi, Grandma," Janey said, giving her a quick hug.

"Good afternoon, Jane. And might I add, Happy Birthday."

"Thank you. I'm glad you're here, you're just who I wanted to talk to."

"I'm always here for you. You're the apple of my eye."

She'd come up with that the other week, during a Saturday when, on a cool crisp morning, they had gone apple-picking, and afterwards had sipped at freshly made cider, just the two of them sharing time. Janey was a student of life, always observing, always curious, and she had watched with awe at the refinement Didi Duncan carried herself with, especially given her loss. Janey felt she understood her, now. They had something in common, sorrow. But it also enabled them to talk and to bond and to grow ever closer. It was a far cry when she had first met her that one holiday. Janey Sullivan had grown up, and maybe, perhaps, so had Didi.

They drove back toward Crestview Road, Janey talking non-stop, her words spilling out of her as though they'd been hidden behind a dam inside of her. Didi listened, and she nodded, and when they turned up the driveway and came to a stop, Didi reached out and caressed her cheek.

"I don't know from where you came, Jane, to have such an impact on our lives. But I am ever thankful. I will see you later tonight, at your party. For now, I think what you have in mind is beyond ideal. Your grandfather would be proud of you. But he always was, you know that, don't you?"

"Do you miss him, Grandma?"

"Every day, and that will never change."

"I love you, Grandma."

"And I you, dear sweet child."

Janey ran from the car, excitement fueling her legs as she made her way around the back of the house, across the field until she came to the edge of the hill and gazed upon the windmill. It still surprised her, this new view, with the cottages lining the northern section of their property. But she liked them; she always felt the windmill was lonely, its sails turning as if beckoning people to it, to keep it company. After all, it was now over one hundred fifty years old, and it had seen so much over that time. Today it would lay witness to more, another miracle to occur underneath its spun dreams.

She saw Kiera and Brian strolling along the walkway, hand-in-hand. She waved to them, and then, with Sully coming up from behind her, she took off, a girl in motion, almost as if she was taking flight, just as she had done as a toddler first learning to walk, then run, and she twirled her arms in the air, something she had done as a child, something she always felt like she would, even if she were a hundred and fifty like the windmill itself. At last she came to a rest beside the great windmill, and she stared up as its sails welcomed her.

Brian and Kiera found their way there, too, laughing at Janey's antics, at Sully's racing around her, barking with delight. It was as perfect a scene as any of them could have imagined, and for a time, the sorrow which had hung over their lives lately took a back seat to joy. Janey asked them to follow her, and they did, curiosity guiding them inside the windmill, up the winding stairs to the second floor. This had been Annie's place, but Janey knew her mother approved of them all being here. That's one of the *things she talked about when she tossed and turned at night. Dunc the purple frog agreed with her.*

She'd been waiting for the right opportunity to tell Brian her idea. Today was it. Her birthday. As if, after today, Janey Sullivan would be reborn.

"Janey, what's going on?"

"I wanted to give you—both of you—a gift."

"Janey, it's your birthday. That's for us to give to you," Kiera said.

"I know. That's great, and I can't wait. But neither can this."

Brian gave her one of his curious expressions, knowing she was up to something special. But he knew not to interrupt her, not with the serious tone in her voice, her giggle silenced. So she said, "I wanted to do this here, where Momma could hear. I've already talked to her, and she's okay with it all. But that doesn't mean I can't share it with her." She paused, making sure she had their attention, and she did.

"Brian, I know there's been a lot going on. Grandpa leaving us, the opening of the inn, the construction on the barn still continuing. What I've learned is that life is a work in progress, you can't count on tomorrow, so you better make the most of today."

"That's very astute of you, Janey."

"So with that said, I don't want you and Kiera to wait too long to get married."

"*We're talking about dates. I think we need to get through the holidays first.*"

She nodded her approval. "*Christmas is always busy here in Linden Corners, you'll see, Kiera. But okay, so next year, the two of you will become husband and wife, and I'll be there, and so that will make both of you my parents. I always called my mother Momma, and I barely knew my father, but I learned a while ago that I could have a father and a Dad. So I'd like to be able to have a Mom, too. If that's all right with you, Kiera?*"

Kiera bent down, took Janey's hand in hers. "*I don't need a piece of paper to feel like your mother.*"

Janey smiled, wide and bright. "*When you do marry, will you become Kiera Duncan?*"

"*I...I suppose,*" she said, turning up to look at Brian. "*We haven't discussed it.*"

"*That's how it's usually done. So he's Brian Duncan, and you'll be Kiera Duncan. But I'm Janey Sullivan.*"

"*Janey, where are you going with this?*" Brian asked.

"*If Kiera gets to change her name, I think I get to also. After all, I'm the one who proposed to Kiera. Asking her to join our family.*"

Brian came to her, taking her into his arms and feeling the warmth which beat within her. She saw *him wipe at a tear, and then he too bent down, the three of them now on equal footing.*

"You want to become Janey Duncan?"

She shook her head vehemently, her decision made. "No, I want to transform into Jane Duncan. I'm growing up. That's what today is all about, isn't it? A new year, a fresh start. That's how I'd like to begin it. Jane Duncan, daughter of Brian and Kiera Duncan."

"I don't know what to say, Janey..."

"Jane."

"Well, the fact you responded so quickly, I guess your mind is made up," He extended his hand, a smile upon his face—more than a smile, really, Janey thought, his face was alight like the sun—and then he said, "I have only one caveat."

Now she scrunched up her nose. She knew lots of big words, but that one escaped her.

"What does that mean?"

"It means I have a condition. No more Brian. Even when I'm silly. I'm Dad."

"You got it, Dad."

"Then we have a deal, Jane," he said, shaking her hand. "But sometimes I might slip up, like you do. Will you give me some time with this?"

"Time," Janey said, "is precious. It's our friend, when it wants to be."

"Time can't be held," Brian said, "just like the

wind. *It's always here among us, sometimes silent,
other times as noisy as Sully. But it's what shapes
our days, and our nights. We have to take the time
we're given, and embrace it. Love, life, loss, they all
go together, bound by time, taken by the wind. Our
journeys take us so many places, some planned, some
unexpected. In the end, we all have out giants we
must slay, our windmills we must tilt at."*

---

*Where life takes you, you never know. When I came
to Linden Corners, it was by mistake, a lucky acci-
dent that landed me in the world of the windmill.
There I found love, and I brought love into this world.
How could I have ever guessed my own fate; how can
anyone? Brian is right, you have to live your live and
enjoy every moment, take each turn of the windmill
as a special gift.*

*I watch over them all. My dear Janey, and the
loving man I entrusted her to, the woman who now
rules their hearts. Theirs is just one story that has
spun around the windmill, just as so many others have over the years, and will continue to do so.
As I watched the three of them leave the windmill
that day of Janey's birth and head back up the hill,
Sully still racing around them, I felt the world begin*

to fade, colors darken. My Janey was disappearing, growing up and becoming someone else. I had my own journey to continue, but I do so knowing that my daughter lives on, protected, so loved, given all she could ever dream of.

Maybe not everything. Not me. That's what life teaches you.

I will still visit, when I can, when the wind takes me there, and I will embrace her even when she is unaware. She may be Jane Duncan now, but she will always be Janey Sullivan where it matters most, deep in a soul no storm can ever silence. But I think she'll know when I'm around. She always does. The bond between mother and daughter can never truly be broken, it endures, just like the windmill does, turning, spinning, offering up wishes upon the wind to anyone who is ever taken into its embrace.

I wonder, always, what other stories await my home called Linden Corners.

AUTHOR'S NOTE

Chasing Windmills is the fifth book in my ongoing series about the lives of the people of Linden Corners. When I wrote the original book, *Tilting at Windmills*, I never imagined a sequel, much less four of them. I thank the readers who have reached out to me for encouraging me to continue the tale of Brian, Janey, and the rest of the gang. It's been a revealing journey.

A few thoughts about this volume.

First of all, I hope you have fallen in love with Kiera, just as the Duncan's have. To win Brian's heart—and Janey's of course—she had to have had a special connection to the windmill, and I hope I offered up a viable reason. I knew little of the past stories of the windmill prior to writing—not Charles, Lars, or even much of Annie's tale. But I tied them all into existing storylines that played out in previous books.

Also, I mention the concept of time often in this book. I realize that in the real world, it would take far longer than four months to build something such as the Windmill Inn. For storytelling purposes, I had to condense that timeline. Otherwise it might have made for a far longer book.

One of the dangers of repeating similar themes over the course of a series is overdoing your metaphors. I hope none of you have tired of the wind, the windmill, and its spinning sails. Such images inspire me as I am writing, and at the time they feel completely new and natural. Brian is never too far from my heart.

Linden Corners exists in its own world, though a modern one. Sure, I have had to introduce technology, such as cell phones, references to text messages and the Internet, all of which were not as prevalent when I began the series years ago. So again, I am playing with time—we don't know what year it is, and some ages are stretched to fit the needs of the story.

The only constant, as the story says, is the windmill. Characters come, characters go. It's a slice of life, as tempting as Gerta's strawberry pie, and just as sweet. Through times happy and sad, Linden Corners endures, and I hope to be back within its borders again. I hope you'll join me. Who knows what celebration awaits us next?

54282506R00262

Made in the USA
Lexington, KY
13 August 2016